BROKEN
PHOENIX

Ashlyn Hades

EXPRESSO PUBLISHING

To all the readers who like their romance with a side of depravity. Who like their men vicious and dark. Who think ruthlessness is hot and cruelty is just another form of seduction. This story is for you.

1

NYX

The high I get from stealing is better than an orgasm—it lights me up like a carnival, and the glow lasts longer than any half-faked pleasure I get in bed, anyway. Right now, I'm beaming bright yellows and reds; my chest is spinning happily like a Ferris wheel.

I'm utterly delighted because I clutch a diamond in my gloved fingers, marveling at how big it is—nearly as tall as my thumb. It's a perfectly shaped and sculpted oval that refracts the green laser lights dancing around the darkened room I stand in.

"Gorgeous," I whisper, more than a little awed, a blissful contentedness rolling through my shoulders now that my prize is in my grasp.

I smirk underneath my black mask, and with a quick flick of my wrist, the jewel disappears from my hand like it was never there at all. Poof.

If I'd been on a street corner, a crowd would have

*ooh*ed and *aah*ed for me. I would be the best damn magician the world has ever seen. People would pay thousands of dollars to watch my sleight of hand, and my name would be displayed in bright lights, illuminating every busy street in Vegas. But I'm not out in Nevada performing.

I'm in the Cartier store on Fifth Avenue in New York City at three in the morning.

The thousands of dollars? Yeah, that's stolen.

My name displayed in bright lights? Ha. That's comical. Unless you count the "Wanted" poster with a horrible caricature of what they believe me to look like, since no one has ever seen my face.

My only audience is my partner and sometimes semi-adequate lover, Taylor. Emphasis on the *sometimes* because semi-adequate doesn't always apply.

He's turned his back to me while he clears out the unset diamonds . . . the loose stones that foolish men— armed with a quick Google search about carat and cut and clarity—put into a tacky engagement setting for the woman of their dreams.

I pretended to be one of those women the other day. A dream woman. *Snort.* As if that exists.

I wore a pair of big Audrey Hepburn-style sunglasses and an A-line dress that I'd "borrowed" from Prada. My long brown hair had been done in beach waves and ratted to have lots of body. I'd tried to offset my normally innocent girlish face with intense bronzer accenting my cheekbones and cat-eye makeup that would hopefully contrast the way my long lashes typically make me look a bit younger and more naïve. The ultimate effect was posh and dim-witted. Perfect for plucking—or so the shop workers had thought when they smiled after I'd walked in. They'd thought I was a target, not realizing they were *my* targets.

Them and this shop, where the floral scent of over-priced perfume lingers in the air even after hours. Where the display cases have been cleaned so meticulously, I can see my reflection in the glass. Where the camera in the corner—currently turned off—usually pans over the occupants of the store, searching for gullible victims to buy their overpriced products.

Though I'm just twenty-three, I'm anything but a dewy-eyed little girl full of innocence and hope for a better tomorrow. Blah blah blah. My parents beat that little girl out of me with every hurtful word and expectation they knew I'd never live up to. That girl didn't just die—she was stepped on and pushed through the meat grinder. Eviscerated. Until all that was left was me.

This little girl now knows how to plan and pull off some of the best heists no one's ever heard of. The hush-hush work. The kind that insurance companies like to sweep under the rug because they don't want to look incompetent or weak. That's what I do.

Taylor helps too. Sometimes. Though, right now, he's making about as much noise as you'd expect of a bull in a china shop. He moves to the next case and sweeps his hands through necklaces, making them clink and clatter.

"Can you keep it down?" I hiss.

"It's impossible to stay down around you, babe. You're too fucking hot."

Oh my god. He did not just make a dick joke. Except . . . he did, because I turn around to glare at him and all he does is smirk in response—while shoving necklaces into his bulging pants.

"Classy, Taylor."

"Keeping it real."

I have to grit my teeth and spin to another part of the room in order to avoid starting up what he calls my "nagging" to be quiet, but I call it "goddamned reasonable logic while committing a felony."

Men.

"If only dildos felt half as good as the real thing," I mutter under my breath.

I sigh as I move over to another case, striding underneath one of the two grand chandeliers overhead, which dangle like the room's earrings.

During our recon, while I was all dolled up and my feet were absolutely hating the pumps I wore, we'd walked into this narrow jewelry shop, and it had stolen my breath. I mean, I know everyone goes on about Tiffany & Co., but for me? This place takes the cake. The store is all plush carpet and wood-paneled walls. As a former trust-fund baby, the old-school money vibe typically doesn't get to me. This store is an exception. I'd had to rein in my surprise at finding myself charmed, though I'd quickly crumpled and tossed out that useless emotion as if it were a dirty tissue.

Like any other job, we'd come here to case the joint first.

Taylor, with his buzzed blond hair and chin dimple, had walked in on my arm that day wearing a polo and some of those ridiculously bright salmon pants that wealthy men sometimes think they can get away with. Newsflash: no one can get away with that look. Not even a Hemsworth.

Gradually, Taylor wandered off to flirt with the hungriest-looking salesgirl and find out about closing protocols by asking totally subtle questions like, "So, what time do you get off? I mean, what time can I *get you off*?" even though we were supposed to be engaged. Luckily, she seemed greedy enough not to care, as if all she wanted was the sale, no matter what kind of dickhead schmoozing she had to put up with to get it.

Meanwhile, I targeted an older gentleman with trembling hands and asked to try on some of the rings. Gerald had pulled engagement rings out one at a time until I'd gotten impatient and insisted that he kept picking the wrong ones. I'd be the first to admit I was channeling Mommy Dearest, right down to the derisive lip curl and haughty eye roll.

When Gerald had brought out a tray of glittering things, I'd become suddenly clumsy—a grin still spreads across my face at the memory of him bent over, plucking rings from the plush carpet like they were weeds. Meanwhile, I'd leaned forward, spouting apologies as I'd slid a stick of moldable plastic into the display case lock to get the shape of the tumblers. Too easy.

Recon is always one of my favorite parts of the job. Getting paid is another. The thrill of the actual heist? I think I might be the only one I know in the business to get off on it the way I do. Even now, the adrenaline engulfs me in a big, warm hug that makes my cheeks flush and heightens my sense of hearing. My clit is flushed and a tiny bit swollen from excitement.

If this were another gig, I might indulge myself and Taylor. But this is our biggest job to date.

The payout from this could mean *bye-bye, shitty studio in Parkchester*. We might even be able to move out of the Bronx entirely. Maybe we should just use the money and buy plane tickets somewhere tropical and steal from the richie riches on vacation.

"Mai tais and mayhem," I whisper under my breath.

The fantasy of a beach disrupts my thoughts for a moment as the vision of the darkened room and dead security cameras is replaced by swaying palm trees and a bright blue ocean. Yes. That sounds like a plan. Maybe I'll even suck Taylor's cock—heaven only knows the pussy-ass won't extend the same courtesy to me. Lazy lover. Still, I can suck a cock like a champ, as Taylor's well aware, and I don't even mind licking a taint from time to time. If my dead, bitchy grandma's ghost truly is watching over me like she promised, she'll be fucking terrified of the little ho I've become.

But in order to make that plan a reality, I have to get back to work.

I press my lips together as I make my way around the semicircular set of tables and use my homemade skeleton key, delicately guiding it into the lock and turning until I hear a happy little click.

"God bless 3D printers," I murmur as the lock opens and I pull back the sliding door on the side of the case before tucking my little printed key away in my black jeans.

I glide my fingers forward, and "Nothing Could be Sweeter" by The Virginians pops into my head. The 1920s happy-go-lucky orchestral arrangement plays in my mind, and I smile as I free a beautiful emerald necklace from her cage. She slithers like a snake up my sleeve, tucked safely away, her stones cool against my overheated, overexcited skin.

My head starts to bob to my internal soundtrack as I move to a tennis bracelet that's gorgeous—if you like boring, which I don't. I prefer intricate, off-the-wall jewelry. Last weekend, I bought a pair of those ear cuff earrings that look like a dragon is wrapping around your ear. They're a far cry from the expensive baubles I'm currently sliding into my pockets, a collection of solitaire rings that is just as mundane and forgettable as the future housewives it was intended for.

"Sorry, Karen. You'll have to get your ring somewhere else," I murmur, sliding a band off the velvet holder.

I also snag a pearl necklace from beneath the glass, snickering. I'm pretty certain the woman this was intended for has never worn the other kind of *pearl necklace* in her life. Nope. This looks like it was made for one of those innocent women who finds blow jobs "icky." Ridiculous.

Her future husband should be glad I saved him from buying this. Now, he can cover her neck with something better.

"I'm practically a sex therapist here," I whisper lightly to myself as I push the pearls into the breast pocket of my black blouse next to the huge diamond I already hid there.

I glance at my digital watch, reading the glowing numbers on my countdown clock, judging our time. We've only got three minutes left before the hack to the security system lets up. My heart starts to beat faster, energized by the thrill of racing against time. I love cutting it close.

I navigate around another lime laser beam with my knee-high black boots, stepping carefully over the light because the hacker I've paid to override this system has done an incomplete job. Nearly a third of the green beams crisscrossing the store remain in place. Annoying but avoidable obstacles. It's disappointing, though—it's so hard to find good help through the dark web these days. Every prepubescent boy wants to call himself a hacker.

I blame YouTube and those Minecraft videos that use that word to describe any mediocre player. Just like I resent any asshole who calls themselves a thief. This job takes finesse and planning. Even Taylor is barely capable, and I've trained him for nearly a year.

I glance over to see if he's finished when, to my surprise, I see him turned away from his case. Instead, he's facing me in the dark, one arm raised, extended in front of him. There's a gun in his hand, and it's pointed straight at me.

What the motherfuck?

Time downshifts. It goes from racing to a crawl. Everything but my heartbeat seems to melt into slow motion. The pounding inside my chest, however, picks up speed until it becomes a thrum. Until I can feel it pounding in my ears, throbbing in my fingertips, sizzling down the insides of my legs—making every bit of my body recognize that it's alive and that it might not be for much longer.

A ferocious burn starts in my cheeks, and I can't identify if it's mottled anger, hurt, or embarrassment. I'm unsure what I feel as my partner stares at me, his expression covered by his mask but his light blue eyes clear and untroubled, as he trains his gun on my heart.

A million thoughts gallop through my head, each one trying to win my attention like this is the Kentucky Derby. I'm not sure what the hell *this* is, but I can see the finish line staring me right in the face, and I don't want to cross it. I don't want to have people ring me in flowers . . . though, who would bring flowers to my funeral?

I have nobody but Taylor.

And clearly, I never even had him.

I stare at the asshole I've been willing to settle for . . . the guy whose fingers always fade halfway through my trip to O-town, forcing me to finish the job myself. The guy who reads his fucking phone when he pees, forcing me to clean the bathroom seat every single time I have to go. The guy I found huddled on the street . . . that I took in and trained . . . the man I pitied as I tried to give him something to reach for, goals, hope, a future.

My heart doesn't break, but it cracks. Because my one good deed in the past four years is now coming back to bite me.

I don't ask why.

I just stare at him as I slowly slide my hand behind me. Not for a weapon. I never bring more than a Taser on these jobs. It's the one line I've never crossed. But I reach back for the lime green light that I know hovers just above the display case. Because if he's going to fuck me, I'm going to fuck him right back. In the asshole, preferably. With a dildo covered in barbed wire and lemon juice.

"You son of a—"

I don't even get the words out before pain explodes in my chest. White-hot heat rips me apart, and it feels like wolves have sunk their teeth into my flesh. My body screams out that I'm being eaten alive. My ears ring. My heartbeat speeds up until there aren't individual beats any longer, just a meteoric vibration thundering through me.

I hardly notice that the front of my shirt grows wet, because I'm fighting. Fighting the nerve endings that snap viciously at me and the instinct making me want to curl into a protective ball. I can't. I can't save myself. There is no saving myself, because I'm not faster than a bullet.

There's only one thing I can do.

I turn my head to the right, telegraphing my intentions, but it's too late for subtlety. I stretch out my right arm behind me as far as it can go, which isn't much, because my limb has become impossibly heavy. With a gurgled gasp and my final surge of energy, I swipe out my right hand. Because it's important—so important—that Taylor not walk away from this . . . from me . . . without getting his own.

Motherfucker. I can't believe I ever gave that traitorous asshole a blow job.

My hand slides through the laser beam, and I collapse as Taylor curses and runs . . . and the store erupts into a soul-piercing alarm.

2

NYX

Seven Months Later

Orange is most definitely *not* my color.

As I sit in the back of the prisoner transport van, my gaze fixed stonily on the chipped paint of the wall, I can't help but allow my mind to wander.

Pink . . . I look damn good in pink. Black too. Even blue and green, despite the fact that my eyes are brown. But highlighter orange? Nah. I honestly don't think anyone is capable of pulling it off.

Prison jumpsuits are *so* last season.

I internally smirk at my own joke while, outwardly, my face remains expressionless, a perfect mask. I've had a lot of time to perfect that mask sitting in jail, in the courtroom...a lot of time for thoughts to roll through my head and for me to overthink every tiny possibility until they swirl around, a constant storm cloud hanging over me.

The inevitable conclusion? Douchebag is a piece of shit with a micropenis who deserves to rot in hell.

And I'm the dumb bitch who got dick-notized by said micropenis, which led to my downfall.

Maybe I should take responsibility for my actions and all of that crap, but I don't feel an ounce of guilt for the crimes I committed. All I did was attempt to survive in a world that chewed me into tiny pieces and then spit me back out. The only regret I have is saving Douchebag's sorry excuse of a life in the first place.

I should've let that fucker starve to death in the alley-way. Curse my bleeding heart.

Latisha sits on the bench across from me, a gun resting across her legs as she stares at a spot above my shoulder. She's tucked her long braids underneath her cap, and her dark brown eyes are serious but thoughtful as we bounce along the poorly paved road.

I've always liked Latisha more than the other cops and guards I've come into contact with. She doesn't speak much, but when she does speak, I don't detect any malice, which is as rare as a diamond without flaw. If anything, I think Latisha pities me—the poor little girl who is facing twenty years in prison. Who will see the light of day when she's thirty-three . . . and that's if I get out ten years early for good behavior.

Fat chance of that.

But unlike her, I've accepted my fate, and though I don't like it, there's nothing I can do. Sometimes life shoves us into a box and tells us to stay there. I'm sure prison won't be much worse than my childhood home. That was just a prison overlaid in marble.

My parents didn't even bother to show up to the fucking trial. The rich, pompous assholes don't want to be seen with their criminal daughter.

Ridiculous, considering they made me this way. But not unexpected.

I try to ignore the pinch in my chest that still occurs whenever I think of them. It's gotten duller over the years, smaller. It's nearly ignorable now. I'm mostly pissed that I still feel anything at all. They certainly don't.

I'm their dirty little secret—the daughter they wish to eradicate from their lives. I'm a disease to them, and that's all I'll ever be. Even after years of trying to prove myself and make them proud, I remain the black spot that tarnishes their preconceived and idyllic notions of family and wealth. They couldn't even spare me a few dollars to pay for a semi-decent attorney, one who actually cared about what happened to me.

My lawyer was one of those shitty public defenders just out of law school who has over a hundred cases and no idea what he's doing. I'm not saying it's his fault I faced the maximum sentence, but . . . it's totally his fault.

To add insult to injury, *Douchebag* wasn't even implicated. Yes, I gave the police his name—I have no loyalty to the traitorous asshole anymore—but they couldn't find him. And since we took out the security cameras, there's no proof that there was even another person on the job with me.

You'd think the gaping wound in my chest would be a clue, though, wouldn't you?

Ahh, modern police work. It's not like on *Bones* or *Lucifer* or any of those detective shows where they actually care.

So Douchebag—as Taylor will forever be known to me—got off scot-free while I'm forced to rot away behind bars. How the fuck is that fair?

Then again, life is never fair. I learned that the hard way when my parents kicked me out the second I turned eighteen and refused to acknowledge my existence, content in their opulent mansion while I spent my nights on the streets. I learned that when I had to fend off my first predator after he found me curled up on a park bench. I learned that when the prosecution team refused to offer me a plea bargain, and I was forced to go to trial, so they could get the headlines they wanted in the papers and then polish their nails on their jackets like they'd done something grand—*Diamond Thief Convicted!* I learned that from my cellmate in jail, who'd been to the pen three times before and liked to yank out strands of my hair while I slept just to keep me off-balance.

Life. Sucks. Ass.

Big ass. Small ass. Plump ass. Every single ass you can think of.

When the van finally pulls to a stop, I release a heavy sigh, my muscles loosening as if all the anticipation I've had so far—all the tiny glimmers of hope during the trial that shone like stars but turned out to be as useless and fake as glitter—is gone.

This is it, Nyx. The end of your life.

I can't even blame myself for having such morbid thoughts. Because prison life? Worse than the color orange. Definitely not for me.

"Hands, please," Latisha says, raising a single finger in a come-hither motion.

I obediently hold my hands out in front of me, and she sticks a tiny key in the cuffs, allowing them to clatter to the ground. I'm confused, mainly because the majority of the crime shows I've watched have the prisoner in handcuffs up until the time she reaches her cell.

Maybe this is different? Did television get it wrong again?

Latisha doesn't meet my inquiring gaze as she continues to stare over my shoulder. I quirk an eyebrow but, as expected, get no response.

"What—" I don't get to finish my question before the back door to the prison van is yanked open, blinding sunlight immediately illuminating the cramped space. I squint my eyes against the blistering rays, my heart hammering like an escaped rabbit inside of my chest.

Thump. Thump. Thump.

"What the fuck?" I demand as three faces peer up at me.

All of them are bedecked in black ski masks.

Terror infiltrates my system, cascading through my veins at the knowledge that something horrible is about to happen. Something very, very bad. It steals the breath from my lungs, immobilizes me, until all I can do is gape like an idiot.

This is definitely not normal protocol.

I turn toward Latisha in alarm, but the woman has reached underneath her seat and is now positioning a gas mask over her face.

"What the fuck?" I repeat as one of the masked men throws a tiny canister into the van with us. Then he slams the doors shut. Immediately, a potent gray gas fills the vehicle and enters my lungs, and the scent settles on my tongue like sweet sugar. I gasp, falling to my knees as my body goes weak and leaden. Dark spots dance across my vision, and I feel myself tilting precariously to the side.

No. No. No. No.

And then darkness consumes me.

I'M AWARE OF A MECHANICAL, roaring noise that deafens me.

It's all I can hear, all I'm aware of. Just that horrible noise that sounds like wind pelting at the side of a house and the *creak, creak, creak* of machinery.

The second thing I'm aware of is how terribly uncomfortable I am. My body is positioned oddly in the minuscule space I find myself in. My knees touch my stomach, and one of my arms is thrown haphazardly over my chest while the other touches a cold floor.

What . . .?

Consciousness returns to me as I drowsily struggle to piece together what just occurred and then articulate it with words.

The last thing I remember . . .

The transport van. After the jury gave their verdict and declared me guilty. After the judge sentenced me to twenty years in a maximum-security women's prison.

And then . . .

My heart races, thrashes, beats erratically inside of a chest that is no longer capable of containing it. Panic courses through me, hotter than electrical cords sparking wildly.

I was kidnapped.

But why?

My eyes snap open, and I realize I'm in what appears to be a small cargo plane. That's the noise I hear—the wind whipping at the steel enclosure as the engine rumbles. Dark gray clouds are visible through the small, rectangular window opposite me. Benches rest on either side of the plane with a single aisle between them, and it's one of those benches I'm lying beneath, my body contorted into an unnatural position. In my periphery, I see black boots, and I know, without a shadow of doubt, that those feet belong to the men who kidnapped me.

Is Douchebag somehow involved? My parents? Someone I stole from? The owner of Cartier, perhaps? I don't even know who that is, but they'd be rich enough.

I go through a mental list of all my enemies as I work on controlling my mounting panic.

Okay, think, Nyx! Think!

I'm still in the hideous orange jumpsuit, and I haven't been tied up. Why is that? If I'm a prisoner, wouldn't they restrain me?

But if I'm not tied up, then that means I can fight . . .

Though I don't know where I can escape to when I'm probably forty-thousand fucking feet in the air.

Think about where you'll go later, Nyx! Right now, focus on how to get the fuck out of this mess.

Keeping my limbs languid, as to not alert anyone to the fact that I'm awake, I tilt my head ever so slightly until I have a clearer view of the plane.

Across from me, a man in an orange jumpsuit lies unconscious on the ground underneath a bench. Beside him, her cropped hair colored a vibrant purple, rests another unconscious prisoner—this one also in an orange jumpsuit.

What the fuck is this?

Is someone . . . kidnapping prisoners?

My already chilled skin grows even colder as goose bumps rise up on my arms.

I was alone in the van, so where did all of these people come from? Who has the influence to kidnap prisoners from multiple locations?

My eyes sweep over the men and women who are conscious and chatting, my heart racing to a tune I can't quite understand. None of those awake are in jumpsuits. They're all in black cargo pants and T-shirts with some sort of insignia on the left breast that I can't make out. None of them wear ski masks, leaving their faces clearly displayed— though one guy still holds his mask in his hands.

So, these are the fuckers who took me.

And they're sitting there, jabbering like goddamned

Boy Scouts around a campfire, almost as if kidnapping prisoners and flying off with them is some kind of bonding exercise instead of seriously fucked-up shit. I can't help but wonder why they would remove their masks in the first place before deciding on two possible scenarios, each one instilling me with ice-cold terror.

One—they never intended for one of us to wake up.

Two—they don't plan on letting us live.

Maybe they're terrorists.

Shit on a brick.

I'm not the praying type, but if I were, I would be on my knees with prayer beads and candles and animal sacrifices. I'm pretty sure the balls I don't have wither into raisins and jump right back inside me.

I've never been big on violence, but right now, I'm regretting that tendency as I look over at my captors. There are six of them in total, twice as many as the ones who kidnapped me originally. Two women. Four men. One of the females has long, shiny blonde hair pulled into a braid over one shoulder, while the other has ruby-red hair and a nose piercing. The four men vary in looks and age as well, two of them looking old enough to be my father and one the age of my grandpa.

And then the fourth man . . .

My breath catches when I find his gaze fixed on me, his brows lifted in surprise. My eyes drag over his hand-some, chiseled features—the ashy blond hair spiked at the top, the elegant swoop of his neck, the verdant green of his eyes—before lowering to the handgun in his lap and narrowing my focus on that little bit of molded metal, the barrel, and the muzzle.

My mind immediately throws me back to Taylor pointing his gun at me and the moment a bullet should have ended my life . . . but a trial ended it instead. I drag my eyes back up to his and dare him with my gaze. Because, after all, what's left for me? I don't even know what I'm daring him to do. Shoot me? Strangle me? Throw me out of the plane?

I half expect him to yell to his little kidnapper friends that I'm awake, but instead, his lips purse into a thin line and he turns away from me.

What the fuck?

"Is it about time we wake them?" the man questions, his low, husky voice reverberating through my system. I can't help but notice he's speaking much louder than is polite, almost as if . . .

Almost as if he's trying to warn me.

I repeat—*what the fuck?*

"You're right," one of the women remarks. "The pilot just contacted me." She touches the earbud in her ear. "We're here."

Here? Where the fuck is here?

They stand as one unit, cohesively creepy.

My eyes snap closed just in time. I hear footsteps clomping, and the floor of the plane vibrates underneath my cheek as they get closer. Less than a second later, I feel a boot connect with my ribs, and pain explodes through me. I grunt, weakly opening one eye and contorting my features into horrified confusion, as though this is all brand new to me and my eyes aren't already looking for things my hands could grab, snatch, steal . . . once we're safely on the ground, of course.

I want to fight these fuckers, but I'm not suicidal. Attacking them in the air, with no escape route in sight, is just plain stupid. And I reached my quota for stupid when I trusted Douchebag not to stab me in the back. Or shoot me in the front, as the case may be.

The oldest terrorist—I preemptively decided they are, in fact, evil terrorists—leers down at me, his wispy gray hair combed to cover up the bald spot on the top of his head. His belly is prominently displayed in the thin black shirt he wears, and I can finally make out the logo on his shirt, which reads, Hoplite Defense Services.

What the hell is that? A company is stealing prisoners? Why?

Oh god. This isn't some fucked-up human trafficking ring, is it?

"Up!" he snarls, and I blink.

"What . . .?" In all honesty, I'm not entirely masking my confusion and fear.

Something's happening. Something awful—I can feel it. My nerves are jangling just like they do when I know I'm about to get caught . . . like they did that time when I was seventeen and my dad's best friend caught me in his safe, the first time my parents discovered my proclivities.

The two other prisoners are roughly forced awake, and it's only when I shove myself into a seated position that I notice that it's not just the three of us. One glance behind me confirms there are at least twenty prisoners on the plane, if not more.

Some are as large as Mack trucks, with muscles upon muscles stacked across their bodies. Some are my age; some are younger. Most are older. The majority are men, their faces grim and angry, though I spot a few women as well, including the one across from me who's wearing a grimace.

God, whatever is going on is huge. This is a massive undertaking. Dread eats at the lining of my stomach.

"What is this?" a heavily tattooed man in a gray jumpsuit bellows, staggering to his feet, his snarl revealing that one of his front teeth is outlined in silver.

I want to know too, but I'm not stupid enough to ask. Defense services . . .

Is that like pseudo military? Who are these assholes?

"Shut up and put these on," one of the kidnappers says, stalking toward him.

My eyes on them, I'm surprised when a backpack is roughly thrust into my chest, and I turn to see the handsome blond man staring down at me.

There's something inscrutable in his expression, something I can't quite put into words, as he watches me. It's not disgust or horror, but when I try to puzzle out what it might be, I can't . . . It's been too long since anyone looked at me normally and not like I was gum stuck to the underside of their shoe.

When I don't immediately move to grab the pack, the blond guy yanks it away and turns me roughly to face the wall of the plane, my body a tiny toy in his grasp. He grabs my wrist and pulls it behind me before he slowly slides a single strap up my arm, his fingers grazing my skin with a calloused touch that sets my nerves alight. He repeats this process with the other side, oblivious to the fact that I haven't been touched with anything even close to resembling care since I've been incarcerated.

The sensation is so overwhelming that it's almost too much. I have to force myself to take slow, steady breaths to counteract the jittering jump of my pulse. When he reaches around my body to the front of my chest, I nearly choke as I swallow a gasp. Of course, he's only about business. He hasn't been locked up and sexually starved for months. He grabs two dangling connectors and snaps them together to keep the heavy bag firmly attached. Then he yanks the drawstring, making the two straps scrape roughly over my nipples, which are wide awake and at attention after the ice-cold plane floor. The sensation sends my already humming pulse into hyperdrive and nearly brings me to my knees.

Though he's attractive as hell with those bulging muscles under his shirt, when I turn around, all I can do is glare at him. Fuck him for making me feel things I shouldn't. Fuck him for taking me. Fuck him for whatever is about to happen.

"Where are you taking us?" My voice is barely above a breath. I don't know why I expect him to answer, to help. He's obviously a part of whatever this *thing* is.

"Quiet," he says, though not unkindly. Almost as a warning.

He bends down and secures straps around my thighs,

touching me in places no man has touched since I've gone to prison, creating an unbidden, unwanted tingling sensation along my spine.

Bastard. Is he doing this on purpose?

I can't tell, because he won't make eye contact. He finishes and shakes his hands out for a second, before standing and stepping away from me to move toward the next person in line.

"Wait!" I whisper. I grab at his arm instinctively, but he stealthily backs away, casting glances in both directions.

"Don't touch me," he warns, his voice loud enough to garner the attention of the nearest kidnapper, who glances over and then away dismissively when he realizes I'm dropping my hands and not actually making trouble.

The handsome man's eyes reach out and do that strange evaluation of me once more, as if drinking me in and savoring the flavor. He takes a step closer, and I automatically step back so that he'll think I'm intimidated.

I am, but I'm also planning because, if I'm not wrong, there's a little spark between us, and I can use that to my advantage at some point. He leans close enough that anyone watching us might mistake his words for sweet whispers. But he only says one word, and there's nothing sweet about it. "Run."

Run.

I don't know if it's a threat, a warning, or something else entirely, but when he steps away, I can't breathe.

Run? On a plane?

"Prisoners! Line up against this wall!" a strident voice

demands, and I turn to see the largest armed man stalking down the aisle, a huge machine gun strapped around his shoulders, the trigger resting in his hands.

"Fuck you!" the tattooed inmate from earlier shouts, throwing a punch at the guy with the machine gun, a very intelligent move. His fist connects with a smack, and every eye in the plane turns to the pair. I watch as Machine Gun Kelly steps closer, removing his hands from the gun . . .

And slices a knife clean through the inmate's neck.

Someone shouts, but most of us simply stare in wide-eyed horror as blood spews like a fountain and the inmate drops to his knees, then onto his face while the machine gun bastard simply wipes off his knife and puts it casually back into a sheath on his belt.

What the hell is happening?

All I can do is stare on in horror, my hands instinctively touching my own neck in some sort of fucked-up solidarity. I swear I can feel phantom tingles, as if a blade has just been swiped across my own skin.

"Peter, was that really necessary?" the blonde woman guarding us questions. It doesn't sound as if she cares either way. A tiny smirk teases the edges of her lips.

"Get. Against. The. Wall," the guard—Peter, apparently—repeats, his grayish-blue eyes narrowing into thin slits.

Yeah . . .

Definitely not going to argue this time.

We all immediately do as instructed, moving to stand against the wall at the back of the plane as the six Hoplite

Defense fuckers sit on the bench to the right of us and strap themselves into the seats one by one. As each one of them straps in, the other five all train their weapons on us to ensure we comply.

My eyes flick to the blond guard's face to find him watching me intently, his eyes beseeching me to do . . . something. Run?

Run where?

Into Peter's goddamn knife?

But I don't have time to ponder that when the rear wall of the airplane starts to lower and the air becomes filled with tangled screams as we're sucked right out of the back, and I find myself tumbling through the sky.

3

NYX

A t first, I see nothing but water beneath me, and a wave of panic rolls through me as I plummet toward the sea, pawing frantically at the straps on my shoulders.

This has to be a parachute, not just a backpack, right? They strapped us in. There were fucking leg straps. At least, that's how parachutes are portrayed in movies. I've never actually jumped out of a damn airplane before.

Movies got this right, didn't they? This one fucking detail. They got it right—right?

My fingers jitter painfully as I try to keep my arms tucked in and not let the screaming air around me whip them out so that they flail like useless ribbons. Finally, tensing all my muscles, I'm tucked in enough to swipe my palm down the right strap.

Come on. This isn't just a cruel joke, is it?

Everything inside me tightens and spasms as terror like no other consumes me. For months, I've pushed my

fear away—shoved it into a steel box and locked it up
tight. But it's resurfacing with a damning vengeance, and
there's nothing I can do but accept it and its cruel,
taunting touch.

I search the left side for a pull ring as the wind beats
at my ears and rips tears from my eyes before I find that
gorgeous bit of plastic and yank on it with all my strength
so that I don't plunge two thousand feet into the ocean,
with no hope of surfacing.

Immediately, it feels like a hook snatches me out of
my fall and drags me back up toward the clouds, leaving
my stomach somewhere in midair below. Once the light-
headedness wears off, my eyes trail across the gray sky,
trying to pick out other prisoners. I only see three others
with their parachutes open.

My throat goes dry.

Does that mean the rest . . .?

I don't allow myself to complete the morbid thought,
though a second immediately replaces it. My brain has
become an expert at sinking into darkness during the long
hours of nothingness in jail. My new thought is a question: *Why did I even bother with the parachute? If we're
in the middle of the ocean . . . then, why?*

Instinct.

I've always been scrappy. Even as a child, I never
backed away from a fight, not even one I was certain I'd
lose. I still remember that time in fifth grade when I took
on Tommy Bent and his gang of eighth graders. It was
five against one, but I was faster than them. Smarter too,
though that's not saying much, since they each inherited

their mothers' good looks instead of their fathers' genius. And while they'd been burdened by societal norms dictating whether they should hit a girl significantly younger than them, I had no such qualms. When they tried to taunt me and called me an *ugly little freak*, I fought like my life depended on it . . . and won.

Stupidity, my parents called it. Right now, I might agree with them. My instincts just ensured I gave myself a slow death instead of a quick one.

I glance down at the waves, trying to judge how far up I am and if wrangling this parachute off now is worth it. The prestigious academy my parents sent me to as a pre-teen legacy had mandatory swimming lessons every day at the ass crack of dawn. But that had been a damn swimming pool—not an ocean with violent waves crested white with sea-foam.

That's when I spot land.

It's slightly to my right, a few miles at least, and I didn't notice it at first because the gray day doesn't lend a lot of contrast. But it's there—this murky, indistinct blob like a forest dusted in starlight.

Hope bursts to life inside of me—small and fleeting but growing larger and larger, like a ball of fire being fed by kindling.

I lick my wind-chapped lips and immediately sharpen my gaze, my hands lifting to my straps. I don't know if I can make it to that island, but I'm damn well going to try. Determination weaves through me, like threads braiding themselves together into something stronger, and I test out my ability to control the parachute by reaching up and grabbing on to the dangling cords on either side of me.

Fuck, which cord will propel me closer to land? Which one will move me farther away? I'm assuming the right one will move me to the . . . well . . . the right, but what do I know?

I need to get to the island. I don't have a choice. Dying is *not* a fucking option. Not now. Not after everything I've been through. I refuse to die before I have the chance to enact my revenge against Douchebag. And dying by either drowning or a shark attack? That's like every nightmare I ever had combined.

Even if I have to survive off the land of this mysterious island, I'll do it. Even if I have to give myself orgasms day after day, never touching a living man again, I'll fucking do it. My determination to live outweighs everything else.

But first, I need to figure out how to use a motherfucking parachute.

Other than parasailing in Bora Bora on a vacation with my parents once when I was in middle school, I've never done anything like this.

"No time like the present," I say aloud, then immediately hate myself a little bit because it's one of my father's favorite sayings, the bastard. I compensate for that slip by yanking hard on the right-hand cord, which is a mistake. I zoom off to the side, away from the little island.

"Fuck!" I try to rectify the situation by pulling on the left side, and there's a disastrous mess of zigs and zags through the air that I'm sure would embarrass anyone who's ever actually skydived. But fuck them all, because I get that lush green island lined up with my feet eventually, and what's more, I even figure out how to work the damn cords enough to veer slightly left, away from the cliff side of the patch of land and toward the beach that looks as peaceful as any postcard, waves lapping gently at the sand.

Yes. Fuck yes. A tear drips down my cheek when I realize that I might fucking live through this insanity. I'm going to make it. A warm feeling swells inside my chest and encases my heart—the primal satisfaction of survival.

As I get near the island, my eyes scan the treetops. The trees are full and thick, not all tropical. There are a few random pines here and there, which means they were imported. That means there are people on this island.

The blood in my veins suddenly grows as thick as honey, and I'm certain that my heart stops for a moment as the blond kidnapper's words come back to me.

"Run."

Shit. My blood turns to ice. *He didn't mean on the plane. He meant once I landed on the island.* I feel like such a damn idiot.

Then again, I really didn't expect to get thrown out of the plane, did I?

I don't have time to do more than think that before I see one of the other prisoners pass beneath me and land on the beach, his green parachute billowing out into the foamy waves behind him and making him stumble. His feet haven't hit the sand longer than two seconds before figures burst out of the trees and run right for him. I can't see much of them, only faceless, nameless, genderless shapes who circle him like wolves surrounding a deer.

His panic shoots straight up into the sky and becomes my own.

Fuck.

I want to watch what happens, but I sail over the scene just then, still several hundred feet in the air. I reach for a cord to twist myself around, but a bloodcurdling shriek reaches my ears and sinks into my skull like the blade of a knife. I drop the cord.

Nope. I don't want to see what's happening. My mind can fill in the blanks.

"What the ever-loving fuck is this? Some kind of prisoner-killing game show? Is that even a thing?" I mutter in a shaking tone.

I wouldn't be surprised if it was . . . Somewhere in the world, some fucker would be sick enough to find it amusing.

Or is this how that private military group practices? Hoplite—that was the name. They drag out prisoners that no one will miss and then use them as living dummies for target practice—

I cut off the direction of my thoughts because my shoes are now nearly skimming the treetops. The scent of pine wafts up to me as I careen through the sky, and a lump flies into my throat, lodging there as I reach down with ice-cold fingers to start struggling with my straps, undoing my right thigh.

Fuck, if I'm going to get caught up in this thing, like a

spider in a web, dangling from a tree branch. I'll be easy pickings if that happens. I move to undo the second strap on my thigh before rethinking my approach. I worked out in jail—there wasn't much else to do—but how long can my shoulders carry my body weight?

I take a deep breath and try to still my thundering pulse enough to think.

Come on, Nyx. You've got this.

Ultimately, I reach up and undo my left shoulder strap instead so that my right shoulder and left leg bear the brunt force and constant yank of the parachute. It's a pleasant sensation akin to being ripped in half.

Forcing myself to ignore what I'm feeling, I look down into the trees, trying to gauge how far I'll fall. I read somewhere that anything over fifteen feet is deadly. I'm pretty certain I'm at least double that. But the mix of pine and deciduous trees form a canopy that's as dense as carpet.

I chew my lip as I weigh my options. The bottoms of my ugly, orange, prison-issue Keds are already brushing against the occasional leaf. I'm not going to have much choice soon. So, do I drop now, or do I let the parachute tangle, getting me that much closer to the ground . . . but also losing precious time to escape from whoever it is that's down there?

Two choices, like the red pill or blue pill from *The Matrix*. Unfortunately, the question I'm asking myself isn't about reality—it's about how I'd prefer to end it. Going splat, or at the hands of some crazed stranger.

Or *strangers*.

People are assholes. That's my philosophical conclusion and final answer.

Splat it is.

I reach up and unbuckle my right shoulder but keep the strap on as I lean down and undo the clasp on my left thigh. I make both motions as solemnly and formally as a pallbearer, because this could very well be it.

Funnily enough, I find that I'm not ready to die. You think I would be, given my propensity toward danger. I knew it when I was staring down the barrel of a gun, and I know it now as I'm about to plunge to my death. There's an innate voice inside of me that screams at me to fight, to persevere, to *survive*.

With a shuddered gasp, I slip both my arms out of my straps and straight up into the air, letting my body plunge beneath the tree line, like I'm jumping into a green pool.

I've already nearly died at some other fucker's hands.

Never again.

———

BRANCHES AND TREES assault me in a cruel initiation to the island, and suddenly, I feel sure I know what it's like to get jumped into a gang, whacked with bat after bat. My legs scissor wildly in the air, and my hands claw at nothing, always reaching out a second too late to grab hold of anything.

My pulse pounds so painfully that I'm certain my skin is about to burst.

All I want to do is pass the fuck out.

No dice.

My consciousness flickers, like a television that momentarily lost the signal but then blares annoyingly back to life, making me experience every minute horror, each precious final second. My raw skin is scraped and pummeled, and agony hacks at every inch of my body.

It feels like I'm falling forever before my foot strikes something thicker and harder than the wispy branches that have been whipping me. My ankle screams in pain, and my arms windmill as I tumble backward, losing my balance on what's clearly a thick branch. My left arm smacks another branch, hard. My entire shoulder to my fingertips protest as pain bites into me, but I fight to ignore it and scramble to grab on to the branch, nails clawing at the tree.

Come on. Come on. Just one—

But my angle is off, and I plunge to the ground.

My body is contorted from reaching for the branch, so I land on the dirt on my side with a thump that feels like a giant just smacked me, stealing all the breath from my lungs.

Fuck.

For a moment, I wonder if I'm dead.

But my eyes still blink, my hands still curl into fists, and eventually, I'm able to breathe again as I roll onto my back and stare up at the banyan tree that probably saved my life by changing my trajectory and slowing my fall. I lift two fingers to my forehead and give the old piece of wood a little salute in gratitude.

The thrash of leaves moving and the sound of footsteps in the forest have me dragging myself onto my knees before I can take a full breath. I glance around for a weapon, but ferns and trees are all that I can see before the shadows of the forest swallow up anything more than ten feet away.

Surprise is probably the best weapon I have right now. It's not my favorite weapon, but it's all I've got.

I hurry over to the base of the banyan, which looks like thirty tree trunks crowded together. My ankle cringes in protest, sparks of pain flaring with each step, but I ignore it as I strip out of the bright orange jumpsuit that makes me a target, keeping my plain black underwear on. Since I don't know what to expect from the inhabitants of this island, I'm a little nervous about being vulnerable in only my undergarments. At the same time, the clothing covers more of me than most bathing suits do, and any fucker who wishes to put his hands on me like *that* will attack me regardless of what I choose—or don't choose—to wear.

I also keep the ugly canvas prison shoes while I kneel in the roots and bury the stupid outfit in fallen leaves and forest detritus. Pain shoots up my leg when I twist to shove dirt over my shoes to make them blend better, but I've ignored worse trying to escape from jobs. Once, I had to ignore a broken arm as I shimmied down a roof, trying to get away from the homeowner who'd arrived early and spoiled my fun.

So, I mentally tell my ankle to stop being a little bitch as I stand and then pull myself up onto the first low-hanging branch I can find. It's slow going because my limbs are sore, the fall having taken a lot out of me. Honestly, it's probably a terrible idea to wear myself out more.

But that soldier's one-word warning turns into a chant in my head. I need to run. If not literally, then at least figuratively. I don't want to end up like that prisoner on the beach.

I give myself a moment against the rather delicate bark of the trunk to just breathe before I reach for another branch, using my arms to pull myself up enough to latch a leg over the side and slide over. Then I center myself on the branch in a prone position so that I'm balanced on my stomach, both hands wrapped around the branch in a hug for this big tree. I stop there because I've reached the end of my strength and because the sounds of hunters and laughter are getting closer. Any more movement on my part might draw their attention.

Come on, tree. You saved my life once. Let's do it again, mkay?

Despite my semi-sarcastic thoughts, my heart feels like a woodpecker trying to get to the tree beneath me, pecking violently at my ribs as I wait for the hunting party to emerge. A strange prickle travels along my neck, and I get the eerie sense that I'm being watched, but when I turn my head to peer up into the forest, I don't see anything but a bird flying underneath the canopy, gliding smoothly from one green shadow to the next.

A figure materializes in the underbrush beneath me. I squint, wondering if the fall made me hit my head and hallucinate things.

But nope.

No matter how hard I concentrate, the scene below me doesn't change.

A single man stands directly below my hiding spot, wearing only a bright-pink Speedo that leaves very little to the imagination. His chest is covered in thick patches of black, curly hair—and I mean "patches" literally. It's almost as if he placed five cups in various places on his stomach and chest and then shaved around them. Contradictorily, he's bald, his shiny white head a blazing beacon that immediately captures my attention, even in the gray mist.

But that's not the strangest thing.

Wrapped around his waist, directly over the skin-tight speedo, is a belt. And connected to the belt are dozens and dozens of Barbie-like plastic dolls.

A few of them are coated in blood, blonde hair stained garnet and faces splattered in the thick liquid.

What the fuck?

As I watch, horrified, the stranger grabs one of the dolls, strokes her hair, and then pushes it into his speedo to scratch his balls. A contented, almost—gag—orgasmic sigh leaves him.

Holy fuck.

Poor Barbie.

The strange man cackles maliciously, still scratching his damn balls with the doll's head, as he continues his trek through the forest, heading in the direction of the beach.

And—no doubt—in the direction of the other prisoners who jumped out of the airplane with me.

I repeat—what the fuck?!

It feels as if I'm only able to breathe again once he disappears amongst the thick cluster of trees. But that breath of air is short-lived as boisterous, masculine laughter and the pounding footsteps ring out.

The tromp of boots gets louder, and fury overtakes me when I hear one of the unknown men call out, "Come out, little bitch!"

"This one's a woman? Let's fuck her before we kill her," another voice says.

"Looked like it from the binoculars. Looked like she had tits. Juicy ones," his gallant and progressive friend replies.

Why does it feel like I should've taken my chances with Barbie man?

My hands tighten on the branch I'm clutching, and while I've never been prone to violence, I hope I get the chance to slit the speaker's throat. He just needs to come a little closer. If I can only take out one before I go, I want it to be him.

The assholes appear as they shove aside the brush and step into the shelter of the huge banyan, which has created a small clearing based on the stretch of its branches.

At first, I think I'm hallucinating a-fucking-gain, because the bodies that burst through the ground cover are clearly human, but their faces are all distorted, noses and chins horrific, monstrous in a way that sends a cold sweat down my spine.

It's only when one of the men turns sideways and I see a black strap over his ear, his hair visible beneath it, that I realize they're wearing masks.

I squint down and realize they look like wolves and coyotes and bears and foxes, carved wooden masks hiding their eyes, though their guns can't hide their intentions. It's fitting that they're imitating predators, because as far as I can see, they're acting like a pack of wild animals. They descended on that guy on the beach without warning. Or, at least, I'm assuming it was them. How many masked dickheads can there be? Unless it was the strange Barbie man, though I didn't see a weapon on him, and he appeared to be by himself. It has to be these men. That guy didn't even get a chance to speak. Criminal or not, he was still human . . . which makes them less. They're monsters.

"Her parachute seemed to land another mile or two south. Let's keep moving," one guy, with a deep, scratchy voice and a red coyote mask, says, causing his three friends to glance over at him.

"Nah, she bailed out. We'll find her sooner rather than later. If she was smart, she would have fallen near one of these." Another tall guy in black with a brown bear mask points at the banyan, making me clutch my branch tighter. My entire body freezes, even my heart, hoping that their stupid masks impede their vision enough so they can't see me.

The other three glance up, and my stomach grows a

knot, my arms feeling weak as noodles for a moment when the black eye slits of a green-and-black wolf mask peer up at me.

Oh, fuck. Oh, fuck, fuck, fuck. This can't be happening.

I can't tell—I can't *fucking* tell—but my heart says he sees me, until he looks back down at the tall bear guy and asks, "Why would she want to fall on one of these?"

"To break her back—so she's dead before we get to her." His laughter chases a chill down my spine. That noise . . . Why does it remind me of my father? Their voices are different—my dad's is rough and raspy, while his could almost be described as high-pitched—but something in the guy's tone . . .

All I can see when I close my eyes is my father's sneering face, his eyes rife with contempt. I hurriedly banish the memory, but one thing remains clear.

I'm dealing with a goddamn psychopath.

"Well, let's move out. Hurry it up. I'll still fuck a dead girl, so long as she's warm. So, quit this dilly dally shit," another says, his mask orange and the nose of it elongated.

"Fox, that's . . ." The coyote shakes his head.

"Hey, I got standards. You can have her when she's gone cold," Fox retorts, starting to stomp off.

Dark laughter breaks out amongst the four of them, and the breeze catches it, carries it, rubs it into my ears abrasively. My fingers finally find their strength as anger courses through me. Sick motherfuckers.

I eye them all speculatively, deciding that the man

with the red coyote mask looks like the easiest target. He's careless with his gun, flicking his wrist casually to gesture . . .

He's also skinny, his form narrow underneath the black clothes they all wear. He'll probably be the quickest to overpower. He's checking his surroundings far less often than the others do. I don't know if he's young or inexperienced, but either way, he's the weak link.

"Come on, pred team. Let's move out." The man with the black-and-green wolf mask marches forward until he's nearly to the clearing. Then he stops, plants his feet, and gives a howl. The others join in, making the hairs on the back of my neck stand up. His tone is laced with amusement when he speaks next. "If that didn't make her shit herself, I don't know what will."

They all chuckle, releasing more howls and yips. This is nothing but a game to them . . . killing us.

And fuck me, but that arrogance does it. All I can see is Douche's grinning, cocky face as he aims the gun at my chest. Something inside me snaps, and instead of staying put and waiting for the opportune moment, my body decides "fuck it, this is a nice time to die" as I launch myself off the branch right onto the man wearing the coyote mask.

What can I say?

I'd rather die fighting than hide like a little bitch, waiting for the Grim Reaper to find me. I have no doubt these sick, sadistic men will continue to hunt me if I don't do something to stop them.

Who else is even on this island? Clearly, not anyone

who's going to stop whatever the fuck is happening. There's no one to save me but myself.

Sheer luck plants my foot near his neck, but I'll take it. I use my knee to add a snap to my movement, and I hear a gasp as my foot connects, and oxygen suddenly becomes a top priority for the asshole as his windpipe is crushed. Momentum would make me sail past him, but I know I can't do that—the other idiots will open fire—so I use my reflexes to grab on to his shirt, swing around behind him, and yank him in front of me as I land. I smash my fist down onto his gun hand, making him fumble the weapon but not quite drop it.

"Oh fuck!" Fox shouts from nearby as he spots me.

I don't even feel my injured ankle, though I know it must be throbbing. But a high has come over me, the same reckless high that I feel when I'm stealing. My vision sharpens, and time slows to a gentle spin. Carnival lights dance at the edge of my vision as the other men all train their weapons on me, and I use the still-gasping coyote man as a human shield.

"Don't shoot! You might kill Coyote too!" The man in the wolf mask is smarter than his stupid, snarling mask makes him look. His two companions freeze.

I honestly don't know what comes over me—if it's bravery, stupidity, or a toxic combustion of the two. The only thing I know, with unwavering certainty, is that I refuse to cower. Not again. Not ever.

It's as though a chill dances across my skin, cooling my emotions as I have that thought. Fear is replaced by smirking arrogance, and shock has been transformed into anger. These men are vile brutes with wicked intentions; I know that without a shred of doubt, and I want them to pay.

Maybe there's always been a hint of darkness inside of me, a monster clawing and tearing at my body, just waiting to come out. And maybe I'm no longer afraid of the beast inside of me. Maybe, just maybe, I've begun to embrace it.

"But if you do kill him, you might get me too. Try it, I dare you. Shoot through him," I taunt, one arm digging into Coyote's neck and the other digging into the back of his pants . . . for the second gun that I feel tucked into his waistband. It slides out easily, and I murmur to Coyote, "Better throw that gun into the trees, sweetheart."

He does what I say when he feels his second gun kissing his spine.

I can't remember why I was against violence.

The lights dancing inside my head aren't a dull red and yellow anymore. They're brighter—hot pink and highlighter yellow strobes, pulsing and whirling. The music inside my veins is louder too. The glorious high I get from watching a man toss his weapon away on my orders is better than any I've ever felt before. I'm absolutely giddy with delight.

If these are my last few moments, so be it.

"We're going to play a game, boys," I tell them, my tone a seductive purr I've never heard before, spurred on by this ravenous bliss that's eating up all my reason. It must be, because what I say next takes even me by surprise. "No weapons. You chase me. If you catch me, I want you to kill me with your bare hands."

"Oh, I will," Coyote growls, his fists clenched at his sides, furious. Hopefully humiliated. I bet his tiny little balls have crawled up inside and hidden after all his horrible little friends watched him become my bitch.

"What do you say? Up for the challenge, little predators?" I let disdain seep into my tone. "Or do you need to compensate for those tiny dicks with big guns?"

I hear a male laugh burst through the trees, but I can't tell if it's from any of the assholes in front of me, because their chests don't shake.

I can feel their contempt build in the air and thicken it, making it taste as sweet as cotton candy on my lips when I deliberately lick them slowly, just to taunt them further.

Wolf is the first to throw his gun aside into the brush and wiggle his fingers in my direction. "I'll bite."

"I bet you will. If you can catch me." I give him a wink as I try to encourage that pathetic looking boner he has going.

Bear and Fox are more reticent, and as they look at one another, I shove my own gun quickly past Coyote's side, underneath his raised arm, and shoot at each of them in quick succession. *Pop. Pop. Pop.*

They wilt as my bullets pierce their chests, and something strange and wild flaps inside my chest. I should be wearing one of their masks because I feel just as wild as the beasts these idiots pretend to be.

"What the fuck?" Coyote snarls as I lift my gun along

his spine to finish him as well. With a curse, he dives to the side and rolls, grabbing a discarded gun from where it landed a few feet away from his friends' bodies.

He rolls onto his back and begins to fire madly, bullets pelting the nearby trees and causing splinters to fly in all directions.

I was right.

Coyote is definitely the weakest link.

But there's a thing called "luck," and I don't want to wait around to see if that bastard's in play. Coyote may not know how to aim a gun to save his life, but there's a chance one of his wayward bullets will hit me.

My heart pounds and my brain screams, "Stupid!" at me, but my mouth erupts into a wild chuckle as I dart off through the shadowy trees.

4

FALCON

I can't turn away. Even if I wanted to, my eyes are glued to this woman's lithe, petite form as she ducks beneath the nearest tapestry of trees, her breathing erratic despite the beatific smile on her face.

Behind her, face down on the ground, Wolf and two of his men lie either dead or unconscious while Coyote hovers over them, cursing up a storm.

Who the fuck is this girl, and where has she been my entire life?

Something percolates in my stomach, something dark and dangerous and teetering that precarious line between insanity and coherence. My therapist would have told me I'm becoming obsessed again, but that bitch is long dead.

By my hand, actually, after she tried to touch me.

Either way, she's right.

There's something about this little female that lures me in, hook, line, and sinker. I'm utterly enthralled, my gaze homed in on her crouched form like a heat-seeking missile. When she shot those fuckers . . .

Amusement curls up the corners of my lips.

How many times have I imagined putting a bullet in their foreheads? More times than I care to admit. They have hurt so many people since I met them nearly two years ago, and they would've continued to do so. Their favorite targets are women—defenseless women in orange jumpsuits who fall onto the island with no idea how they got here or why and are typically dead before the sun rises.

They're weak.

Prey, despite the masks they wear and the idiotic name they give themselves: Predators. Preds, to be cutesy and pathetic about it. They're nothing but posers. Not true killers.

But not me. Never me. I've always been a hunter. There's a reason they call me an apex predator.

Crouching on the low-hanging branch, I grip the trunk, the coarse bark rubbing deliciously against my calluses. It has already drawn blood, but I relish the sting of pain, the decadent sensation that has my eyes rolling into the back of my head.

Blood, pain, and lust. They're all I'm good for, all I know.

Oh, and obsession.

Definitely obsession.

I jump from branch to branch, as soundless as the wind rustling her brunette hair. She doesn't see me; then again, they never do. It's easy for me to keep pace with her as she hurries away from the scene of the crime, stopping only when she's certain they're not chasing her.

I shift on the branch, my bare feet digging into the wood, as I watch the girl slowly regain her bearings. Her breathing slows down, her hands stop trembling, and fierce determination enters her eyes. The sight has my cock hardening in my jeans, and I resist the urge to release the tree trunk and stroke myself.

There'll be time for that later. For now, I have to watch. Learn. Obsess.

I know, if she were to see me, she would be terrified. How could she not be? As usual, I'm wearing only a pair of jeans that cling to my skin, sans shirt and shoes. Blood covers my chest from one of my victims.

Normally, I'm cleaner when I make my kills, but not today. Today, I'm distracted.

Or is it tonight?

Brows furrowing, I glance toward the sun ducking beneath the tapestry of trees. The sky is gray, and I know that, in only an hour or so, it'll turn pitch-black.

Another cruel smile dances on my lips.

Birds of prey like me . . .

They revel in the dark.

I know, by now, my team will have discovered I'm missing, but they won't dare search for me. They know better than anyone that, when I want to be alone, you better leave me *the fuck alone*. No doubt, they're chasing down prisoners and either recruiting or killing them.

There is no other choice on this fucked-up island

we've all found ourselves on—either you're murdered by one of the teams present, or you join them.

We haven't taken any new members since Eagle last year. But how could we not want the huge, scary-as-fuck Russian with a penchant for machetes? Raven took one look at him and declared that the brute was now Eagle. That, to become one of us, he had to rid himself of his birth name and become one with the birds.

We have no "official" leader, but there's no denying who's in charge.

Raven.

He's the smallest of us all . . . but also the scariest. What he says goes, and we never dare question him.

But today, I just might.

I want the tiny female with umber locks and eyes that almost appear caramel in the waning sunlight. The need is unlike anything I've ever felt before. Carnal, primitive, and downright terrifying . . . for her.

"Carter, you have a problem," my therapist said, her eyes wide behind her wire-rimmed glasses. That was mere seconds before I stabbed her own pencil into her neck. She should've learned by then that I didn't like being touched —I didn't want her hand on my thigh or my cock, and I definitely didn't want her lips anywhere near my face.

Carter, you have a problem.

I may have a problem, but I'm no longer in a world that dictates whether my behavior is socially acceptable. On this island, we are all free to be ourselves, which comes in handy when the worst of the worst drops from the sky. Literally.

Murderers, serial killers, thieves, rapists . . .

We all live here.

And we all train.

Wicked Island is full of monsters and beasts wearing human skins, and it's where the worst of us thrive.

The tiny female moves in my periphery, drawing my attention back to her. She stealthily dances out of her hiding spot and ducks behind a second tree, plastering herself flush against the bark. I watch her in confusion, my eyes narrowing as I try to figure out what threat she sensed, when high-pitched voices reach me.

Fuck.

The Baby Dolls.

Licking my upper lip in anticipation, I watch as a second team meanders from the tree line, talking and giggling amongst themselves. This team of four is made entirely of women, and I just know they will scoop up my little female for themselves the second they see her.

Fierce possessiveness and jealousy steal the breath from my lungs as the team enters the clearing.

A woman we only know on the island as Annabelle—cleverly named after the famous doll—stops and pauses. Like her teammates, she wears a cherubic mask constructed entirely of porcelain. Her eye sockets are accentuated with ridiculous black lashes, and a red mouth is drawn in the center of the white mask. Two brown braids fall over her shoulders.

"I thought I heard her this way," she says, turning to her teammate, Chucky. The second woman wears the exact same mask as Annabelle, but her hair is a red tangled frizz cascading down her back.

"I could've sworn I heard her," Chucky insists.

My eyes drop to the girl—*my* girl—currently crouched behind a tree, only a few feet away from the Dollies. She slowly reaches forward, her hand closing around a rock.

Then she waits.

She still has her gun, but the smart little thing must have counted her shots. She's only got two rounds left, which will leave at least two attackers alive.

I have no doubt that, if they were to step in her direction, my petite female would attack with all the fervor and vigor she did before.

A tiny, *tiny* part of me wants to tell her to show herself—they're one of the only teams who won't kill her but take her in and befriend her.

But I'm selfish, and the second I set my eyes upon the girl, I knew she was meant to be mine.

Mine.

My toy, my plaything, my fucking pet. She'll be what I want her to be, and any argument will be stopped by my cock between her plush lips.

One hand gripping the base of the tree, I drop the other beneath the waistline of my jeans, cupping my cock as I watch the scene below.

My eyes track the delicate curve of the newcomer's neck as she waits with bated breath. I'm actually worried she might pass out in her quest to be silent. This angle draws attention to her perfect ass, currently sticking out behind her as she crouches.

I free my length from its denim prison and then rub my hand over the pre-cum leaking from my dick, using it for lubrication to stroke myself, base to tip.

What I wouldn't give to have her tight little body underneath mine as I take us both to the peak of pleasure. I might kill her afterward, but it would be fucking worth it. Her tits strain against the hideous gray sports bra she's required to wear, and I imagine ripping the fabric off and devouring her perfect tits.

The only thing that would make this image even better is her skin covered in blood—whether that be her blood or the blood of one of my enemies.

When did I last get laid? Fuck, if I remember. Very few women survive on this island longer than a day, and those who do get claimed become Baby Dolls, who say they won't touch a man with a ten-foot pole.

The Baby Dolls are already moving away from her, swinging their machetes and axes as if they haven't got a care in the world, but I can't focus on them. Not even when they stop almost directly underneath me and begin to whisper amongst themselves once more.

They still don't notice the female hiding, but that's okay. I notice her enough for all of us.

Oh, do I notice her.

I wonder how pretty her unblemished skin would look covered in wounds from my knife.

When they move out of earshot, the woman rises, her eyes flashing dangerously as she creeps forward. She's still holding that damn rock tightly, and I can't help but picture my dick in its place. I love it when my women squeeze hard enough for me to black out. That visual careens me over the edge, and I come with a groan, ropes of cum erupting from my dick.

"What the fuck?" the woman exclaims in alarm, and I glance down through the tapestry of leaves and branches obscuring me. My sweet, sweet pet has her head canted backward as she squints up at me, though I know she'll be unable to see me. I made a living out of hiding in the shadows.

My female brings a hand to her cheek and wipes at the white cum, my cum, that shot through the trees and landed on her face. Desire sparks in my bloodstream like fireworks, and I feel myself growing hard again.

"Is that fucking bird shit?" she hisses, her face twisting adorably as she continues to wipe my cum off of her. A tiny trickle of it cascades into her bra, and I watch in rapt fascination as she pulls the material away slightly, allowing me to stare straight down at her bare breasts.

Fucking hell.

Her tits are fucking magnificent. The best pair of tits I've ever seen.

I stiffen further, and I stroke myself leisurely, almost lazily, watching as she attempts to clean herself up. Every time she pulls at her bra, I see her sharp nipples, and it amplifies my desire tenfold.

If I wasn't already positive I was going to keep her, this would cement it all.

This tiny female is mine. Her body. Her soul. Her

fucking heart. I just have to convince Raven to let me keep her instead of killing her.

But for now . . .

I grin wickedly as I come a second time, but unfortunately, she steps away at the last minute.

Damn.

Oh, well. Soon, that delectable body is going to be mine and mine alone. If I want to paint her body in my cum, then I damn well will.

No one, not even Raven, will stop me.

5

NYX

I slither through the forest, trying to be as silent and invisible as a snake. Trying to blend, avoid any sounds, curl my body up tight whenever something tromps through the leaves and shadows nearby. My confidence grows as that group of masked women gets farther away. But my grandmother always used to say that confidence is a match. If you don't keep an eye on it, it'll burn you.

Just as my limbs go limp and I let out a sigh of relief, a man drops from the trees above me. I can't do more than gasp in surprise—because I had no idea he was there—before he lands less than a foot in front of me in the dirt.

My gut lurches with fear before I force myself to act. Because if I give in to the terror ensnaring my heart, I'm a dead woman. I didn't survive being pushed out of an airplane, dropped onto an island I know nothing about, and shooting down a team of masked psychopaths, only to die at the hands of one man.

I kick out at him, my foot catching on his kneecap, but he simply laughs through the pain, wrestling me for control of the gun.

And I know I *can't* let him have it.

I ball my hand into a fist and prepare to throw it into his side, but before I can move, he has a knee in my stomach and both hands around my wrists, tightening until I fear my bones will break. I grunt, wiggling wildly underneath him, but his laughter only turns more manic. The sound is . . . broken. It's beautiful and haunting, but there's something about the noise that isn't quite right—the discordant ping of a broken piano key.

Still, I don't stop fighting, don't stop bucking my hips with the force of a raging bull. I'll fight until I die if I have to, but he won't win.

God, he *can't* win. I've met my fair share of deranged men and women throughout my life, but none of them made my stomach twist with fear like he does. There's something so predatory about him, something so innately lethal, that I know he won't just kill me—he'll make me suffer first.

"Little killer, are you *trying* to excite me?" His voice is raspy, hoarse, as if someone strangled him until his vocal cords stopped working correctly.

And I must be extremely fucked in the head, because a sliver of heat travels down my spine at the low, gravelly tone.

But that sliver of heat turns into ice-cold fury when he wrenches the gun out of my hands, ejects the maga-

zine and the round in the chamber, and then places the
weapon into the waistband of his jeans.

It feels like he's taking away my umbilical cord, my
lifeline, when he takes that gun, and my heart gains speed
as I glance up into his pale face. His brown eyes study me
with an intensity that feels more like a dissection.

In Biology class my sophomore year of high school,
we had to dissect an unborn pig. Study every organ, learn
each of its muscles, slice through its flesh. That is what
his stare feels like—I'm the pig, and he's the eager high
school student about to cut me open.

Is he about to kill me?

He could have just used the gun, so I feel a flicker of
hope, but as I search his gaze for the answer to that question, I can't find it. His eyes are so dark that they're
impossible to read, almost as if I'm staring at a book
written in another language. The harsh lines create words
with no meaning, nothing but slashes and curves on
paper.

The man looks like he's in his mid-twenties. He's got
a strong jawline, but it's a bit narrower than is popular
now. He reminds me of a 1920s mobster, with his unruly
brown hair that's parted on one side. Or perhaps a surfer,
with his trim physique, which is clearly on display
because he's shirtless, wearing only jeans and no shoes.
His washboard abs tighten, and I make out a tribal tattoo
on one of his shoulders as he peers down at me.

He's so fucking sexy—exuding an aura of danger—
that I don't know whether to run as far away as I can or
give in to every dirty fantasy I've ever had. Tension builds

in the air between us, and either impending death is hot as fuck or he is.

God, the fact that I find him attractive when he's no doubt thinking about killing me just proves how broken I am.

That slanted grin is still firmly in place, giving him an unhinged look as he jumps gracefully to his feet and drags me up with him. Before I can back away—before I can run or fight—he has his hands on my shoulder and his nose in my neck, nuzzling the skin there and inhaling deeply.

"Smells good. So good," he purrs, bringing his nose to the shell of my ear. "My favorite scent. Did you know I can smell your fear, little killer?"

"Get the fuck away from me." I shove at his chest, and surprisingly, he moves backward, that damn grin still curling up the corners of his lips.

My spine liquifies, and I step back as well, fern fronds caressing the backside of my knee and adding a tickle to my fear. I consider screaming, but that might bring those women back here. And unlike them, this guy is unarmed, other than my useless gun tucked into his pants. Was he a prisoner on the plane? Did he get shoved off too?

My question is answered when I spot a string around his neck and the mask hanging loosely between his muscular shoulder blades. A falcon mask. A hunting bird.

My throat grows as dry as the Sahara. No. Definitely not a prisoner from the plane.

"Sweet little killer," he says with a grin, his voice a dark scratch against my ear.

Every single one of my muscles grows tense as I realize he saw what happened between me and the men in the predator masks. There's no other reason he'd call me that.

Oh, fuck. Is he pissed? Were they friends? That was pure dumb luck. It was adrenaline and fury fused together into a once-in-a-lifetime chance occurrence. I don't think that explaining "I didn't actually think I'd kill them" will suffice, however. I'm pretty certain it will only make him realize how helpless I really am.

He takes another step toward me.

This time, my adrenaline converts from its typical carnival sideshow into a horror flick, complete with an evil clown and demented music.

Fuck.

The man's hand comes forward, and I turn to run, but he catches my upper arm before I can get two steps away. He yanks me back against his torso, and I feel his coarse chest hair tickle my spine as he slides one arm across my breasts and pins me to him. His other hand leaves my arm and traces down my side.

"So soft and yet so hard," he murmurs before leaning down to sniff my hair.

I feel like a rabbit caught in a trap, and I hate that feeling. Goose bumps cover my body, and I'm treading water, trying not to drown in panic.

Think, I order my brain, trying to force it to shove aside whatever instinct has me freezing up. I need to

fight. Attack. Get away. I try to slip into my thief mental-
ity, see this as just another lock I have to pick. If I plan
this just right, I'll be able to outmaneuver him. I shift my
feet so that I can stomp this fucker's instep, but he feels
me move.

"No, little killer. Don't even think about it. Be a good
pet for your new master."

Fuck him. And fuck his condescending attitude and
his dumbass nickname for me.

Trepidation transitions into anger and adrenaline—a
similar sensation to what I felt when I shot those men
down. I retreat to a place in my mind where darkness
resides and monsters come out to play.

I toss an elbow backward, ramming his solar plexus.
To my absolute fury, it doesn't even make him flinch. His
hold on me doesn't loosen whatsoever.

"Now, I'm going to have to punish you." He makes
his threat sound so utterly sexual. His tone is an eager
purr as the hand that was caressing my side comes to rest
on my low belly.

My limbs lock as he drags his hand up and tugs down
one side of my bra, folding it so my breast is pressed
upward. Then he slowly pinches my nipple. To my
horror, it's already swollen and hard. He hardly tugs
before it's standing at full attention.

What the hell is wrong with my body? I wonder as
heat licks up my thighs.

My mind tells me to hate this, but my body has
another idea.

"You excited by death, little killer?" His grip on my

nipple becomes punishing as he pinches down hard, and I let out an involuntary squeal. His other hand quickly releases me and moves to smack my ass, jolting me forward, making me take a step to regain my balance . . . and making the pressure on my nipple tug painfully. "You're mine now. I've claimed you as my own—my own, perfect pet."

It's demeaning and horrible, but an itty-bitty part of me—the part that feeds off the thrill of a job well done—gasps in pleasure, arching into his skillful hand. I hate myself for it, I really fucking do, but my body seems to have a mind of its own. My parents were right. Maybe I am broken beyond repair.

But fuck him. Fuck this shit. If he's going to play with me before he kills me, then I'm at least going to get in a few good swings.

I move back, tilting my head back against his chest and arching. I breathe hard, as if he's made me hot. It's not entirely an act, but I'm not willing to admit that, even to myself.

That's when I grab his dick and twist. Hard.

His hiss of pain might as well be the chorus of angels. He drops his hold on me to grip his precious cock as I spin around to face him, ready to fight for my life.

He body-slams me to the ground, and I barely miss cracking my skull on a tree trunk. The ringed bark of the palm tree scrapes my cheek as we fall. The man's dark eyes gleam with wild excitement as he grabs my hands and pins them above me.

And though I feel the natural ribbon of fear at being

held down, it's braided together with a sick wantonness that comes from a thousand different memories of being held down and fucked hard. The position isn't capable of making me that afraid anymore. But I pretend it is. I widen my eyes and wait for this fucker with the wind-blown hair to lean down toward my exposed breast.

Just before he can latch on, I shove my knee upward.

He lets out a breathy grunt of pain, and I push him off, scrambling to my feet and tucking my breast back into my bra as he staggers to his feet, smiling.

What the fuck? Is he a damned eunuch? What guy recovers that quickly from two back-to-back ball hits?

"I like this game, little killer." An emotion I can't quite read enters his eyes—some combination of impish delight and anger. Whatever it is has every muscle in my stomach knotting. "You're fun to play with. But fair warning." His smile grows, curving at the edges the way I imagine the Joker, enemy of Batman, might. "I always cheat."

I dart off into the trees at his final words, fear clasping at my airways, but a huge black hand reaches out of the darkness and clamps down on me.

Fuck!

A man the size of a truck walks me backward, and as he steps out of the shadows and into the light, I notice a bird mask covering his face. It's painted brown with a sharp, curved beak. A hawk.

The first man behind me calls out, "Hey, Hawk! Glad you could make it. I was just about to initiate our newest member."

Confusion rockets through me, but then I start to make the connection . . . they both have bird masks. Just like all those women had fucked-up doll masks and those other guys had wild animal—no, *predator*—masks.

"If by *initiate* you mean rape," I snarl at the handsome psycho.

"Your body was willing. Your mind was playing catch up," the man asserts with a dismissive flick of his hand.

I glare at him, because he's half right. At least about my body.

"Besides," he narrows his eyes at me, "I don't *rape* unwilling women. You would've wanted me by the time I was done with you."

"Fuck you. There's no way in hell I'll ever want you," I retort scathingly, but the crazy man simply laughs, as if I amuse the shit out of him. Maybe because he can tell I'm lying through my teeth.

The huge man holding me—Hawk—shoves his mask upward, back into his hairline, so that I can see his face.

Damn.

While the first man who found me is pale and angular, this man with the hawk mask looks like he could win a body-building contest. His muscles bulge into sleek curves everywhere, and his black T-shirt struggles to contain him. I'm five foot five, but he makes me feel tiny and delicate, especially when his huge hand encases both of my wrists, clamping down on them like he's a human set of handcuffs. He could probably lift my entire body with one hand. God, my interaction with the crazy man behind me has scrambled my brains, because the idea of

Hawk picking me up and dangling me in front of him as he has his way with me seems incredibly hot.

I stare at his huge, dark fingers curled around me and then up at his face, which has a perfect square forehead and straight brows, big lips, and thick stubble lining his chin. He'd definitely win a Mr. Universe contest. He's hot. He's handcuffs. Hotcuffs.

Shit. My mind is spiraling downward into a strange space, where it combines words and thoughts and nothing is clear. Perhaps I've had too much adrenaline pumping through my system. I've been out of the game for nearly a year . . . but even when I was in the game, it wasn't life and death. I've never had to deal with levels of panic like this before.

Maybe that explains why my tongue blurts out, "Well, at least you're a hot rapist."

Not that the first guy wasn't sexy as hell too, though I won't admit that in a million years.

A crooked grin transforms Hawk's face, immediately followed by a glare as he shoots a look over at the guy who jumped out of the trees. "What the hell, Falcon? Is that how you treat a lady?"

"She's mine. I found her first." Falcon, apparently, holds out a hand in midair, as if he expects Hotcuffs to just release me and turn me back over to him. There's something dangerous in his dark eyes, something predatory and intense that has goose bumps rippling across my skin and the hairs on the back of my neck standing on end.

Hawk shakes his head disapprovingly at the other

man before he turns and looks at me. In a gentle, deep voice, he asks, "Miss, do you want to go back with Falcon?"

I quickly shake my head.

Falcon's brows lower, and he pushes himself against my back, his hot breath fanning against my neck as he crowds against me and presses me up against Hawk's ribs.

Falcon whispers, "Finder's keepers." With one finger, he traces gently up the back of my thigh, toward my panty line. His finger teases the edge of the fabric, and I suck in a gasping breath.

My heart trills inside my chest, especially when I feel Hawk start to grow hard in front of me. The huge man's eyes, though, remain earnest as he gazes down at me. I can't help the tiny flicker of trust I feel. Maybe not every person on this island is out to get me. Maybe Hawk will protect me—though I've proved time and time again that I can protect myself. But to have a little backup, especially against men like Falcon, the predators, those masked women, and the crazy Barbie doll guy?

I'm not complaining if Hawk decides to be my knight in shining armor.

"What the fuck is going on here?!" A new voice breaks through the trees. The sound of tromping feet makes both men turn to the side, away from me.

Relief and gratitude seep into my bones for the newcomer, who's currently emerging from behind a huge pine. Until he speaks again.

"We don't play with the newbies. We kill them." A

man who's only a couple inches taller than me, wearing a black raven mask, pulls a gun from his waistband and points it right at my forehead.

Fuck.

My vision blurs red for a millisecond, as if I've been hit hard by an object. But the men around me move quickly as a unit. Hawk releases my wrists and slides in front of me as Falcon smoothly steps in behind me, and his arms wrap around my shoulders once again.

"She's joining us," Falcon announces stubbornly. "She's my new pet."

The man in the raven mask leans around Hawk. "What the fuck, Falcon? You can't just go around fucking adding people. There are fucking rules—"

"She took out the entire Predator team. Except for Coyote, but he's such a dumbass, he'll be dead in days without a team," Falcon argues, hugging me closer, like murder is something to be proud of. Of course, based on what I've seen thus far on this island, killing is something of a sport to them.

In that case, I'll just tuck the knowledge that those shots hit their targets accidentally right into my chest pocket and button it up tight. There is absolutely no need for these men to know that information. Especially not when two other men have stomped out of the trees behind the Raven-masked man, both also in bird masks. All the masks have swiveled to stare directly at me, and Hawk has even given up his position as my shield so that he can turn to stare at me after the truth-bomb that Falcon just dropped.

Five men.

One of me.

I do not like these odds, especially if they intend to—a shudder rumbles through me—*keep* me.

"No." The man in the raven mask shakes his head, a strand of pitch-black hair dislodging and tumbling forward. "Not possible."

"Yes, Raven. Go a half mile northwest, and you can watch the flies gather on the bodies," Falcon responds proudly.

The night grows thick with the humidity and the power of their gazes.

A soft tenor voice asks, "Is that true?"

I search the masks, trying to identify the voice, but I can't at first, because the carved wooden faces they wear cast black shadows over their lips. But then one man, the largest of the group, pulls his ugly vulture mask up. And he doesn't look at Falcon, who's holding me, nuzzling against my cheek. He looks right at me.

Something in his gaze pierces me, but not in a harsh or disapproving way. There's a sort of insane clarity that radiates from his calm demeanor, and he asked the question so gently that I almost feel compelled to answer. Why do I feel like he can truly see me? Not as a toy or a pet or a prisoner . . . but *me?* "Did you shoot three men?"

I press my lips together and give a solitary nod as I take note of his features. While his mask has the hooked beak of a vulture, his own nose is wide and straight. His hair is cropped close to his head on either side with a faux hawk strip of hair that could be any shade of brown or black . . . I can't tell in the darkness. He has a barrel chest and biceps the size of dinner plates and skin that's bronzed, as if he spends a lot of time on the beach here. Tattoos wrap his forearms, and my eyes lock on to his dark brown gaze as he slowly holsters his gun at his waist.

"She's in," he declares.

His simple statement sets off sparks amongst the rest of them, rippling flames that ignite this forest on fire.

Raven turns to the vulture man and smacks him on the chest with the back of his hand. "What the fuck, Vulture? Just because you wanna fuck her does not mean she's in."

Okay, fourth bird name in a row. Apparently, they use codenames. And not clever ones. My thoughts process that fact as I look between Vulture and Raven, watching the testosterone build to a sizzling peak in front of me. For some reason, the smallest man seems to think he runs the show. I try to dissect their dynamic as they argue. I always try to dissect marks, so I suppose dissecting potential killers isn't that different.

We have Falcon, the unhinged one who wants me as a pet.

Hawk, my smiling knight.

Vulture, with that soft, lilting voice.

Raven is still wearing his mask, as is the man wearing an eagle one behind him. Eagle remains a mystery, but Raven's need for control broadcasts as bright as a spot-light to my eyes. I'm not sure how I can use this informa-tion yet, so I store it away. I'll keep watching and adding to it.

"She knows weapons. She's hot. I'm claiming her," Vulture says simply, offering a nonchalant shrug.

As if he didn't just act like he has a say over me and my body.

As if he didn't just make both fear and lust slither down my spine, twining together until I can't differentiate one from the other.

Fuck.

"She's a goddamned untested liability!" Raven throws a hand on his head as if to grab his hair, forgetting his mask is in place. His fingers scrape against the wood while the hand holding the gun remains trained on me, surprisingly steady.

"Can't claim her. She's *my* pet," Falcon interjects with a petulant pout and foot stomp.

What is with these guys and claiming? And why do I find it so damn attractive? Oh, right. I have terrible taste in men. Douchebag—case in point.

Vulture turns to glare at him, and they have a stare off. The air around them practically crackles with electricity, and I don't know which side I want to win. I definitely don't want to be someone's pet or toy, but at the same time . . . am I ready to die? I've never contemplated my mortality until today. Even after I got shot, my thoughts focused more on revenge. But now that I'm staring the Grim Reaper in the eyes, I find that I have a lot to live for. Not for other people—they can all go to hell —but for myself. There's so much I still want to do, so much I need to accomplish. I was just headed to prison, and now . . . I'm here with a chance at something more.

But every second I remain in this intense tug-of-war, my hopes and dreams begin to trickle away from me, like water in a wrung-out sponge. Fear occupies the space that hope once was.

If they don't win and the Raven man does . . . I'm dead.

As they debate, their words become muffled because my pulse thumps so loudly in my ears it eclipses all other sounds. I don't think I like that claiming statement, though Vulture is one of the handsomest guys I've ever seen. He has a dark and dangerous biker vibe, the kind that's always drawn me in back home.

But if it's either death or claiming, I choose the latter. At least for now.

"She's just been tested and took down three guys with minimal blood splatter on her. Her panties aren't even ripped . . . are they, sweetheart?" Vulture asks, stepping closer with a gleam in his eye that transforms his friendly demeanor into that of a scavenger who could rip me to bits.

My throat dries out, and I shake my head, even though what I want to do is find a way out of Falcon's hold on me and flee. I have to remind my panicked heart that they outnumber me, and I don't have the element of surprise like I did with the group I shot.

I'm better off observing them and finding their weaknesses. Biding my time.

"Goddammit! Her panties aren't the point! The very fact that she could wipe out a team should tell you something. She's a plant! They sent her here to spy on us! Or take us out! Someone wants us all dead." Raven retrains his gun on me as he rants. Though his chest heaves as he spits out paranoid vitriol, his eye contact never wavers. All I can focus on are those dark slits, barely visible through the raven mask he wears.

Falcon chuckles into my ear and circles a finger on the skin of my hip, his finger slipping just below my panty line.

"I don't know. I think her panties *are* the point," Falcon replies. "They're in the way."

I stiffen, his statement sending a shiver down my spine that makes goose bumps spring up along my arms, and my nipples tighten in the chill.

Vulture narrows his eyes when he spots Falcon's fingers. "Hands off my merchandise."

"I found her. She's not yours," Falcon retorts. "She's my pet. My little killer." He nuzzles my head, and I resist the urge to cringe away. The last thing I want them to know is just how much I fear them.

But is it only fear I feel?

The thought slips into my head unbidden, but I shove it off the metaphorical airplane, the same way I was.

"Now, guys, is that any way to talk about a lady in her presence? I don't think so. I don't know about you, but my momma would spank my ass for that kind of thing," Hawk interjects, his eyes softening and radiating kindness, which feels so out of place in this scenario. It's like a sunbeam suddenly appearing in the middle of the night. Hawk has an incredible smile, I realize. He's also got the type of grin that makes grandmothers everywhere melt.

I'm instantly certain he's a master manipulator, even as my chest grows a smidgen warmer at his words. The guys around him quiet down. I'm not sure if that means that Hawk is the actual leader of the group, or he's second in command to Raven. But . . . he's at least not aiming to kill me instantly.

I stare at him for a moment. "Thank you, Hawk. I always appreciate when a guy recognizes that I'm a human being and not an object," I say, deciding I'd rather negotiate my life or death with someone who maintains at least the illusion of manners. Unlike Raven, who's still muttering a bit wildly under his mask.

"Hawk, hmm? Catch on quickly, don't you? And who might you be?" Hawk offers another one of his charming smiles. Or perhaps *disarming* would be a more accurate descriptor.

I let my eyes scan their masks. Two of them have claimed me. Going along with that seems like the best survival strategy right now. "Well, I'll call myself Phoenix. You don't seem to have one of those yet."

"Because it's not a real bird," Raven instantly retorts, his gun wavering slightly in agitation. "And you're not fucking joining. We are not adding a fuck doll. Come on, Hawk. Please tell me you aren't fooled by this little act. Obviously, she knows exactly what she's doing and who we—"

"*Obviously,* your codenames are the same as your masks. It's not rocket science," I retort.

I can't see his expression, but Raven stiffens, as if offended. "I say we nix her."

From the back, the man in an eagle mask steps forward. The pale painted feathers of his wooden disguise are lighter than all the others. When this man lifts his mask, I see eyes too light to be brown but too dark to be blue—hazel, perhaps. His jaw is strong beneath the scruffy hint of a beard that coats it. He props his mask up on his forehead as he tilts his head and studies me just like a bird might.

"I agree," he states in a stilted accent that sounds Russian or Eastern European.

"With who?" Hawk turns to look at him.

"You." Eagle nods at Hawk. "She stays. And initiation will test. Prove her."

My stomach sinks at those words as Hawk and Eagle both nod at one another. Of course, Hawk does so with a wide, friendly smile in my direction while Eagle's eyes pierce me like twin spears.

"Goddammit! But no fucking. Not one of you is allowed to stick your dick in her. Fucking Venus flytrap pussy has you idiots slobbering like dogs. It's going to get you killed. Fools." Raven turns on his heel and strides off, angry mutters floating back through the trees behind him, though none of the other men seem to pay his anger any mind. Their eyes are all on me, and I'm still processing exactly what went down just now.

Initiation, they said. It looks like I'm going to be put to the test.

But the question is . . . what kind of tests do a bunch of psycho murderers give?

Raven growls, "I don't agree with this. I think we need to run her background. One five-second interaction doesn't make her worthy of the Birds of Prey."

I swallow down the natural sarcasm longing to erupt because they've given themselves a group name like this is summer camp. This would be the most warped version of camp, ever.

Instead of eating s'mores or singing a riveting song about love and friendship around the campfire, as far as I can tell, the activities on this island include stabbing one another or gunning one another down. Camp games here are epic.

I focus on the fact that, behind several of the guys, the trees have low-hanging branches that stretch out invitingly, as if they're beckoning me to climb in and hide amongst their leaves. If I can disarm and get away from all these guys, of course.

I estimate the likelihood of that as less than the likelihood of a whale growing legs. But stranger things have happened. I just need to stay alert for an opportunity.

Falcon yanks and snaps the waistband of my panties, making me yelp, and all the other guys stare.

What the hell is he doing?

I try to pull away from Falcon and fail. His arms tighten like vises around me, pinning me to him while he stares right at Raven. "Fine. How about this? Phoenix, you want to live, you give Raven here your real name. And while he searches a million websites and sorts through thousands of false hits all by himself, the rest of us will test you out in much more *fun* ways."

That sounds like I'd get fucked fifty ways to Sunday —literally—and then killed, because Raven seems like an unstable asshole.

I debate Falcon's ultimatum as I eye them all, weighing them as much as they're sizing me up. Well, I haven't had sex in a while . . .

Behind me, somewhere in the trees, a gunshot goes off, and a wretched scream fills the air. It's so loud and long that it could be mistaken for a howl from an animal . . . but I know it's not. I swallow hard as cold reality sets in.

There's no getting away. It's either these fuckers or the monsters out there. And for some reason, these Birds of Prey want to keep me, even if it is for unsavory purposes. Once again, my survival instincts kick in.

I may hate myself for this decision down the road, but

it's my only choice if I hope to live another goddamn hour.

"Nicholette Bettencourt." I give my legal name haltingly. "But I've gone by Nyx for as long as I can remember."

Raven stares at me long and hard, as if he can mentally twist me up and wring the truth out of me. But he doesn't have to. There used to be a time when some people might have found that information valuable. Found *me* valuable. Not anymore.

"When you find my parents, don't think you've hit the jackpot. They won't pay a dime for me. I was disowned and written off when I was sixteen," I tell him.

His head cants to the side, ironically birdlike, and he studies me through his mask, taking in this new tidbit as if it's a delicious little treat.

"Mafia?" he asks.

"Heiress," I respond. "Or I used to be. Now, I'm just an ugly memory."

Immediately, he turns to the others and shakes his head. "No way. I'm not letting someone that soft on the team."

"Well, she *is* awfully soft," Falcon adds, his fingers tracing down my arm.

"If you're going to taunt us with the pretty lady, you should at least offer to share." Hawk's thick lips grow thin as a frown mars his perfectly symmetrical face. His words become increasingly tense, and all the protective vibes he was emanating shrivel up as he stomps forward. A growl erupts from his mouth as he yanks me out of Falcon's grip, and the hard look in his eyes makes my stomach acid curdle. Fuck.

When I glance down at his huge hand clamped on me, I feel trapped, and the instinctive urge to run makes my leg muscles tense.

Another horrid scream cuts through the night and makes the chirping insects surrounding us go silent. I force my legs to relax, my lungs to take a steady breath, and my lips to get the next words out without my voice wavering.

"Look, I gave you my name," I say, as my eyes dart into the darkness, my mind etching out pictures of horrors that I don't even want to imagine. Body parts being hacked off. Women being held down by men like those damn predators. Blood soaking the tangled grass. "Can someone tell me what the fuck this place is?"

Hawk's arms encircle me, his biceps bulging near my cheeks. But unlike Falcon's touch, which volleyed between shackling me and seducing me, Hawk's huge muscles feel comforting, and he keeps his grip loose and polite. Protective instead of possessive. The scent of orange blossoms, musk, and honey drift over me.

He's wearing nice cologne? On an island full of killers? This place baffles me.

"Please," I add. "Where are we?"

Hawk gives me a friendly smile as he stares down into my eyes. "This place is basically hell on earth. And we're all demons."

Vulture blows out a raspberry. "Fuck that. There's no such thing. We're all convicts here, Phoenix," he explains as he pulls his mask off completely and runs a hand through his faux hawk and along the backs of his ears, as if the wood irritated his skin. With the mask off and the moonlight giving me a slightly better look at him, he doesn't just resemble a biker. His looks are classically Italian. "Private prison owns this place. Company called—"

"Hoplite Defense Services?" I ask.

"You've heard of them?" Vulture cocks a brow up as he runs a hand down over his black beard and mustache, smoothing them. His expression is cold, but unlike the other guys here, he doesn't direct that ice in my direction. He just looks like the kind of man who has no emotions, a statue brought to life. While Raven might rant and rave, or Hawk might run hot and cold—sweet one second and cruel the next—and Falcon might be slightly unhinged . . . none of those things are quite as bone-chilling as Vulture's no-nonsense distance. He looks like the kind of guy who could flay a person without batting an eyelash.

I suppress a shiver as I shake my head. "It was on the shirts the fuckers wore before they tossed us from the plane. I thought they were terrorists at first."

"In a way. Yes. That's true." Eagle looks at me, his mouth a flat line and his accent even more pronounced with his agitation. "They use fear. Yes?"

Hawk nods his head, his giant hands tightening slightly before he realizes that he's squeezing my arms, and releases me, taking a step back. When he speaks, he suddenly has a prim and proper British accent that is quite ridiculous given his mask and the black combat gear he wears. "I've always been a fan of fear. But only at the right moment. It can be an art form, you know? But these pathetic wankers have no subtlety. I'd never have lasted outside these walls as long as I did if I hadn't managed to control—"

"Yes, we know. We've heard this. A million times. And your British accent. It's horrible," Eagle shakes his head. "Is like broken glass on my ears."

"Well, then, how about Texan?" Hawk changes his voice mid-sentence, shifting his weight to widen his stance.

It's surreal, what is happening. These men are having a casual conversation—with theatrical accents included—in the middle of a tropical forest while people are being killed all around us.

"Um. Excuse me, but can someone fill me in a little more on this private prison stuff? And maybe, you know, the murders that are happening right now?"

A shot goes off nearby, and it makes even Raven jump. His eyes dart around like mine have been, though I hope I didn't look quite so startled and afraid. "Yes, let's go turn in our weapons and talk back at the bunks while I look her up."

Before I can blink, I find myself scooped up into Hawk's arms, bridal style. I swallow my exclamation of surprise but can't stop my jaw from dropping. "Excuse me, but that's not very progressive of you." The words leave my mouth unbidden, but before I can think too hard about the consequences of my sassy retort, Hawk speaks.

"Well, now, ma'am, I was just thinking I'd spare you having to keep an eye out for all the snakes."

"Pretty sure the snakes I need to worry about are in all your pants," I quip back, though underneath my bravado runs a vein of fear.

Don't let it show, I coach myself. If there's anything a life on the streets and time in jail taught you, it's not to let the fear paint your face.

Hawk chuckles. "If any of their snakes try to bite you, you just let me know, and I'll take care of it."

"Will you?" I peer up at him questioningly. Of all the guys, he comes across as the least threatening and most friendly. The friendly giant. The BFG. But my trust has eroded over the past year, and I can't quite bring myself to believe him. He's got an angle. They always do. The accents also prove he's an actor. So, the friendliness could just be another accent he tosses around, a façade.

Hawk gives me a playful double eyebrow raise. "Oh, I've been looking for an excuse to go head-to-head with Vulture since I got here."

"Fuck you," Vulture retorts from Hawk's right, just past my dangling feet. "I'm gonna pierce your dick while you sleep."

"Not if I cut off your fingers first."

The men begin a round of violent banter back and forth as they shove aside ferns and weave through a forest full of bullets and dying screams, as if tonight is a regular occurrence. With a shudder, I realize maybe it is.

I bring a hand to my forehead and swipe across my eyes, checking, wondering if I'm still passed out in the back of that transport van and this is all some horrible nightmare. But my eyes are open, a pinch to my arm hurts, and reality bitch slaps me back.

Hawk gives me an understanding look, as if he knows exactly what's going through my head. "We've all been there." He juts his chin toward me in empathy before ducking to take us underneath a tree branch and over a ridge. I clutch his T-shirt, totally and completely oblivious to the hard planes of his pecs and the tiny nubs of his nipples as he slides along some wet leaves and we go down a steep hill in the nearly pitch-black darkness. I'm not distracted at all by the first hot male I've touched since before going to prison. Nope. Not me.

"What *is* this place?" I ask again, but this time, my voice is as thin as a reed and the words are no more than a whisper.

Thankfully, that polite streak of his allows Hawk to indulge me. "Hoplite Defense takes the worst of the worst criminals. Or so they say. And they bring them here. New deliveries once every few months. They call these deliveries 'hunts' because those of us already here can hunt for members to add to our team or . . ."

A scream finishes his sentence for him.

"Or you hunt the new people down." The words drag like dry cotton across my tongue.

He nods. "Falcon's never chosen anyone before."

"None of you have," Raven's voice pipes up from somewhere in the darkness, and I turn my head, trying to spot him. But it's impossible. The leaves overhead block the moon with alarming efficiency, and I have no clue how these men know where they're going right now. Not until I see Hawk slide his own mask back down and realize that there are actually night vision goggles embedded in the eyeholes. Hmmm . . . and I thought I saw people's eyes. I scold myself for overlooking a detail like that. It's the details that make or break a thief.

That makes me wonder . . . "What kind of prison arms its own prisoners?"

"Have you ever seen that show, *Squid Games*?" Hawk asks, no accent or chipper tone to his voice this time around. It's low and raspy, a baritone rumble.

A chill runs down my spine. "Where people basically play fucked-up games and prove how evil and selfish they are?"

"Yup. You got it."

My stomach plummets. *This can't be right. This can't be right. This can't be right!* My mind repeats the same thing over and over again, as if thinking the thought louder and more frantically will make a difference. Goose bumps rise on my arms. What I believed was a twenty-year sentence full of monotony transforms into a much more violent, much shorter future. I chew my lip, trying to hide my panic with what could be thoughtfulness.

Hawk continues talking as he curves around a giant tree trunk. "Falcon was an assassin for hire. Raven was a hacker who took over some nukes. Vulture worked in interrogation."

I'm not sure if I'm impressed or about to puke. I force my face into neutral as I nod.

Interrogation . . . what kind of interrogation gets you

arrested? My throat grows dry as I connect the dots and realize that he was probably the sort of guy who tied people up and asked questions while he unrolled a black cloth sewn with special pockets for all sorts of medieval instruments. Dammit. I need to stop. Any more mental images, and I will probably vomit. I try to tell myself this is just another job, not my new reality. This is just another job with one objective—get the fuck off this island. These are my teammates. Not threats. Fuck. The bile coating my throat rejects the lies I try to sell myself.

Eagle's Russian accent drifts through the dark. "I was weapons dealer. And you, Phoenix?" He steps closer behind Hawk's shoulder, and as we move through a break in the tree canopy, I can see his white mask turned in my direction, the hooked beak like a question mark.

Dipping my head, I stare down at my lap, wondering if I can pretend I didn't hear him. What the hell am I supposed to say? I'm just a thief? I don't belong here?

I'm a petty criminal in comparison to all those things listed—I mean, come on, a freaking nuke!

I half wonder if I should lie about my crimes, make myself sound bigger and badder, so the men come to fear me. But then I remember that Raven plans to look me up, and if he's skilled enough to steal a fucking nuke, he can surely find my criminal record, even though my parents paid to have it sealed.

I press my lips together and glance up at Hawk. "And what did you do?" I only ask the question to deflect the one aimed at me, but I am curious, and slightly hopeful, that Hawk's crimes are much more minor . . . like my

own. Could he be a scissors thief? Is that a thing? Maybe
he doodled a penis on a wall in downtown Chicago? Or
maybe he streaked down Main Street with his ass cheeks
flapping? No, correction. That ass wouldn't flap. You
could bounce quarters off that thing all day long. But
still . . . I hope he was a streaker. And maybe that there's
footage of it online somewhere.

Hawk steps up to a chain-link fence topped with
barbed wire. His eyes study mine carefully as he gently
sets me down on the ground. Tension weaves between us,
tying our breaths together.

Why isn't he answering?

Something dark and sinister cascades through me. I
don't want to call it a premonition, but it feels oddly
similar.

Raven breaks the moment when he yells, "Guard!"

I glance over at Raven, who bangs impatiently on the
fence, yelling about priorities and deadlines, like he's
some entitled brat instead of a prisoner.

That's when Hawk pulls his gun out of the holster at
his belt. I stiffen as I turn back toward him. Was this all a
hoax? This joining them? Did they just want to wait and
kill me in front of a guard?

Hawk's eyes stroke up and down my skin as he gives
himself a moment of slow perusal, the kind that makes
my breath catch and my skin pebble. He looks almost
sensual in this moment, which only amplifies my trepidation as he brings the gun up and uses the side of the
muzzle to caress my neck and then my cheek.

Dread encases my entire body like a block of ice, and

I'm frozen. I can't move as his weapon slides along my skin, back down my neck, and then the tip traces over the top edge of my bra.

Hawk leans down and whispers in my ear. "Your fear is so beautiful, Nyx. You look like the statue of a goddess."

A guard comes around the corner, an irritated expression on his pug-like face. His appearance breaks Hawk's concentration, and the big man straightens, turning and pointing his gun at the ground, his hand off the trigger.

The guard shakes his head, a hand on the machine gun slung around his neck. "You fuckwits. No one else is back yet. There are still plenty—"

"I caught one, and we're keeping her," Falcon announces proudly as he lifts a bare foot and pulls a burr out of it, casually tossing it aside. "We're done for tonight."

The guard grumbles as he glances over at me. His startled bug eyes clearly convey that he has no idea why these idiots would keep me.

That makes two of us, buddy.

"You know you can't keep women just to fuck—"

"We know the rules," Raven growls. "Now hurry up, so I can run a background and confirm this choice."

The guard mutters under his breath as he digs a key out of his pocket. He reaches for a radio that's attached to his shoulder. "Cover me. Birds of Prey is back."

"Affirmative, over." A voice crackles through the radio.

Two seconds later, the gate opens with a horrible

screech, and the five men who claimed me tromp inside. Hawk offers me his elbow, but I pretend not to see it, walking faster, unnerved by his caress with the gun.

All the Birds of Prey stalk over to a folding table set up in the grass near the gate. Then they disarm, leaving their guns, knives that were tucked into their boots, and masks behind.

More guards come out from behind a cement building and pat all of them down. Even I get a pat down, though I'm wearing practically nothing.

Hawk and Falcon stare at the guard who touches me with menacing expressions on their faces until his hands leave and he announces, "She's clean."

Falcon winks at me, and when we walk forward, he throws a possessive arm around my waist.

I need an ally, I tell myself, as his warm hand combats the cool skin on my hip.

And he wants to keep me.

I force myself to look up at his clean-cut face. I realize how young he looks with a tendril of dark hair falling across his forehead, this madman plucked from a twenties era mob and shoved into the future. I make myself give him a thin smile and am shocked when his returning smile makes my heart skip a beat.

It's fear. Just adrenaline doing odd things, I try to reassure myself. My body is out of whack after everything that's happened tonight. There's zero chance that I'll develop hero worship for the fucker who fell from the sky and claimed me. Or at least, that's what I tell myself.

I turn away from Falcon and force my eyes to take in

the prison. It looks nicer than a normal prison. The cinder-block buildings have more windows, for one thing. For another, most of the buildings are only one or two stories, instead of big boxes stuffed full of as many people as possible. A few wooden cottages rest farther back, oddly resembling bunkhouses from the one summer camp I went to in fifth grade. There are golf carts here and there. I see a Jeep without doors sitting behind one building. And tons of Hoplite Security guards walk around with machine guns that are as thick as my thigh.

So, running back into the forest doesn't seem like much of an option . . . not that I really consider it for more than half a second. Based on my hour or two here, this fucked-up place would just start another "hunt" if I ran.

No. If I want to survive this and not end up on some stupid suicidal mission that I'm completely unqualified for, I'm going to have to play it smart. Make Falcon my ally.

I glance over at Hawk, who's walking beside me. As soon as he realizes my eyes are on him, he snatches me away from Falcon, ignoring the shorter man's protests. Hawk scoops me up so that I'm facing him. He wraps my legs around his waist and slides his massive hands across my ass.

He gives me a friendly smile again, that boy-next-door grin that I suspected, but now know, is a lie. My pale hands grip his massive shoulders as he says, "Our fun little conversation was interrupted earlier. Want to guess what I'm in for?"

Fuck. Is this a game? Guessing criminal convictions? If so, I don't want to play. But what I want doesn't really matter on this island full of wicked souls. What I need to do to survive does.

"You were a torturer too?" I shrug my shoulders, trying to keep my tone and face as casual as I can. Based on the way Hawk slid that gun along my cheek, I believe he's done that before.

"Of a sort. But not like Vulture. Sadly, I didn't get paid to play."

That sentence tells me a lot. He wasn't a criminal for hire, so an assassin is ruled out. And he thought of it as play . . .

Chills don't just creep down my spine—they invade every nerve ending in my body.

As we walk around the corner, Hawk cheerfully says, "Time's up. We're home, pretty girl." He slides me down his front, deliberately rubbing me against his dick, which is rock-hard and thick as my fist. Then he leans forward and whispers, "I was a serial killer. And I had a thing for brunettes."

Fuck.

7

NYX

I'm in a daze as the guys lead me to a small, nondescript wooden building located near the edge of the cleared land housing the prison. Behind the cabin, a towering silver fence erupts from the dirt like razor-sharp silver teeth.

Eagle yanks open a creaky front door and roughly shoves me inside, shouldering past me and heading toward a bunk.

As my eyes adjust to the sudden light inside, I realize the bunkhouse is insignificant in its simplicity. From what I can see, there are no guards present, though the windows are fortified by steel bars. The walls, ceiling, and floor are all constructed of distressed wood, a fine layer of dust visible in the rafters overhead. The cheap fluorescent lights illuminate six bunk beds lining the walls—three on each side—though not all of them appear occupied. There's a bathroom directly opposite the door-way, consisting of nothing but a metal toilet and sink. No showers. There are no tables or chairs, so the only places to sit are the bunks themselves.

Charming.

Eagle has already perched on a bottom bunk in the far corner, running a hand down his cheek. I take a brief, brief moment to survey him without his mask in place.

He's huge—over six feet tall—but in this group, he's only the third largest, coming in after Hawk and Vulture, who has probably another five inches on him. He has a strong, prominent jawline covered in brown scruff and even darker hair. His hazel eyes have crinkles around them, almost as if he's someone who smiles and laughs often. But that smile is completely absent now as he pulls at the strands of his hair in agitation. He moves to recline back in his bed—

Before jumping to his feet with a curse in Russian. Ah, so his accent is likely real, unlike Hawk's.

"You!" He points an accusatory finger at Vulture—the man with the faux hawk—whose face remains completely impassive. "You do this."

Vulture's expression doesn't change, though I swear his eyes sparkle with amusement.

"What are you accusing me of, Eag?" Vulture asks in a low, baritone voice devoid of any inflection.

Still cursing, Eagle gives Vulture his back, where I can see two nails protruding through his T-shirt. One glance at his bed confirms that it's full of nails, all of them pointing upward.

Vulture bursts into laughter.

Oh my god.

I'm surrounded by fucking psychopaths.

I knew that before, but this—whatever *this* is—only reaffirms that idea.

Who the fuck puts nails in someone's bed? And laughs?

I half expect Eagle to leap across the tiny bunkhouse and strangle Vulture, so I slide carefully over the wooden floorboards away from the convicted interrogator, a.k.a. torturer. But instead of lunging, the large Russian's scowl disappears instantly, and he throws his own head back with booming laughter. The noise has me flinching, taking an instinctive step backward, and I find myself in Falcon's arms.

His nose immediately lands in my hair before lowering to my neck. His arm bands around my waist, his fingernails digging into my skin.

"Hmmm, you smell divine," he whispers as he moves his lips to the shell of my ear. Then he drags said lips up and down my lobe, causing a tingle to travel across my skin. Stupidly, I think that if I remain very, very still, he'll forget I'm here, as if he's a goddamn T. rex or some shit. Completely illogical, but a girl's gotta do what a girl's gotta do.

"I get you back," Eagle warns Vulture in stilted English, releasing another throaty chuckle. Then he proceeds to say a flurry of words in rapid Russian as he extracts two long, bloody nails from his back and tosses them to the floor, where they land with a *plink* before rolling and leaving red half-circles on the wooden boards.

"Enough of this!" Raven stalks to the center of the

room before turning and placing his hands on his hips. My heart races in trepidation as he levels a cold, distrustful glare in my direction.

Holy crap. What the hell is in the water on this island? Hot juice?

Raven's easily the sexiest man I've ever seen, though I don't think he realizes that. While he reeks of arrogance, there's an unease underneath it, maybe an insecurity or something, that makes me believe he doesn't know how attractive he truly is.

He might be shorter than the rest, but he's got these plush pink lips, that would look gorgeous on anyone, and dark eyes framed by eyelashes so long that I'm envious. He has bronze skin and broad shoulders leading down to a tapered waist. Though he's not as muscular as the other guys, I can see every line and dip of his six-pack through his skintight black T-shirt. Dark hair, longer on the top than the sides, is tossed haphazardly across his forehead in loose waves, spilling into his eyes as if he can't be bothered to brush it away. His features themselves are perfectly proportionate—dark brows over flinty-black eyes, those biteable lips, and a smooth-shaven jaw. He's the sort of man who could go viral in two seconds on social media if he were to growl at the camera.

If only he didn't want to kill me . . .

The direction of my thoughts takes me by surprise. I know I shouldn't be admiring his looks, especially when my death is imminent once he discovers I'm not an asset, but I've already decided there's something inherently wrong with me. Maybe that's why my parents treated me the way they did. Or maybe the single good piece of me died when my so-called partner shot me and left me to the pigs. Maybe it perished when I sat in the courtroom awaiting my sentence. Or maybe it occurred when I was pushed out of an airplane and forced to fight for my fucking life on an island full of convicts.

Either way, I'm broken.

Irrevocably and happily so.

Rough hands grab my chin, and I jerk in surprise, finding Raven's furious stare connected with my own. He's close enough to kiss, though I'm certain kissing is the last thing on his mind.

Or so I believe until his eyes drop to my lips. But when his gaze travels back up, he seems twice as furious, as if angry with himself.

"Did I give you permission to look at me?" he hisses, squeezing down on my jaw to the point of pain. I try to contain the desperate whimper that wants to escape by biting down on my lower lip. "Are you a fucking idiot?" His fingers dig in even tighter, and I honestly fear he's going to break a bone in my face.

"Raven," Vulture, of all people, warns. "Ease up."

Apparently, I need a torturer to stand up for me.

Raven gives me a look of barely veiled disgust, releasing my chin and shoving at my shoulders. Of course, with Falcon still behind me, I can't go far. My back ends up plastered against his, his hard cock digging into my ass. I struggle, but that only seems to spur Falcon on as he grinds against me, his lips and nose traveling up and down my neck again.

Raven turns and gives Vulture a look of disgust, but the large man with the faux hawk stares back impassively. "You've always been a bleeding heart for whores." Raven's face distorts into a hideous sneer. "I thought after Rachel—"

"Enough." Fire enters Vulture's eyes, his stone-cold façade cracking as he takes a threatening step closer. I don't know what or who Raven's talking about, but apparently, it's enough to break through Vulture's apathetic exterior. I store that little nugget away to dissect at a later time.

"What do we even plan to do with her?" Raven peels his gaze off Vulture and redirects his glare onto me. Pure vitriol spews from his deep brown eyes as both of his hands clench into fists. "Do we even know how to take care of this thing? Feed it? Wash it?"

"I'm not a dog, dumbass!" I seethe, though I know I should keep my mouth shut. But I'm feeling claustrophobic all of a sudden. I'm in their cabin alone with them. And while they could have done terrible things to me out in the woods, I somehow feel like here . . . inside their home . . . I'm in far more danger. It makes me crack and say things I really shouldn't.

These men are devils wearing human flesh.

And, perhaps, a part of me wants to be a sinner.

Raven's brows rise to his hairline as a thunderous expression crosses his features. "What did you just say to me?" His voice is a dark, husky murmur promising pain and vengeance.

"Oh, snap. Our little pet has a backbone," Hawk hollers, laughing maniacally. I whip my head in the serial killer's direction, having forgotten he was still behind me. A wide grin pulls up his lips as his eyes sparkle with mirth and joy . . . but now that I know what he is, now that I've been made aware of his darkness, I see something else in his eyes. Something dark and malevolent. Something that has the fine hairs on my arms standing on end, saluting the world.

He's absolutely insane.

They're insane.

They're all fucking insane.

I'm going to die here tonight. The thought creeps into my head unbidden as Raven continues to glare at me, Vulture and Eagle give me curious frowns, and Hawk grins, that friendly look his face relaxes into so fake that he's clearly toying with me.

I can't see Falcon's expression, but I can feel his length against my backside and his hands caressing the underside of my breasts over my bra.

I'm going to be raped and murdered here tonight. I don't care what they said about not raping unwilling women. I can see the intent in their eyes.

I need to get the fuck out of here. Only . . . there's nowhere to go.

"I'm waiting for an answer, you dumb cunt," Raven hisses. A part of me wants to rip him a new asshole, but I can see in my mind's eye how that interaction will play out.

Namely, my death. In a horrific and bloody manner.

Probably with my eyes removed from my sockets and my ears where my mouth should be.

I rather like my face the way it is, thank you very much. If I'm going to get plastic surgery, I'll hire a professional.

I have to snark inside my head to keep tears from forming in my eyes. Because these men are far scarier than Taylor with his gun pointed at my heart could ever be.

"You stupid, dumb bitch." Raven's face twists as he leans closer. Instinctively, I ram myself farther against Falcon's hard body, wanting to disappear inside of his muscles, but Raven simply walks past me, ripping the door open. "I'm gonna see the guard about using the computer to get details on . . . Nicholette." He practically spits my name, his features screwing up in disgust.

"Gonna suck a guard's dick again to get special privileges, are you?" Hawk asks, putting on an Irish brogue.

Raven glares at him, then seems to remember that I'm public enemy numero uno and glares at me instead. He races outside, the door slamming shut behind him.

But his absence doesn't leave me with any relief. If anything, my tension ratchets up a dozen notches when I realize I'm alone in a roomful of predators, all of whom are staring at me like I'm a tasty morsel they're desperate to devour.

I'm quite literally *flush* against a batshit insane stalker as though I think he's going to save me from the rest of the world.

Deluded for one hundred, anyone?

Racking my brain for something to say, I point toward one of the bunks. "So, this is where you guys sleep?"

"Ah. She's a smart little pet, isn't she, Falcon?" Hawk grins down at me. "Perceptive."

"I'm not a pet," I seethe through gritted teeth, though I don't know why I even bother. My sharp tongue is only going to get me one thing—a bullet to my head. Or a knife to my throat. Or a nail to my eye.

Or however else these men like to murder their victims. They seem like the creative sort.

"I wouldn't be too certain about that." Falcon's teeth graze my earlobe, and I squeeze my eyelids shut as panic bombards me. "You're my little killer."

"I'm not," I whisper, my body trembling, especially when he tenses behind me. "I'll never be yours. I'll die first." Fuck. Why did I say that? And why did it come out so pathetic? *Goddammit, Nyx! You know better than to show fear.* I sound scared. I look scared. I try to rein it in, but the damage is done.

"You are mine. Even if you don't know it yet." He releases me as if my touch burns him, shoving me between the shoulders until I fall to the ground.

My hand smacks against the wooden planks, barely saving my face from colliding with the floor. Exhaustion immediately sweeps through my entire body, and I just want them to stop. But I've already shown a moment of weakness; I can't show another. I lift my head defiantly, my eyes radiating fury.

Hawk continues to grin, laughter swirling in his dark eyes, as he stares at my crumpled form. Eagle regards me blankly, his head tilted to the side and a curious expression on his face.

Only Vulture looks distressed, his brows lowered, but when he meets my eyes, he smooths his features into neutrality.

I scramble to my feet when it becomes apparent none of them are going to help me up. Not that I want them to. They're all fucking assholes who can rot in hell.

"I hate you," I seethe, glaring at all of them, who've lined up to stare at me, not-so-subtly blocking my access to the exterior door.

So much for playing along . . . I have too much dignity to be their whore and live, apparently.

Hawk *tsks* in disapproval. "Hate is such a strong word, sweetheart." His voice lowers with a posh English accent, though that damn, blinding smile never leaves his face. I mentally begin to call it his "crazy" smile. It's too wide, too open, too . . . fake. It's just as much a mask as the hawk one was.

Falcon glares down at me. "Apparently, our pet needs to be housebroken."

"Whatever *shall* we do with her?" Hawk queries, maintaining that ridiculous accent.

Tension and expectation fill the air with crackling, wild energy.

My heart squeezes in a fist as blood rushes to my ears, sloshing around inside of my head. I can barely breathe as I see hours upon hours of torture and rape laid out before me. Hopefully not on that goddamned bed of nails.

I'll fight. I'll fight with everything I have, and if the consequence of that fight is my death, then so be it.

"Make her take the first shift," Vulture suggests in a monotone voice, barely sparing me a glance. "She shouldn't be able to sleep until she proves herself."

Hawk begins to cackle, while a sinister smile pulls up Falcon's lips. If there's one thing I've learned so far, it's that I need to be the most cautious of those two. If Hawk's mood swings are any indication, he's the most volatile. But Falcon . . . he's the most psychotic.

I don't know enough about Vulture and Eagle to get a read on them, but so far, Eagle appears unconcerned with my existence—as if he doesn't give a shit if I live or die—while Vulture seems slightly more cautious. Still, he doesn't make a move to stand up for me, despite the flicker of unease on his face.

And then there's Raven, who hates the very ground I walk on for no reason, except for the fact he's a fucking cunt.

"Guard duty . . ." Hawk absently picks at his trimmed beard, a devious light entering his dark brown eyes as I glare up at him towering over me.

"What the fuck do you psychos want me to do?" I demand, once again finding my backbone.

Because, apparently, I still have my ovaries, despite the fact I sorta want to piss my pants and cry.

"Just guard our bunkhouse, little killer." Falcon steps forward and rubs the back of his hand gently down my cheek before grabbing my neck and squeezing. It's not tight enough to choke me, but he applies just enough pressure that I know he could snap my neck in seconds if he felt the desire to.

I meet his stare, trying to remind myself of my mantra from before.

I'd rather die on my feet than be forced to my knees by these assholes.

"Sometimes, naughty inmates like to sneak inside and try to stab us." Hawk laughs, as if the mere concept is hilarious as he pantomimes cutting his own throat and dying dramatically. His arms flail in all directions as he collapses onto one of the bottom bunks, his tongue lolling out.

"We always have one person on guard," Eagle interjects as he carefully removes all the nails from his bunk, piling them in his hands and then shoving them into a tiny box underneath his bed. I try not to let my gaze focus too hard on what he's doing, on the entire box full of potential weapons. Instead, I let my eyes travel over his exposed forearms, the delicious veins exposed to my view. Veins that could easily be opened if I could get my hand on those nails.

God, two seconds on this island and I'm thinking about violence. I've already killed three men, and I'm imagining more. This is a truly fucked-up place.

Eagle collapses with a sigh on top of the scratchy gray blanket, his hands behind his head and his eyes already closed. "Protect us."

It takes me a second to realize that he's continuing his prior thought and explaining the purpose of their night shifts.

"That's right." Falcon, seemingly over his anger from earlier, wraps his arms around my waist and nuzzles my cheek. His strained, breathy voice gets even thinner when he adds, "And tonight, you're taking the first shift."

"And second and third," adds Hawk with a grin.

"But I—"

Before I can mount a protest, Falcon takes one of my arms and Hawk takes the other, though the latter's touch is significantly gentler. I kick and scream, attempting to break free of their holds, but their grips could be fucking iron with all the good that does me.

Falcon leads me to the doorframe, turning me to face it as he accepts a rope Hawk hands him.

Where the hell did he get a rope?

Terror inflates my lungs like poison in a balloon, just waiting to explode and seep into my bloodstream. I renew my struggling in earnest because I know I'm fighting to survive.

This is it.

All of this buildup, and they're just going to hang me from the rafters. They're going to make a noose and kill me. I know it. I can feel it. My heart darts wildly, as if it will help me escape. But I'm already caught, and Hawk's huge hands make excellent handcuffs, just like I imagined they would. Now, however, it's not hot. The current situation makes me buck and lash out, my feet smacking against their shins and sending red ribbons of pain up my spine.

"Calm down," Vulture leans in from the side and whispers, his voice too low for the others to hear. His dark brows furrow, and his eyes, while not concerned, don't seem quite as icy as before. "You'll just make things worse, and I don't want to see you hurt."

"A little too late for that," I hiss venomously as my hands are extended above my head. My left wrist, held by Falcon, is tied up.

Wait. My hand? Just my hand? Distracted, my gaze drifts over Falcon as he stretches upward, his arm muscles straining and the jeans that sit low on his waist dipping down enough to reveal the V of his hip bones as he tosses what's left of the rope over the rafter directly above the door. When he's satisfied it's secured, he tosses the coil of rope to Hawk, who quickly ties my right wrist. I fight with everything I have, but with one of my hands incapacitated and two of the men holding me, it's a losing battle.

"It's either us or death," Hawk hisses in my ear as he tightens the knot. "It's either us or another team. We weren't fucking lying when we said we won't rape you . . . despite Falcon's *issues*. But the other men and women here?" He shakes his head ruefully as he drops down to his knees. Instinctively, I kick out at him, but he captures my knee and squeezes until I whimper in pain. "They'll eat you alive, baby."

"Fuck you." A single tear slides down my cheek before I can contain it, and suddenly, Falcon's face is taking up the entirety of my vision, his eyes wide in wonderment as he leans forward and licks the salty track of water. He groans, almost like he's having an orgasm, and his lashes flutter shut.

"You taste fucking delicious. I wonder how good the other half of you will taste . . ." His eyes travel down my body, tied up and displayed for him now that Hawk has been able to tie up both of my ankles as well as both of my wrists. My breasts are practically spilling out of the bra issued by the prison, and Falcon's eyes drift to them before lowering to my panties. Without removing his eyes from my pussy, he brings a finger down my throat and between my cleavage, trailing down my stomach before pausing just above my panty line. He cocks his head to the side curiously, fascination filling his gaze, but before he can continue his exploration, Hawk shoves Falcon's shoulder.

"We need to get to bed. We have an early morning ahead of us."

Hawk's words seem to pull Falcon out of whatever daze he found himself in. He rips his eyes and hand away from my underwear and turns toward the other man.

My heart frees itself from the barbed wire wrapped around it when I'm no longer the sole occupant of his attention. I can finally suck in a slow, jagged breath.

"But . . ." Falcon pulls at his hair, his eyes dipping to my breasts once more, before releasing a disgruntled sigh and ducking beneath one of my outstretched arms.

"We can all have a good night's sleep knowing that our phoenix is guarding us," Hawk continues in an amused voice. He follows Falcon until he's behind me as well, and I can see nothing but the door and a section of the rough-hewn wooden wall.

It's terrifying to know that I have four dangerous

predators at my back, but I can't do anything to stop them. I tug at the ropes restraining me, but after the tenth yank, when my wrists feel nearly rope-burned raw, I decide it's futile.

Fuck. Fuck. Fuck.

Someone smacks my ass, and masculine laughter fills the room. More and more tears of indignation burn my eyes, but this time, I refuse to let them fall.

"How the fuck am I going to fight off any intruders when I'm tied up like this?" I hiss, struggling once more but only managing to make the knots bite into my wrists more viciously.

Warm hands rub across my bare stomach, and Falcon's breath washes over my ear. "Because you're not meant to be the attacker, little killer. You're meant to be the alarm."

Eagle's accented voice reaches me, drowsy with sleep. "You scream, we fight. You probably die. We probably live. Win-win."

Win-win, my fucking ass.

As soon as I get free, I'm going to steal a weapon from one of the guards, stab them all in the fucking face, and then bathe in their blood.

8

VULTURE

I never sleep well. Not even with a human alarm guarding the door. Especially not on nights someone mentions Rachel.

Fucking bitch.

When her face pops into my dreams, her sharp cheekbones lit with flashing red-and-blue lights as the sound of sirens fills my head, I jerk awake, kicking off the scratchy gray sheet and sitting up in bed.

Dammit, it's hot in here. Muggy. Tropical weather is shit, as far as I'm concerned. Give me cold-ass Colorado mountains any day.

I run a hand down my face, swiping a small line of sweat from my brow. Then I dig my fingers into my faux hawk, combing through it as if I can brush away the sick feeling that creeps across my skin at the memory of Rachel's bright blue eyes.

My one foolish weakness. But never again.

Women are good for fucking, but that's about it.

I glance over at the doorway, at Falcon's new pet. Moonlight from a window on the right side of the cabin traces her curves. She's got amazing hips, and my eyes zero in on that plump ass. My dick twitches. It's a good view, better than I've had since I got here. But as blood starts to flow to my cock and my hand reaches down to touch it, I realize Nicholette's head is drooping.

Not good.

I'm off my bunk and slinking silently across the room seconds later, my arms going around her waist and picking her up. Her small body is easy to lift, and I have to mentally scold my skin for tingling at the gentle rub of her skin against mine. It's been years since I've touched another human without the intent to kill them, and it's a slight overload for my system. Excitement crackles through my veins. I have to calm myself down and remind myself that this is practical. I'm only trying to relieve the pressure on her shoulders before she accidentally dislocates them. If she does that, then Raven's argument to kill her will hold more weight. We can't keep a liability on the team.

While I'm not psychotically obsessed with this girl the way Falcon appears to be—or even the way Hawk is because I know she ticks all the boxes for him by being a sassy brunette—I don't think she needs to die of torture. That death should be reserved for those who deserve it.

Like Rachel.

Or the Specter.

I toss aside thoughts of my mortal enemies as I gently shift Nicholette in my arms until she's facing me. Her skin is so soft. And the way her hips curve down and then her calf muscles flare back out . . . I swallow hard.

Her eyes blink wearily at me, and while they're brown like my own, normally such an ordinary color, I find the shape of them fascinating. They're perfect little almonds and large for her face, making her appear a bit young. Not too young. But fresh and lithe. And she has long lower lashes that make her seem vulnerable. Not like Rachel, who always appeared years older than her actual age, with a sharp chin and piercing eyes that were just a little too cruel.

"Not falling asleep on the job, are you?" I question, already knowing the answer but wanting to see what guilt looks like on her face.

It's one of my key techniques whenever I work. I always begin with a question I already know the answer to, so I can get a read on a person.

Nicholette shakes her head determinedly, but I see her swallow a yawn.

I drop her roughly, letting her stumble around in her boots and scramble to stand in order to relieve the pressure on her shoulders. "No lying."

"Sorry. My body's shutting down after all that fucking shock, okay, asshole? I'm not falling asleep on purpose." Even half asleep, this girl has a mouth on her, which is both good and bad. Hawk and Falcon like that kind of thing. But she's only going to drive Raven insane with it. Me? She can't get to me. No one can.

I stare Nicholette up and down in disdain, noting the fact that she's got scratches all along her arms, welts on one side, and more gouges along her legs. I try to judge if her landing here was as rough as mine was when I was dropped onto Wicked Island nearly three years ago. I nearly fell off one of the cliffs and had to hide a broken rib from the team for weeks so that Raven wouldn't off me.

"Don't let your body be your excuse," I chastise as my eyes roam over her, checking for injuries we might have overlooked.

I tell myself it's because I need to know if she's a liability or an asset. I tell myself I'm merely looking for things we can exploit. I tell myself I don't give a damn whether she's bleeding out.

I'm a liar.

There's just something about her wide, guileless eyes . . .

"What? What does that even mean?" she scoffs.

"Your mind should always control your body. Always." I jab a finger into her sternum to emphasize my point. She doesn't grunt in pain, so I assume she hasn't broken any ribs. Good.

"Right. Says the guy who got a nap."

I've always liked complacent women who do as they're told, but either I've been here too long, or my preferences have changed—maybe that bitch Rachel truly did break me—because I can see why Falcon and Hawk are drawn to her sass. Not to mention her body, which is balancing the thin line between soft and muscular. The way her ass is spilling out of those panties is downright sinful. And the way her tits strain against that hideous sports bra, her tiny nipples poking through the fabric? I don't want anyone else to see her like this. Ever.

I can't help but wonder how she would look in lacy lingerie . . .

I let the left side of my mouth curl into a smirk. "Want to make a deal? If you say yes, I'll untie you."

Her eyes narrow, but those lips of hers stop talking. She's interested but hesitant. I already know what she thinks we'll do to her. We could do it too, if we wanted. But that wouldn't be nearly as fun as getting her to beg for it.

Yes. My mind wraps around the idea of getting Nicholette so worked up that she begs for my body, despite her clear vitriol. What a pretty picture that would make—her brown eyes wide and desperate as her hands clutch at me, trying to convince me . . .

My cock gives a little thump of approval as it hardens and jerks against my thigh.

What to offer her . . . I debate my options and have to hide a grin as I decide on one I think she might hate the most. The one that will get her exactly where I want her.

I take a deep breath and then give her a careful shrug as I lay my cards on the table. "If I stay up with you until four a.m., then you have to kiss me for five full minutes," I say, my eyes carefully blank and disinterested. As if I'm not rock-hard and desperate to steal the air from her lungs.

God, just imagining the kiss—the electricity of her anger mingling with the potency of my attraction to her right now—then piling on the fact that the rest of the

Birds of Prey are asleep, and it will be a stolen moment. The factors combine to make this little offer into something I find I really want to happen. Of course, I would never let her know that. And it's not because I want her. I want the control it will give me.

Only that. I breathe carefully, exhaling and wiping the mental images from my mind, regaining my equilibrium.

I let the offer dangle in the air between us and don't bother to mention the fact that I'm wide awake, insomnia in full force now. I wouldn't be able to go back to bed if I tried.

Nicolette instantly recoils, fear and disgust clear in her expression.

"No hands, no other touching. Lips and tongues only," I clarify.

"What? You sick—"

I interrupt. "If you're going to survive here, you're going to do terrible things. And you need to learn to compartmentalize. You'll have to shove aside your anger for our kiss. Then let it come right back after." Or during. That's fine too.

A false sense of gratitude crosses over her face, and sarcasm pours from her delightful mouth. "Oh, so this is a little lesson to *help* me—"

"No. This lesson will give me something to jerk off to later. But it might also keep you from dying of suspension trauma. I'm pretty certain you'll suffocate if your arms stay up like that all night." I glance at the ropes, which the idiots on my team have pulled too tight. I'll have to have a private word with them about it later.

Nicholette's eyes widen. "Why didn't you say anything to those fuckers when they did it, then?"

I shrug, moving to untie her left wrist, assuming she's going to take the deal. She did earlier—take our deal to join the Birds. I don't think her death wish has gotten any stronger since then.

She doesn't fight me as I work to loosen the stubborn knot. Her dark brown eyes just latch on to my hands. I try to make minimal contact with her skin, which is far too cold for the warmth of the night. She's got goose bumps and is clearly affected by shock, and I don't want to make things worse by pushing too hard too fast.

They're fucking idiots sometimes, Falcon and Hawk. They know how to kill people, but have no clue how to keep them alive, how to draw the game out for days on end. Weeks, even.

We all have our weaknesses, I remind myself. And mine just happens to involve a stone-cold bitch who used me for her own gain.

I free one delicate wrist, annoyed by the rope marks I see there. Unintentional wounds are just sloppy. Every bit of pain should be earned. But I keep my face impassive as Nicholette hisses in relief.

I move toward the other side while she answers her own question. "Silly. How dumb of me to think you might say something to stop them. I'm just a fucking pet. Of course, you wouldn't protest."

"I was going to say *bros before hoes*, but you go with

whatever makes you more comfortable," I retort, just to rankle her.

That gets me the glare I expect as I free her second hand. She drops her arms down and rubs at her sore wrists, which are chafed, the marks from the rope leaving deep, dark-red tracks.

Part of me wants to offer to massage her arms for her to get the circulation going again, but from the way she's tensed up all night, I know that touch is going to be off the table, especially if I want that kiss later.

And I do.

Not for the kiss's sake.

But my eyes drift to her lips. They're this soft pale pink, and I instantly think about trading with one of the guards to get Chapstick, so her mouth doesn't become cracked and worn like most everyone's here. Of course, as soon as I have a thought like that, I shove a bag over its head and smother it.

Her lips have one purpose. My pleasure. That's it.

"Nicolette, you never said what you were in for," I state as she sits down on the wooden floor and starts to work at the knots binding her legs.

She glances up at me for half a second before turning and scanning the beds. She spots Raven asleep in the one farthest from the door, his paranoia that someone is after him seeping even into our sleeping arrangements.

I'm honestly surprised he was able to shut his eyes, considering there's a virtual stranger in his private space. The crazy bastard sleeps even less than I do. His mind refuses to shut down, as if his thoughts continually barrage him, even in unconsciousness.

He returned only an hour after we tied up Nicolette, smirked deviously at her hanging body, and then declared, "I know all about the little phoenix we stole from the ashes."

Stole.

Because that's what criminals do, after all—steal what they want, when they want it.

"He knows. Isn't that enough for bros?" Her eyes look even bigger when she's seated on the floor, staring up at me.

Hmm. Interesting. She doesn't want to say. So, either she's very notorious or out of her league. Before I can decide from her posture which it is, the ropes fall away from her hands.

She killed the Predator team. But she's also quite young. She's an heiress. Hence, spoiled childhood. But Nicholette is neither simpering nor arrogant. No, her sass comes across like a wild opossum digging through the trash. There's a hiss to it—not a lacquered sense of entitlement.

I'm intrigued.

I'm hardly ever intrigued.

In my line of work, you're only ever allowed two emotions—anger and lust. Anger fuels a good torture session, and lust is the release valve.

Rachel and the Specter currently occupy all my anger. There isn't even room in my head for Hoplite and this whole ridiculous human experiment they're conducting. The other guys have enough anger for all of us there.

This new addition, with those round breasts that fill out her bra so nicely, is checking off the lust box.

But intrigue is a bit too far.

First, thoughts of Chapstick and now intrigue? Three nights of insomnia in a row is clearly taking its toll on me. I take a step back and decide to deal in facts.

The facts are that she's here and we're going to play with her. I like my toys to last a few weeks. In order to live long enough to beg me to fuck her, Nicolette needs to know a few things about Wicked Island.

"You need some basics. There are about ten groups in here. Most aren't trouble for us. Stay away from the Dollies, a.k.a. Baby Dolls. They may act like you're their best friend, but they're stone-cold bitches who will slice your throat for even talking to a man. You understand? Predators were a bunch of assholes, but since they're pretty much out, you don't have to worry about them. There's one other group of prisoners you need to ignore— Dragons. Watch your back around them. Got it? And don't even *look* at Old Twinkle. Quiz time. Who do you avoid?" I don't pause, just speak right on through, watching her. She's going to have to be quick on the uptake if she doesn't want to get her throat slit on day one.

"Stay away from Dollies and Dragons. And . . . um . . . Old Twinkle?" She says the name with a frown, but she doesn't know how deranged that fucker truly is. "Any chance you idiots wear your masks around inside the gate? Otherwise, I don't know how I'll identify these dicks."

"I'll show you soon," I reply, deciding to sit down on the ground near her. I place myself between her and the door, and she rolls her eyes when she notices. No gratitude for my sacrifice, though perhaps, the severity of this island hasn't fully sunk in for her yet. She heard a lot of screaming. But she has yet to watch a full dismemberment.

Baby steps.

Hearing nothing approaching, I decide to stretch my back and straighten a leg, reaching for my toes as she continues to rub her sore limbs. If someone does show up to attack us tonight, it can't hurt to wake my muscles up a bit.

The silence between us becomes potent, broken only by the occasional sounds of the birds and crickets outside, not enough to cover up her shaky exhales.

"Favorite ice cream?" I ask.

"What? Why would you care?"

I shrug. "I don't. But questions are kind of my thing." I give her a wink as I pull harder on my foot and deepen my stretch. It's not lost on me that her eyes drift over my torso and the tiny gap between my shirt and pants.

Yeah. She's going to enjoy this kiss later. First, a kiss. Later . . . we'll work up to more. If I've learned one thing from my career, it's that patience is the key to success.

Everyone breaks eventually.

When her dam of anger breaks, the lust she's been

holding back is gonna be a fucking waterfall. I, for one, intend to get wet.

And she'll get soaked.

"This is stupid." Her mouth purses into a tiny bow that's completely insincere. She wants to tell me. She's annoyed that she wants to tell me.

"You have something better to do right now?" I query, glancing around the cabin. "I'm sure we've got Scrabble stashed away . . ." I layer on the sarcasm.

"Mint chocolate chip," she responds with a roll of her eyes.

"Really? Me too." Always try to find something in common with the subject. Trust starts with commonalities.

"Liar," she snorts. "Were you any good at this job?"

I stop short and stare at her, wondering how she knew I was lying. No one ever knows.

"For real, what is it?" she asks, wrapping her arms around her knees and finally relaxing her posture around me. Her head tilts.

I study the pulse in her neck, notice how the thrum has steadied. She's calming down. And she's good at reading people. Either that, or insomnia is making a poor liar out of me.

Falcon makes a noise in his sleep, and Nicholette stiffens instantly, her head whipping to the side so she can look back at him. Her shoulders only relax when she realizes he hasn't woken up.

She seems afraid of Falcon and Hawk more than any of the others. How long will it be until she realizes Raven is the true threat in the room? He's the one who determines whether she'll live or die, after all.

He's the craziest bastard of us all.

"Are you going to get in trouble for letting me go?" she asks as she turns back to gaze over at me before her eyes slide contemplatively to the door. She doesn't move for it, so she's baiting me. Interesting.

I raise a brow. "You're not going anywhere. You're simply guarding the door from another position."

"Actually, you're first in line to die if someone gets in."

I glance back at the door and shrug. "Fine. Go sit with your back against the door."

She stares at me.

"You'd rather I tie you back up?" I ask.

That does it. She stands and hurries over to the door, those breasts bouncing prettily for me. I swing around in my spot on the ground and extend my legs before I stretch toward the other foot. I watch as her back slides down against the door until she ends up sitting with bent knees, her elbows resting loosely on them.

"You could have tried to run," I tell her.

She gives me an annoyed glare. "I'm not that stupid. Between guards and these other prisoners, I wouldn't last a minute."

"True." I give her a wink and deepen my stretch. At least a tiny bit of her new reality has begun to sink in. I can't wait until that knife digs all the way into her flesh.

Silence takes up the space between us for a few minutes, me stretching my limbs after running through the forest most of the night, her staring at me, trying to unravel the knots inside my brain. But she doesn't know that there are so many, even I can't unravel those fuckers.

I give her a straight look. "My favorite ice cream flavor is chocolate. Now, tell me what you used to do."

Her tongue traces the edges of her teeth before she says, "Thief."

I can tell she doesn't want to admit that, notice the way her throat tightens after the word comes out and her hands ball up defensively. Her answer is the truth.

It's clear she expects mockery, so instead, I stand up and reach for my toes in a forward bend as I try to decide why Hoplite might have chosen a thief. Most of us are neck-deep in body counts. Is it her connections? Is there a job coming up where sleight of hand is going to be essential?

"Don't make it weird with your silence or anything," she mocks.

I pull out of my stretch and stare down at her. "Biggest job?" I ask, since she's clearly more comfortable with confrontation.

"Cartier. Thirty-two mil."

"Your cut?"

She laughs bitterly. "All I got out of it was this." She yanks aside her bra and points to a scar on her breast I hadn't noticed. It glitters slightly, and I lean down, leering a bit, in spite of my resolution not to. But her supple curves are delectable, especially when she's baring them for me, teasing me with the sight. My eyes eat up her skin the way my mouth wishes it could. Naturally, I go to check on her nipples, to see if they've hardened into points, but I cock my head to the side when I realize there's a little bit of clear stone embedded into her skin. It winks in the moonlight drifting in from the windows behind us.

"Diamond saved me when my fuck of a partner betrayed me."

My teeth clench together, and I can feel my jaw tighten to a point where I might crack my teeth. But I force my limbs to relax. To loosen up. I clearly need to stretch more if her little admission is tinting the edges of my vision red. I'm overtired.

I don't give a shit.

We're all here because someone, somewhere, betrayed us.

She's nothing special.

Nicholette gives me a grin as dark and full of fury as the ones I've seen from Hawk. His looks are the type that make a man's balls consider crawling up into his ass crack to hide. Hers has the opposite effect. My balls are practically thrumming, and my dick's threatening to get hard again.

"Doctor estimates I've got almost a carat still in there. So at least I got some bling out of it." Her nonchalant sarcasm is a familiar sort of armor. We all wear it here. But I'm not interested in armor—I want to strip her bare and see what's underneath.

"What happened?" I ask, coming over and sitting next to her, leaning my shoulders back against the door and turning my head so I can watch the brown locks tumbling down her shoulders.

She shrugs. "He sold me out."

"Why?"

"No clue." She doesn't look at me, but I can hear the break in her voice. That broken sound of wrath and hurt and betrayal, the kind that comes from working with someone you consider more than just a partner.

Nicholette endured the same thing I did.

I reach out a hand and turn her chin toward me. Her big brown eyes gleam, just like the bejeweled scar on her skin, and fury rolls through me. Not directed at her, but at that nameless asshole.

"It's four a.m.," I say.

"No, it's not—"

I cut off her protest with my lips. I brush mine softly against hers, reveling in the smooth, silken texture of her mouth.

Mmm. Yes. This. I'd nearly forgotten what mindless bliss a kiss could be.

I drag my lips gently back and forth over hers, teasing her lightly with my mouth before I press a firm kiss down and then change back to softer brushes. After a minute of light pecks, I move to open-mouth kisses, not using my tongue, just hinting at what's to come. And to my delight, she responds. Nicholette's lips start to move against mine, and she becomes an active participant.

I nip her bottom lip with my teeth, swallowing a grin when she gives a breathy little gasp.

And then I go for a real kiss, my tongue plundering

her mouth, exploring her, fucking her, stroking. Letting her have time to anticipate everything my tongue will eventually do to her. I imagine it all myself in full detail.

One day, I'm going to spread her thighs open on my bunk and eat her until she's screaming. I'll drag this tongue up and down her seam until she's writhing, pumping those hips up toward me to increase the pace. I'll shove my tongue deep inside her pussy and find it soaking already, just waiting for me to lap up her juices, which I will, all while I hold her in place and force three orgasms out of her.

Then I'm going to fuck her while the other guys watch. Maybe even share her. The image of us all fucking her one by one in our bunkhouse, of her legs sprawled open sideways on my bed and her pussy dripping with load after load of cum, makes my balls tighten inside my pants.

I suck her tongue into my mouth and show her all the techniques I'm going to use on that clit. The figure eights. The circles that grow faster and faster. The little taps. The steady lapping up and down.

Her breathing grows shallower. My own head is full of a euphoric rush.

I have to clench my fists so that I keep my word. Tonight is only about kissing. I won't touch her and dive into another fantasy as our tongues battle one another.

I'll fuck this perfect mouth with my dick while Hawk ruts her pussy and Falcon reams her pretty, round ass. I'll feel every squeal and moan on my cock as they pound her into a wanton mess. We'll make her feel so good that she'll shyly ask for it . . .

Who am I kidding? This girl isn't shy. She'll fucking hit us with insults until we have to put her back in her place. Again. And again. And she'll love it.

She'll hate that she loves it, but she's going to love it all the same. I'm going to make damned sure of that.

I reach down and touch myself through my pants while we kiss. My dick hasn't been this hard—ever. Not even with Rachel. I stroke it a second through the fabric, enjoying the torture of drawing everything out so long.

When Nicholette's hand reaches instinctively for my face and drags down my cheek, I trap it in mine and pull back to look at her. The sight is every man's wet dream. Her eyes are hooded, her breathing is short and raspy, and her lips are swollen. She tries to lean toward me and reconnect our lips, but I back away.

"Time to get back into your ropes," I tell her.

Her brow furrows in confusion as she slowly descends from the lustful cloud she was floating on.

"But . . . they won't be up for hours."

She clearly wants to keep going. Which is exactly why we're going to stop. I stand and gently pull her up with me, shuttering my expression and walking her back to her "guard" position.

She's so confused that she doesn't protest when I retie her left hand. But when I get to the right, she asks, "Why are you doing this?"

Because she wants me to answer her, I don't. And her

frustrated little growl is too adorable to resist. Oh, she's mad at me. Good.

"I said kissing, no touching," I remind her. It's important that she learns to follow orders without question.

"From *you*. No touching from *you*." She immediately twists my words.

I walk around behind her and give her a single, hard smack on the ass. It's only half satisfying, since she's still wearing panties and I can't see my print marking her.

She bites down on a whimper. "Dick." She doesn't clamp down on the insult.

"No. You don't get this dick. Not until you learn to follow the rules."

"Well, I don't want your dick," she growls. She's utterly pissed and sexually frustrated, and it's delicious.

"Who's lying now?" I grin as I circle around to face her.

Her face is picture-perfect fury. I debate jerking off right then and there, standing in front of her, so that she'll have a mental image stuck inside her head for days. But then I decide that mystery might be more effective. After all, the first day of questioning, the goal is to leave them wondering about how much worse it's going to get.

For her, I think I'll take the opposite tactic. I'll let her know just how much better it could get.

So, I walk back to my bunk and lie down on top of the covers, unzipping my pants and pulling out my dick, then arranging myself so that I'm comfortable. I spit loudly on my hand and then start to stroke.

Oh. Fuck. Yes. I needed this. My cock swells under

my hand, hard and ready. Pleasure gathers at the base of my spine and infuses every pore. I imagine the way our little Phoenix yanked aside her bra for me, and I picture her going further, showing me those glorious, perky little nipples.

Thwap. Thwap.

The sound is obvious in the dark room, and I see Nicholette's back tense when she realizes what I'm doing. What I've tied her up to ensure she *can't* do. I let my eyes roam over her tied-up silhouette outlined by moonlight, those prison-issue panties so thin that I can see the crack of her delectable backside through the fabric. God, how it's going to feel underneath my hands . . .

"Asshole," she calls out.

"Torturer," I correct her just before my balls tighten in pleasure and my dick shoots out a huge stream of cum.

And, sweetheart, you're my newest victim.

9

NYX

My arms and shoulders ache from being held above my head for so long. Everything hurts, if I'm being completely honest—my body, my mind, my fucking soul.

Morning sunlight streams through the barred windows, dispersing the shadows that had clung to every surface. The light dances happily while I'm about to cave in like mushy cardboard.

My brain feels groggy as I squeeze my eyelids shut, dropping my chin so it rests against my chest. I'm so unbearably tired that I'm afraid the second I'm released, I'll collapse.

Yesterday . . .

Well . . .

If I believed in hell, I would say with certainty that I died and descended there.

Even when I was in jail, I always used to remind

myself that it was a better prison than my parents' house. I'm not sure that saying is still true.

My stomach muscles clench and tighten at the memory of all I endured yesterday—falling from the airplane, killing those masked men, hiding from the women and that doll-wielding creep, and then . . . and then Falcon. Hawk. Raven. Eagle. Vulture, that bastard.

They're dangerous, sadistic, unhinged, and apparently, I'm theirs.

Until they tire of me and choose to put me down like a feral pup.

My blood simmers with tension and rage, fear and hopelessness, the feeling almost corrosive, as I finally peel open my eyelids.

To find myself face-to-face with a familiar, angry man. The only one in the group who doesn't tower over me.

Raven's lips are slanted into a hard line as he glares at me, body thrumming with hostility. His shrewd brown eyes—eyes that see and know too much—narrow, emanating pure, unbridled rage.

Slowly, the angry scowl transforms into a taunting grin as he swipes at a strand of dark hair that has fallen over his left eye. "Sleep well, little heiress?"

I don't bother to give him a response. It's what he wants, after all, and I refuse to be a willing participant in his macabre game.

I lift my chin stubbornly, attempting to turn away, but he grabs my throat, his fingers squeezing ever so slightly.

His other hand moves to my mouth and forces it open. He presses so hard and fast that my jaw pops uncomfortably, and I can't help but feel like a fish on a hook.

"What? No witty retort?" he snarls, grabbing my tongue, which gags me. I try to bite down on his fingers, but he simply moves his other hand from my throat to my jaw, holding me still. Squeezing my tongue, he flashes me a dark smile. "Bird got your tongue?"

Asshole isn't even fucking clever.

I try to speak—the words garbled with my tongue still in his hand—but he simply chuckles. God, I hate that sound. I hate *him*. I didn't think it was even possible to have such intense loathing for a single person before, but here we are.

Wait. No. That's not true. I'm pretty sure I hate my parents and Douchebag just as much, if not more, than this flaccid dick.

"What was that?" he asks tauntingly, finally releasing me. My poor tongue already feels bruised and tender from his touch, but I refuse to let him know that. I spit at the ground by his feet, making sure not to actually hit his shoes. I can't imagine the pain he would rain down on me if I did that. My tongue throbs, punishing me for that move.

"Real fucking mature, asshole," I snap. Now my tongue has joined my entire body in the aching department.

"Watch it." His voice is an icy chill that resembles the breath of winter itself. "You would do well to remember that *you're* the one tied up and at our mercy. Show us a little respect."

"I'll show you respect when you fucking earn it."

Remember when I vowed to myself that I wouldn't stir the metaphorical pot?

Well . . .

Someone needs to take this fucking spoon out of my hands before I whip, beat, and agitate him to death—*my* death. I'm cooking up wrath, and I know it. I can't seem to help myself, though. This unwarranted cruelty makes me want to lash back.

Raven's eyes flash with anger, and his hands raise, as if he's preparing to strangle my neck, when Vulture's voice penetrates the morning air. "Let the girl be, Rave." His voice is groggy with sleep, though I can't see his face.

Heat surges through me as my mind drifts to our kiss. The one damn pleasant thing on this entire island. I never thought about what kissing him would be like when I made that deal—and I can't say I even wanted to then—but I have to admit, it was one of the best damn kisses I've ever experienced. It was the kind that left my toes tingling and my mind sparkling.

Even though he used coercion and trickery to steal it.

I hope he stayed up all night long thinking about me, that fucking bastard. From the sound of his voice, he didn't, and I'm more than a little bitter about that. I've had hours, literal hours, to replay that kiss in my head. His skillful tongue, the soft scratch of his beard against my skin, the way he knew how to push but also how to retreat until I was completely tantalized. Suddenly, I'm glad Raven's injured my tongue and it's pulsing with pain. Otherwise, I might want to kiss Vulture again. And heaven knows, he would just smirk like the arrogant psycho he is and deny me—even get off on denying me.

Fuck. Why'd I have to be sucked into a group of psychos? Couldn't I have fallen in with some nice, stable bomb-builders instead?

The pressure on my shoulders is instantly relieved as someone comes up behind me and slices at the ropes holding me hostage. My very bones sing in relief as my arms fall to my sides, and the blood rushes back through my limbs. They almost feel too heavy.

The faint scent of bleach identifies my savior as Vulture—a scent I noticed clung to his shirt during our kiss last night—though his footsteps instantly retreat once I'm released.

I nearly collapse onto the ground, my legs wobbling precariously, but manage to right myself before I can topple face-first at Raven's feet. I imagine the asshole would like that—me, falling at his knees like some sort of servant.

Well, fuck that shit. And fuck him too, while I'm at it. I'm not a servant any more than he is.

I'm a goddamn queen, assholes.

If anyone's falling to their knees, it'll be him to shove his mouth against my pussy. Perhaps that acerbic tongue of his can actually be put to good use.

Raven's lips twitch in amusement as he takes in my disheveled appearance and the pain in my eyes, but he doesn't comment. Instead, he stalks past me, moving toward his bunk.

My eyes follow him instinctively, watching as he leans over his bed and fluffs his pillow like some sort of pampered prince. Unlike the rest of the bunks, his bed is already made, not a crease visible. He's also already dressed for the day in a skintight black shirt and cargo pants.

At least we don't have to wear hideous jumpsuits like the prison getup I arrived in. Those are impractical when you're fighting for your life *and* uncomfortable.

"Here. Wear." Eagle, the man with the thick Russian accent, marches forward and thrusts a pile of black clothes into my hands before turning away dismissively.

I eye the shirt and pants he gave me distastefully, half expecting them to be covered in poison, and the large, scary man turns back and raises a scarred eyebrow. "Or go naked. You choice."

I glare at him but take the clothes without complaint. Also without gratitude.

Eagle's lips curve upward in stark amusement before they wobble, replaced by a pained expression. He grunts, rubbing at his shoulder as if it's sore, and moves to perch on the nearest bed—Hawk's, if the large lump beneath the blankets is any indication.

I don't see Falcon anywhere, though that doesn't mean shit. The crazy asshole who found me originally is probably hiding beneath one of the beds, waiting to jump out and scream, "Boo," when I walk past. It seems like his kind of thing.

"Get the fuck away before I slit your throat," Hawk murmurs, and knowing what I do about his history, I don't entirely believe he's joking. As a serial killer, he might even enjoy it.

Raven pauses where he's smoothing out an already impeccably straight blanket and frowns, glancing in Eagle's direction. Even Vulture has stopped getting ready for the day to stare at him.

"Back hurting you?" Raven's voice is taut with concern—concern I know he will never, *ever* direct at me.

"I am fine," Eagle says, his stilted accent even more pronounced as he shifts on the bed and attempts to rub at his shoulders. I want to scoff at him. Can't he see that the tension is coming from his neck? I mean, I can practically see his blood vessels bursting.

But, of course, he doesn't know. Most men aren't that observant, in my experience. That's why they're easiest to rob face-to-face. They get caught up in their tasks or by your boobs and you can easily slide your hand next to theirs and come away with a watch or a wallet . . . My thoughts trail off as I come to the grim realization that I won't get to do that anymore. Sometimes, I forget.

I glance back over at the big Russian, who's a giant to me, but only middle of the pack in the Birds of Prey. Unlike Hawk's fake smile, Eagle's face is normally stoic. Not now, though. Currently, it contorts as he hits a sore spot and hisses.

"We can't get any more medication." Raven's words are both a warning and a question, almost as if he's willing to disregard his own statement if Eagle truly says he needs it.

Interesting. So, his asshole persona only applies to me. My gaze glides between the two men, fascinated by this new dynamic revealing itself. First of all, it tells me there's more to their relationship than a simple alliance to survive. It gives me a dangerous, tiny bit of hope that I might become more than a tool to them. More than an alarm or a pet. Or maybe that's just wishful thinking on my part. Still, I stay quiet and try to take in as much of the scene as I can.

"No. No." Eagle waves his hand in the air, his large barrel chest straining beneath his black T-shirt. "No medication." He clearly needs it, though he's being a stubborn, prideful male right now. While the other guys shrug it off and go about their business, I watch him. Thinking. Pondering.

"You can stay in your underwear for all I care, but we're leaving here soon." Raven's harsh words interrupt my thoughts, his glare a zillion degrees hot and burning a hole in the side of my cheek.

Resisting the urge to flip him off and keeping my eyes on the men—and making note of all their positions, besides Falcon, who I still can't see—I pull on my own black shirt and pants. The shirt is way too large on me, falling to nearly my knees, and the cargo pants slide down my hips. These are clearly men's sizes. Great. Either they didn't ask the guards to give me a new set of clothing, or the guards simply chose not to. So much for having more comfortable clothing. I desperately wish for a hair tie or something to keep the damn material in place. I feel like a gangster wannabe with my pants constantly sliding down my ass.

Excellent. Today's going to be awesome. I pinch the side of the pants and make my way over to the bathroom to use the facilities and finally get a drink of water.

"Leave the door open!" Raven calls out, his cruel streak returning. I want to snarl at him, but I also don't want to piss myself. Luckily, the shirt is long enough to hide everything from view, though I absolutely hate the fact that every single one of them can hear me pee.

Whatever. I've been through worse. I finish and wash my hands, splash some water on my face, and bend to lap up some water from the faucet. I haven't had a drink since yesterday, and my body almost sags in relief as I gulp the water down.

"That's not drinking water," Hawk calls out in an overly cheery tone that tells me he's on the verge of laughter.

Of course, he waited until after I drank it. Of course. Well, fuck him. I know whose sheets I'll shit on if I get the runs. I swipe the back of my forearm across my mouth and shut off the faucet, pretending I didn't hear him.

When I turn back around, Raven is pacing near the door, muttering to himself. Eagle is still perched on Hawk's bed, rolling his shoulders and groaning.

"What happened?" I ask tentatively when Eagle releases another grunt of pain.

"None of your damn business," Raven snarls, but Eagle simply points at his back, his face creased in pain.

"Accident. Hurt back."

I roll my eyes and walk over to stand behind the Russian, ignoring my own body's protests as I force it to move more than it has in the past twelve hours. I'm not entirely sure what I'm doing until my hands are millimeters from his shoulders. "You need to release some of the tension. May I?"

What the fuck are you doing, Nyx? These are your enemies, your tormentors, and probably, inevitably, your killers.

I guess I'm just a fucking bleeding heart, or whatever the kids call it these days.

Or, maybe, I'm just trying to make the best of a bad situation.

"Errr. Ya?" Eagle stares at me over his shoulder in confusion, but with a sigh, I grab his chin and force his gaze straight ahead. I then bring my small hands to his shoulders and begin to knead the skin there, making sure to rub my thumbs into some of the more tender areas. The entire time, my arms are shaking, muscles as limp as deflated bike tires. Part of me wants to sag onto the bed and sleep. But I just keep telling myself, *You need allies, Nyx.*

"Oh . . . fuck!" Eagle curses, his voice ending on a moan. The look of disgust Raven throws us? Makes this entire thing worth it. I realize I receive great joy in life from pissing off the paranoid computer genius or whatever the fuck he is. Particularly if I can do so while getting one of his friends on my side.

I move my hands to Eagle's neck, paying extra attention to the muscles there, and he begins to make noises that sound damn near sinful. Meanwhile, my own hands are soaking up his warmth, marveling at his body heat, wondering how he's so sculpted when the most I ever got was an hour of workout time in the women's prison.

Hawk, finally jerking himself upright, sits up in bed, resting on his elbows, and flashes us a dark, dangerous grin. The scratchy blanket pools down around him, baring his dark, naked chest to my eyes. When he catches the direction of my stare, his smile broadens.

"Why, darling, if you look at me like that, I might need to show you the benefits of Southern charm," he purrs in a deep Southern accent.

I roll my eyes, finally pulling my hands away from Eagle. The large man makes a noise of distress, jumping off the bed and then spinning to face me. Those hazel eyes of his pin me in place and make me feel oddly vulnerable, which is ridiculous, considering I just tried to do something nice—without strings. Well, without any overtly stated strings attached, anyway.

"Does it feel better?" I query, crossing my arms over my chest, refusing to acknowledge just how much that massage physically cost me. My arms aren't going to be able to do much of anything today. The muscles feel dull and heavy, a hot ache in the very middle of my bones. But if Eagle's a bit closer to trusting me, it's worth it.

The Russian gives me a look I can't quite read, his eyes narrowing contemplatively, his tongue tracing the inside of his mouth and making his lower lip bulge. "Why did you help me?"

"Because you needed it?" I throw my hands up in the air as he continues to give me that strange, unreadable look. Dammit. Maybe that massage was a mistake. He seems suspicious.

Fuck my life. If I'm mean back to them, then I get my tongue nearly yanked out. I'm nice, and I get an arctic glare. This is a great start to the morning.

Before Eagle can respond, I become aware of a presence directly behind me, his warm breath brushing against my skin. I tense automatically—a reaction I'm not sure will ever go away when it comes to the deranged man known as Falcon—but he doesn't give me a chance to pull away. One of his large arms closes around my chest, just over my breasts, while his other hand moves into my line of sight. He grips something white and red and quickly brings the strange item to my lips, poking at them repeatedly, and with a start, I realize it's an apple slice.

"What the blood fuckery are you doing?" Hawk questions with a heavy British accent.

"Feeding my pet," Falcon purrs in my ear, his tongue sneaking out to lick the shell of it. I tremble, and not entirely in revulsion. My ears have always been a bit of an erogenous zone for me.

"She's not a fucking pet!" Raven rages, scowling at me as if his team's behavior is all *my* fault.

Yes, asshole. Because I purposely got caught with millions of dollars of diamonds on me, sentenced to prison, kidnapped and tossed into an airplane, thrown out of said airplane, chased on an island of psychopaths, and then stolen by masked men with a superiority complex who see me as an item to covet and possess.

But instead of allowing his look to get to me, I tilt away from the apple and smile at him broadly.

"Thank you, Raven, for agreeing with me that I'm a human fucking being," I say cheerfully. Might as well needle the overly gorgeous bastard by misinterpreting him.

Falcon takes the opportunity to all but shove the apple slice into my mouth. I chew—because what else can I do?—as the sweet taste of the apple erupts on my tastebuds. It's fucking delicious, and my stomach growls its assent, pissed at me for keeping it empty for so long. As though I had a choice in the matter.

Raven stares at me as if he has eaten something sour. God, I love that frustrated look on his face. And if he's determined to be a dick to me, then he deserves a middle finger right up his ass. Dry. And if I still had the means or ability to get pointed acrylic nails, oh, he'd deserve that too. His next words are a pathetic attempt to cut me down. "You're nothing but a filthy maid."

"Did somebody wake up on the wrong side of the bunk this morning?" I taunt as his eyes darken with rage. "Let me guess? You woke up on the bottom, even though you think you're a top. Is that right?"

Everyone freezes at my words, their eyes volleying between me and Raven like they're expecting their team-mate to charge at any moment. And I sure as fuck think so—there's something deeply unhinged about the striking man with ebony hair and eyes so brown, they almost seem black. Something dark and dangerous that heats the blood in my veins as effectively as any eroding acid.

But now that Falcon's back, arms wrapped around me, I highly doubt Raven will be quite as cruel as he was this morning. Not when my "owner" has me in his arms. The psychopath almost seems to be a shield, of sorts. Of course, there will be no protecting myself from him. I try to suppress the shiver that rolls down my spine, but Falcon presses harder against me, and I'm certain he knows exactly what I'm thinking.

Raven closes his eyes and takes deep, shuddering breaths, as if praying for patience.

Eagle, almost imperceptibly, moves slightly in front of me. I have no idea if he means to protect me from Raven's rage or if he simply wants to help his friend if they decide to get rid of me. Either way, I appreciate his broad back obscuring Raven from view.

And a tiny piece of me hopes that my massage tilted Eagle's favor in my direction.

When the silence becomes almost deafening, I stand on my tiptoes and peek over Eagle's shoulder.

Raven's eyes have finally reopened and now freeze me in place. Pure, unadulterated rage traps me, though he doesn't take a step closer. He doesn't need to. That look alone is enough to make me rethink all my life choices, including my most recent one—poking the beehive until the fuckers attacked and stung.

Though Raven isn't as large or as muscular as the others, there's something so predatory about him, so innately lethal, I know that, if he ever chooses to kill me, I'll be dead in seconds. Not even my body will be found.

The question is if he'll choose to kill me while Falcon still wants me . . .

I have to bet he won't.

But that's gambling everything.

"You think you're so smart, don't you?" A sneer distorts his handsome face, one that has insidious fear slithering through my veins. "Did you think you were so smart and witty when Daddy snuck into your bedroom at night?"

No.

Pain fills my veins, dark and caustic, but my face remains completely impassive, closed off, as icy as his. My pulse doubles, though, and my hands grow clammy as I press them against the huge black pants encasing my legs. For a split-second, my brain glitches and there's nothing but white noise inside before my thoughts can regain control.

How did he . . .? No. No. No.

I believed that part of my past was buried, I thought I'd escaped it. I know my parents buried it under millions of pretty little green dollar bills. But it's coming back to haunt me like any poltergeist tethered to a living spirit.

Images flit through my brain—memories I thought I turned off long ago—a pillow wet with tears, the rooftop above my window where I'd climb and hide, the awful scent of vodka—

I try to shut myself down, turn off my emotions and retreat to a place where hopelessness can't reach me, but it gnaws at me, tightening all my muscles until they physically spasm. I can't shut it out, no matter how hard I try.

I'm vaguely aware of Falcon's arm tightening over my chest as he presses me back against him so that I stay upright.

My heart migrates to my throat as I hold Raven's pitch-black stare—the eyes of a fucking demon coming to claim my soul and drag it down to hell. God, he let me think I was winning, only to smash me down further than I've been in years. He's a demon.

Burn. Burn. Burn.

He wants me to burn.

"Raven . . ." Vulture warns, standing, not a hint of the guy who untied me last night in his expression. His eyes are cold, dark, angry. And when he glances at me, they remain as icy, as cold. A fucking tundra most travelers would be too afraid to venture across.

I'm past dissecting what his looks mean right now. I simply don't have the bandwidth. I'm still scrambling to put back the pieces of my brain that Raven just toppled—all the progress I thought I'd made tumbling over like a game of Jenga, like pathetic toy blocks. I thought I'd built something stronger than that, but all the weakness and resentment comes rushing back. Bile coats the back of my throat as a brief sensation of trapped helplessness—the same feeling that drove me to the streets—churns inside my stomach.

Raven's cruel smile grows as I try and fail to hide how he's rattled me. "You forget, little Nicholette, that I know all of your dark and dirty secrets." He very carefully smooths a hand down the front of his pristinely ironed T-shirt, not at all concerned by the fact that my body is practically trembling with rage.

So much rage, it drowns me. Buries me in a coffin crafted from knives.

"I hate you," I manage to gasp out.

"Good." He finally takes a step closer, though Eagle still doesn't move from where he stands in front of me. It doesn't deter the coldhearted hacker, though, as he smiles around Eagle's muscular body. "It will make it all the sweeter when I destroy you." He snaps his finger like I'm a dog. "Now, come. We have to drop her off in less than ten minutes for orientation." He says the word *orientation* mockingly, as if that word fails to truly encapsulate what I'm about to experience.

I don't want to know what horrors are next.

Raven glances over my shoulder at Falcon and adds cruelly, "Don't bother to feed your pet. I have a feeling she won't last long, anyway."

He might be right.

Falcon *does* feed me in defiance of Raven, sweeping me up into his arms, turning me to face him, and wrapping my legs around his waist as the other men finish getting ready.

Thank goodness. I'm starving, and I need—and deserve—a second of reprieve from Raven and his horribleness before I have to face whatever atrocity this island has ready for me next.

I wrap my arms around Falcon's neck in order to keep my balance, though I don't make a ton of eye contact with him. I'm not ready to see pity or disgust in his eyes, not even ready to know which one he feels after Raven spilled a secret from my past as casually as someone spilling a spoonful of sugar into their coffee.

"Here, pet," Falcon whispers softly, one hand clenching my ass to hold me up as the other proffers the apple slice.

I lean forward to take a bite, and Falcon deliberately

moves the slice, making it spray across my lips when I chomp down.

Dammit! I almost curse at him, but he grins knowingly down at me—he made a mess of me on purpose—before he leans in. His tongue darts out, and he licks the corner of my lips, where a bead of juice from the apple remains.

I freeze as Falcon's warm, wet tongue drags slowly from the corner of my mouth across my lips. All the swirling sick and sad feelings I was wallowing in evaporate, fade like fog under the sun, as the scariest man I've ever met breathes against my lips. I tense, waiting for him to take it further. But he doesn't. He swipes his tongue once and hovers for a moment before retreating, leaving behind a trail of fear and the tiniest, most ridiculous bit of desire.

I sweep it away without a second thought, blaming my reaction on my hormones that Vulture built up and left wanting last night. Or maybe my desire to feel anything other than the horror Raven induced.

When the men step outside, Falcon doesn't set me down. He carries me out into the bright morning light. I squint as my eyes adjust, and my skin immediately warms. It's going to be a hot day. The birdsong can't overpower the sounds of prison life, however. Human chatter and the gritty noise of tires rolling over dirt and gravel reach my ears. At first, since I'm facing Falcon as he carries me, I don't see much, other than the Birds' cabin getting smaller as we leave it behind.

Gradually, other cabins appear. They look identical

to the one the guys have, and none are numbered, though my eyes roam over them from top to bottom. I spot a distant guard tower near the trees. It's manned by several men with guns. But the prisoners inside the complex—all of whom seem to be wearing the same black clothing as my team—roam freely. No cuffs. No ankle monitors that I can spy. Just hard looks and hard bodies, most of them nearly as cut as the men surrounding me.

The guys march silently through the prison complex, ignoring the stares of the other prisoners. Falcon follows behind the rest of the Birds of Prey as they tromp down the middle of the road.

The glares must roll off the men's backs, but they don't roll off mine.

There's a huge man with dreadlocks, who's missing a front tooth, who gapes at me as he wields what looks like a white plastic throwing star.

Where would he even get something like that? Why isn't he hiding it?

This place makes absolutely no sense.

Another cluster of men, all of them with mustaches that droop over either side of their mouths, give me dark looks as they whisper to one another in a different language, one I don't recognize.

A third group stops talking and stares, sending a sharp chill down my spine.

I don't like the way the other prisoners look at me—as if I'm a big glass of water and they're wanderers in the desert. How many of these guys will be allies? Enemies? Based on their leering glances, I'm gonna have to go with the latter option. They'll stick their teeth into me, rip out my throat, and bleed me dry if they get even a fraction of a chance.

"You doing okay?" Falcon's voice is a breath of air by my ear. "Are you still hungry?" His hands shift on my ass, and he digs into his pocket to pull out a lint-covered apple slice.

"No, I'm fine," I reply, grateful my voice doesn't shake.

Falcon's attention doesn't make me feel comforted or coddled, despite the fact that my aching limbs absolutely need the rest. Instead, I'm nervous as hell, because if he's being this nice, it means something terrible is about to happen.

We pass several more bunkhouses made of wood and cinder blocks on a muddy trail. All of them are over-grown by vines and surrounded by flowering bushes, like the island is trying to reclaim its territory from human civilization.

If I didn't know this place was a penitentiary, it would almost look like a postcard.

The prisoners whisper as they watch us, but they don't approach.

I assume that's because Falcon turns to glare at them and hisses, "*My* pet!" in a tone that's more than a little unhinged.

I don't argue.

In fact, I might lend a little credence to his claim when I lean in closer to him, though I'm honestly just trying to make my profile smaller for the guy with the throwing star, who's started trailing slowly after us, licking his lips.

Once Hawk turns and glares at the guy, he backs off a bit, walking more slowly.

I can't decide if the guys are parading me through the middle of the complex as part of some male pissing contest, or if I'm like some Greek sacrificial virgin about to be tossed into the ocean. With my luck, it's probably the latter.

I attempt to shake off the fear encroaching on my thoughts about what's to come and try to get the lay of the land while Falcon stares down his rivals. I count two larger buildings that look like they might hold either a cafeteria or administrative offices. There are guards up on the flat rooftops of these slightly-nicer-than-shit brick buildings. Guards with guns, who frown down at all of us in equal measure. I count them, just in case an opportunity ever arises to . . .

To what? I question myself. *Steal a boat and go . . . where? I don't even know what part of the world we're in.*

I count them, anyway. Just in case. There are six.

Dragonflies flit around uncomfortably inside my chest as I see nearly a hundred other prisoners file in through open double doors into a huge building just behind the maybe cafeteria. It's a solemn parade of black ants marching one by one.

No hurrahs, though, my fritzing brain says sarcastically, thinking of the childhood song I used to sing before life went to shit.

The fact that each and every one of these prisoners is probably a murderer or terrorist is not lost on me, and I can't help reflexively clutching Falcon a bit tighter as the crowd grows closer. He's still not wearing a shirt, so I'm unable to hide my reaction when my fingers scrape over his tattooed shoulders.

The madman nuzzles my neck when I do so. "Don't worry, little killer. I won't let anything happen to you."

I lean close to his ear and whisper, "What exactly happens during orientation?" I hate revealing how nervous I am, but my body feels like it was placed between two clock gears and is slowly, painfully, being squished. Without a single ounce of sleep, and only a couple of apple slices in my belly, I don't have a lot of calm and collected fakery left to work with right now.

"Don't you worry about it. I took care of it." Falcon's teeth nip at my neck, and then he sucks a tiny bit of flesh into his mouth, giving me a hickey. The suction of his mouth makes me want to close my eyes, but I don't, because we have a dangerous audience.

I let the psychopath mark me, because who knows? In here, that sort of thing might be protection. It certainly was in jail. There, women wore string through their pierced ears to mark them as protected by Dana Maldonado, Mamacita, the most badass bitch in the place.

My eyes roam over the building that Falcon leads me into, which is not in the same building all the other prisoners are pouring into. No, this is a separate building right behind that one. A shack, more than anything. It's a tiny, cinder block square about the size of a dorm room.

Definitely only large enough to hold maybe a dozen people standing shoulder to shoulder. There's a door but no windows, which immediately sets off my Spidey-senses. What could possibly happen in here? Nothing good.

Medical examinations? Horrifying images of being strapped down and prodded with metal instruments by pseudo doctors who get off on torturing prisoners pop into my head and dance around like deranged clowns. My throat dries out, and it takes all of my stubborn pride to keep from hiding my face in Falcon's shoulder when he stops walking, catching up to the rest of the Birds of Prey.

Hawk sidles up to me when Falcon stills, his thick lips curving into a smile as he stretches in the sun, his muscles on display underneath the bottom of his shirt. He runs a hand over his forehead, where sweat has already begun to bead in the tropical morning humidity. Then he reaches for me.

I try not to stiffen in Falcon's arms, partially because I know that would amuse them both, and partially because the serial killer basically told me he gets off on fear. Instead, I narrow my eyes and glare at the huge black man.

"What?"

Hawk gently lifts my hand from Falcon's shoulder and raises it to his lips like he's going to kiss it. "I just want to give you something to remember me by."

I relax a fraction. Fine. Let him play his little mind games. I'm immune. I stare off into the thick tree line as

Hawk kisses the back of my hand, and then his lips feather over each one of my fingers. When he sucks my right index finger into his mouth, though, he gets my attention. My head whips back toward him as his tongue drags slowly across my finger.

His eyes are on me, dancing, like he knows exactly how to toy with me. I open my mouth to tell him to take his tongue and shove it where it belongs—up Raven's ass —when he bites down. Hard.

A hot line of pain shoots right from my finger up through my arm, and a scream erupts from my lips, drawing the attention of everyone around us. Hawk's teeth clamp down so hard that I'm certain he's going to break a bone. I slap reflexively at his face with my other hand, thoughts muddled because the red haze of pain from my right index finger is so thick and all-encompassing. My movements are jerky and ineffective. I only know I have the vague goal of breaking his nose.

But Hawk's huge hands easily capture my free one and hold it hostage as he continues to press his sharp, razor-like teeth into my flesh.

I can't help the tears of pain that come to my eyes. When the first one falls, despite my efforts to blink it back, Hawk's jaw finally releases me. His lips part, and a throb rushes through my veins as the pressure he puts on them suddenly lifts. I pull my aching, mauled, wet finger back to my chest, curling over it as I try to yank my other hand away, worried he's going to give it the same treatment. He lets go, freeing me only when I'm off-balance and have to clutch at Falcon in order to avoid toppling backward. I tuck my head into Falcon's neck and try to make myself as small as I can to make sense of what just happened and—more importantly—*why* it happened.

Insane motherfucker. I'd rail him with all kinds of curses if I didn't truly believe he'd gut me tonight and string up my own intestines in front of me as I slowly expired.

All of these men are unsettling, but I truly believe Hawk is the most dangerous, even if he isn't the scariest. One moment sweet, the next, he's cold and brutal, and there's no telling what's set him off, making him bounce from one persona to the other.

Falcon shushes me gently, petting the back of my head like one might caress a nervous puppy at the vet. I want to yell at him too, for standing there and letting this happen. But I'm all too aware that I need him, that I need someone to hold me, that I don't want to be alone. So, my teeth saw at my lip instead, until, gradually, my breathing slows enough that I glance up.

Hawk's face is right there, watching me. He gives me that friendly, too-wide grin—only now, it looks like the smile of a shark.

"Now, you'll remember me all day," Hawk states calmly as he circles around to my back, which is exposed because of the way Falcon's holding me. Hawk brushes my hair behind my ear, his touch so gentle and unwanted that my shoulder rises automatically to reject him. Then he whispers so that only I can hear, "You're going to be throbbing for me all day, just like I'm throbbing for you."

That bastard! Can you believe the arrogance? I wish I

still had the gun from last night. I'd shoot him in the balls. Then in the face. As it is, I've got nothing more than my acerbic wit to whip him, and I think the only one who'll be hurt by that is me. But I can't stand doing nothing.

So, instead of directly lashing out at the serial killer, I do something stupid instead.

I pretend I can't hear Hawk, like he's not there. And then I lean closer to Falcon, toward the psychopath who thinks I'm some sort of toy. A pet.

And I kiss him, gently, just lips.

Why? I'm not thinking fucking rationally. But part of me wants to piss Hawk off. Part of me wants to strengthen my alliance with someone in this godforsaken place. And part of me wants the reassurance that Falcon won't turn around and do the same as the crazy behind me. Otherwise, I'm going to make a run for the fucking fence and let those guards shoot me down. Because what's the point?

Thankfully—or regrettably, I'm not sure which— Falcon returns my kiss eagerly. His hand comes up to gently trace the back of my head and trail through my hair. His kiss isn't studied perfection like Vulture's was. It's actually a bit sloppy, in an innocent and eager sort of way. His lips open and close rapidly as he gives me a series of light pecks, and I return his preferred sort of kiss, softly caressing his mouth with mine.

Hawk gives an annoyed grumble and stomps away.

I try not to smile in satisfaction, because I don't want Falcon to think I'm using him. The only thing worse than one psychopath messing with you is two.

We keep kissing until a bell rings somewhere, something that yanks out old memories of middle school tardy slips. That's when he ends our kiss with a final peck. He sets me on my feet and says softly, "All right, pet. Time to go learn all your tricks."

I glare at him, but playfully, because I know, right now, he's my best shot at making it through this place. Thank fuck thieves have to be good actors, because I'm able to contain my shiver at the unhinged look that crosses his face as his gaze travels down my body.

He points a domineering finger toward the cinder-block building, and I turn hesitantly toward it. I glance back once, deciding a pet would look at her master for reassurance. That seems to please him, and he flutters his hands in a gesture that urges me forward.

I grab the knob awkwardly with my left hand, still cradling my right protectively. When the metal door swings open inward, my eyebrows shoot up in surprise. Instead of a medical room of horror, like I was expecting, there are five desks set up in the room, just like a classroom. But there is no chalkboard, no teacher, nothing that indicates I should be here right now.

I step inside slowly, my feet dragging across the floor, which is still just dirt.

What the hell is this?

I wander toward one of the desks, which has graffiti on it. Etched into the surface of the desk is a sentence. *The Endgame is Death.*

Seems like my little troupe of birds aren't the only fucking crazies here. Great. I move to another desk, wondering if orientation is sitting in here all day. Were the guys just riling me up? Was all that talk about orientation and all that buildup . . . a joke? Were they trolling me? An emotion that mingles disgust with a muted sense of amusement crops up in the vicinity of my chest.

I glance around the empty room again, noticing a light switch. If I turned that on and locked the door . . . I could use a fucking nap without them leering at me. But what if this is a set up? Something about this feels off, though I'm not sure what yet.

I switch the light on, and an annoying fluorescent buzz starts up as I sink into my seat, careful of my throbbing index finger, which has already turned an unsightly shade of red. I can tell the bruise is going to be massive.

I wait and wait, worried that someone's going to come.

Horrible scenarios dance through my mind—torture sessions, interrogations, and more.

But an hour—or what feels like an hour—passes and no one comes. Eventually, I slump my head against my arms, blinking wearily down at the scratched desk my elbow rests on, wondering where the guys have gone. If they're out hunting more humans, if I should go look for them or if that will get me good and dead . . .

I'm out for all of five seconds when a hand shoves me back roughly, and I jerk awake, heart galloping, my left arm immediately flying up to defend myself. I end up smashing my fist into someone just as they step back.

"Calm the fuck down, or I'll Tase you," a male voice says. I look up and see a guard in all black, Hoplite

Defense Services embroidered on his left pec, a black beanie on his head, and a belt with a very big gun hanging from it.

Aw, shit.

"Sorry. Sorry." The words spill from my lips as I rub the sleep from my eyes. My brain is hazy, and it takes a moment for everything to come into focus. As my gaze adjusts, I realize with a start that I'm facing the very fucker who was with me on the plane. The handsome blond guard I'd noticed before I'd plummeted from the sky. His jaw is covered in stubble today, but I'd remember those blue eyes anywhere.

His Taser is out already, so I'm certain he means what he says. I lower my left arm reluctantly, not a fan of how close he's standing. It's close enough that I can smell his minty breath, which makes me run my tongue over my own fuzzy teeth.

"Falling asleep during orientation? I could put you in the stocks for that," he observes as he slides a step backward, having determined I'm not going to resist.

I shrug. "My 'bunkmates' are assholes, so I didn't get much sleep."

He barks out a harsh laugh. "That's a pot calling the kettle black, isn't it?"

I don't bother arguing. I've learned guards like to maintain the upper hand in a verbal spar. If you don't let them have it, then they'll take the upper hand in a physical one. And that's not a fair match, since I don't get a Taser, baton, cuffs, or—in the case of Ken-doll guard here —a gun.

I press my lips together and refrain from tapping my foot as I wait for him to tell me exactly what orientation is.

I feel like I'm in front of Lucifer's throne, just waiting for him to dole out my punishment, to crucify me because of my past sins.

It's a disconcerting sensation.

The blond guard smiles at me, and though the curve of his lips is devoid of any warmth, it also lacks the wild, unhinged quality of Hawk's smiles. There's a simpler sort of cruelty to it. "We're going to be spending some quality time together, you and I."

"Yippee," I deadpan.

He chuckles in amusement as he decides I'm not a threat. He holsters the Taser before walking back over to the door and grabbing a black canvas duffel bag I hadn't noticed before. Hefting it onto one of the desks, he unzips it while keeping a wary eye on me and then pulls out a tome. A huge, bigger-than-the-dictionary, black book. He then retrieves looseleaf paper and a pen and eagerly trots over to me with all of them.

"This is our book of guidelines and regulations." He sets the literary monster on my desk with a loud thunk. The paper and pen are next. I gaze at them before his voice causes me to glance up. He pins me with a no-nonsense stare. "For orientation, you get to copy every single word in here. Orientation will occur daily until you're finished."

Motherfucker.

My thoughts immediately fly to the guys. To Raven,

making me believe I'd fucking die from this—like it was some sort of deadly challenge like yesterday's. But then my anger takes a sharp ninety-degree turn and focuses on Hawk. I stare down at my throbbing index finger, which has turned a ghastly maroon. Writing a single line is going to be torture, not to even speak of the thousands of lines I'm going to have to do. That bastard knew exactly what he was doing.

I throw aside all my instincts that swear to be cautious around Hawk. I'm getting that fucker back if it's the last thing I do.

JAYCE

I knew from the very moment I got the phone call telling me my family was dead, I wanted to change the world. Make a difference. Be a positive change. Which is a fucking load of shit, because this world is beyond saving.

The criminals on Wicked Island are the worst of the worst, maniacs who must be kept on tight leashes, or they risk snapping and hurting anyone who dares to come too close.

When Hoplite first approached me about this job—promising adventure and excitement to a fucked-up young detective—I accepted it graciously. How could I not? This was my chance to make a positive difference in the world, to rehabilitate the types of criminals who took my family from me.

But then I met the fuckers who live here and realized there was no saving them, no changing their malicious ways. There are some people in this world too broken to ever be fully mended back together, too twisted to be sane.

Including the beautiful girl with haunted eyes before me.

It's always the gorgeous ones, isn't it?

I watch, legs crossed, back against the wall next to the door, as she scribbles the rules out, her face scrunched in agony. At first, I thought it was just from writing, but I gradually notice how stiff her index finger is, just like I notice almost every detail about her.

Brown, slightly wavy hair cascades around her face, giving her an almost angelic look. Unlike the other prisoners who enter this island, she doesn't appear hardened by time. Of course, she might be too young for that yet. Her eyes are flinty, yes, but there's a vulnerability to them that conjures up images of a different girl in my life. The harshness in her expression is juxtaposed by the softness of her lips and the long curl of her lashes.

Beautiful.

She's beautiful, and I fucking hate her for it.

She's going to be a problem. A distraction for me. A reason for all the other prisoners to fight—which means more work for me. I'm tempted to throw her into the hole right now, just as a preventative measure. That face alone of hers earns it, not to mention the fact that I can see her nipples occasionally press against the bulky shirt she wears. I wonder whose shirt it is, and then immediately scold myself for having such thoughts.

See? Distraction.

She needs to be eliminated. And soon. It will make

all our lives easier. Suddenly, I feel dizzy and unbalanced. But it's not at the idea of her death. It can't be. I don't even know her. I don't want to know her.

When she pauses in the midst of writing out a sentence from the orientation book, I push myself off the wall and stalk toward her. "Keep writing," I bark. She throws me a glare full of defiance and indignation, and God help me, I feel my cock harden in my Hoplite-issued pants.

There's a spark in her eyes that I don't want to see dissipate, regardless of what is to come.

"I'm trying," she grits out, focusing her attention on her injured index finger. I have no idea what happened, but there almost appears to be . . . bite marks? What the fuck?

Fierce protectiveness crashes over me in a torrent, though I quickly shove it away. I imagine the feeling stems from her similarities to Shelby, nothing more.

"Well, try harder," I reply lamely, clearing my throat and stepping backward to place my back against the wall again.

This job is just as monotonous for her as it is for me. I fucking hate this part of it. Every few months, new recruits will fall onto the island, where they're either claimed or killed. And every few months, in this exact room, I'm forced to fend off psychopathic murderers who think they'll be able to escape this island.

The only escape they'll find is in a body bag.

"Can't you just tell me what I need to know?" she asks, her voice laced in irritation.

She's the first one who's ever asked that. Most bastards just keep trying to attack me for the first hour or two. Then, once that game's run out, they'll write until they think I'm complacent. That's usually when they try to launch a desk my way and discover that, underneath the deliberate disguise of a dirt floor, the desks are bolted to the cement beneath. Nobody ever asks about the rules of this place . . . or tries to figure out how to survive it. They're always focused on the wrong thing—leaving.

I mull over the fact that she's at least a little original and debate whether originality merits a response. When I don't immediately answer her, she huffs out a breath and ducks her head once more, focusing on her paper. As I watch her in silence, she bites down on her plush lower lip, devouring it with her teeth.

Fuck silence.

There's a reason I rose to detective before I turned twenty-four, and it wasn't because of caution. My intuition has always been my biggest ally, and right now, it's telling me to speak.

"What's your name?" I demand, and her head snaps up, her eyes widening. Fuck, why does she have to look so innocent? So sweet? I'm liable to get a toothache just from staring at her.

"Um . . ." She hesitates, that damn lip of hers disappearing between her perfectly straight and white teeth. "Phoenix," she decides at last, jutting her chin upward.

"Phoenix." My brows raise as I give her a disbelieving look. "You know I could just look in your file and find your real name, right?"

"Then, why don't you?" she quips back.

I smirk, amused rather than annoyed, and fold my arms over my chest. "Are you testing me, inmate?"

She huffs again, her nose scrunching, and sets down her pen. "So what if I am? I'm screwed already simply by being here." The last part is said as a grumble, heady with disbelief and pain.

My eyes sharpen. "You don't think you deserve to be here?"

Everyone deserves to be here. Sometimes I even think that includes me.

Once again, she hesitates, biting down on her lower lip as she glances at something over my shoulder. Finally, she pierces me with an eloquent look worth a thousand words. "No. No, I don't."

My curiosity piqued, I move to stand in front of her. This close, I can see the individual freckles dotting her nose and cheeks. They're barely dark enough to be visible unless you're staring directly at her. Which I shouldn't be. I most definitely should not be staring directly at her. Fuck. "So, you're saying you're not a criminal."

"I didn't say that," she points out.

"But you don't think you deserve to be here." It's not a question, and I can't help but be *fascinated* by this woman. Which is very, very dangerous.

Appearance wise, she's the exact opposite of my little sister—if she looked like Shelby even a little bit, there's no way in hell I would be attracted to her—but it's the vulnerability in her gaze that reminds me of her.

It's that vulnerability that made me whisper to her on the plane, when I shouldn't have.

Maybe it's an act?

I've seen my fair share of female prisoners—usually swooped up by the Dollies or whatever the fuck that misfit group calls themselves—attempt to play the *woe is me* card. Funnily enough, they're usually the most deranged psychos on this island.

"I'm not like . . ." She waves a hand in the air with a defiant downward curl to her lips. "I'm not like the others."

Of fucking course.

That's what they all say.

However, their rap sheets tell a completely different story.

I cock an eyebrow, waiting for her to continue.

"And?" I press, when it becomes apparent she isn't going to.

"And," she blows out a frustrated breath, "I don't kill or hurt people to get what I want. I just . . . take."

"Take," I repeat drolly. "You're a thief?"

She nods.

"A thief and . . ." I wait for her to list her other convictions.

"Just a thief. Stole some diamonds."

That can't be right. We have murderers, rapists, and terrorists on the island. People who have committed crimes so despicable, normal prisons are too lenient. There's no way in hell the island would admit a damn thief.

A jewelry thief, at that. There's no way she's telling the truth. She couldn't just be a burglar.

Not unless she stole uranium and made a bomb. We've had one of those before. But Wicked Island is primarily made up of killers, each with a body count that rivals the number of their teeth.

Which means she must be lying.

"You don't believe me." It's not a question, but her words catch me off guard. Normally, I'm better at keeping my emotions under lock and key.

I debate how to respond before settling on honesty. "We don't have thieves on the island."

Something dark flashes in her gaze, there and gone faster than a bullet leaving a gun. Her lips purse slightly. "Apparently you do if I'm here."

I scoff and turn away from her, stalking back toward my wall. I won't admit this out loud to her, but the second I'm out of this room, you can bet your ass I'm grabbing her damn file. I don't appreciate being lied to.

Almost an hour passes, the room filled with the quiet scratch of pen against paper. More than once, Phoenix releases a pained groan, though she works to quickly stifle the sound.

Still, I hear it. I always hear it.

When she's only thirty pages into the seven-hundred-page book full of rules and regulations in legalese, I release a heavy sigh and push myself off the wall once more. Her head snaps up, eyes widening in alarm, as I take the pen out of her hand and glance down at her chicken scratch handwriting.

"Your writing's shit," I point out conversationally as her lips pull away from her teeth.

"You try writing with a bruised index finger, asshole."

"Asshole, huh?" I feign hurt as I slowly close her book, pushing it to the side. "And here I was going to do something nice for you."

Her brows rise suspiciously—not that I blame her. I imagine her experience in this shithole has been every man for himself. Nobody will do anything for anyone without some kind of personal gain, be it leverage or blackmail or whatever. It's what makes the people here no better than filthy animals.

"You probably already gathered that this island isn't like a normal prison," I begin, summarizing what's in the book. She straightens almost imperceptibly, her gorgeous eyes fixed on my face.

"I honestly have no idea what the fuck is going on," she confesses, and for some unexplainable reason, my heart clenches. I remember the terror splayed across her face just before she fell out of the airplane, her scream echoing through the air.

Five years on the job, and it never gets any easier.

"Hoplite Defense Services works independently of any government, military, or penitentiary," I begin, gauging her reaction carefully. "We have no idea how the director chooses who will join, only that she recruits for the teams using different prisoners from different countries."

"Teams?" she pipes up, her voice sounding frail and small.

"When you fell out of the plane and landed on the island, it was a test." I watch as her eyes flash with some unknown memory, some indescribable horror. "Currently, there are about a dozen teams on the island, all made by the prisoners themselves."

"Like the Birds of Prey," she whispers, referring to the deranged psychopaths who claimed her as their own. My jaw clenches tight enough to break. If they chose her, it's not because of her skills. There's only one reason men like that would choose a sweet, beautiful thing like herself.

Pussy is very, very rare on the island.

Unlike me—I can fly to the mainland on a helicopter when I need to get my cock wet—these men are stuck here. The only female prisoners who've survived the first night's hunt before this are the Baby Dolls, and they would sooner cut off any dick than allow one to enter them. Most of the men have taken to having sex with each other to soothe the ache—or forcing sex on each other.

But now that this beautiful woman is here . . .

Maybe she should be fighting harder against me. Getting Tased or shot and ending up in the med ward . . . no. That would leave her a sitting duck. No matter what's to come, her future is dark. Darker than I realized. I shouldn't have told her to run, because now, that future is my fault.

I shake my head roughly, realizing she's expecting me to continue. Those big doe eyes are blinking up at me, and it takes me a moment to remember where our conversation left off. That's right—teams.

"Exactly. The teams have a little bit of independence that way." I move to perch on the desk in front of her, kicking out my legs. Her lips purse, almost as if she's surprised I'm relaxing in her presence, but I continue before she can comment. "The new recruits are placed on the island while the various teams can scout them out. If a team claims you as their own, you join. But if they don't . . ."

"They kill you," she breathes, another memory darkening her features.

I nod. "They're only allowed to kill on game days." I don't bother to add that *allowed* is a term that doesn't mean shit around here, and guards will often look the other way if a murder takes place. I'm sure that's already clear.

She swallows hard, and I find myself drawn to staring at the tender muscles of her throat before glancing back up to realize her face has grown ashen.

What the fuck did she experience in the one day she's been here?

I almost want to ask. Almost. The bile in my stomach rises, coating my tongue in a bitter acid.

Maybe it makes me the biggest asshole in the world to allow her to stew in her pain. But if there's one thing Wicked Island has taught me, it's that sympathy, even the tiniest bit, gets you killed faster than you can say "fuck me." It's better to hide your emotions than allow anyone to believe you have them in the first place.

"The teams are trained on the island until they're cleared for missions."

"Missions?" But I detect she already knows what I'm going to say before I even say it.

"Suicide squads," I confess, watching her reaction and noting every minuscule tick of her features. The way her jaw clenches, teeth lock together, and brows furrow. The glimmer of fear that bursts to life in her eyes, along with a healthy dose of pain. "They take on missions that are too dangerous for normal army operatives. Stuff that might look bad politically. Stuff with big death counts. And a lot of the time, they do the shit that governments don't want to acknowledge."

She swallows, dropping her gaze to the wooden desk. A muscle in her jaw twitches. "This isn't a prison sentence, is it?" She slowly lifts her chin to meet my gaze. "It's an execution."

For the first time in all the years I've been a guard here, I'm at a loss for words. Because she's right.

AFTER DISMISSING PHOENIX FOR LUNCH, I stalk down to the administrative building. It's the second largest on the island, rivaling only the arena in size, and is constructed out of gray cinder blocks in a box-like shape. It's really fucking gorgeous—like a concrete turd in the middle of the orange and pink jungle flowers.

I give the guard out front my ID badge and then

travel through three security checkpoints before I'm officially inside.

The interior is in direct contrast to the exterior and the rest of the prison. The russet mahogany floorboards give the building an elegant feel, and the cream-painted walls add a soft flare. The main lobby consists of a desk, a collection of leather couches that guards can sit on for quick breaks, a flat-screen television, and a hearth, which is just for show because there is never a reason to light a fire in this god-awful humid mosquito-pit. Hallways in the back lead to individual offices, the records room, and the cafeteria for the workers. It's small but cozy. At least Hoplite gives us a bit of normalcy to escape into, away from the wild assholes outside. Without this retreat, I doubt I'd have lasted at my post this long.

"How'd it go, man?" my friend and fellow guard, Lance, queries from where he sits on one of the sofas watching a football game. A bulky guy with a scar striping the right side of his head, he's also former military. And a former football QB to boot. A little on the slow side, but we can't all be Einsteins. "I heard you got the only sane pussy on the island." He waggles his eyebrows suggestively as fierce indignation—and frankly, irritation—crashes over me. As if I'd rape a prisoner. I ball my hands into fists and grit my teeth to keep from doing something I'd regret.

Instead, I simply nod at Lance before heading toward the front counter. Sarah, the woman who works there, has soft, dewy features, silvery blonde hair, and wide,

fuck-me eyes. It's probably why I *did* fuck her years ago—
a mistake I regret to this day.

As soon as she sees me, a soft, wistful expression
distorts her face. The love in her eyes is plain to see,
despite the fact it'll never be reciprocated.

Mainly because I can never and will never love her
back.

I don't love.

At first, I thought her attention was flattering, but
when she began to follow me on dates with other women,
when I found her creeping up behind me when I went to
my apartment on the mainland, I realized her obsession
with me went beyond a crush.

Curse my cock for doing such an incredible job. I
need to learn to be a taker, not a giver. It's just that
nothing gets me harder than a woman squealing and
yanking on my hair as I eat her to climax after
climax . . . because then, once she's putty, she'll let me do
anything I want to her. *Anything*.

Unfortunately for Sarah, she's too sweet. And desperate. And needy. And everything I don't want in a girl. I
prefer my women to be a little wilder, a little more
cutting edge, with big tits and brown hair. Sorta like
Phoen—

I shut that shit down fast and offer Sarah a smile
that's probably more of a grimace.

"Hey," I say lamely as she flutters her lashes.

"Hey," she breathes, biting on her lower lip the same
way Phoenix did. Only, I don't get hard.

At all.

The little fucker in my pants is softer than Play-Doh.

"I was hoping to get the files for the new inmates this rotation," I say, flashing another constipated smile. Especially when she leans forward far enough that I can see down her shirt, no bra in sight.

I look away before I can unintentionally encourage her any further.

And her boobs? Not even a solid two. They're way too small.

"I'll grab those for you." She smiles softly at me and stands, brushing her hand over my arm as she passes and stalks to the records room.

Alone, I try to think of anything but the girl with haunted eyes. *Anything.*

But then my mind travels to the one and only time I fucked Sarah, and how she screamed "cowabunga" when she came, fondling her teeny tiny breasts while I struggled to actually get hard inside of her.

Maybe not *anything.*

Sarah returns a minute later, dropping five files into my hands. Five survivors last night? Dang. That's quite a few, though Phoenix seems to be the only one who made it through the night without ending up in the hospital wing. My little orientation room is going to be full really soon.

"So, I was thinking that we could—"

"I'm on the clock!" I wave my hand in the air like a dumbass and quickly turn away from the counter and Sarah's disappointed gaze, heading toward the cafeteria.

As I walk, I open the files for the new recruits and thumb through them.

Richard Pierce.

Arnold Shaw.

Henry Lever.

Terry Grock.

Myles Peterson.

My brows furrow as I stop mid-step. I flip through the files a second time, fingering the edges of each of the blue folders, counting to make sure I didn't miss one.

"Hey." I turn around to face Sarah, her eyes lighting up instantly at my attention. "This isn't right."

A frown touches her lips. "Huh?"

"What about the girl?"

I watch her brows knit together as confusion splays across her face. "The girl?"

"Yeah, she goes by Phoenix. Hasn't been assigned a number yet on the island." Numbers don't come until a day or two after a hunt, since prisoners have been known to die of mystery causes—like pissing off their new group members or if other groups end up thinking the power balance is too off.

"Jayce." Sarah takes a step around the side of her counter, coming toward me like she thinks I'm losing my mind. "There isn't a girl. No woman survived the fall from the plane. They either couldn't get their parachutes open or were taken out by the hunting teams."

"Huh?" What the fuck is she going on about? "She was in my orientation class. I just want to see her file to know why she's here—"

"I don't know what you're talking about," Sarah snaps, spinning on her heel and reclaiming her seat behind the desk. "Those are the only files I was sent for the new recruits."

That can't be right.

I stand in the hallway, the sound of the air-conditioning kicking on a sharp contrast to the thudding pulse that's pounding in my ears. What's going on?

Either Sarah's lying to me—maybe due to some misplaced jealousy because she is batshit—or there's something else going on here. One thing's for certain.

I need to get into the records room.

I walk into the cafeteria, a tall, one-story building that the hot blond guard, Jayce, pointed out for me. And it's not at all what I was expecting.

First off, there are actual windows in here, which makes the room almost pleasant because the view of the jungle is exotically enticing. The second surprise is that the cafeteria is full of round wooden tables instead of long, rectangular, metal tables like the ones in jail and prison. This gives it the feel of a high school lunchroom or something. It's a definite upgrade.

Perks of this place being death row, I guess.

The final astonishing tidbit is that there are geckos everywhere. On the walls, on the floors, some on the tables getting hand-fed scraps by prisoners. Their speckled bodies dot the room.

I hate geckos. Or lizards of any sort. They're just nasty little snakes with legs. as far as I'm concerned. And now I have to eat with them?

No—worse.

I have to eat with them and pretend that I don't give a shit about it because, if I so much as cringe, the other criminals in here will notice my weakness and swoop in to exploit it like the monsters they are. I'll find lizards in my bed, dead and dripping lizard guts in the shower, curled inside my shoes. That's how prison rolls.

I swallow the trembling, high-pitched shriek that wants to erupt when a stupid, green lizard waddles three feet in front of me and instead gaze out across the cafeteria, trying to focus on something else.

I search for the Birds of Prey.

They're assholes, and I still haven't forgiven Hawk for biting me, but better the assholes you know than the hundreds of those you don't. Unfortunately, all I see are assholes I don't know.

I try to find each of the different groups Vulture started telling me about, but without their masks on, it's impossible to know who's a friend and who's a foe. I spot a guy rocking a "baby" made out of tin cans and swaddled in a blanket, his husky voice whispering to it. Another man is stabbing himself in the thigh repeatedly, blood dripping onto the floor as his eyes remain fixed on me. A third man is twirling his cock around in his hands like it's some sort of flaccid baton. Whenever an inmate gets close to him, he whips him with his unnaturally long dick.

A sea of unfriendly and lustful looks turns my way as prisoners all around the cafeteria stop eating their mystery meat sandwiches and canned pears. All eyes land on me.

Great. Fresh meat and fresh pussy; I can tell that's what most of them are thinking. If only my brain was such a hot commodity. I see a lot of fights in my future, and I suddenly wish that my life on the streets had focused more on getting into scraps than avoiding them.

I sigh, thinking I'd better see what kind of shank material the cafeteria might house. I'll probably need to spend tonight making one. That is, if I don't end up tied to the front of the door again like a virgin sacrifice. Those assholes. My eyes do another pass, looking for said assholes, but I fail to find them. I find trouble instead.

At a far table, close to the window, two guys shove back their chairs and stand when they spot me. Immediately, I tense. I don't recognize them, but they sure as fuck seem to know who I am. The first is tall and dark-haired, with his arm in a sling. The other, shorter guy laser beams a glare in my direction. Their cold attention pours ice water down my spine, chilling me to the bone.

Luckily for me, that pair is across the cafeteria, and a dozen tables are between us. If I have to run for it, I will.

But someone stomps behind me and grabs my waist. I turn, shocked to see another woman standing next to me. She has frizzy red hair and black liner smudged all around her eyes so that she resembles a raccoon, and when she smiles, I notice she's missing two of her lower teeth. "Hey there, pretty princess," she coos at me.

Her tone instantly puts me on guard. She sounds like one of the women who ran my old prison, the alpha bitches who'd make newbies kneel in the hallway and eat them out in front of the guards.

Fuck.

I wouldn't expect a woman to be in charge in this place, not with the number of psychos around, but pussy does come with a certain amount of leverage—especially if the rest of your body is deadly.

"Are we going to have a problem?" the raccoon alpha bitch asks me.

The Baby Dolls, I recall belatedly. The only female team in the entire prison—she must be one of them.

And one of the only groups Vulture warned me to steer clear of.

I must have done something to offend her. I have no idea what, but I know how the women at my old prison wanted to be treated. And if I can make an ally out of her instead of an enemy, maybe she'll tell me who the hell those guys across the room are, or why the hell the Birds of Prey are so fucked up, or any of the other million questions I have zooming around in my brain.

I drop my eyes and step back, gesturing so she can walk ahead of me to the cafeteria line.

"Hmmm, good. Glad to see you won't be a problem for me, princess." She taps my shoulder lightly as she steps forward to pass me. But at the last second, she digs her fingers into my shoulder. "I'm Chucky. Head of the Baby Dolls. Watch your back around the other groups. Word on the island is that your pretty little tongue will fetch a good price. Some of them might let you suck their cock before they do it, but make no mistake, princess, they're gunning for you. Price on your tongue is a whole box of Twinkies."

"Twinkies?"

"Only dessert that could outlast the apocalypse or this shit humid weather. So be careful. Lotta sweet tooths here."

I nod my thanks.

She leaves me stunned and scared, though I fight not to show it as I watch her grab a tray and get served noodles and a fresh salad, instead of the gruel the other prisoners get.

I stare at her back, wondering whether I should believe Vulture's counsel. This woman just gave me a heads-up and didn't ask for anything in return. I glide my tongue along the inside of my teeth as I debate whether I should ask her to let me switch alliances. Of course, she didn't offer. She might not want me. With a price on my head, who would?

Fuck. Who the hell put a price on my head?

And why the hell is my life only worth a single box of Twinkies? Not even two boxes. *One*.

It's sad, really.

My eyes drift back over to the two guys who were eyeing me. Did they do it, or are they just looking to collect?

They're still there, glaring, but another random prisoner hops up on top of the table in front of them, jabs a fork in his hair so that the handle sticks out like a fucked-up unicorn horn, and starts screeching *The Little Mermaid* lyrics as blood drips down his forehead. His tablemates chuckle, not even fazed.

I quickly turn away, heading for the cafeteria line,

wondering what I could have done to earn a price on my head. It could just be because the Birds of Prey publicly claimed me. I've got zero doubt that the assholes have made enemies. Or maybe those guys across the cafeteria were friends with those guys I shot. Or maybe they're just the welcoming committee for an island full of insane assholes.

Regardless, the guys don't stride over and immediately attempt to shank me, so I get in the cafeteria line, determined to snag something to eat before they do. One of the things I learned in prison was that fights are easier to handle when you don't have an empty stomach.

And then . . . I see *him*.

The man I spotted in the forest, dressed in only a speedo with his hairy chest on full display. And just like before, those fucking dolls are tucked snugly into numerous holsters around his waist.

I expect the other prisoners to taunt or attack him—he's a walking target with his ridiculous getup—but they actually move out of his way in fear.

Fear.

Wide, terrified eyes hone in on his face as he moves toward the front of the line, bypassing even Chucky, and begins to scoop up a pile of mystery meat.

Whispers reach my ears, none louder than "Old Twinkle."

The fuck?

Is this the man Vulture warned me to be leery of?

My confusion is only amplified by the tense, wary silence that fills the cafeteria. All eyes are on the tall man as he shakes his hairy ass—the red cheeks hanging out of his Speedo—from side to side, dancing to a tune only he can hear. Or maybe it's to the off-key rendition of *The Little Mermaid* that's still going on.

When Old Twinkle finally moves away from the cafeteria line, it's to stop at a table where a familiar man sits, pale-faced and bruised. I recognize him belatedly as one of the guys who was on the airplane with me. His cerulean-colored mohawk is unmistakable.

Old Twinkle stares intently at the newcomer, a muscle in his jaw ticking like a tiny clock, before he leans down and grabs the milk carton off Mohawk's tray without a word.

The entire cafeteria seems to collectively hold its breath.

And then . . .

"Hey! What the fuck?" Mohawk demands, jumping to his feet and balling his hands into tight fists. I imagine, back in the prison he came from, he was the hot shit—muscles for days, gang tattoos lining his rippling fore-arms, teardrops etched beneath both his eyes. But right now, he looks like a child confronting a man five times his size.

And five times more terrifying.

I don't need to be a genius like Raven to sense the tension saturating the air, the fear seeping from the other prisoners' pores.

Mohawk's table-mates flash him unreadable looks, but not one of them gets up to help him. I can see the resignation on their faces. The knowledge that something is about to happen, and there's little they can do to stop it.

Something bad . . .

Quick as lightning, Old Twinkle shoves Mohawk's head down against his tray hard enough to elicit a cry of pain from the younger man. He grips the blue tips of Mohawk's hair, dragging the man's face to the side so that his cheek presses against the table while simultaneously reaching for one of his blonde-haired female dolls.

With a growl of pure, unbridled rage, Old Twinkle slams the doll into Mohawk's eye, causing it to spurt blood.

The scream the other man makes has me fighting the urge to place my hands over my ears. Terror pools in my stomach as I take an automatic step backward, farther away from the mayhem.

Holy crap. What the fuck is that? Did he put a *blade* inside of the doll? Is that even allowed?!

Where are the guards?

Why aren't they stepping in and doing anything?

But the few I spot are chatting casually among themselves, their fingers resting lightly on the trigger of their guns, not the least bit surprised or horrified by this revolting display.

Oh god.

Old Twinkle twists the doll once in Mohawk's eye socket and then rips it back out, causing blood and what appears to be a squished eyeball to splatter on the table. Then the old man shoves the bloody doll into Mohawk's mouth hard enough for the other man to gag. And he keeps shoving and shoving and shoving—

Until the doll pops out of the other side of his neck.

Mohawk falls to the floor, his one working eye vacant, blood pooling around him like a macabre red blanket.

Without a word, Old Twinkle grabs the doll from his victim's mouth, wipes it on his Speedo, and then casually places it back in the holster. He grabs the lunch tray he discarded on the table—the food soaked religiously in blood—and whistles as he leaves the cafeteria.

Oh.

My.

God.

As soon as he leaves, it's like nothing bad just happened, like there isn't a body in the middle of the cafeteria, like we didn't just witness a goddamn murder.

Am I the only sane one here?!

Apparently, because the guy behind me shoves my shoulder and hisses, "Grab your food or move, bitch."

Okay, then.

Not really sure I'm hungry anymore, but fuck . . . My feet shuffle forward anyway as I try to feign the same nonchalance as everyone else.

As soon as it's my turn to grab a tray, I feel a hand slide around my waist and squeeze, spinning me around. I expect to see Falcon, who's always the handsy one. But it's the short, angry guy who was staring at me earlier. I'd completely forgotten about him during Hurricane Old Twinkle.

Now that we're face-to-face, he doesn't seem so short.

His brown eyes bore into me from a couple inches above mine. He's got a massive scar on his chin and a chipped front tooth that's visible as he snarls at me. He's gripping me so hard that I know I'll bruise later in that spot.

Goddammit.

Considering a fight in the women's prison is never fair, I'm not even sure what I'd call the inequity here. The muscles on this fucker tell me that, if I want to live, my best option is running. But running will make me a target tomorrow and the day after.

I can't show fear, or I'll be marked a pussy and a toy. It's one thing for me to be Falcon's pet. But people who run on the first day in prison end up the bitch of anyone nearby. Bottom of the food chain.

So instead of running, I hope that he won't get in too many punches before Falcon or one of the other Birds of Prey arrive, and I toss out arrogance, using the only weapon I've got on me—my tongue. "If you're looking for a 'special hug' from me, you'll have to check in with my keeper, Falcon." I let him know I'm taken immediately. I don't know the kind of weight Falcon has here, but I'm about to find out.

A couple of the guys at a nearby table snicker.

"I want a special hug," one guy tells his buddies.

His friend cuffs him over the head. "Shut up, fucker. If Falcon hears you've said that, he'll go apeshit."

I try to hide my grin and the shaking sense of relief coursing through my kneecaps right now. I think I bet right. Falcon is a level of fucked up that goes beyond even most of the killers here. He's got a deranged sense of danger that makes him unpredictable. At least as unpredictable as that Old Twinkle bastard.

Scar Face doesn't look amused by my snark. And, unlike the other guys at the table nearby, he doesn't seem cowed by Falcon's name. He leans in close, and I can smell his putrid breath as he says, "Yeah. I'd like to hug your neck real good. 'Til it snaps."

It's fucking hard not to shiver at that. My toothy grin is entirely fake as this stranger lifts his hands from my hips and reaches for my throat, brushing his fingertips over my pounding pulse.

Not a guard in the fucking room even glances our way.

Then again, they didn't stop the man from stabbing his thigh or the one singing Disney tunes with a fork in his head or the man who *goddamn speared a man with a doll.* They aren't currently stopping the two men who just started fucking on a table near the back or the fight going on at the opposite end of the cafeteria.

This island is survival of the fittest, and even the guards know not to get involved.

I'm deliberating how to get out of Scar Face's hold when a blue cafeteria tray slams down on his head. He doesn't fall, but it startles him enough to make him drop his hand from my neck and turn—only to have the tray slam into the side of his throat. Scar Face crumples, and I turn to see who my savior is.

Vulture stands there, his chest heaving, fire in his dark brown eyes. He glances at me, steps over the fucker on the ground, and reaches for my neck. His fingers drag gently over my thundering pulse, and I stare at the angel wing tattoo on his left forearm, thinking how ironically accurate the tattoo is at this moment. He's my guardian angel.

"Did he hurt you?" Vulture asks in his soft tenor voice.

I shake my head. "He didn't quite get around to it."

His nostrils flare, and he turns and kicks the asshole on the ground twice in the back, making the other man shriek.

I glance up. Other prisoners are watching the scene with interest, just like they did when Old Twinkle attacked Mohawk. Who needs television when you have murder and mayhem to entertain you?

Vulture turns back to me and gestures toward the cafeteria trays. I grab one for myself, and he uses the one still in his hands. We proceed through the line in silence, picking up whatever mushy crap the prisoners on cooking duty today have managed not to burn.

I start to shake, items rattling on top of my tray, before I tense my muscles as tight as I can to hide the tremors. I'm surprised Vulture doesn't comment. I can't help but think about what could've happened if he hadn't stepped in. What *almost* happened. Fear lights a fire in my belly, but the knowledge that I need to be brave keeps it adequately contained. I've been close to death numerous times since I fell onto this island, but I've never seen my life flash before my eyes like it did then. Scar Face had every intention of killing me—I could see it in his eyes.

I don't think he was going to do it for a box of Twinkies, either.

When my tray is full, about five items before Vulture's is, I wait behind him so he can lead me to a table. He might be an asshole orgasm-denier, but he also stood up for me in public. That means I'll watch his back.

Or try to.

I'm not really sure what I can do against a roomful of murderous assholes, but ehh. Problem for another time.

He leads me over to a table next to the windows, which makes me smile. It really is a gorgeous view outside.

"How was orientation?" I don't know if he's actually curious or simply trying to make polite conversation, but I answer honestly.

"Learned this is a prolonged death sentence here."

"Beautiful place to spend your last days, though, isn't it? If you like sweating to death, that is," he states before biting into a very questionable burrito. He swallows after chewing for what seems like way too short a time and follows up with, "Did you get to all the island rules yet?"

I hold up my swollen index finger, which—thanks to fucking Hawk—is turning a lovely purple. "Nope."

Vulture rolls his eyes and grinds his teeth as he stares at my bruised appendage but doesn't say anything. I glance around again, wondering why his little friends aren't with him. I don't know much about them, but prison gangs typically seem to roll together, so I find myself surprised he's here alone. "Where are the others?"

"Practice yard."

"Practice yard? What's that?"

"Exactly what it sounds like." He takes another ungodly bite of the burrito as if he fears it's going to be taken from him if he doesn't finish it soon.

I kick him under the table, and his eyebrows shoot up in surprise, like no one's ever dared to do that before. "Don't be an ass," I seethe.

His head cants to the side as he studies me. "You aren't afraid of me?"

"Why should I be? You gonna kill me? Apparently, I'm just waiting to die here. You gonna deny me more orgasms as punishment? Let me tell you, that's a woman's normal existence. Half you fuckers don't know how to get a girl there, anyway," I mock with a shrug.

"I'm not in that half."

I roll my eyes. "No guy thinks he's in that half. Because women are better liars than men."

"Are they?"

"Yup."

"Tell me a lie."

"You're ugly as fuck," I say as I use my fork to slice up one of the canned pears into bite-size pieces.

Vulture cracks a smile. And damn if it isn't the most beautiful thing I've ever seen. His cheeks stretch, and part of me wants to reach out and run my hand over the scruff of his beard. He really is a beautiful man. It's a shame he's so fucked in the head. Why do the beautiful ones always have to be broken?

His foot nudges mine underneath the table. "Eat. You're gonna need your strength."

"What, for writing more lines this afternoon?" I mock.

He shakes his head. "No. We have combat practice this afternoon."

All the color drains from my face, because that does not sound like something fun.

"Exactly." Vulture points at my cheeks, noting my reaction. "And since the Preds are going to be out for your blood—"

"Wait," I interrupt, panic slicing through me like the barbed end of a whip. "I thought you guys said that Coyote wouldn't be a problem, that we wouldn't have to worry—"

"Coyote isn't the problem," Vulture agrees nonchalantly, acting as if he didn't just announce a team is already gunning for me before my second day is half over. "But Wolf is."

"He isn't dead?" I screech, making some of the guys at nearby tables turn their heads.

I knew I wasn't that good of a shot! My generic fear of humiliating myself during combat morphs into a very specific fear of dying at the hands of one of those masked freaks.

"Nope. He survived. And Wolf . . . well . . . he isn't someone you want as an enemy. He makes Falcon look sane." A frown touches his full lips. "Sane-ish," he amends, snorting in amusement.

My throat goes dry. "Wolf?"

My head swivels to find the guy in the sling, who's standing near the doorway talking to the prisoner that

Vulture attacked with a tray. Scar Face holds a hand to his neck, and I can only imagine his throat hurts with each word he speaks. Both of them cast death glares in my direction, which sends a dull ping of certainty from my brain right to my puckering asshole. That's why they hate me. The one in the sling must be Wolf. That makes Scar Face . . . Coyote.

"Those two?" I jerk my head in their direction.

"Yup." Vulture's tone is calm and unconcerned, as if he just answered a question about the weather.

Fuck. Great. Now I have to watch my back twice as much as before, because those guys won't just want to fuck or kill me. They'll want to draw it out in vengeance.

"Why did you stop them?" I ask.

"You belong to us," Vulture replies simply.

"*Belong* to you?" I scoff. "Excuse me. I'm one of you now. I did your little initiation ritual. I picked a stupid bird name—"

Vulture's knees smash into mine, and one of his legs comes between my own. His thighs line either side of my right leg and squeeze painfully, making me want to yelp. I barely keep the sound in.

"Don't ever call it stupid again, you hear me?" His voice is hardly louder than a whisper as his knees dig into either side of my thigh.

I nod, and he releases me. Instantly, blood rushes back into my leg, and I let out a low gasp. "You don't have to be so dramatic."

"That was *understated*, Phoenix. If I want to be dramatic, you'll know."

I rub resentfully at my thigh, annoyed he can put me in my place so easily. Maybe combat practice will do me some good.

"And what, exactly, is combat practice?"

"Normally, it's no big deal. But one of those dudes from the Predators is a Krav Maga expert. And he's scheduled for combat practice at the same time as you. So, I hope you have some tricks up your sleeve."

Turning, I stare again at the assholes I shot at in the jungle, the ones who would have killed me otherwise. And instead of finding the cocky confidence that normally sees me through most things . . . it feels like my sleeves are very empty.

I might be out of tricks.

13

NYX

"Fucking hell. You do know how to fight, don't you?" Vulture intones in a low voice so that no one at the next table can hear.

"If I say no, what are you going to think?" I ask, my tone thin and reedy. I don't want to admit this weakness to him, but if he's telling me the truth, then I'm really and truly fucked and could do with a bit of advice.

"Shit. Why the hell did you get dropped here?" he grumbles.

I shrug a single shoulder, because I've been wondering that myself. I certainly don't fit the MO. "Guess I've got enemies in high places?" I deadpan.

"Come over here." Vulture gestures with his finger for me to come around the table.

I stand and follow his orders, hoping he's going to whisper some kind of plan to me. Or maybe tell me he's got a stash of guns hidden somewhere. I'm not the greatest with those, obviously—I only killed two-thirds of my intended targets last time—but it's still better than nothing. I pull the seat out next to him, but Vulture grabs my left arm and yanks me onto his lap.

"What—"

"Shhh," he shushes me as a wolf whistle erupts at the next table. "Turn around and straddle me."

"How is this—"

His hands come to my hips, and he digs his thumbs in just above my hip bones, pinching a tendon or something. I nearly screech, but he lets up just before the pain becomes unbearable. Then he pats my hip, urging me to comply with his command.

A protest dances on the tip of my tongue, but common sense wins out. So far, Vulture hasn't led me astray. Not where it matters, anyway. Denied orgasms aside, he did take pity on me and untie me last night. If I were to trust one person on this island, it would be him.

I turn around, straddling the handsome, psychotic fucker with a deadly glare on my face that turns into wide-eyed shock when he immediately palms my ass with one meaty hand as the other comes up to wrap around my neck. He leans forward, and his tongue pops out and drags along my earlobe.

I have no clue what to make of his actions. Is he fucking with me? Is he playing with his toy before it gets broken? Dammit, I thought he was going to help me. Serves me right for assuming anything good about him.

You can't trust anyone, Nyx. You know this, I scold myself.

I try to shift my hips away from his greedy hand, but

that just shoves me closer to his stiffening dick. And despite my alarm, Vulture is hot as hell, and after he worked me up last night, my body turns into a confused tangle of sensations. My nipples harden and my breath quickens while I try to sort out what the hell he's doing and how I can get away.

"Shhh, calm down, Nicholette," he whispers into my ear before nipping at it. "I'm going to teach you some pressure points. But we can't let everyone know what we're doing, or they'll realize just how innocent you are. My little violence virgin." His lips glide down my neck over my pulse, and he sucks on it.

Oh god. It's like he's pushed a button and deactivated every single one of my muscles just by sucking on that little bit of my throat. I go limp on top of him, unable to resist the sensation as his lips draw my skin in and his tongue flicks along the sensitive skin of my neck.

When he finally pulls away, I lean into him, my hands gripping his shoulders. "Is that one of the pressure points? You want me to suck on my opponent's neck?"

He gives a slow, cocky grin. "Nope. That was just for fun. We're going to be mixing a little business and pleasure here." Darkness suddenly radiates from his eyes as something occurs to him, and his hands dig into my skin hard enough to hurt. "You don't kiss anyone but the Birds."

I open my mouth, fully intending to protest that I don't plan on kissing anyone, but then he leans up and smashes his lips to mine. And damn, I'm immediately drawn back to last night. His lips are strong, and he's forceful and commanding, his tongue sweeping out like it's ordering mine to do the same. I can't resist.

I lean into him, let him steal my breath. My pulse starts to pound when I hear a wolf whistle go up nearby and realize that we're drawing attention to ourselves. I suck in a shocked inhale but am surprised to find my stomach isn't clenching in embarrassment but delight. I might like the fact that we're putting on a show. My hands go up to touch Vulture's hair and then glide down the stubbled sides of his faux hawk. I want to drag my fingertips all over him the way I couldn't last night.

His hand on my ass slides to my thighs, and he grips them tightly through my baggy prison pants. Then, without warning, his thumb digs into the muscle on one of my inner thighs, and *zing*! Pain shoots through my body so quick and fast, it might as well be a bullet. A radiating, ricocheting prickle burns through my veins.

I almost shove up to my feet in a bid to get away, but the combination of dizziness and Vulture's grip stops me. His hands clamp down on my legs, transforming my attempt to stand into little more than grinding against his lap before he removes his thumb from that aching, delicate spot.

I pull back from the kiss, furious, ready to lash him with every curse word in the dictionary because whatever pressure point he just used, the bastard made my entire foot go numb.

But he simply grins back mischievously before diving down to kiss the base of my neck and working his way back up to my ear, where he whispers, "Sciatic nerve. Want to try it on me?"

My fury abates a little, like clouds parting for the sun. "You want me to hurt you?"

"Only fair, isn't it?" A dark chuckle punctuates that question, one that has goose bumps pebbling on my skin.

I'm not sure if it's the promise of violence or something innately *Vulture*, but heat pools low in my stomach.

God, yes. I want to hurt this man. In so many ways.

I brush my breasts against his chest, well aware that at least two dozen prisoners have full-on turned their chairs in our direction to watch the show. One or two are even jerking off the alphas of their respective groups.

I can't help but think that, if Falcon were here, he'd blow a gasket. He doesn't seem the type to share his toys or even have his toys *looked* at by others.

"Is that smart?" I question, even though, as soon as he offered, I felt a thrill surge through me like a wave. I really, really do want to give it back to him.

"You'll have to be sneaky about it," he advises. "Think you can do that?"

He drags my hand forward toward his dick, curving my fingers so they wrap around his girth through the fabric of his pants. I'm struck by how I can feel the heat of him right through the pants, how the shape of his mushroom tip is so clearly defined . . . It makes me think he might not be wearing underwear.

Wetness pools in my hideous cotton panties at the thought, and I'm sure my nipples are hard enough to cut glass as my veins practically bubble with boiling heat. I want to curse my body for betraying me, for loving the feel of him, but I can't muster up an ounce of ire. After all, this is my new life, for better or worse. I better get used to it and learn to wring a little pleasure out of this sick, twisted place whenever I can.

Vulture's hand caresses the back of my neck, sending an involuntary tremble through me.

"I think, for revenge's sake, I'll be able to manage a little sleight of hand," I whisper softly, though I feel like crowing in delight. Sleight of hand, I can do all day with my eyes closed and a hand tied behind my back.

He gives me a sultry grin as I lean forward and peck him on the lips. Then I use my right hand to slowly stimulate his dick as my left wanders down his thigh in between us. To our captive audience, it probably looks like I'm trying to cup his balls. But instead, I search for that little crease in his thigh muscle.

"A little lower," he pants, when my thumb tries pressing into his thigh. "Two more inches."

"That's what she said," I tease, as I glide my hand faster over his rigid dick and slowly slide my other hand down like he suggested. I angle my body forward so that my thighs block any onlooker's view of just how low that left hand has gotten. My breasts end up flush against Vulture's chest, and I know there's not a chance in hell he doesn't feel how my nipples have grown rock-hard during our little game.

He tilts my head so that I'm facing the middle of the room before he kisses me quickly. He probably wants the horny fucks in here distracted by my parted lips, hooded eyes, and quick breathing while I search for his "special" spot. I think I find it and circle my fingers experimentally.

"There," he confirms. I press, digging the tip of my finger into a part between the muscles. He stiffens underneath me, grabbing on to the back of my neck and staring at the window as he curses. "Fuck!" he growls as his legs straighten in pain and everyone else in the cafeteria assumes he's coming.

"So damn hot," a random onlooker calls out.

"Can you do this every lunch?" another asks.

I'm pretty sure one of the alpha prisoners just shoved another man face-first onto his cock so he can suck it, but I don't look up at what's going on in the periphery. Instead, I stare down at Vulture as I slowly release the pressure on his thigh and then my grip on his dick.

I turn back to him and lean in close until my nose nuzzles his gently. "I hope you didn't actually come."

Vulture smiles enigmatically. "Maybe I did, maybe I didn't."

My jaw tightens and my eyes narrow as I pull away slowly, but then I spot movement in the reflection of the window. In less than a second, Vulture has both my hands gripped in one of his as he stands, shoving me roughly to the side as the two Predators from before leap at us, trying to take advantage of our distraction.

They rush at me, wielding meat cleavers they must have stolen from the kitchen staff. I freeze, panicked, because I know I have a window at my back and absolutely no weapons.

Holy fucking shit.

For a millisecond, I almost wish Douchebag had killed me. Gunshot wounds sound better than being hacked to death.

Panic slimes my brain, making every thought thick and gooey and slow. My body struggles to catch up, to jolt abruptly from seduction to fear, but my synapses and the tips of my nipples haven't quite gotten the message yet.

The fact that a gecko scrambles down from the window and across our table at that very moment only adds to the horror of the moment. Those stupid lizards will probably crawl all over my face as I'm dying, and I won't be able to stop them.

My stomach finally clenches as my body registers what's going on, anticipating pain as Scar Face—a.k.a. Coyote—jumps up onto my former chair and then leaps across the table.

Vulture grabs the back of his metal chair, swinging it through the air like a baseball bat. It hits Coyote's cheek with a resounding crack so loud that I can practically feel the sound reverberating through my own teeth. I watch in horror as the guy's face distorts in slow motion. I literally see his jaw dislocate and his eyelids flutter before he falls sideways across the table, his head cracking against the windowpane as his chest smears across the leftovers of my disgusting meal. He's knocked the fuck out.

I suppose I was right when I thought of him as the dumb one of the group. No wonder the Birds of Prey didn't think he would survive on his own.

His weapon clatters from his limp hand to the floor,

and I dive underneath the table to get it, my heart pumping wildly.

I need a weapon because pressure points aren't going to stop the other guy's wild hacking swings with his miniature hatchet.

God, why did I listen to Vulture? Why? Why? Why? Pressure points . . . that's never going to work in here. There's no fucking way I can get close to any of these maniacs to use them, unless I'm being forced to suck their dicks.

I grab the handle of the machete and shove up onto my knees underneath the table, ready to swipe at Wolf's shins.

Turns out, there's no need, because Vulture still has his chair in hand. He jabs the chair legs into Wolf's chest twice in rapid succession until that guy falls back onto his knees, gasping for air. I watch from beneath the table as Vulture circles the table and kicks Wolf's wrist—the one that isn't in a sling—to disarm him and then roundhouses the guy in the face.

Wolf falls to the ground, his brown hair fanning out above his head.

"One, two, three, four, five. And he's down!" a prisoner shouts. "We have a winner!"

Warped cheers erupt around us, along with a smattering of applause, though I do hear one British accent call out, "Fuck off, Preds. You ruined our sex show, you wankers!"

"All right, that's enough," a guard calls out lazily from his post on the far side of the cafeteria. He leans against the wall, a huge machine gun—one that would have been very useful if he'd bothered to use it seconds ago—drooping lazily in his right hand. "Inmates, you know you're not allowed to take supplies out of the kitchen and blah blah blah." He waves a hand in the air dismissively. "Return all the weapons, and I won't have to write you up."

That's it?!

They try to kill me, and they don't even get punished?!

I glare at each of the Predators in turn, gripping the handle of my weapon and wondering if I could get away with a few hacks. Or does the guard's word really stand, now that he's finally spoken?

Vulture bends and picks up Wolf's machete before moving to the table and offering me a hand. I take it, trying not to acknowledge just how much I love the feel of his huge hand enclosing mine. Trying not to let gratitude or the shakes from the adrenaline show.

"Never attack a guy who's in the middle of getting laid," Vulture says as he sternly points his weapon at first an unconscious Coyote and then Wolf, who blinks dazedly back at him.

"Amen, brother!" some dude from the back of the cafeteria calls out. Then he thumps the table with his fist.

The sound erupts around the cafeteria as others join in with a chorus of "Amens" and fist pounding.

Vulture gives them all a stoic nod before he leads me from the cafeteria, machetes still clutched in each of our hands.

The guards don't bother to stop us, though the one at the door extends his hand. Vulture hands over his machete, and I reluctantly do the same, though I instantly miss the cold, certain weight of the weapon in my palm.

When we reach the relative calm of the jungle outside, which is full of birdsong instead of the chitchat of murderers, I turn to Vulture with narrowed eyes, suspicion creeping up my neck. "You knew they'd try and attack in there, didn't you?"

He lifts a shoulder lazily. "If we gave them an opening. It's what most village idiots would do."

"So . . . pressure points . . ."

"Gave them an opening."

I narrow my eyes at him, glaring through slits sharp enough to cut. "Does one of them really know Krav Maga?"

He deadpans, "They could."

Motherfucker. He gave them an opening . . . so he could take them out. So they couldn't come after me during combat practice later.

I run a hand through my hair at the revelation, my thoughts just as knotted as the strands. "I can't decide if I'm angry at you or grateful."

"I'm fine with both. Or either. Whatever you decide. But we accomplished three things. First, the other prisoners know you belong to the Birds of Prey. It won't stop all of them from going after you, but the majority are too terrified of us to risk it. Secondly, the fucking Predators now know you have our full protection if they're stupid enough to attack you again. And finally . . ." He gives a dark grin as he shamelessly looks me up and down. "I definitely think I've proven women aren't the better liars."

He turns and strides away, giving me the view of his tight ass as the humidity enfolds me like a wet blanket. But that's not the reason I can't breathe.

Well, motherfucking dammit.

I want to ball up my fists and yell that I don't need his protection. But that isn't true, and we both know it. I don't want his protection. Or at least, on the surface, I don't. But some little piece of my chest sparks up at that thought, flickering like a little flame in a dark tunnel. That tiny little part of me doesn't just want his protection —she adores it.

14

EAGLE

"You fucking bastards," Chucky snarls at me, her nose scrunched and her teeth bared as she leaps at me, both hands wrapping around my neck, legs around my waist. Her red hair has been haphazardly tossed into a braid, and her canines, which are on full display, have been filed to sharp points. Her eyeliner, which is always thick and smudged so that she resembles a panda, is smeared worse than normal. She's glaring at me as though she plans to kill me. Perhaps she does.

Of course, fate would have it that the day after we get our new recruit, I am paired up with a Baby Dolly for combat. What a coincidence. Makes me wonder if the guards know more about our secret arrangement with them than Raven suspects.

In any case, Chucky is livid. She ran at me the second our code names were announced, not even squaring off within the fight circle like a good little prisoner. If she wants to be riled up, fine. I know just what to do about it.

I fall back to the wrestling mat, letting her think she has the upper hand, allowing her to land on top of me. Then, to piss her off, I mimic humping up into her through our clothes.

"*Da*. Call me bastard. Call me bastard like you mean it!" I cry out. "Choke me harder, baby."

Several of the other prisoners laugh, stopping their own combat matches to watch us—they're well aware of what public sex acts do to provoke the Baby Dollies. Trying anything with them is a good way to get your dick cut off.

Of course, the other prisoners don't have what we have.

Leverage.

Secrets.

Agreements.

Chucky lets out an animalistic growl before smashing her heel into my ribs.

I fake a gasp. Though her kick makes my ribs squeal like butchered pigs and sends bands of pain through my vision, so the metal ceiling of the combat room swims slightly above me, it's not enough to take me out. But I sell it the way Hawk has taught me. I allow her to think she's going to win. Sometimes, it is fun to play with the other prisoners that way.

In weapons trade, you mess with others, you lose trust, you die.

There are no games.

No play.

Here, though . . . play has become life. Play is the only reason to wake up each morning. I spend hours planning out each little method I use to play with Vulture. Like the fact that, last week, I pissed into an empty Gatorade bottle in front of all my Birds, winking at him as I did it.

He's gone on high alert, knowing, just knowing, that frothing piss was all for him. It's made him lash out. Spiders in my underwear. Nails in my bed.

But it will be worth it when I finally reveal what I've done to him . . .

"Motherfucker!" Chucky's punch gets me right in the eye. Pain shoots through me as she leans down and spits in my face, whispering, "She was our recruit. Ours! We get first shot at any of the decent female prisoners. You stole her."

I laugh, knowing that will only enrage her further. And then I grab her ass and flip us over so that I'm on top, dissolving her illusions of grandeur and control.

The guards do nothing, just as they always do. One is smoking, watching us, and the scent of his cigarette tempts me more than the bitch beneath me.

I smash my forehead into Chucky's, relishing the dazed look that comes into her nut-brown eyes. Then I say, "Listen—" Nothing enrages a woman more than telling them to listen. Except for, perhaps, my next words. "Be reasonable, *da*."

Oh, that does it.

Chucky growls, "No, you listen. Orgasm trades are

done. You hear? Finished. No Dolly will touch a Bird
from here on out—"

I chuckle darkly as I grab one of her legs and force it
onto my shoulder. To others, it might look like a sex position, but I lean forward until I see her expression tighten.
Then I push a tiny bit more, just until I see her facial
muscles clench. Enough to make my point but not
enough to dislocate her hip, which I could do. Easily.

I don't hurt women . . . not physically, at least. Not
unless I have to. But I don't mind putting them in their
place or reminding them who actually holds the power.

"We don't *need* this alliance," I tell her as she gasps
beneath me.

It's true, the orgasms were convenient. It was an easy
way to clear one's head.

But a sloppy, full-of-obligation-and-resentment blow
job from the lowest Baby Dolly on the totem pole is no
great loss. My hand does better work than they often did.
The information they sometimes let slip is more valuable
than the orgasms. But Raven has more contacts among
the guards now. The Baby Dollies rarely provide
anything we haven't already heard.

Trading with them has proven unnecessary.

Particularly now that we have a woman—a
gorgeous woman—for our pleasure. True, Raven says
no fucking, but we'll see how long that rule lasts. I, for
one, would love to see those ripe breasts of hers
covered in my cum. But not if the price is our unity.
And Raven might have the right of it there. I stare
contemptuously down at the Baby Dolly pinned to the

old, cracked blue mat beneath me and reflect on the
fact that sex is one of the most stupid and ridiculous
things to get angry over.

And yet, so many murders spring from it.

Power lasts longer than pussy.

But too many small-brained men worship the
wrong one.

I worry that some of them are my teammates.

Perhaps we should have let the Baby Dollies take
Phoenix . . .

I don't like that I'm second-guessing things.

What's done is done, and we'll live with the consequences. Vulture is supposed to be bringing our new toy
to combat shortly. I wonder if she will prove to be an asset
or a colossal mistake.

The woman beneath me hisses, tone full of spite,
"You're going to regret this. You sorry cocks will come
crawling—"

"In Russia, we have a saying," I interrupt her and stop
her speech with my palm over her mouth. "The titmouse
claimed to set the sea afire."

Her eyebrows arch in an expression of confusion she
attempts to hide with disdain.

American criminals.

So uncultured, many of them. Unable to think
through metaphor.

"The sea does not burn. Especially not for you, little
mouse. Don't lie to yourself."

With a final shove at Chucky's shoulder, so she can't
quickly follow me, I stand up. "Match over," I tell a

guard, who hasn't bothered to look up from his little ledger the entire time. "I win."

The balding man simply shakes his head and makes a mark in his book before I stride off to check on the other Birds currently also in combat practice. The scent of the room, gym socks and sweat, hits my nose hard the farther I walk away from the propped-open door near my original spot. The door provided air flow, but it cannot defeat the stench of the entire cinder-block building.

I pass by two of the Mountains. Everest, the tallest man on the island, crouches and circles around Denali, a one-eyed Italian with a mean right hook. As two lifelong mafia members, they care more for their ridiculous plots to escape this island than anything else. I ignore them and they me as I search for my other teammates.

I find Raven standing over a much bigger man—one who clearly threw the fight to appease the leader of the Birds.

Physical brutality is not Raven's strong suit. Never has been. I suspect he was on the receiving end of some at one point, because his mental violence game is the strongest I've ever seen. The man knows everyone's ghosts.

Ghosts? No, skeletons, I think it is.

He digs up the bones with his keyboard . . . fingers tapping away . . . unearthing all the secrets.

At one point, I begrudged him. But now, I can admire such ruthlessness.

I make my way over to him, where he hasn't even

broken a sweat. Still, his hands go up to check his hair.
Smooth his shirt.

If others could see past what they think is vanity, they
would know the truth. He's nervous.

I move to stand beside him, at attention, a foot behind
him like a security guard—just the way he likes. Raven
enjoys showmanship. Power. His priorities are aligned.

I see some of the tension leave his shoulders as his
opponent gives him a nod and then shoves up off the mat
to walk away.

Of course, once he is out of earshot, I must under-
mine Raven's sense of bravado.

"Your ass is looking fine today," I coo at our leader.
Never in public, but in private, I absolutely love to piss
him off. "Did you pull that . . . what's the word? Branch?
Did you pull that branch out of it?"

Raven turns and glares at me, and I smirk in return.

"We don't have time for your stupid jokes," he grumbles grumpily.

He's always in a bad mood, for one reason or another.
I used to take offense to it, until I realized that behind all
his bluster and anger is the anxiety of a guy who's
escaped more murder attempts than I have kisses from
my great-aunt Olga with the whiskery mole. Thoughts of
her make me chuckle as memories roll through my mind.
I still think mostly in my native tongue, but I don't speak
it, though the memories of my great-*tetya* cursing me
make me want to call out to her under my breath. She
lives inside my head rent-free, though not in the way the

other prisoners say it. She moved in, brought a bag of her things, and remains there like a squatter inside my skull.

Raven claps his hands behind his back like some sort of military general and gestures with a jerk of his head for me to follow him down the line of fighters. Thus, we walk the complex. It's one of the oldest buildings in the entire prison and looks like it's survived a hurricane or two. One of the cinder-block walls tilts at an odd angle, like the builders were a bit drunk when they assembled it.

It works as a combat practice room, though, because there are no windows—no glass to shatter as prisoners bodily throw one another—and the walls are padded. With weak, old batting that escapes from the leather mats at every opportunity. Still, they are softer than elsewhere. The guards could have done worse. At least no one has to sleep here. They could have made it a barracks.

And no matter how I feel about this desolate, concrete cube, it's better than the arena.

Of course, a vise to the testicles is better than that fucked-up place.

In the distance ahead of us, at the very back corner of the room, Falcon and Hawk square off on a muddy, black gymnastics mat, forced to wrestle with one another.

I shake my head at it. In their idiocy, Hoplite Defense Services insists that our missions will include lots of hand-to-hand combat and therefore make this part of our daily routine. Beating one another. I personally think that they just want to wear us out to make the jobs of the guards easier. Or perhaps they're perverts who like to watch us grapple with one another. From the way one of the guards is eyeing Falcon and Hawk, his tongue lazily tracing his lower lip and his hand continually dropping to his crotch? I wouldn't be surprised.

Fuckers.

For all the years I was in the family business, there was almost no hand-to-hand combat. That is an American action movie myth. Gunshots? Yes. But exciting car chases down the street with people precariously balanced on the roofs of vehicles? Multiple chances to use a round-house kick? *Please.*

Bet if I mention that we should try this vehicle surfing thing, Falcon would sign right up. That man has more than a few screws loose. He has lost so many, he could fill up Olga's spare button jar.

"Eagle," Raven intones, putting a hand over his mouth to disguise his words, so neither the guards nor our compatriots can see what he's saying.

Immediately, I'm intrigued. I move a little closer, despite the fact that Raven already underwent his wrestling match and smells like the taint smear on old underwear. Faintly gross but no longer gag-worthy.

"Yes?" I say, annoyed that my accent is still so strong after all these years, even on such a simple word.

"The girl is a problem," Raven says just as Hawk manages to get Falcon into a headlock. The massive black man flexes his bicep, and Falcon's hands come up to futilely scratch at Hawk's muscles. I'm not even sure the serial killer has nerve-endings. Falcon is fucked.

"Why is this?" I ask, unsurprised by the venom I hear in Raven's voice. He's always plotting and planning.

My father used to say, "Little thieves are hanged. Great ones escape." It was a common saying in our hometown. Or, at least, in our circle. Raven is what I would call a great thief. He never lets down his guard. Of course, he did once. Otherwise, he wouldn't be here. But I feel in my bones that he deeply regrets that moment and never wants to repeat it. Hence, the constant agitation.

I honestly wouldn't be surprised if Raven planned contingencies for all the members of his team. And when I say contingencies, I mean *ways to kill us without arousing suspicion*. Raven blatantly went up to me a year or so back and said, "If Falcon gets out of hand, I'll need you to put him down. I don't care how."

He's ruthless, vindictive, and the most neurotic fucker I know, putting even Hawk and Falcon to shame. Others may not see this. But I do. He trusts absolutely no one . . . not even himself half the time.

Vulture once joked Raven's a ticking time bomb just waiting to detonate, and I have to agree. His paranoia is what makes him valuable, but it also makes him dangerous.

Raven grinds his teeth, and his lips pucker as he sourly says, "She's going to be *useless* on the field. A liability. She's going to drag us down. And in the meantime, before we even get an assignment, she's going to tear us apart. Those fucking horndogs. And! And we know nothing about her. Not really. The paper trail of the socialite daughter was pretty well erased when her parents disowned her after she got fed up with Daddy diddling her. They hired some decent people to wipe her from the web. I could only dig up a little. But she's basically a ghost after that. Very few documents, and documents can be forged."

He steps closer, eyes shining wildly as he glances quickly at me, agitation vibrating through his very bones as he whispers, "Doesn't it seem odd to you that a thief would be sent here to play ball with murderers? She's a ghost . . . which means she *must* be a spy." He becomes more animated with every word he says, snapping his lips together only when a guard looks in our direction. As soon as the guard is watching, Raven forces his entire body to relax into a lazy pose, and his eyelids droop over his eyes as if he's bored, tired, complacent.

Hawk would be proud of that transition.

"She does not seem . . ." I search for the stupid English word that means *intrigi*. ". . . Does not seem scheming to me."

"She doesn't have to scheme." Raven points a finger at Hawk, who's maneuvered himself and Falcon down to the mat.

Hawk rolls on top of the much slimmer man, crowing, "Say she's mine."

"Never," Falcon growls, wriggling underneath Hawk's muscular thighs and flipping onto his back so that they look very . . . intimate. The perverted guard appears to like that as he not-so-subtly places a hand beneath his waistband, the gun slung over his shoulder forgotten.

Falcon's hand flies up to Hawk's balls.

"Awoooooooo!" Hawk shrieks in a way that would

have made my father *tsk* in disapproval. He thought men should bear their pain in silence.

Not that he bore his own quietly when his final days arrived . . .

The two Birds of Prey start to grapple more viciously, rolling and clawing and scratching and punching and even kicking whenever they have an opening. But then, they've always fought hard. Not all Birds hate this combat nonsense.

"I thought this anger was why you chose them." I nod at my two cellmates. Raven has a thing for taking damaged, broken, deranged souls underneath his metaphorical wing. I half wonder if that's why he named us Birds of Prey. The crazier, the better.

Raven shakes his head, his gaze flicking from side to side, as if he worries someone will overhear him. "It is. But that wildness needs to be directed outward. And she's going to fuck all that up."

"Well. What are you proposing?" This was one of my father's favorite questions to ask, ever the businessman.

Always calm.

Always allowing his opponent to lay their cards on the table first.

That's how he survived the weapons business so long.

Until, of course, he didn't.

"Falcon's already too attached. We can't outright kill her, or he'll go berserk." Raven bends down and reties his boot as a guard passes by. He always stops conversations if they are within five feet. At one point, when I first joined the Birds, he would only send us hand-scribbled notes that always told us to eat the note after reading. They tasted like shit. I'm pretty sure Falcon "convinced" some of the other prisoners to eat the notes for him because he didn't like the taste, a fact which infuriated Raven.

But now, our ruthless leader has had ample time to investigate all the parts of the island, and Hoplite apparently is sadly lacking in technological spyware in several buildings, including this one. Since I prefer the struggle of mental translation over the taste of paper and ink, I do not mind that Raven's arranged the schedule so that most of us have our combat time together.

Once the guard is sufficiently distracted by a few other prisoners betting on their upcoming match, Raven stands back up. He scratches at his nose as he mutters, "If we can't kill her outright, then we're going to have to be strategic."

Sometimes, he can be a bit over-the-top with his monologues. You cannot rush him to make his point, though. He'll only start over, determined to piss you off. And then he will make sure to treat you like a child who needs small words to understand.

I grit my teeth into a counterfeit smile. "*Da?*"

Raven licks his lips, and I can see the shields come down inside of his eyes. He goes from a living, breathing man to a computer that calculates actions and outcomes, running the numbers and not giving a single fuck.

Whenever he gets such a look, my spine turns as cold as a Siberian winter. Because I know that I'm not going to like what he has to say. In the weapons trade, you give out machines for money. The bloodshed is very little. In here, it is not the same.

Whenever Raven gets that look, it ensures evil will follow.

Falcon smashes his hand twice into the mat in defeat as Raven whispers, "We're going to have to torture that little spoiled princess until she kills herself."

I never truly had a home before.

The mansion I lived in with my parents? It felt more like a prison than anything else. The bleak white walls and mahogany floorboards did very little to make it seem welcoming. A cement block with a door carved into the side would be more appealing. And the secrets that hid behind those carved doors at my parents' mansion were far darker than the ones I learned in prison. Criminals typically want money. But rich people? They have money, so their desires are a lot more fucked up.

It's ironic that prison is exactly where I've ended up, in another kind of jail cell. Maybe that's all life is . . . a series of cell blocks. Some people realize they're trapped in one. Others don't.

I recall the first time I became conscious of the dark underpinnings of my parents. Of how I was trapped and bound to them, no matter that I didn't want to be.

I used to own a pet parrot, and every day when I arrived back from school, it would squawk, "Welcome home. Welcome home. Welcome home" in an increasingly high-pitched croak. One day, though, when I stepped into the opulent living room, I was greeted by silence instead of the incessant cries of my favorite bird. I'd run from room to room, searching for him, to no avail. When I asked my mother what happened to my beloved pet, she stared at me coldly over her reading glasses, her ruby-red lips pursing, and declared, "If I had to hear the damn thing say 'home' one more time, I would have lost my mind."

To this day, I still don't know exactly what happened to Ruffles.

After I left my parents' house, I simply lived from day to day, never settling in one location for long. Some days, my house consisted of a cardboard box I found on the side of the street or behind a dumpster in a dark alleyway. Other times, it was beneath a bridge or under an awning of a storefront, particularly this abandoned old-school photography shop that was killed off by the digital era. There were a few times when I managed to score enough money to rent apartments or hotel rooms. I actually had an apartment with Taylor the Douchebag before the sick fucker betrayed me and left me for dead.

But this cabin the Birds of Prey claimed as their own, with its log siding, unwashed windows, and pitched roof? That'll never be home. The mere sight of it has a shiver of unease rippling up my spine.

After an hour-long session of "combat," where I knew

absolutely no one and was forced to fight a fifty-year-old man, I was finally released for dinner.

Before I could even take a bite of my food, a greasy concoction that the inmate serving it called "Cannibal's Wet Dream" while flashing me a cheeky wink, Hawk arrived with a cheery smile on his handsome face.

"Raven told me to bring you home, lil' miss," he said in a ridiculous Southern accent.

I grimaced but didn't protest. I grabbed my bread roll, so that I'd at least have something in my stomach, and silently followed him. The eyes of all the other prisoners burned my skin, as if someone lit an entire package of cigarettes and decided to use me as an ashtray. Every little look seared my flesh, and I tried not to focus on that feeling but on Hawk's words as we strode through the prison yard while I ate my meager dinner.

Home.

Now, we're at the cabin, and I stare at the moss-covered log walls and notice a little cluster of wild mushrooms growing out of one corner. As if this cabin could ever be considered home.

I'm a firm believer that home is where the heart is or however that clichéd saying goes. And my problem? I don't have a heart. Not anymore. It's been beaten out of me, mauled to death by life itself, and then dropped into a blender for good measure. That fucker has been swirling around and around for years, becoming increasingly more shredded with every second that passes.

The only thing left inside my chest is a glittering, one-carat jewel.

I'm sweaty, tired, and covered in bruises. My nose aches from a punch that old guy landed—I swear he had brass knuckles on, but I didn't call out his cheating use of the weapon because I feared retaliation—and all I want to do right this second is take a long, steaming hot shower.

Hawk gestures to the front door of the cabin, but I shake my head. Enough is enough. They've deprived me of food for nearly twenty-four hours. The Birds have deprived me of sleep. But I reach my limit at being deprived of a shower. I fucking reek of sweaty old man armpits, and I'm over it.

"I need to wash up."

"This way." Hawk doesn't even bat an eye at the change of plans, despite the fact it will probably drive Raven insane. Good. Any opportunity I have to irritate the evil fucker, I'll take.

I haven't forgotten that I owe Hawk one, either. But revenge is best served cold, right? So they say. I'll find out later.

Hawk takes a sharp left turn and tromps off into a path between two frilly, overgrown ferns. I sigh but follow. He brings me to a showerhead located in the middle of the forest, the pole coming right out of a cement pad in the ground, only one handle on it. There are no walls whatsoever.

I glance at him, waiting for a second to see if he'll do the polite thing and turn. Of course, the serial killer doesn't. He shoots me a cocky grin.

My hesitation only lasts a second before I decide— why the fuck not? I'm dirty, stinky, and drenched in sweat. I won't let him win by refusing to partake in the one thing that might give me a modicum of pleasure.

I flip him off, and he just chomps his teeth at me, as if he's threatening to bite another of my fingers.

Bastard thinks he can rile me? Fuck him.

I drop my hands and turn. My shirt and pants come off. It takes only a second to shed them, since they're so big. I lay them over a nearby bush and kick off the women's prison shoes I've been wearing since my arrival, which are now so mud-covered they could be mistaken for brown shoes instead of orange. My ankle gives a hiss of protest as I slide the shoe off, and I realize it has a solid bruise forming from my forced skydiving lesson. I reach a hand down to touch the tender flesh but stop when Hawk's voice reaches my ears.

"That's not going to work." His tone is sharp and scolding and immediately makes me pop upright to turn and look at him.

"What isn't going to work?"

"Putting your ass on display."

"Oh, trust me," I grit out, disdain as thick as peanut butter oozing through my tone. If I could make my fury manifest and choke him, I would. "I'd *never* try to seduce you."

"Wouldn't you?" His brow arches as if he doesn't believe me.

I hold up my swollen index finger and the one next to it. "I'd flip you off, but some asshole tried to cannibalize me earlier today."

"Not into that, huh?" His tone turns playful, eyes sparkling at the painful results of his madness.

"No." My answer is clipped and curt.

"Better watch out for Old Twinkle, then. He's been known to eat a prisoner or two."

"That man's a sweetheart in comparison to you," I retort roughly as I turn back to the shower pole. I leave on my underthings, refusing to give him a show, and reach for the knob to turn on the spray, unsurprised to find it colder than Douchebag's balls after I refused to sleep with him for an entire month.

Fucking great.

When I turn to look for some soap, I find Hawk staring intently as I stand underneath the ice-cold water. There's something sinister about it, doubling the number of goose bumps on my arms. Something that's far more chilling than the water splashing into my eyes. It almost reminds me of the night Taylor shot me. Not Douchebag himself, but the gun in his hand, the finality of death peering back at me through the barrel, the smoke puffing out of it as the bullet sliced through air.

My teeth chatter as I wrap my arms around myself, fighting off the chill.

Eventually, I spot a tiny container of liquid soap half-hidden underneath a leaf. Sweet relief! I dive for it and lather it into my hair, using my fingernails to dig into my scalp in comforting circles. Then I experience another tiny burst of gratitude for the fact that my wealthy upbringing means all the hair was lasered from my body, and I'm not turning into a hairy beast out here in the jungle.

I've barely had time to wash my hair before the shower shuts off.

"What the fuck!" I screech, pissed. I try the knob again, but it doesn't turn back on. My shower is over. My sopping brown hair falls forward to hang in my eyes, and I agitatedly push it away.

Does this island come with a damn hairbrush?

There has to be one somewhere. Raven may be a condescending dick with murderous tendencies, but his dark, silky hair is fucking magnificent. He must use product in it.

"Timer," Hawk chimes, as cheerful as ever. "But I don't think your nipples could have taken much more of that water, anyway."

I look down and immediately cover my chest. Keeping my sports bra on has done nothing to prevent Hawk from getting a show.

Rather than glare at him, which would be a waste of energy, I bend to grab my clothes, and a wolf whistle hits my ears.

What the hell? Why is he suddenly appreciating my ass when, two minutes ago, he warned me against bending over?

"Damn. Is it peach season? Because you're looking ripe," Hawk teases me with a groaner of a joke, one that almost makes the unhinged man seem human for a moment. Until I look back at his eyes and see his smile fade back into that hungry, dangerous look he wore while

I washed. It's not the same as Falcon's crazed possession. There's something far more eerie about Hawk, something that warns me that, if I don't run now, I might not be able to run at all.

I swallow hard, but the lump in my throat doesn't fade. It pulses with the beat of my heart, making me all too aware of just how jittery Hawk makes me.

I promised vengeance against him earlier, and if I hadn't just seen the look in his eyes, I might be okay with teasing him, bantering like we did before or even deliberately drying myself off with those prison clothes—rubbing them lewdly across my body under the guise of drying off—making him wish he could have me right before I raced off to find Falcon. But that look sends a warning tingle up my spine, stopping me from playing with him.

I narrow my eyes at him for talking to me so crudely but don't say anything else, because we're alone in the middle of the rainforest and no one will come if I scream. He very much looks like he wants to make me scream. Tension radiates from his deep brown eyes, his thick lips smiling but tightly drawn. His dark fingers flex, almost as if he wants to grab me and hurt me.

I'll have to piss him off another time. This isn't my moment.

Cautiously, I bundle my clothes in front of me, covering up the peep show as best I can while I'm forced to walk back to the cabin with soaking wet hair and skin. Not even the heat can dry me, because the air here is as moist as an armpit. Even if the heat was dry, it would probably be useless. Chills travel up and down my spine, not only from the water, but from the fact that the serial killer is two steps behind me and breathing heavily.

By the time we reach the cabin, I've run out of all the shits one woman is capable of feeling. I suppose you can say that my shit-o-meter is at a record-breaking low. The anticipatory fear he's wrung from me on the walk has drained me to empty.

The sun dips beneath the tops of trees as Hawk gestures for me to step in front of him. The door to the cabin looms ominously, and my stomach feels like a brick has been shoved inside of it, because I really don't want to deal with anything else today. But I'm pretty certain there's no warm welcome awaiting me inside.

"Right this way, my lady," he purrs in a haughty British accent.

As I move forward, his dark hand snakes out to pinch my ass. I jump, whipping my head around to glare at him before remembering he's a goddamn psycho and I need to proceed with caution.

Like I did with Falcon earlier, I dip my head submissively like a good pet—gag—and bat my eyelashes, hoping like hell that passive responses have the same effect on both men.

Hawk takes a step closer to me, his heat surrounding me like an inferno, and places one hand beneath my chin, guiding my head up. My pulse sizzles as his dark eyes ensnare my own and his huge hand covers the length of my jaw.

"My, my, my," he drawls in an exaggerated Southern

accent. And then his hand tightens on my chin to the point of pain, and I have to bite down on my whimper. "Don't go pretending to be demure, Nyx," he purrs, leaning even closer, so his face consumes my vision. "We both know you have the claws of a tiger, not a kitten."

God, I want to bite his hand. If I could just turn my head slightly . . .

I think he can read my intentions based on my expression. And by the excited glint in his fathomless dark eyes?

He likes that.

A lot.

A thread of alarm unfurls in my stomach, curling around the knot of tension already there.

What does a serial killer do with a girl he . . . *likes*?

He releases me as abruptly as he grabbed me, shoving me forward so my shoulder hits the closed cabin door. Pain splinters through my already abused body as a dozen acerbic retorts dance on my tongue.

I don't say any of them, though, as I walk inside with my head held high, Hawk a step behind me.

Don't annoy the unhinged serial killer, Nyx.

But isn't there also a rule that I shouldn't give an unhinged serial killer my back? No? Well, then, I'm officially adding that to the rule book.

My skin practically prickles as I venture a step farther into the cabin, keenly aware of Hawk directly behind me, his heat migrating to my own body, his hands brushing my waist in a touch that could be a taunt or a promise.

The rest of the men are already lounging around or lying on their bunks, talking amongst each other, and they don't pay us any mind as we enter. None of them bothered to shower after combat, except for Raven, so the cabin is ripe with the tangy, musky scent of sweaty men.

I scan the bunks, searching for a friendly face—or as friendly as possible on an island full of monsters—but Vulture pretends not to see me and Falcon is already asleep, I think.

The man lies on top of his blankets with his hands folded over his chest and a motherfucking sausage link fisted in one. Despite the fact his eyes are shut, I have a feeling he's aware of everything going on around him and that he'll jump to his feet at the slightest provocation and kill whoever bothered him with that damn sausage.

I wonder what my obituary would say in that scenario?

Here lies Nicholette Bettencourt, who died from being whipped to death by sausage. Rest in peace.

Then again, do the criminals here get obituaries?

Do we even get burials or gravestones or funerals?

Probably not. Even if I did, who would mourn me?

Something leaden settles in my gut, swirling the contents—that meager roll I ate—around like a boulder.

Hawk grabs my shoulder from behind to halt me and places his lips directly beside my ear. His rough stubble grazes my lobe as he whispers, "Want another love bite?"

I attempt to smother my irritation, knowing the last thing I can afford to do is poke the beast. And this beast is a six-foot-three killer who's proven his cruelty to me.

Hawk chuckles, apparently not expecting a response, and moves away with a wide smile on his face. If I didn't know the monster he truly was, the devil beneath the man, I might've believed he was a genuinely good guy. Happy-go-lucky. His fake smile is convincing. He even somehow manages to pull off that friendly aura that eases people, which probably lets him get close to his marks. I would know, because we have that in common. But unlike Hawk, I felt genuine happiness every once in a while, like the time I rescued a baby kitten from the gutter. The two of us are not the same.

I don't believe Hawk is capable of feeling any real emotion, outside of bloodlust. That smile is nothing but a mask, one he wears with the skill and ease of a seasoned pro. I doubt he even knows what joy is. That smile seems to be ingrained inside his sadistic mind, the only facial tic he's capable of utilizing.

If he weren't batshit crazy, I might feel sorry for him.

"Oh, look!" Raven moves from where he was standing beside his bed, straightening out the covers. He fixes his black hair where it flopped across his forehead, and I note the untangled waves of his hair with more than a wisp of jealousy flitting through me. When he smooths his black shirt, he says, "There's our precious little Phoenix."

My unease amplifies as I stare at his grinning face, clothes still clutched to my body. He's using a tone I don't like, one that almost seems worse than the fiery disdain he slung at me this morning. I know he hates me, maybe more than any of the others. The old me might've constantly wondered *why* he resents me so much, *why* he seems to envision taping my picture to a dartboard and then bombarding it with darts, *why* he glares at me like I'm the piece of shit under his polished shoe. The new me doesn't give a single damn.

I don't rise to the bait.

Raven, unperturbed, stops directly in front of me, and it's then that I notice he's holding something in his hand.

Is it . . . a shiv?

Oh god. It's a shiv. He's going to motherfucking shiv me.

I'm not ready to be shivved, dammit. I'm meant to do the shivving, not the other way around.

Why isn't anyone putting a stop to this?

My eyes unwillingly flick to Vulture again, almost as if I—I dunno—expect him to stand up for me or something, but he remains on his back on his bunk, his arms folded behind his head.

Fuck.

Falcon's asleep, his back moving up and down with regularity.

Eagle's biting down on a grin as he pushes himself up to a sitting position to watch. I guess a massage didn't earn me enough credit to help with this.

I'm on my own.

These sick fucks will all just sit around and watch him kill me. Cold dread slithers from my toes and reignites the goose bumps on my wet arms. I smash my clothes against my chest, no longer caring that they're wet. I'm just wishing I had gotten dressed, that I had some kind of armor, some weapon, something more to prevent Raven from gutting me with a homemade knife.

"A present," Raven practically purrs, his chocolate eyes glittering with malice as he slowly extends the object toward my torso. I brace myself for the pain, for the piercing sensation of metal slicing me open, but it never comes.

When I glance down, I see that Raven is holding out . . . a blue toothbrush?

The fuck?

"A peace offering," he tells me, still flashing that sadistic smile. My unease from before? It transitions from a simple firework to an entire circus inside of my head, complete with acrobats and jugglers and men who breathe fire.

Accepting the gift can only mean bad things for me. But refusing the gift can also only mean bad things for me.

The conclusion of this story? I'm fucked. So, so fucked.

My hand trembles as I close it around the toothbrush, but I keep my gaze locked on Raven. I have a feeling he's irritated by my response, but if he expected me to be a sniffling, sobbing mess, he picked the wrong fucking girl to torture.

I grab the toothbrush with my left hand, jerking it quickly back to my side and holding it almost like I would a knife.

Raven's not kind. He's not like Hawk; he doesn't bother to put on a veneer of fake friendliness, to smile enigmatically as if the entire world's a show and he's the star performer. So, I very much doubt that this toothbrush will help me with any hygiene issues.

Raven's grin widens, and he steps closer until his minty breath fans against my face.

Suddenly, I wonder if the toothbrush in my grip is used. Does he have some kind of disease conveyed by spit? Is he going to try to make me use his old toothbrush? That seems like the sort of backhanded cruelty that would suit him.

I swallow hard.

"Clean the floor," he whispers, his eyes hardening, becoming empty orbs. He really is dead inside.

"Excuse me?" I ask in disbelief but also partially in relief, because it's better than what I literally just imagined.

Raven places his hands on my shoulders and roughly forces me to my knees. My clothes tumble to the floor at my side as my shins hit the ground. I stare up at his unnaturally handsome face. I could resist him—and I almost do—before I decide that playing his game might keep me alive long enough to find a way off this island. It's a thin hope, as meager as a narrow beam of light shining under a locked door made of solid steel, but it's all I've got right now, so I cling to it. I lean forward a little and extend the brush toward the floorboards.

"Good little slut," he hisses, his fingernails digging into my skin as I stay put on my knees.

He has no idea, but that phrase automatically kindles heat low in my belly, because *little slut* is what an old ex who had dominant tendencies liked to call me during sex. I remind myself that Raven isn't Edwin, and that this asshole has zero interest in anything other than degrading me. That douses the fire quickly enough, though shame does creep up, because I'm still only wearing my sopping, see-through underthings.

My underwear and panties cover more than a bathing suit, and it's not like they haven't seen it all before. But god, I feel so fucking vulnerable right now.

Raven's eyes burn into me, and the air between us thickens with tension. His fingers dig deeper into my shoulders, pinching a nerve so that I involuntarily hunch and look weak and cowardly. Loathing builds up deep inside my soul as he stares down at me, pressing harder and harder, making me curl until my back is shaped like the letter C.

At some point, the line blurred between pretending to be docile and actually becoming it. I no longer know if I'm faking being this meek little creature . . . or if the guys have turned me into one.

Even as the errant thought forms, I sweep it away in a tidal wave of anger.

No. I won't let them get to me.

I won't let them break me.

My bare knees dig into the hard floorboards, exacerbating a newly forming bruise I must've gotten from combat training.

A second later, he drops a rusty bucket of brown water beside me, liquid sluicing over the rim.

Raven's hands leave my shoulders, finally satisfied that I'm not going to resist him.

But I take my spite for him and turn it onto Eagle, facing the other criminal with narrowed eyes, spitting flames at one of the men in the bunkhouse that I'm least scared of...the Russian with the scarred eyebrow who just delivered the water bucket.

He simply shrugs at me as if to say, "What can I do?" and moves toward his bunk. I notice that he surveys his bed intently, pulling back the blankets and checking underneath the mattress for any unwanted surprises.

Yeah, he'd better keep checking, because I'm going to leave him an unwanted surprise first chance I get.

Vulture bites his lips to keep from smiling as Eagle curses in Russian under his breath.

"Paranoid, little fellow?" Vulture deadpans, sitting up and swinging his legs over the side of the bed.

Eagle grabs his pillow and whacks Vulture with it. "You pay!" he warns the other man with a grin. "You still pay!"

"Yeah. Yeah." Vulture waves a hand in the air dismissively. "You keep threatening that, but so far, nothing has happened. Your threat is a little *impotent*." He emphasizes the last word and then sticks his index finger up in the air. He makes it sag as he utters a "deflation" sound.

"I'll show you potent!" Eagle snarls, jumping onto Vulture and wrestling with him.

Vulture cackles madly. "Impotent. Not potent."

They'd almost look silly if I didn't know they were wildly unhinged maniacs.

"Hey!" Raven bends down and grabs my chin tightly, forcing my attention away from them and back to him. "Get to cleaning." He releases me with a disgusted hiss. "That's all women are good for, anyway—cleaning, fucking, and cooking."

Anger flares inside of me, white-hot and defiant, as I angrily thrust the toothbrush into the bucket and swirl it around.

Play their game, Nyx, and get out when you can.

But his foot kicks at me as if I'm a fucking dog, and I snap. "One—I haven't cleaned something in my entire fucking life," I tell him with a sneer. "I had maids for that when I was younger. And when I was older?" I offer him a cruel smile. "The men I fucked didn't hesitate to do what I asked. And that brings me to number two—I'll never in a million years fuck you, Raven. I'd rather fuck a dildo wrapped in barbed wire than put your disgusting dick anywhere near my body."

"You tell him, love!" Hawk goads me from behind, his British accent bright and sunny.

Raven's eyes flicker over to Hawk to shut his teammate up, and when his gaze turns back to me, it's so hard and angry that I almost fear I crossed a line I can't come back from. Still, that doesn't stop my big, stupid mouth from continuing its verbal rant. Apparently, my mouth met its take-it-in-silence quota for the day and has decided to shoot off like a loaded gun. "Finally, if I ever cooked you a meal, it would be your own ground-up testicles laced with poison. Do you understand me?"

Shocked silence permeates the room as everyone gapes at me.

Are the big, bad killers not used to their pets talking back?

I realize that I'm being stupid, impulsive, reckless, but my body thrums with a type of courage that I thought had been leached out of me days ago. Maybe months. These men are nothing but bullies, and if they believe they can push me around, they'll continue to do so.

And if they decide they want to be done with me? Well . . .

I don't think I'm ready to die, but I'm also not quite sure I still want to live in this fucked-up world characterized by chaos.

Raven simply glares at me, his expression like thunder, before he roughly grabs my hair and wrenches my head back.

"Listen here, you little slut," he hisses, baring his teeth. "The only thing I understand is that I'm the leader of the Birds of Prey, and by default, you. Falcon and Hawk want you as a pet and plaything? Fine. They can have you. But these breasts . . ." He pulls a shiv out of his pocket, reaches out, and swiftly cuts my sports bra down the middle, nicking the tiniest bit of skin so that a trickle of blood slithers down my chest. He bares my naked chest with the makeshift knife, the flat side of the blade dragging over each of my nipples before he replaces it in his pocket.

I want to step back, but I don't let myself. I lock my limbs and stare at the middle of his forehead, picturing the emerald earrings I stole in a solo heist just weeks before everything went wrong. I plucked them out of a woman's jewelry chest, freeing them from their velvet prison. I focus hard, trying to mentally picture those emeralds. Their glimmer and sparkle . . .

Raven's hand cups one of my heavy breasts, his thumb rolling across my nipple. A bolt of purely physical reaction vibrates through me, but I counteract it by chanting "asshole" inside my mind. I try to recapture the image of the emeralds, but I can't. I can't picture anything. My mind goes blank. My body goes blank. I just cease to exist where I stand as he violates me.

"And this pussy . . ." He pulls my hair again, yanking it by the roots until my scalp is screaming, forcing me up to my feet or I'll risk losing a chunk of it. My body moves on autopilot, and that's the same way the tears erupt—automatically. Suddenly, I'm not Nyx anymore. I'm back to being young, vulnerable Nicholette, who didn't know what to do or what to say, so she simply floated away.

Pain sprints down my skull as Raven grabs my under-wear, though it hardly registers inside the place I've retreated to—the mental cage I've locked myself into. He yanks me toward him using the hem of my panties so that my thighs press close to his. I can feel the bulge of his desire beneath his pants. He clearly loves cruelty. Though, in my experience, most men do.

I start counting my breaths.

He grabs my nipple and twists until I shriek. The pain unlocks my cage for a moment and thrusts me back into the dark pit of reality, my senses crackling with red-hot agony.

My glossy, tear-laden eyes scan the room, but not one of the other men steps closer. They aren't going to do anything. Not even Vulture, though he turns his head from the sight, ironically. He's a torturer. He should be used to shit like this, shouldn't he?

I want to hiss and snarl at the rest of them, but my throat is tightening up with panic over what might come next. And who am I kidding? They don't give a shit about me. We've only had tentatively friendly interactions before now, if you can even call it that. Vulture . . . I thought . . . well, I thought wrong.

One denied orgasm and then dry humping in the cafeteria, a friendship does not make.

They've known each other longer. Their loyalty is elsewhere. And apparently, Raven is the king of the birds.

If they aren't going to help me, then there's nothing to stop Raven from outright killing me. Or humiliating me in every way he can manage, which is what he's clearly trying to do. I want to fight fire with fire. I want so badly to be the badass persona I've created for myself over the years. But I'm just wrung out.

Hawk calls out, "Where's your sarcasm now, sweetheart?" using his Southern accent. And something about his tone stings, disdainful enough to make my head whip up so that I can glare at him through my tears.

He simply arches a brow, waiting for my reaction.

And somehow, the challenge I clearly see issued on his face spurs me to try one more time. Just one more.

I have to swallow, and my voice starts out clogged, but I get the words out with an increasing amount of venom as I say, "I thought Raven would be more used to girls crying when he plays with them than screaming for more. I don't think he knows what ecstasy looks like in a female. Do you?" I turn my head and cock it to the side as I glare at Raven.

Behind me, I hear Hawk moan. But Raven's eyes shutter as he realizes I've turned the tables on him. That cold, calculating mask of his slides over his features.

His hand releases my aching nipple, and I let out a relieved breath that I try to transform into a disappointed sigh to keep up the façade. "Aw, did you come in your pants already? I wasn't done playing."

That line must be too much for him. In the very next moment, he yanks on my panties until they dig painfully into my skin before he rips them clean from my body. Then he shoves his hand down between us and cups my heat.

That rat bastard.

The same thumb that played with my nipple jabs inside of me hard enough to hurt. Goddammit. Nothingness threatens to close in on me again, shield me like before. New tears sting my eyes, but I refuse to let them fall. Visions of how I want to hurt Raven flare inside my mind as the asshole calls my bluff and ups the ante.

"You're a toy, a pet, not even an asset. You're a liability, and you know it. Every breath you take is a gift from me," Raven whispers softly, but his words slap me across the face with their stark, solid truth. If I want to survive

in this insane place, with Predators hunting me, and
death-sentence missions hanging over my head, then I do
need him.

Superiority flickers across his expression when he
sees the wheels turn and the realization click into place in
my head.

"Fuck you," I manage to grit out, though every fiber in
my legs wants to give out from underneath me so that I
collapse to the floor and give in to the need to sob hysteri-
cally. I struggle to push the hurt and violation away,
focusing only on the strands of rage tying up my chest in
emotional knots. But then his finger curls and taps just
the right spot to make a tiny dart of unwanted pleasure
pierce the negative emotions bombarding me.

And through it all, I can't help but think of those late
nights when I was a child . . .

The creak of a door opening . . .

Raven cocks his head to the side and studies me with
keen intensity, as if he knows exactly where my mind
has gone and is wondering if he's tipped me over the
edge.

I rein myself in, but just barely. I try to relax my
thighs, because I don't want him to see that he's found my
G-spot. I don't want him to know that he's not only won
this little game, but he has the power to humiliatingly
make me come in front of all these other bastards. If he
does that, I will shatter.

I don't know if it's hilarious or terrifying that the
thing betraying me here most of all is my own damn
body. My toes start to curl, and I suck in air between my

teeth as my lower abdomen blazes with a fire I wish I could put out.

"Not even in your dreams, baby." He yanks his finger roughly out of me before he shoves at my shoulders again, forcing me back onto my hands and knees. I kneel there, gasping, hating him but also grateful, in a twisted way that shouldn't even exist, because he didn't make my body forsake my mind. I know it's not something I should be grateful for . . . but I am, and I hate the fact that I am.

"Clean. If you're going to act like a defiant whore, you're going to be treated like one. No clothes for you until you learn how to behave."

His eyes are obsidian as he leans down one last time, getting right in my face as he grabs one of my dangling breasts and twists it hard enough to bruise.

"Birds . . . I don't think this floor is dirty enough yet. I'm sure this slut would love to scrub your semen up."

Low chuckles echo from the other men as humiliation and shame wash over me.

The sound of fabric rustling, the hock of spit, and then the slap of skin on skin reaches my ears as the men all start to stroke themselves to the sight of me naked on the ground.

"Now, get to cleaning," Raven hisses, releasing my breast and rising to his full height. He smooths down his shirt as he glares at me. "This floor better be spotless by the time I wake up in the morning, or there will be consequences."

Just before he steps away, he kicks at the water

bucket, brown sludge staining the wooden floor and wetting my skin.

"Clean that shit up," he hisses, and the other men laugh again.

I grit my teeth as I turn my face to the floor, all the emotions piling up on me like an inverse pyramid, pressure pressing down on a singular point behind my eyes and threatening to crush me.

I bring back the thought of those emeralds, try to remember the exact setting they were in, the diamond chips sparkling all around them.

The first splatter of cum hits my cheek and drips down my face.

I don't bother to wipe it away because it helps hide my tears.

FALCON

I stare at the tears trickling down my pet's cheeks. The others have already fallen asleep for the night—even Vulture, that insomniac fuck—but I remain awake.

Watching.

Studying.

Learning.

As my pretty Phoenix crawls on her hands and knees across the cabin with that damn toothbrush, angrily wiping at her cheeks with the back of her hands, I feel something twist in my chest.

Not guilt.

No, the little temptress needs to understand that she's not the boss around here but merely a pet for us to play with. My eyes study the gap between her pale thighs when she has to lean around a bedpost to scrub a corner.

Lust, perhaps?

No, that doesn't seem right, either, though she always awakens that side of me.

Pity?

I nearly scoff as that one word flits through my head. No, definitely not that. I can't even remember the last time I've felt pity toward another individual.

Perhaps that lack of empathy makes me a psychopath. I've certainly been called that on more than one occasion when I've crept into my victims' homes, slit their throats, and then disappeared into the dead of night like a wraith itself. Even my many therapists used that word over the years.

Psychopath.

Sociopath.

Crazy.

Never taking my eyes off Nyx's pussy, the tiny bits I can glimpse from behind, I sit up in bed and place my feet silently on the floor beside me. She doesn't hear me— not that I want her to. I'm content to watch the show as she sniffles and tries to mask the cries that so desperately want to escape.

Poor little bird . . .

I've been a bad owner to my pet for allowing this to go on for so long.

I reach for a shirt lying haphazardly over the side of the bed. It's one of mine, obviously, and it'll fall to her knees. She's so adorably tiny compared to all of us.

My cock stirs to life in my pants at the thought of seeing her in my clothes, enveloped in my scent.

My pet . . .

Mine.

On silent feet, I move until I'm directly behind her, eyeing the curve of her back, the arch of her spine, the soft globes of her ass. I tighten my grip on the dark shirt as I rein in the desire to spank her, brand her, stake my claim.

Jerking off over her wasn't enough.

It'll never be enough.

The only thing that will satisfy the beast within me is pounding into her tight cunt as she screams my name and drags her sharp nails down my back. Once she's trained, of course. But right now, I don't want to wake the other bastards in this cabin.

Nyx finally seems to become aware of the presence directly behind her—the monster looming over her shoulder—and I watch her entire body stiffen as if a bolt of lightning just shot through her. The sight of her fear makes me smile.

Before she can turn around and face me completely, I grab her under her armpits, force her to her knees, and then release her just enough to drag the shirt over her head. I make sure to graze her pointed nipples as I lower my hands down her soft skin, straightening the shirt in the process. She flinches instinctively at the contact, and my smile only broadens.

Soon enough, she's dwarfed in my large shirt, the hem cascading around her knees like a dress.

Fuck, I love seeing my pet in my clothes.

Arousal trickles through me, just enough to have me forgetting my plans for tonight. I'm tempted to turn her around and force her to nuzzle my hardening cock, but I force back the lust with an iron-like will and then extend a hand toward her.

She eyes the proffered limb warily, fear igniting in her eyes, and I smirk at her obvious distrust of me. Good. She's going to need her wits about her if she's going to survive this island.

And she *will* survive.

I'll make damn sure of it.

An owner has to look after his pet, after all.

"Falcon . . ." she murmurs in confusion.

I simply smile and press a finger to my lips, indicating for her to be silent. When she continues to regard me with that wide-eyed, guileless look, I nod toward the others, who are still fast asleep.

For now.

I wouldn't be surprised if more than half of the bastards are actually wide awake and listening to our conversation. At least I know that Raven is still asleep. If he weren't, he would be in my face like a damn pit bull, barking and snapping and biting.

I tug on Nyx's soft hand until she's forced to follow me toward the exit of the cabin. Once again, fear splays across her face as she swallows heavily.

"Are you sure this is a good idea?" she whisper-hisses.

I grin. "All my ideas are good ones, my pretty little killer."

I begin to stroke her hair, relishing how soft it is beneath my fingers, and she flinches away from the contact. But she'll get used to petting. One day, she'll even crave it.

Somewhat belatedly, I notice Vulture sitting slightly up in bed, looking at us with an unreadable expression. His hard eyes narrow in my direction, but I simply wink at him. He knows better than to fight me on this—she's my pet, after all, not his, and as her owner, I know what's best for her.

With a nearly inaudible sigh, Vulture settles back on the bed, folds his hands over his chest, and shuts his eyes. I know he's not sleeping, though. His muscles are too tense to be considered relaxed.

Ignoring him, I pull Nyx out of the cabin and inhale deeply as the piney scent of the wild amalgamation of trees in this man-made forest barrages me from all directions. There are so many trees here that it's nearly impossible to decipher only one scent, but the potent smell of pine . . . I'd recognize that anywhere.

It reminds me of home.

Nyx trembles beside me and wraps her arms around her stomach. "What are we doing out here, Falcon?" she whispers, darting her gaze from side to side.

I grin and then lean down to nip at her earlobe. She jumps but doesn't pull away.

Good.

My pet is learning.

"I'm going to murder you and hide your body where no one can ever find it," I whisper in a low, seductive voice. When she gasps and turns toward me in horror, I burst out laughing. She continues to gape at me, at a loss for words, as I struggle to get my erratic breathing under control. "You should've seen your face!"

She frowns and takes a step away from me. "That's not funny."

Nope.

Not having that shit.

I growl and tug at her arm, forcing her flush against me yet again. I wrap my arms around her and lower my chin until it's able to settle on her bony shoulder. Then I squeeze just hard enough to elicit a cry of pain from her, the discordant noise like music to my fucked-up ears.

"Don't you ever walk away from me," I hiss, panic causing my heart to race. "You hear me?"

She trembles but doesn't respond.

Fear continues to assault me as worst-case scenarios play on a loop in my mind.

Nyx, wandering alone in the woods, stumbling upon the two remaining Predators . . .

Nyx, accidentally walking into a group of deranged men, their hands on her small body, their knives grazing her curves . . .

No one, outside the Birds, is allowed to touch my pet.

I'll rip their eyes from their sockets and force them to eat them before I'll allow that to happen.

Nyx continues to shiver in my arms.

Is she cold?

Is my pet chilly?

I tighten my grip even more around her, and her trembling increases.

"Shhh. Shhh. Everything is okay, my little killer.

Everything is okay." I brush my lips across her temple, and she squeezes her eyelids shut, capturing a tear before it can cascade down her cheek.

Why is she crying?

I continue to whisper reassurances as she shakes in my embrace. I stroke the length of her arms, her sides, her neck, though nothing I do seems to be working.

Finally, I force myself to step away from her, and her trembling immediately ceases. Her breath hitches as she stares up at me with wide, terrified eyes.

I offer her what I hope is a friendly smile.

"Come, pet. I have something I want you to see." I extend my hand for her yet again, but this time, she doesn't take it. She does, however, walk beside me, her arms once again coiling around her waist as if she wishes to hold herself together. Fear paints delicate lines across her cherubic face.

"W-what do you want me to see?" she stutters, glancing at me out of the corner of her eye.

I lead her toward the edge of the forest, where the trees are even denser. Hopefully, they'll provide us coverage from the guards patrolling the island. If they find us out of our cabins after midnight, they'll shoot us on sight. All of the cabins are supposed to have locks on the doors, but Raven managed to nab the keys years ago. Or maybe he bribed someone to get them. Either way, we don't have to worry about locks anymore.

And Vulture made it his mission to memorize the patrol routes. Yes, the guards try to be spontaneous, but even their spontaneity is predictable. Take Gary, for example. That fat fuck works every Monday and Tuesday at night. He tries to take random routes through the forest, but we've noticed he never strays too far from the main guardhouse, because he runs out of breath quickly.

And Miles . . . That guard always streams a sports game during his shift when he's supposed to be watching the video feeds.

There may be over a dozen guards on this island at one time, but we've studied them the way you would a dissected pig under a microscope. We know what makes them tick, what allows them to function, what their vices are . . . and we work to exploit them.

I continue to weave my way through the trees as Nyx follows me. More than a few times, I find myself looking over my shoulder in alarm, not hearing the sound of her footsteps. But each and every time, she's there, her face a blazing beacon in the glow of the moon, her eyes shadowed. She's nearly as quiet as I am.

What a perfect little shadow.

We don't speak as I continue to guide her through a forest that is now as familiar to me as my house back home. Perhaps more so.

I take every opportunity I have to caress her skin, rub my hand down her arms, stroke her brown hair. She flinches but doesn't comment.

Maybe she's finally come around to the idea of me owning her. She's going to have to.

We reach the edge of the forest, where the sounds of hoots, screams, and jeers reach my ears. I'm certain the guards know about this particular nighttime activity, but they choose to ignore it. I think the lazy fucks are too scared to get involved.

"What?" Nyx stops in her tracks, the blood draining from her face in a way that makes it impossibly paler.

I give her hand a tug without answering her and lead her toward the very edge of the clearing. Before she can take a step into it, however, I tug her down until her body is hidden behind the twisted branches and decaying leaves above.

Like before, I place a single finger to my lips, signaling for her to be silent. She swallows but nods quickly in agreement, obviously sensing the tension in the air.

The violence.

I swear it saturates everything in the immediate vicinity until I feel it racing through my bloodstream like a sickly poison.

Slowly, never allowing my grin to falter, I poke my head up to stare at the clearing. After only a moment of hesitation, Nyx does as well.

Her breath hitches, as I knew it would, and she has suddenly turned rigid beside me. I thought she'd looked fearful earlier, but that's nothing compared to now. She's practically translucent, almost like a ghost.

My pretty dead bird.

Choppy breaths escape her as she focuses on the clearing, and I force myself to look away from her face to study it as well, despite knowing what I'm going to see.

Over a dozen male prisoners stand in their prison-issued

black clothes. Unlike during the island hunt, they don't wear their masks, though I know who they are immediately. There . . . that's the Dragons, one of the meanest groups on the island. And there . . . those are the Predators, at least the two who remain, their features set in tight scowls, their eyes as hard as stone. Almost all the groups are here, excluding us, the Dollies, and a few of the newer teams. And of course, Old Twinkle. The doll-wielding man is here all on his own. Though cabins are typically locked for the night, sometimes guards can be bribed to look the other way. Clearly, a guard is walking around with heavy pockets tonight. The inmates don't do this often, however, so as not to draw attention to themselves. Only when blood needs to be spilled.

Wyvern, the leader of the Dragons and a terrifying man with numerous scars running down his face, jumps onto a fallen log and spreads his arms wide.

"We all know why we're here, don't we?" he calls to the silent crowd, his voice a knife that cuts through the potent air of quiet expectation. A slow, malicious grin stretches across his face as he eats up the attention aimed his way. "Bring him out, boys!"

Two more Dragons—Ice and Fire—materialize out of the darkness opposite us. They each hold the arm of a small, trembling man with a receding hairline, wire-framed glasses, and a black-and-gray goatee.

Embers doesn't look like much, but I know him to be a serial rapist and killer with over fifty girls under his belt, most under the age of eighteen. I've wanted to take care of the sick fuck myself, but Raven insisted that I stay out of it. After all, Embers used to be a member of the Dragons.

Until now.

"Please," Embers begs, huge tears cascading down his face as he stares around helplessly. "Don't do this."

Ice and Fire ignore the old fuck as they shove him to his knees before a grinning Wyvern.

"It seems we have a traitor in our midst, boys!" Wyvern bellows, lifting his hand into the air.

Nyx gasps harshly, and I know it's because she sees the machete in his grip. I have no idea where he got it from, but I wouldn't be surprised if one of the guards snuck it to him earlier today.

"Embers, here, has been giving the guards information on us," Wyvern continues, his words immediately followed by boos and jeers from the crowd. Wyvern merely grins, enjoying the attention, relishing it. "Isn't that right?" He leans down until he's directly in front of the trembling man's face. Wyvern's eyes are hard, practically chips of obsidian, and his smile has disappeared completely.

Embers begins to sob.

"I-I'm sorry," he stammers, the words barely audible over his sobs.

I snort derisively.

As if apologies will help him whatsoever right now.

I begin to sway with restless energy as I fight the urge to join the crowd calling for Embers's death. I could—no one would deny me—but Nyx couldn't.

And I won't leave my pet alone, not in this clearing of predators and beasts.

Out of the corner of my eye, I watch Nyx place a hand over her mouth in terror. Tremors rock her body as tears drip down her face.

I want to tell her not to cry for this man, not to pity him, but I can't say a word. Not here. Not this close to the very people who would love nothing more than to see her bruised, bleeding, and naked underneath them.

Nope.

Won't allow that to happen.

Refuse.

"You know what we do to traitors, don't you?" Wyvern's voice is practically a hiss as he spits at Embers's feet. Embers cringes, almost as if that glob of saliva is acid, and I silently begin to cackle. Nyx looks at me as if I'm insane—which I am—but I ignore her to focus on the show.

Embers has been grabbed by two men and is now being tied to the trees behind him, one wrist and one ankle connected to each branch until he's splayed like a X. Another prisoner steps closer with a pair of scissors and slices right down the middle of Embers's shirt and pants before forcing the fabric off his bony frame.

Soon, the former dragon is naked, his body trembling, huge tears rolling down his cheeks.

Wyvern grins maliciously as he steps toward his former friend and lifts the machete.

"What do we do to cock-sucking traitors?" he bellows, his voice reverberating through the forest.

The crowd all shouts at the same time, their voices blending together until I can't differentiate one from the other.

Without removing his gaze from Embers's face, Wyvern reaches down to grab the other man's dick, pulling it upward.

"Please!" Embers screams in unbridled fear.

I turn away, already wincing in sympathy, just as Wyvern drops the machete.

Nyx cries out in horror, though the sound is eclipsed by the woots and cheers of the crowd. I don't turn away from my little pet, however, and watch her face the way I would an art piece at a museum. I want to study every angle of her and read the emotions emanating from her haunted eyes. There's a story depicted in her expression, and I'm suddenly desperate to uncover it.

What is she thinking?

Where did those shadows come from?

Why does she cry for this despicable man?

With great reluctance, I peel my eyes off her and turn back toward Embers.

Blood pools around his feet, and his head has rolled forward. In his mouth is his bloody, severed dick.

But he's still alive. I know that with unwavering certainty. Wyvern prefers to leave his victims kicking for as long as he can.

"Let's show this guard-kissing traitor what happens when you fuck with us!" Wyvern roars, throwing a fist in the air and stepping away from Embers. A sly smirk teases the edges of his lips.

This is all a show for him, after all. A performance.

The crowd surges forward like the rippling waves of an ocean. All I can hear is the sound of flesh hitting flesh as the prisoners quite literally beat Embers to death.

But my pet doesn't need to see this.

I've made my point.

I tentatively grab her upper arm, ignoring her flinch, and begin to drag her back the way we came. This time around, she isn't nearly as silent or stealthy. She stumbles over every root and runs into every branch. She seems to be in a daze, her eyes wide and full of horror.

Only when we're far enough away that the shouts and screams are a distant memory does Nyx whisper, "Why did you show me that?"

"Because—" My hand tightens around her bicep almost imperceptibly— "you need to realize that we're not the only monsters on this island. And no matter what you think of us, we're not the worst." I spin her around to face me and then lean forward until my forehead is pressed against hers. I need to be touching her. It's not just a want but a need. "So, you need to fall in line with the others, or you're going to die. And not quickly. Do you understand?"

I don't give her a chance to respond before I spin away and all but drag her back to the cabin.

I did what I could to convince her, but if she continues to be a disobedient bitch, not even I will be able to protect her from the others.

No one can.

The next morning, I wake up to several pinching sensations on my ankles. I sit up, hazily rubbing at my eyes, and that's when I realize there's a trail of tiny ants marching across my ankles.

"Motherfucker!" I skitter backward, my hands and feet quickly crab-walking me away from the surge of nasty little biters before I reach down and start smacking the survivors off my skin.

Around me, the guys laugh. They're already up and dressed, and Eagle's just sitting on his bed, clearly watching this ant invasion occur and doing nothing to stop it.

"You must be too sweet," Eagle taunts me.

His poking comment makes me suspicious, but when I glance around at the floor by my feet, I don't see a pile of sugar or a line of honey. Still, I'm certain he had something to do with this, and I wish I could throw something at his arrogant face.

Instinct drives me to snarl at him, but I shut that down because, after what Falcon showed me last night, I'm inclined to agree with the crazy bastard. There are worse fates out there than falling in with the Birds, so I just lick my lips and say, "True. I'm sure you'll fix that, though," as calmly as I can manage.

Standing up and pulling Falcon's shirt down around my legs self-consciously, I walk over to the sink at the far side of the one-room cabin and rinse off my face. I clean myself up the best I can, washing away the dried cum splattered across my back, my neck, my ass—all the marks that I didn't dare wash away last night because they were all staring so hungrily, and I'm sure they would have used any excuse to humiliate me further.

Then I finger brush my teeth until Falcon comes to stand behind me, tilting his head as he watches me for a moment in the mirror.

"Here, pet, let me." He holds up a toothbrush already prepared with toothpaste, and I'm forced to stand there as he carefully, with a gentle calmness that I didn't think was possible for him, reaches around me from behind and starts brushing my teeth for me.

It's an odd sensation to have someone do that for you. It's simultaneously humiliating and just a tiny bit tender, and I don't know what to make of it at all. His arms are warm and his grip is gentle, his expression focused. I'm in a pseudo embrace as Falcon brushes and my mouth fills with minty suds and confusion. His free hand reaches up to grip the back of my neck and holds me still as he slowly strokes the bristles over the roof of my mouth, then my tongue. I tense, expecting him to go deeper, expecting him to force the toothbrush farther, to turn this phallic at any moment. But he doesn't.

He simply says, "Good girl," when he's finished and then retracts his arms over my shoulders and steps back to let me spit into the sink.

I think I might have preferred if he'd choked me. Instead, I've built up all this anxious anticipation that has nowhere to go. I can't convert it into righteous outrage like I was expecting. I simply have to let the emotions slowly deflate inside my chest, and it's utterly infuriating as I cup my hands under the water to rinse out my mouth.

Then I have to stand still while Falcon produces a brush I've never seen before and carefully brushes my hair, even taking the time to part it in the middle. I close my eyes and allow the soft, steady sensation of the brush to soothe me, trying not to think about who's doing the brushing or why. The surrealism of this treatment is just too much for me to comprehend, so I stop trying. With my eyes closed, I let my brain float away.

Has anyone ever brushed my hair before? I try to remember, try to recall a time when hands smoothed down my disheveled brown locks with painstaking gentleness, but come up blank. I'm not sure my mother ever found the time to run a comb through my snarls, even when I was a little girl.

Once he's finished, I turn to get ready for the day. But he grabs my hand and leads me to his bed. "Guards delivered clothes for you."

Thank god. Another day in oversized pants might have killed me.

"Arms up," Falcon commands, his eyes changing from the calm he's been exuding. Now, they're blazing with a frantic sort of energy, and his unruly brown hair is mussed from sleep, so he looks utterly wild. I wonder what I did wrong. What I might have done to make him breathe this shallowly, almost as if he's upset.

I thought he wanted my submission.

He's no longer gentle as he undresses me. He yanks the shirt he gave me last night over my head before tossing it aside. His fingers come to my hipbones and flex, digging in for just a moment.

I inhale sharply, expecting the calm to be over and the storm that is Falcon to rain down on me. But he takes a shuddering breath, lets go of me, and points at a pair of panties laid out next to my black prison garb. Panties that are way too nice to be prison issue—red silk edged with lace.

Someone must have called in a favor.

But which of them would bother doing that for me?

I swivel my head, my eyes scanning each of their faces, but they all remain stoic, no one giving away a single clue. All their eyes are on me, though, dark and hungry in a way that I'd love . . . if they were anyone else.

I'm not about to look a gift horse in the mouth, so I simply reach for the panties.

"Uh-uh-uh." Falcon snatches them up before I can and lifts them, dangling them out of reach. "Masters dress their pets," he scolds me, his voice gravelly.

God, that's a hard pill to swallow. I suddenly feel like Falcon's testing whether his little lesson last night has had any effect. But if this is a test of my mettle, I'm not going to have a meltdown. Not over simple things like him brushing my teeth and dressing me. No, I need to reserve my rage for things that actually matter. Right now, they see me as meek, timid, and malleable—a girl they can mold and shape in whatever way they see fit. If I hope to survive my time on this island, then I need to play the part they see me as. That way, when I inevitably strike, it'll be all the sweeter.

I inhale carefully to calm the angry pounding of my heart before giving him a single nod of acquiescence.

He steps around me and kneels in front of me, his eyes level with my pussy. When he pauses to stare at it for a long, drawn-out moment, I forget for a second who holds the power here. The blatant desire in his eyes heats my skin, and I expect him to lean forward and taste me with his tongue.

He doesn't.

To be completely honest with myself, I'm not sure if I'm relieved or disappointed. Heat floods my belly while despair creeps its slow, icy fingers down my spine. The two opposing sensations clash in a maelstrom of violence and something akin to anticipation.

I'm practically vibrating with expectation, and I can see his muscles clenched in restraint, the sharp lines on his neck visible.

He doesn't give in.

Instead, he glances down and taps my foot in a businesslike manner. "Widen." I slide my feet apart. "Lift." The rest of our interaction consists of single word orders as he gets me dressed quickly and efficiently, not caressing or teasing me like I expect him to, and by the end, I'm slightly wistful and disappointed.

Wait, what?

I get pissed at myself for even thinking that way. How could I possibly be wistful? I don't want this! Fuck, he's getting in my head by not acting the way I expect.

This is just a trick, Nyx. Just a trick.

Once he's tied my shoes, he straightens. He starts to stroke my hair, and I think he's going to tuck it back behind my ears, but he simply repeats the gesture. Patting me. Petting me. Like I'm a puppy.

Motherfucking—God, I want to give him a black eye for this.

I grit my teeth and do my best to ignore him, turning to look over at Hawk and Vulture, standing by the front door.

"Let's get to breakfast before the good shit's gone," Vulture says, with a nod in the direction of the cafeteria.

His announcement makes Falcon remove his hand from my hair and plant it on my ass. "You heel while we walk, pet," he orders as he nuzzles my ear.

I wonder how pissed he'd be if I snap at his fingers. I am a pet to him, after all, and don't most pets bite when they're threatened? Tension coils around my throat, but I force my instinctive reaction away and silently fume.

I'm forced to walk all the way across the prison with his hand resting right on my ass. Not caressing. Not pinching or grabbing. Just making my nerves skitter with sexual energy that has nowhere to go, even as I'm unable to stop a fearful shiver from working its way up my back.

By the time we reach the cafeteria, and he selects all my food for me, I'm so wound up and stressed by his attention that the fact he removes his hand is a relief.

The Birds stalk through the room with their trays, and Raven eyes a group of three men sitting by a window. They quickly evacuate the table, though they aren't finished eating.

Hawk pulls out my chair for me like a gentleman, though I eye him warily before I claim a seat by the window. Then I dive into my food, tuning out the world around me as I devour everything in sight. When Falcon tries to scold me, I snap, hands pulling my tray closer.

"This is my first fucking full meal since I got here, so don't even." I don't know where my burst of courage came from, but exhaustion, both mental and physical, prods at me. I'm hungry, tired, and goddamn furious at the world as a whole. If any of these guys even think to mess with my meal, I might go batshit crazy and stab them all.

He tilts his head, and it looks like he's weighing whether to scold me for my behavior or not. In the end, he slides his uneaten yogurt cup my way. I practically inhale it.

And then each of the Birds does something I don't expect. Each one of them gives me a little tidbit from his plate. It feels almost symbolic. Like some kind of strange public declaration.

I'm too hungry and wound up to decipher it, so I simply accept their offerings without comment.

Vulture gives me a strip of bacon. Hawk gives me a strawberry. At a glare from Falcon, Eagle shoves over a few almonds. Raven's nostrils flare as he stares at me, trying to decide if he wants to humiliate me or show solidarity, since the eyes at other tables keep drifting over to us. He ends up spitting on a small hash brown circle and smugly handing it to me.

Out of spite, solely to show the bastard I won't be defeated, I lean forward and eat it right out of his hand, mouth sliding over his fingertips and pushing down on them lightly, just enough to pluck the little hashbrown from him, before pulling back and smacking my lips.

Falcon groans lewdly at the sight. "Dammit. I'm feeding you tomorrow, pet."

I give him a wink, as if I'm okay with that plan. Honestly, right now, I might be okay with any plan that gets food in my belly more regularly. My standards have fallen that low.

A bell rings in the distance somewhere, and a few groans erupt around the room as everyone stands, taking their trays to the nearest trash can to dump out their trash. Unlike the rest of them, I'm actually excited. If breakfast is over, that means I get a break from the Birds and all their ridiculous, controlling expectations. All their puppetry.

It's basically going to feel like unwinding on a tropical beach in orientation. I'll relax, unwind, get away from this shit reality for a second. And the view isn't half-bad either.

I know better than to touch a guard, but sneaking glances at him, even if he's a bit of a jerkface, can still be fun. A small way to have my own game, instead of being a pawn in someone else's.

The guys have a different schedule this morning than yesterday. They don't bother to tell me what it is as they talk among themselves, but when Raven nods to the others, everyone but Hawk stands up. Apparently, he's my designated babysitter for the moment. Great.

I can't say my spine isn't tense the entire walk to orientation, because it is. It's stiff as a board. The only benefit of having Hawk marching behind me is that the other prisoners give us a wide berth.

A man with dark skin and a scar slashing across his face, that makes him look like a cartoon villain, backs the hell away when Hawk's big hand comes down on my shoulder in a claiming gesture. The guy practically trips over his own feet as he reverses course rather than walking our direction. He stumbles toward the tree line, ignoring the way a few guards nearby laugh at him.

In my mind, the moment only provides more proof that Falcon's right. The Birds give me a tiny bubble of protection from the evils surrounding us. But inside their nest . . .

I need to figure Falcon out. What he wants. Then maybe, maybe, I can get him on my side. Maybe Vulture too. I don't know about the others.

I turn to glance up at Hawk, following the huge, dark hand planted on my shoulder, tracing my eyes over the long arm and giant bicep, to see Hawk grinning down at me.

"You were surprisingly submissive this morning." His tone is playfully conversational.

"I decided eating and clothes outweigh pride."

"Shame. I think you look better without clothing."

I shake my head and have to resist the impulse to roll my eyes because, even though his friendly persona is in play right now, I'm fully aware that—with Hawk—friendliness is only ever a persona. His dark brown eyes might be twinkling down at me in the sunlight, but behind the smile is a predatory evaluation as cold as ice.

Maybe the meal has given me my fire back, or maybe it's the fact that I spot Jayce, the handsome guard, strolling in our direction, so I know Hawk can't do anything to me. But for some reason, I find myself brave enough to speak the truth. "What you really mean is you think I'd look better without skin."

Hawk throws his head back in a deep, bellowing laugh, one that ripples up to the sky and seems to part the very clouds. "There's the fire. I was worried you were already going soft, Phoenix."

I'm surprised that he uses the group name I chose for myself. Surprised but also pleased because I think it might be a sign that my submission this morning, and their subsequent public claiming of me in the cafeteria, is the first step on the path to acceptance into the Birds' fold.

I decide not to push Hawk any further right now. I

simply shake my head at him before turning and wriggling out of his grip.

When I notice Jayce getting closer, I turn and stride
quickly into the classroom ahead of him, feigning that I
don't want to be near him. There's no way I want a Bird
to see the little crush I have on this guard, even if it's only
a matter of me enjoying the eye candy. Hawk's far too
observant for my liking. And I don't need another drop of
drama, as far as the Birds are concerned.

When I enter the ugly little classroom and spot the
rulebook—that massive fucking tome—already on the
desk and waiting for me, I sigh and wiggle my index
finger. It's not nearly as sore as yesterday, but this is still
going to hurt.

I grab the book and trudge over to a different desk
than the one I sat in yesterday.

Why?

Because I can.

Because I actually have a tiny modicum of self-deter-
mination in this room, whereas in the Birds' cabin, I'm
nothing more than a servant or a pet. A stupid choice like
a chair suddenly represents freedom to me, and I realize,
a little bitterly, just how much it feels like I've come full
circle, because when I lived at my parents' house, I had to
make tiny little decisions like this so I wouldn't go insane.

Damn.

Slamming the door shut on that line of thought, I flip
the book open and find the place I stopped copying
yesterday. It's tragically few pages in.

Jayce's shadow appears in the doorway, and he drops

a bag near the door, just like he did yesterday. "Nice to see you're on time."

"You kidding? This is now the best part of my day." I point at the book and try to hide the way my gaze drinks in how good he looks in his tight black polo shirt. While he's strikingly handsome, with his blond hair and chiseled features, he carries with him an air of unattainability that the old Nyx would have seen as a challenge. The new one simply tucks her tail between her legs like a good little bitch and pants from afar. How the mighty have fallen.

The guard chuckles, and the trickle of warmth that emanates from that sound feels like a blazing fire after the cold laughter of the psychopaths I live with. I find myself staring at him almost longingly, not just because he's hot, but because I realize how rare simple things like true joy are going to be for me from now on.

However long that might be . . . maybe not long at all.

When he catches me watching, I quickly drop my eyes to the book and pretend to be scanning it.

"I know I'm not the best part—"

"Don't be so sure," I murmur under my breath, to the millions of tiny letters printed in miniscule type in this damn rule book.

"What was that?"

"Hmm. Oh, just . . ." I flick through recent events to come up with something mundane to tell him. "Combat practice is just gross wrestling."

"Wait until you get to the games," Jayce returns with a shake of the head. "You'll be glad for it then."

I give him a little nod because that's what he seems to expect, and for some reason, I'm feeling timid instead of sassy right now. Normally, I'd ask him about the games, maybe make a "bedroom games" quip, but he's giving me these confusing vibes that alternate between attraction and suspicion, and I don't really know how to handle them.

Awkwardness hovers in the air as he goes about unzipping his bag. A notebook is tossed on top of the book in front of me, but I find him holding out the pen.

I try to reach for it without making eye contact, but he pulls it back, and I'm forced to look up into his baby-blue eyes. His gaze travels over my face, as if he's trying to decide something. Finally, he says, "Tell me something about you that I can verify online."

I sigh. So, suspicion about me has beaten out attraction inside of his head. That sucks.

He waits expectantly while I chew my lip, thinking. Thinking.

"Or not. Fine." He throws the pen at my feet and turns to walk away, going from normal to offended in two seconds flat.

Over what? A sigh? Geez.

"Excuse me, it's not that easy. I lived on the streets for years. Not like I had a lot of social media going," I grumble as I slide out of my desk to pluck the pen off the dirty floor.

"Sure. Yeah."

I roll my eyes at him. Like I owe him anything.

What the hell? Why would he even ask something like that? Why does he care?

He doesn't.

I press the pen too hard into the paper. So hard that I rip it. I don't give a shit. He can have an ugly assignment. I start copying down words from the book, not even noticing what I'm reading.

I'm so irritated.

This is my break from the Birds.

This, right now, is the only breathing room I get.

And Mr. Hottie Guard Pants has to ruin it by asking questions about my former life. The only online info I can think of revolves around my parents . . .

I rack my brain for something else I can tell him. Something that doesn't feel like it's taking a can opener to my insides and prying open the lid to all sorts of horrors I don't want to let out.

Finally, when the room is starting to bake because the sun has gotten close to the peak for the day, I settle on something. "I was booked for petty theft in San Fran when I was seventeen. You should be able to find the arrest record online."

"What did you take?"

"Food."

He doesn't say anything else, and I try to ignore the way my cheeks heat up, but then I scold myself. There's no reason to be embarrassed about that arrest. It's nothing. It was so long ago. And I'm not that girl who doesn't know how to fend for herself anymore. That girl's gone.

An hour passes.

Then another.

Finally, I hear Jayce clear his throat. "Nyx?"

I reluctantly look up from the paper I'm writing to see him reclining against the dingy wall, a phone in his hands. The regretful twist of his mouth tells me he clearly found the record. That's a pitying look if I've ever seen one, and I've seen more of them than I've ever wanted to see.

Tension curls like a whip in my stomach—cracking down my spine and ripping apart my skin. I hate that damn look more than anything else. It's the look of someone who'll never understand what it's like to find shelter beneath a flimsy cardboard box or search for food in garbage cans. It's the look of someone who has never had to fend off wandering hands in the middle of the night because you're unable to find a safe place to sleep. It's the look of someone who doesn't see the resilience of a mind and body refusing to break.

"You're really a thief?" he asks.

I nod.

He bites his lower lip as he tries to decide if he believes me, and his evaluation makes me feel off-balance, like I'm attempting to stand still atop a swaying teeter totter.

Finally, he says, "Prove it. Steal something for me."

E agle scoops me up from orientation with a scowl on his handsome face. By scoops, I mean literally. He walks right up to me and throws a shoulder into my stomach as his big hands clamp down on the back of my thighs. Then he throws me over his shoulder and carries me in a fireman's hold so that I'm slung head down, my hair swaying around my eyes.

A sharp and belligerent, "Hey!" sends poison ivy unfurling down my throat and prickling the flesh there.

No one yells at the Birds.

No one.

Eagle goes perfectly still, his muscles rigid and unyielding beneath my stomach, the hand gripping the back of my thigh curled into an unforgiving fist.

Rocks settle in my stomach, rolling around and grinding against one another, as I place my palms in the center of Eagle's massive back and push myself up so I can see Jayce's face.

I'm stunned by the raw, unbridled *rage* distorting his features. His eyes home in on where one of Eagle's hands rests precariously close to my ass.

Is Jayce . . . *angry*? On my behalf?

A strange feeling whirls through me—a burning sword that cuts through my meticulous defenses and reduces them to nothing but flaky ash.

Why is this sensation so alien? Logically, I know Jayce can't care about *me*—he barely knows me—but it's completely understandable that he'd be worried about some poor, defenseless girl being manhandled by a guy three times her size.

He's a guard. He's probably not allowed to stand by and watch one prisoner manhandle another.

Still, those stormy blue eyes, hard as they are, flay me open, peeling away layer after layer of skin until my very essence is revealed. It's unnerving, terrifying, and exhilarating all at once.

Eagle still has his back to Jayce, and Jayce's hand rests on his gun holster, but there's no illusion about who the true predator here is. Aggression pulses up the weapons trafficker's body in response to that one word from Jayce. I can feel it in the way he holds himself, in the way his fingers clench on my thighs, the way his jaw locks together audibly.

Jayce remains perfectly still as well, the only sign of his unease the twitching of his fingers near that damn gun holster.

Tension saturates the air, and I'm not even sure I'm breathing. We seem to be at an uncomfortable stalemate, and every second that passes has daggers of dread scraping over old wounds.

Finally, Eagle bites out through gritted teeth, "Do we have a problem, officer?"

There's no mistaking the threat in that one innocent question.

And . . . Jayce deflates. That's the only word I can think of to describe the sudden change in his posture. His shoulders seem to sag forward, and the tension holding his spine up snaps in two. His jaw sets with a tumultuous emotion I can't quite read before he grits out, "No problem."

Without another word, he turns on his heel and stalks back inside the cement building I just vacated.

Why does Jayce's dismissal sting so much?

I know he can't say or do anything to protect me from these monsters—not only would it make me an even bigger target, but he could lose his job if any of the higher-ups got the wrong idea—but a tiny morsel I wish to smother expected *something* from him.

My throat is nothing but a narrow tunnel blocked by a mountain of dry cement. Breathing is impossible.

Eagle chuckles, the cold noise scratching at my skin like a million ice pricks, and shifts his hold on me slightly.

"Come, *kotenok*. We go somewhere. Late." The strange, foreign word flows off his tongue like caustic honey, but I don't have the mental capacity or grit to ask him what he just called me. Probably *evil bitch* or *fucking loser*.

I don't look up again, because my cheeks are flaming

right now, and I don't want to fight Eagle on the off chance he's pushing my buttons in an attempt to get me to mouth off so he can smack me back down. Sometimes you can just tell when a man is in a violent mood by the energy he radiates, and Eagle is pulsing with fury right now. I want to say it has to do with his standoff with Jayce, but I know that's a lie. Eagle was angry even before he faced off with the blond guard.

I don't bother asking who put razor blades in his oatmeal . . . because with what I know of this island, that's definitely a possibility.

Beneath my humiliation, I'm too busy pondering the proposal that Jayce gave me. A part of me wants to focus on the way he tried to protect me, the fierce indignation brimming in eyes the stormy blue of a tempest sea, but I push that thought away. No, I can't think about what he almost did for me. Not now. It's one of those uncomfortable thoughts that burrows deep and makes itself a nest in the darkest recesses of my heart. So, instead of allowing that foreign sensation to mutilate my heart and turn it into ribbons of red, bloody meat, I focus on the deal he made me.

The guard asked me to steal for him. In exchange, he'll meet with me and give me information I need in order to get through each set of games as they come.

It's a tempting fucking offer because I know I'm useless. I don't have the brutality or the violent know-how that everyone else roaming this island seems to have.

Without his help, I'll be wiped out like a little red smudge.

I don't understand why he'd want to help me.

What's the trick? Where's the catch?

Does he just want to make me steal something so that he can be the one to reveal me? So he can get the glory of throwing me into solitary? A promotion?

But what he wants me to steal is so insignificant.

So stupid.

I can't imagine I'd get into a ton of trouble over it.

He wants a pen.

One pen with Hoplite's logo, from the records desk. He even took me to the doorway of our classroom and pointed out the building to me.

The pen has to be a test.

But why?

What for?

Nervous bees buzz in my belly and tell me that I shouldn't take this deal. That I should leave it alone to fester in the dark parts of my mind where unanswered questions go to live and eventually die. This whole proposal would be better left as an unanswered question. It should be shoved right next to the moldering query, "Why did my mother let my father do those things?" and I should never think of it again.

I press my lips together.

Yes.

I'm going to have to refuse him.

To even consider his request, I'd have to sneak past the Birds . . . past the guards . . . My mind sketches out routes inside my head automatically, as if this is a job. Just another heist.

It's nothing of the sort.

I'm only able to shove the niggling thoughts aside when Eagle walks right through the gate at the edge of the prison yard. When I spot him striding past the chain-link fence, I put my hands on his back and push myself up just enough to see a Hoplite guard closing the gate behind us, a smirk on the scruffy man's face.

The bees inside my stomach start to sting.

The last time I was outside the gate was a nightmare.

"Where are we going?" I ask, finding my voice raw and breathy.

"You'll see." Eagle's response gives no comfort as he tromps off the path and through the trees. It almost seems as if he deliberately steps through bushes and leans so close to trees that the trunks brush roughly against my arms. I end up having to try to flinch away from them.

He spanks my ass roughly, hard enough to send a sting all the way through to my thighs. "Stop squirming."

I open my mouth to argue, but I'm pretty sure he's expecting that because I hear his breath catch in anticipation and can almost feel his vicious excitement. He wants me to argue. He wants me to fight, out here, away from the guards, where he can punish me however he sees fit. Though his background appears less violent on the surface than the rest of the guys, I have a dark certainty that's an illusion. My heart beats in slow, shallow claps—nothing like the pounding from before.

Eagle wants to play a game? Fine. I can do that.

And I'll make certain I win.

I bite my tongue and let branches hit me and brambles tangle my hair. I don't protest when my feet start to tingle and get prickles because of the lack of blood flow from being slung over his shoulder. I simply exist. I turn my mind back to Jayce's proposal to keep me distracted, running through the options until I have a shaky semblance of a plan I might be able to pull off.

I hear the ocean waves growing louder as we approach, and I try to peer around his body without moving too much and earning myself another spanking.

What is our destination?

Why would the guards let him out with me midday?

Haven't I been through enough hazing with the Birds?

Of course, as soon as I have this thought, I'm scoffing at myself because I'm pretty sure these psychopaths will never stop.

Suddenly, I find myself tossed backward through the air. The breath flies from my lungs before I land on beach sand with a hard thump that radiates pain up my spine and down my legs.

Around me, coarse laughter starts up, and I blink, brushing sand from my hands as I turn my head side to side and drink in the sight of prisoners lining the beach. The sun washes over what seems like miles of bare skin because all of them have stripped down to their under-wear and are standing at the very edge of the surf, ocean foam lapping at their feet.

I notice Old Twinkle at the end of the line. Like the others, he's stripped down to his prison-issued under-wear, but while the rest of the men are wearing boxers, his are brown-stained tighty-whities that leave very little to the imagination. I can see every curl of coarse gray hair on his stomach and thighs.

The longer I stare, the more I note a bulge in the front of his underwear. Horror cascades over me in a torrent, almost painful in its intensity, before I realize that the bulge is not—in fact—his cock but the head of a doll peeking out.

A doll with gray curly hair.

Wait. Nope.

Those are his pubes.

A shudder reverberates through me, and bile claws at my throat. The only saving grace is that Old Twinkle doesn't notice me staring at him and mistake my attention for desire instead of revulsion. He's too preoccupied with staring stonily at the rippling ocean water while he lazily strokes the hair of the doll peek-a-booing out of his briefs.

Hoplite guards pace behind the men, guns hanging at the ready from their shoulders.

"Hurry up! You're the last," one of them barks at us as he adjusts the ball cap on his head and then glares. His jaw works a wad of chewing gum as Eagle starts to strip.

I struggle to my feet clumsily. The fact that my limbs fell asleep on my involuntary ride over does not help make me more coordinated. Then I shuck off my shoes, socks, and my pants.

I hesitate for a long moment, my hands tangling in the hem of my shirt, before I take a deep, modulated breath. Anger has already frayed the edges of my temper. Any second now, I'll lose the tenuous grip I have on my emotions and bubble over like a kettle left for too long on a stovetop. This is just another stopping point on my descent into madness.

You can do this, Nyx.

You can do this.

When I toss off my shirt, wolf whistles erupt because Falcon didn't bother to put a bra on me this morning. The breeze from the ocean quickly stiffens my nipples to peaks as I debate whether covering myself would look like a show of weakness. My arms jerk by my sides, but I don't raise them. I refuse to give in to the self-consciousness and fear barraging me from every direction. Even still, it feels as if a burning fist has formed in my chest.

Eagle grins down cruelly, his eyes glittering with savage mirth, as if he knows just what I'm thinking. But then, unexpectedly, he grabs his own shirt off the sand and shoves it at me. "Wear this. Only Birds get to see you."

A part of me wants to refuse him just to see what he'll do. Will he yell at me? Scream? Berate? Hit me?

I can say no. I can shake my head, jut my chin up, and treat him like nothing but a pesky gnat buzzing around my head.

But even as the ridiculous thought forms, I remember my mantra from before. I need to pick my battles. And arguing over something as inane as a shirt? That's not a battle I'm willing to raise my sword for.

I shake the sand off his shirt before I don it and take my place in line next to him, raising my chin and staring out at the dark expanse of ocean defiantly. Jeers still drift over as different prisoners proposition me.

Only Old Twinkle remains silent, though I do feel the pinprick heat of his eyes scouring over my face. Unlike the others, the look he levels at me isn't lecherous. More . . . curious. One of his caterpillar-like brows arches upward, as though he's attempting to solve a particularly difficult math equation.

One of the Mountains, whose name I think might be Everest—if the names that Vulture gave me at breakfast this morning are true—lines up on my left side. He's even taller than any of the Birds, and one of his hands looks like it could cover my entire face. His light blue eyes bug out on his face, and his voice washes over me in a deep, throaty rumble. "Don't cover up your tits on my account, love."

Shit.

This man's got the kind of accent that Hawk wishes he had.

I hate the fact that the smoky baritone of it is marred by the scowl distorting his features and the savage intensity lacing each word.

"Don't talk to her." To my utter shock, Eagle gets territorial. He crosses his huge arms over his chest and narrows his eyes at the other man. If looks could kill, Everest would be dead in point-one-seconds flat.

"Why the hell not?"

The two men stare at one another like two rams about to clash horns. I take a step backward on the warm sand, in case this turns physical. I'm honestly not sure who I'd want to win. Go with the enemy I know . . . or the one I don't.

Maybe they can both fall over, cut their heads open on some of the jagged rocks jutting up on the beach, and then drown?

"Claim your own the next time one falls," Eagle simply ends up saying. I might think he's attempting to end the fight before it can begin if it weren't for the bunching of his muscles. His eyes never leave Everest's face, staring at the Mountain with a ruthless intensity that has my skin pebbling and every hair on the back of my neck standing at attention.

"Nah, don't want a bitch holding us back," Everest retorts, his gaze lazily dragging over my bare legs before coming to rest on my now-covered tits. A malicious gleam enters his dark eyes. "We're going to win the next game."

Game? I know both the Birds and Jayce have mentioned these deadly games on more than one occasion, but I've never given them much thought. What exactly are these games that have every male in the immediate vicinity posturing and attempting to show off their feathers?

"Like hell."

Everest scoffs. "You just added a weak link. She won't be able to keep up."

Eagle's hand shoots out and wraps around the back of my neck without warning. Then he drags me five feet to the right, forcing another prisoner to swap places with us in the long line of inmates. Everest's laughter—dry and brittle, like old bones rattling around in a coffin during a hurricane—washes over me.

Why do I have the impression that he's going to be a problem for me?

A guard yells at Eagle, but he ignores him, turning to me. "You." His nostrils flare and his voice is practically vibrating with pent-up aggression.

Is he going to blame me for Everest's comments? Blame me for the truth?

Fuck, though, it's a painful truth.

Shame flames across my cheeks, though I quickly toss the emotion away, stomp on it, and then kick its mutilated remains into a hole thousands of feet below. Anger uses my ribs as a punching bag as I curl my hands into fists.

There's no reason for me to be ashamed. I may not be as strong as Eagle, as cunning as Raven, as depraved as Falcon, as sadistic as Hawk, as impenetrable as Vulture . . . but I'm not weak. I have my own unique skill set that has allowed me to survive most of my life. I have no idea what these "games" are, but I know that I won't lose without putting up one hell of a fight.

I watch Eagle swallow hard. I can practically hear him mentally count to ten before he speaks again. "I bet you can't beat me today."

What the hell? That's a massive change of direction. But maybe he's trying to distract himself from his anger. Or maybe . . .

"At what?" I cock an eyebrow as I surreptitiously try to scan the area around us. Is there a game happening right now? One I haven't been told about? No. Surely Jayce would've mentioned something.

"Swimming."

I glance over at the ocean, studying the swells. They seem calm and placid enough, the small breaks near us no bigger than three feet.

A bet? Is this his way of motivating me to keep up? To prove Everest wrong? I chew my lip because it doesn't sound that bad.

But do I even dare make a deal with the devil himself? For all I know, he'll ask for my soul and drag it down to hell with him.

"What do I win?"

"My dessert at dinner."

Do they even have dessert here? Or is that a trick?

God, why are you even considering this, Nyx?

Perhaps a part of me wants to prove myself to these merciless Birds. Perhaps I want to show them that my presence on their team won't be a hindrance but an asset. It's not because I crave their approval or anything as ridiculous as that. It's self-preservation—if they see the value of having me on their team, they'll keep me around and protected. And if they don't . . .

"I want your roll instead," I counter because bread is a sure thing.

"Done."

"What do you win?" Because that's the way bets work, after all. Tit for tat.

My heart stops between one beat and the next as I debate what he's going to ask me. Will he want me to steal something like Jayce had? Would he ask about my past? An army of goose bumps stands at attention, and heat rushes down my throat, ravaging my insides with burning claws.

He presses his lips together, and his eyes shoot down my body for a moment. I would guess he's looking at my nipples, which are still as hard as gemstones from the ocean breeze.

"A blow job."

My breath leaves me. A heady combination of anger and fear splatter against the glass that has kept the majority of my emotions at bay during this entire encounter.

A blow job. Fucking typical. And hardly fair stakes.

"Your boyfriend won't be pissed?" I shoot back. When Eagle narrows his eyes, I add, "Raven said no sex."

"Is not sex."

"Two months of rolls, if that's what you want," I counter.

"Think you'll be here that long?"

"If you've made it here that long, I'll be just fine, fuckwit."

"I agree. You?"

Can I do it?

Can I sell myself to him like that?

But . . . that's assuming I'll lose. Which I won't.

This asshole doesn't know I grew up with a pool in my house. And I kind of want to prove to that Mountain dickhead that I'm not a weak link. It's one thing for me to think it. To know it. It's another for every asshole on the entire island to be staring at me like I'm some kind of burden.

I lick my lips and give a nod. "You're on."

God, I hope I don't regret this.

I tell myself that giving Eagle a blow job isn't the end of the world. He's not exactly an ugly man, if I'm being completely honest, and I give damn good head. I'll easily be able to shut away the part of myself that always makes me feel too much, too deeply. Compartmentalize. Lock away the insidious emotions that call me "whore" and "slut" and every other derogatory term it can come up with. Even as my mind wails with panic, I close my eyes and remind myself to breathe.

It's just a blow job.

Just a blow job.

But I won't lose.

Then I reach my hands overhead and stretch, ignoring the wolf whistles that erupt when the bottoms of my red panties become visible again. I'm regretting the T-shirt right now, because it's going to weigh me down, but I tie it into a knot and bunch it up so that it won't mess with my legs. I know better than to ask to take it off at this point.

The Birds aren't exactly merciful types.

"Inmates!" One of the guards speaks through a bull-horn, the blast of noise so loud that my shoulders jump. "We've placed buoys out in the water. You'll swim out to a buoy, touch it, and swim back. You'll start on my signal." He raises an air horn, and the blast rips through my ears.

As one, the line of inmates surges toward the water

ungracefully. With whoops and cries and gasps, we enter the lukewarm waves. I settle on a breaststroke that keeps my head above water, but I can see men struggling on either side of me, pathetic doggy paddles showing that they never learned how to swim.

Unfortunately, Eagle does a lazy side stroke next to me, clearly showcasing that the Russian had training. I try not to notice his form or how his shoulder muscles bunch and release perfectly. I turn away when he ducks his head under the waves and emerges with rivulets streaming down his neck.

I have a race to win.

Briefly, I debate not stopping. Swimming forever. How far would I have to swim before I ran into another plot of land? Until a shark ate me alive? Until my body gave in to the seductive pulls of unconsciousness and I drifted away, lost at sea?

The prospect is scarily appealing.

No. I can't think like that. I'm a survivor, and I refuse to give up—and not just during this damn race.

The cresting waves batter at me, and I feel like a piece of debris caught in a hurricane. Still, I don't give up, don't slow down, don't allow my emotions to turn into weighted shackles that steer me toward the ocean floor.

I switch to freestyle as soon as we are past the crests, kicking hard and trying to recall all those years of private lessons. My arms scoop smoothly through the water, and I start up a good rhythm. My muscles are singing in ways they haven't in years, and while I know I'm going to be sore tomorrow, I'm not yet.

I push harder.

When I turn my head to take a breath, I glance back to see most of the men are well behind me. Old Twinkle is lazily floating on his back, his penis doll resting on his stomach.

But I don't spot Eagle.

What the fuck?

I pause, treading water, eyes stinging from the salty ocean as I scan the waves around me. I don't see him.

My heart rate kicks up, because I do see Everest, doggy paddling, his eyes cruel as he glances at me.

I swivel my body and kick myself in a small circle, rotating, looking for Eagle.

Fuck!

That son of a bitch is already tapping the buoy!

I dive back into the water and chase after him with everything I've got, hoping like hell it's enough.

I'm the second person, after that asshole Bird, to tap the buoy and start the journey back, but I don't take any joy in that fact. I'm frantically pinwheeling my arms and kicking my legs, straining my lungs past their capacity in an effort to catch up with Eagle.

I reach his feet, and my heart starts thumping madly, anticipation and desire crowding in against the lack of oxygen. Almost there. Almost there! I push my body to a point that it burns. But suddenly, sand is scraping against my belly.

I've reached the shore and didn't even notice.

I scramble to my knees, spitting out ocean water and floating particles of dirt, swiping at my eyes only to see

Eagle's massive feet standing right in front of me. I glance up to see his hands planted on his hips, a dark smirk on his lips.

"Crawl to me," he commands.

Fuck.

Fuck.

I lost. And he wants to collect now?

I slap at the water, furious, angry, my chest heaving from both a lack of oxygen and disappointment.

Do I fight back?

Refuse?

Choose your battles wisely, Nyx.

Strangely enough, my inner voice sounds like a wise old grandpa speaking ominously into a microphone.

Weeds threaten to grow through the cracks in my control, but I toss my mask back into place before even an ounce of my ire can slip through.

It's just a blow job.

Not the end of the world.

Just a damn blow job.

So what if you're losing what little dignity and respect you've managed to gain since you've been here? So what if you've officially reached a new low for yourself? So what if you're basically selling your body in exchange for protection?

Just a blow job.

The sand is rough and gritty against my knees as I obey. The wet shirt feels like it weighs a metric ton, dragging behind me like a cloak made of iron.

None of the guards even question us, their eyes

simply staring out dispassionately. They might as well be statues. The ones who do pay us any attention seem almost . . . excited. A sick feeling manifests in my stomach, bulbous and threatening to burst at any moment.

When I find myself between Eagle's spread legs, glancing up along the flat plane of his stomach to his jeering face, I swallow hard.

I remind myself that I need the Birds right now.

Inhaling, I try to steady my heart rate and find my courage.

I reach for his underwear.

He slaps my hand away forcefully. "Changed my mind. I don't want it now. I'll save it for later."

Then he turns and walks up the dunes, leaving me on the edge of the beach, on my knees in front of everyone.

I'm not sure what kind of game Eagle is playing, but I suddenly think that this arms dealer might be just as dangerous as the other Birds.

Perhaps even more so.

19

NYX

The next few weeks prove to be relatively the same.

Wake up, let Falcon dress me and often feed me as I kneel between his legs, go to orientation, think about Jayce's strange request to steal a pen, and train. Then I eat again, do chores assigned by the Birds, they stand in a circle and make me pose as they jerk off over me, and then I sleep on the cold ground beside the bunk meant for me. I want to complain, put up a fuss, fight back . . . but I don't. There's a monster prowling just beneath my skin, peeking its head up and sniffing the air, but it knows that now isn't the time to fight back. Right now, the two of us are focusing on survival.

And to do that, we need the Birds on our side.

Something has changed between all of us as well, though I can't put my finger on what it is.

Yes, animosity still saturates the air, growing claws

and canines that pierce flesh and draw blood, but it isn't as potent as it was when I first arrived.

Am I mistaken . . . or are some of the guys actually warming up to me?

I tell myself the notion is ridiculous, but when Eagle passes me his breakfast biscuit for the third time this week, I can't stop the strange flutter that comes to life in my belly. It's not a crush—I'm not stupid enough to develop feelings for the men who've basically come to own me—but it's the tentative stirrings of *hope*.

I've been without that emotion for so long, it feels almost unfamiliar now as it batters against the confines of my chest, demanding freedom and acknowledgment.

Of course, that hope is constantly accompanied by a little sliver of terror as the huge Russian Bird builds up the list of favors I owe him. He still has yet to collect on that blow job. He teases me with it, calling me over, making me kneel, often in front of the guys in the cabin. I think he loves the way all their eyes lock on to the sight, staring with either longing or disgust, depending on their mood at the moment. He's let me go so far as to yank down his pants and get his dick in my hands before inevitably saying, "I changed my mind. Not yet." It's a game that's become both infuriating and exciting for me.

I'm not quite sure what he's trying to prove—that he's got control over me or control over himself.

But I get down on my knees each time he calls.

Because I gave my word.

Because I need them to trust I'll keep my word, so they'll keep theirs.

Raven is currently sitting across from me at one of the round tables in the cafeteria and taps his fingers against the surface. His icy disposition still terrifies me, but I no longer feel he'll physically hurt me. Yes, he'll slay me open with his acerbic words and caustic tongue, but I can handle a verbal berating.

I'm not sure my tired and broken soul will survive another physical one.

"The games are coming up." His cold, angry voice is directed at no one and everyone. I don't know how he manages to do that. He's not even looking in my direction, his gaze intent on the various other prisoners surrounding our table, yet I have the distinct impression he reserves the ire in his voice for me. Then again, I always think it's aimed at me.

"We win." Eagle rolls his eyes and throws his apple up into the air, catching it deftly before taking a huge chunk out of it. Juices dripping down his chin and tangling in his recently grown-out beard, he continues, "We always win."

Raven's upper lip peels away from his teeth in response. "We've never had a liability before, have we?" Yet again, he doesn't turn to stare at me, but I feel his words as if they've been injected directly into my bloodstream.

I don't dare respond.

I've been training with the others for two and a half weeks now—cultivating skills I didn't even know I had and developing new ones—but I'm still far behind the others. The few times we've had to battle in a mock fight,

I found myself on the ground in two seconds flat with a grinning Bird hovering over me.

Raven mutters something inarticulate, but fortunately, he doesn't suggest that they cut my throat while I sleep.

I'm not stupid enough to believe the leader of the Birds likes me now, but I can't help but think that maybe, just maybe, he doesn't want to kill me, either. I call that a win.

"And the fact that we still don't have any knowledge of what this quarter's game is . . ." Raven blows out an irritated breath and, once again, swivels his gaze to encompass the entire room. Morning shafts of sunlight beam down on all the unruly, mostly unwashed prisoners. I try to follow Raven's gaze to see who's gained his ire today. His eyes narrow on one inmate in particular, almost as if he's expecting the man to leap up and charge at our table, before his shoulders relax and he continues his observation of the dining room.

Currently, it's just me, Raven, and Eagle at the table. The others still haven't arrived from an early morning run the guards initiated with several prisoners. The first time I was left alone with the two foreboding men, icy terror skated down my spine and froze all my joints until even breathing was impossible. But when Eagle didn't wrap his huge hands around my throat and squeeze the life out of me, when Raven didn't jab his fork into my eye . . . I began to relax. And the second time I found myself alone with the two of them? I only flinched once.

I can still taste their hatred for me in the air, but it's

muted, stilted, even, eclipsed by other matters that they've deemed more important. I suppose I'll take what blessings I can get and duck my head like a good little Birdy. The last thing I want to do is find myself on their bad side yet again.

Raven's fingers continue to tap away on the table as a muscle in his jaw twitches. "You'll be having private lessons with Hawk today to prepare you for the next game."

It takes me five seconds to realize Raven's addressing me.

"I . . . what?" I blink at the striking man in alarm.

Finally, he rips his gaze off the crowd and spears me with a look that has frost seeping across my skin and chilling my flesh. Why did I find his lack of eye contact annoying only moments before? It was a goddamn blessing. Being the sole focus of those ebony eyes—so penetrating and ruthless in their intensity they're capable of slicing off ribbons of flesh—is about as pleasant as I imagine being skinned alive would be.

Not that I've ever been skinned alive . . .

"Are you daft, woman?" he snaps, that twitching muscle in his jaw commandeering my attention. "Are all females imbeciles, or is it just your particular breed?"

An outraged retort settles on my lips, but I suck it back in before it can escape. I found that riling Raven up only exacerbates his acidic anger. I'm honestly afraid that, one day, I'll push him too far and he'll burn me. *Obliterate* me.

So instead of saying what I so desperately want to

and defending all of womankind, I press my lips together and lower my gaze. I hate the sign of submission, but it's one of the only tools in my arsenal if I hope to survive these Birds of Prey.

They need to see that I'm not a threat, that I only want to keep breathing, that I'll never do anything to put their lives in danger because that would put *myself* in danger.

And I want to live too damn badly to fuck it up.

Raven opens his mouth—and I just know whatever he's going to say next will be either an insult against me or my gender as a whole—when a warm hand comes to rest on the top of my head. Petting me.

Falcon.

"Hello, pet," he purrs in a dark, husky voice that makes my blood chill and my toes curl simultaneously. The conflicting sensations teeter like a seesaw in my brain, and I'm not sure which emotion will win in the end—fear or desire.

Without waiting for me to respond, Falcon scoops me up, settles in my vacated seat, and then positions me on his lap. I stiffen instinctively at the contact before forcing myself to relax.

Routine.

This is routine.

Falcon's never taken it any further than this. He'll touch me, pet my hair, brush his lips against my neck, feed me . . . but he's not demanding more than I'm willing to give. Once in a while, his hands will stroke my breasts, and he'll moan at the restraint he's showing, but he never presses his point. Even though I can feel the hard ridge of his cock nestling against my backside, he won't do anything about it.

He simply holds me, telling me what a good pet I am. How close I am to becoming trained. How close I am to perfect.

And I've come to slowly crave his touch. Adore it. Sometimes, in the dark of the night, I'll even dream about his palm skating over my skin.

A gnawing pit opens in my stomach.

"It looks as if my pet has already eaten without me." I can hear a pout in his voice. If there's one thing I've learned, it's that Falcon loves to feed me. I think it's because he believes it's the sign of a good pet owner.

I ignore his sad mewl and the way he nuzzles against my neck, ignore the scent of his freshly washed hair, focusing instead on the man with all the true power in this room.

Raven.

Don't get me wrong. Each of the Birds is powerful in his own right, but none more so than the intimidating man with jet-black hair, tan skin, and obsidian eyes that chip away at my defenses. He's the one who'll decide if I live as their slave or die at their feet.

He's still staring at me, his gaze almost assessing, and I watch as his eyes zero in on where Falcon's arm winds around my chest, directly underneath my breasts. Those arctic eyes narrow with something akin to suspicion before he smooths his features over once more.

"Falcon, I'm going to need you with me today,"

Raven demands briskly, already diverting his attention, as if I'm not worth even a morsel of his time. And maybe that's true, at least for him.

Falcon goes perfectly rigid underneath me. The arm banded around my center tightens almost imperceptibly, an iron vise that I'm not sure I'll ever be able to remove.

"Why?" he all but growls. His nose slides against the side of my head, pushing away strands of brown hair in the process. A full-body shudder reverberates through me, and like before, I'm not sure if it's one of desire or fear. Can it be both?

I've never considered the two conflicting emotions to be closely related, but there's no denying the heat surging through my bloodstream like molten lava accompanied by a frost that chills me to the bone. Fire and ice—lust and fear. Both trail tantalizing fingers down my spine, causing goose bumps to erupt in their wake.

"Because I said so." Raven's eyes narrow even farther. He has such pretty eyelashes for a man—dark and sooty— and they look like feathers against his cheeks. Ugh.

"I want to stay with my pet." Falcon bites down on my earlobe hard enough to sting, but I don't jump. I've learned that showing any sort of reaction only adds fuel to the fire of Falcon's madness. The tiny embers of insanity are only a container of gasoline away from turning into a raging inferno.

Raven abruptly slaps his hand on the table, causing the entire surface to rattle. A few nearby prisoners glance over, but one incandescent look from Eagle has them turning away immediately.

"That is not how this works." Raven speaks through heavily gritted teeth.

Why have I ever thought his eyes to be icy before? Now, they're pure fire—the flames of hell themselves rising from the ground and clawing at my insides like burning claws. "I say something, and you listen. No arguments. No objections." His upper lip curls away from his teeth in disgust. "Not even on behalf of the irritating, vexing . . . female."

If I thought Falcon would argue or defend me, I was sorely mistaken. Then again, I'm not sure if Falcon even sees me as anything other than a pet. I'd never be stupid enough to mistake the reverence in his eyes as adoration or even admiration. It's *ownership*, plain and simple.

"Fine." Falcon releases a huff of air, stirring the hair by my ear. "What do you need, boss man?"

Raven's face pinches at the title, but he doesn't comment. Instead, he says simply, "Do what you do best, assassin."

"And what is that?"

"Get me information." That tapping begins again as Raven shifts his gaze over the other inmates in the cafeteria.

"On the next game?" Falcon begins to nibble on my neck, and I let him. What else can I do? Fight him off? The mere thought is laughable.

The fact that his nibbling sends tiny sparks of pleasure down my spine is also irrelevant.

One of Raven's perfectly manicured brows begins to twitch, the only outward sign of his irritation. Those plump, pink lips push out into a scowl. "No, of course not, you blubbering imbecile." Sarcasm slathers each word in its sticky poison. "I want you to tell me what the weather will be like tomorrow and if I need to wear shorts or pants."

Strangely enough, Falcon doesn't seem offended by Raven's acerbic wit. Then again, none of the guys seem particularly upset when Raven stares them down like they're the shit stains on his underwear. I wonder if they're just so used to his domineering attitude that his words slide straight off their shoulders, or if they see a part of him I never get to.

Raven? Being anything other than an overbearing ass?

Puh-lease.

"Aye, aye, captain." Falcon keeps his face pressed against my temple as he speaks. "I'll pick you up sunscreen if you need it."

"Idiot." Raven rolls his eyes, but I swear I see the barest hint of a smile tugging at his lips. But then I blink, and his impenetrable mask is once again in place. I half believe I imagined it.

No, there's no "half believe" about that.

I definitely must've imagined it.

Raven only smiles when he's skinning people alive, eating babies, or sucking the blood of children in sacrificial rituals.

"I arranged your training and got it approved by one of the guards," Raven continues, once again addressing me without even glancing in my direction. How does he do that? How can I feel each word like the lash of a whip against my skin, even when he seems to be a million miles away? "I told them that you won't survive the next game without one-on-one help." His lips twitch in the makings of a cruel smirk. "They didn't care, of course. Said that if dumb bitches like you can't live through one measly little game, then what's the point of natural selection? But I insisted, and I can be quite persuasive when I want to be." His eyes glint with unfettered malice that has a chill skating down my back and freezing the tangle of nerves in my stomach.

"What you do this time?" Eagle asks jovially as he flicks a piece of his hash brown at Falcon's head. Of course, Falcon shifts at the last second, so the hash brown ends up hitting me square in the forehead. I reach up to swipe the oily spot away. Assholes. "Suck a dick, hack a computer, or teach old farts how to work a phone?"

My mouth pops open before I can stop myself. I quickly shield my reaction before Raven can see the malicious glee spreading across my face.

I've heard the guys joke before about how Raven is able to get special privileges on the island, but I always thought they were exaggerating. I mean, my underwear is one thing, but this? Does he really exchange sexual favors with the guards in exchange for added benefits? Does he really do . . . illegal things to receive that extra pillow he has at night? I tuck that little nugget of information away to dissect later.

Blackmail can be quite effective when utilized properly.

Raven's eyes narrow into thin, unyielding slits. "You know I don't do that shit," he hisses, and I can't help but wonder which one he's referring to.

The dick sucking? The hacking?

Both?

Eagle doesn't seem perturbed by Raven's glare. He simply throws his head back and guffaws, one of his huge paws coming to land on his stomach.

"Anyway—" Raven savagely rips his attention off Eagle and resumes his perusal of the cafeteria— "Hawk has been made aware and will meet you on the training grounds. He should be there already."

A ball constructed entirely out of razor blades forms in my throat.

"Um . . ." I swallow and rub my damp palms down my prison-issued pants. "Just Hawk?"

Just me and the terrifying, huge serial killer? The one who blows hot and then cold without a second's warning?

Raven's lips curl up into what I almost want to call a smile but I know isn't. It's nothing but a ruthless baring of teeth that has the meager contents in my stomach swirling rapidly. Those cold, cruel eyes of his seem to lock in on my face like heat-seeking missiles, intent on exploding everything in sight.

"Is someone afraid of the little serial killer?" he taunts.

"Little?" I snort before I can stop myself.

"Don't be afraid, pet." Falcon's rumbling voice slashes at my skin like a thousand knives. "Hawk won't hurt you." He pauses, considers, and then amends, "Well, he won't *kill* you. Probably."

Oh, fuck.

The clearing that I'm directed to is outside the gate. It's my third trip beyond the chain-link fence and into the wild, and it doesn't look like this one will be any better than the previous ventures. While tropical trees and blooming birds-of-paradise edge the cleared circle, this place looks nothing like paradise.

There are four tall wooden posts stuck in the dirt, and rotting bodies are chained to the first three of them. The fourth one remains empty, the pole looming ominously. Waiting.

The bodies are all in varying states of decay. The first one has no real face left, just bone glinting under the morning sunlight, though hints of innards remain in his neck. His shirt has been stripped, though he wears black prisoner pants, and his chest has been pecked apart, like an apple left for the birds.

The second body still has flesh on his face, though his

mouth is open and the tip of his tongue is jagged, bits ripped off and nibbled by some unknown creature.

The third man looks fresher than the other two. His tan face still maintains its normal coloring as compared to the mottled gray of the others. His face lifts to the sky, as if pleading with it. His eyes are gone. Just two black holes remain where his eyes once sat, while the rest of him is still intact. Intact, that is, but for the bullet wounds.

I do a double take and look back at the first prisoner, realizing his chest hasn't been pecked apart by animals, but by bullets.

"What is this place?" I murmur, disgust and terror mingling in my tone.

Someone steps up to my left, and I startle, skittering backward only to hear Hawk's fake laugh blare like an alarm. An alarm that should send me running.

"Don't you like our targets?" he queries, tilting his head and grinning, though those eyes of his are jet-black ice.

"Lovely," I retort, trying to hide the way my voice quivers slightly. "What'd they do?"

He sweeps his arm to the side. "They lost one of our games. Such fun, Hoplite games."

My breakfast threatens to come back up, and I swallow hard, looking to the side, focusing on the spiky orange petals of a bird-of-paradise flower, so I don't end up yakking in front of him.

"You're too soft, Phoenix," he states, his big hand moving until it rests on my shoulder. "But I'm going to fix that." Suddenly, the weight of his hand doesn't feel comforting. Instead, it presses down with the weight of his expectations.

Can I do this?

My entire life, I've tried not to cross that line into true violence. But it seems that Wicked Island has no lines. The Birds certainly have none. The weeks have started to blur the lines for me, their cruelty almost becoming routine. I no longer cry when I crawl around on the floor to scrub it each night. In fact, sometimes, I enjoy the way their eyes are epoxied to my ass.

"You know that when you lose a game, you get tied to the pole while you're still alive, right?" Hawk asks.

"What?" My eyes flicker back to the bodies, my horror doubling.

What the fuck are these games?

And why do I feel they're not as simple as red light, green light?

Hawk's huge hand slides up and down my arm in a gesture that might have been comforting if it came from someone sane. "Yes. It's in the handbook. This is just one of the possible outcomes if you lose a game. The guards get to lock you up here to starve to death or be live prey for target practice. Often, if a team member falls behind or fails their group during the games, the team itself will be the first to come out and get to shoot. Of course, the guards demand only gut shots. They don't want any prisoner dying too quickly." He gestures toward the first prisoner. "That used to be Weasel. He was a Predator, once upon a time."

I close my eyes, breathing in and out slowly, though I

feel certain that Hawk can see the way my pulse is jack-hammering inside my ribs. The way my heart pounds so hard that it feels like it might burst through my chest.

I've been holding out hope that Jayce is a good guard and that not all of them would drag me out and let a thing like this happen. I've been hoping Jayce is a diamond in the rough amongst the otherwise heartless assholes here. I've also thought I've been making inroads with the Birds.

This revelation makes me question everything.

Each time I think I've clutched on to a sliver of optimism, something new rips it away.

Wicked Island is truly the lowest ring of hell.

I know Hawk's words are meant to intimidate me—possibly incite me to be that mouthy bitch he seems to enjoy laughing at—but they just smash through my ribs and shatter them.

I end up turning toward him and impulsively throwing my arms around the waist of the giant serial killer. My fingers dig into his back, and I clutch at him as if I'm adrift and he's a life preserver.

He's not.

I know he's not.

But for a second, I allow myself to pretend.

The need to cast some sort of illusion becomes stronger than the reality I simply can't face.

Hawk's big hands push down gently on my shoulders, almost as if he wants to peel me off him, but I don't allow him to. I clutch harder, press closer. I step one of my thighs between his and soak up his body heat, listening to the jagged rhythm of his heart, which seems as off-kilter as mine.

He relents.

To my surprise, he relents and hugs me back, his arms squeezing tight around my back, engulfing me in his strength, lending it to me for just a moment—long enough for me to gain my bearings and my sanity once more.

When I pull away, I look up at him. I don't say thank you aloud, but my eyes shine, and somehow, I feel a tether linking us together. An invisible strap winding around and binding us.

Or maybe that's just another illusion that I need right now.

When he straightens and pulls his arms away, relaxing into a casual pose as if I didn't just teeter on the edge of an emotional breakdown, his lips purse. Then an accent, one of the most ridiculous Western movie accents I've ever heard, drips from his lips. "Well, now, lil' lady. I've got a mind to teach you how to shoot. In these parts, a girl needs to know how to defend herself." He hitches up his belt, an item most prisoners don't get but the Birds have somehow managed to wrangle.

"How?" I don't even try to disguise the breathy quality of my tone.

There's no hiding how I feel. I mean, I basically just used him as a child's stuffed animal to counteract the dark. I've shown my hand. I simply try to roll my shoulders back and straighten up when he points to a flattened area in the grass, and I see an array of weapons that I hadn't even noticed, thanks to the dead men.

Hawk has laid out a picnic blanket along the ground, as if we're on a date. A date with death. On top of it are five different guns. Only one resembles the small handgun I stole from the Predators weeks ago.

Ignoring my dry throat, I take a deep breath to try to gather whatever calm I can. Then I nod at Hawk. "Okay. I'm ready."

"Pick one," he instructs.

I glance first at him and then around at the trees, suspicion suddenly coming over me. "Where did those come from? Shouldn't a guard be supervising?"

"Raven paid for the privilege of privacy, and that's all you need to know about it," Hawk replies evenly, crossing his arms. "Pick one, or I'll pick for you."

I walk tentatively over to the red-and-black checked blanket, staring down at the guns. I really have no clue what I'm looking at, so I just crouch down and select the gun that looks like it's the largest of the handguns but not quite as large as the shotguns. The weight of the thing surprises me, and I have to lock my wrist as I lift it.

"Desert Eagle. Fierce gun."

I stare down at the gleaming weapon. I assume from the weight that it's loaded.

I test it out, lifting it up, and aiming down the barrel at one of the bodies, trying to think of it as a man made of straw or a paper target instead of a corpse.

"Your stance is wrong," Hawk states, marching over and then planting himself behind me. His hands come to my hips and wrap around them. He rests them in place for a moment, and my breath catches at the feel of him touching me and looming over me while I have a weapon in my hand. If I wanted to, I could whirl around and shoot him. Blow a hole right through his chest.

Fuck. It's a tiny bit tempting.

As if he senses the violent direction of my thoughts, he bends down, his fingers squeezing harder on my hips. "Try it. I dare you."

"Try what?"

He chuckles, the sound feathering across the top of my hair and making my nerve endings prickle—whether in nervous delight or pure fear, I'm not sure. "You know exactly what." Those fingers squeeze again, and this time, that press of fingers heats the space between my thighs. Warmth flickers in my low belly, and I can feel my nipples start to pebble. My time with the Birds has warped my libido, and I'm certain that I'll never be able to be turned on by anything vanilla ever again.

Flowers? Fuck those.

Chocolates? Pathetic.

But daring me to kill you? Damn. That's fucking hot.

When Hawk's giant hands slide up my sides, I inhale sharply in anticipation. But he doesn't reach up to cup my breasts or roll my nipples. No, his hands come up and then travel down the length of my arms, correcting my grip on the gun. "Thumb here." His thumb caresses mine and his hands splay over my own, possessively, obsessively.

When his thigh slides between mine, I groan at the friction.

"Spread," he commands, and by his tone, I can tell

he's just as affected by this position as I am. I widen my thighs, almost bemoaning the loss of touch from his thigh, but he simply presses up against my back harder and shoves his leg farther against my ass, keeping the slight pressure against me. But even that light pressure builds the heat inside of me until it's inferno-level. And when he deliberately rocks back and forth against me, I stop breathing.

"Exhale," he coaches. "Breathe. You're going to have to focus through distractions, Phoenix. If you want to survive, prove it to me. Shut everything else down. Focus on the target."

I try. I narrow my eyes and stare at the chest of the dead man chained fifty feet away. I inhale and exhale slowly. But when Hawk drags that thick thigh back and forth against me again, my eyes want to roll back in my head. I want to arch my back and lean my head against his torso and let him erase all my panic and pain with a few seconds of pleasure.

But this is a test. A test.

I grit my teeth and try to ignore the sensations skimming across my inner thighs. Try to ignore Hawk's movements, which are dislodging my panties and slowly edging them closer to the center of me, into my slit, rubbing against my pussy lips. I lift my arms, and Hawk keeps his hands atop mine.

"Feel the wind?" he murmurs, and only then do I realize that a slight breeze is blowing. Luckily, it's not dragging the scent of the bodies toward us but coming in from our right. "Aim a little to the right of where you want to hit to compensate for the wind."

I nod and inhale, knowing at least that much about shooting from television shows. On the exhale, I pull the trigger.

BAM.

The kickback from the gun rattles me, and if I wasn't held up by Hawk on three sides, I might have lost my balance.

"Shit," I murmur, staring down at the barrel.

"Yeah, you showed your hand when you picked that gun. You know nothing about weapons. The Desert Eagle is known for its recoil."

"Thanks for warning me," I toss out sarcastically, tilting my head to glare up at him.

But he simply raises a dark brow. "Not here to warn you. I'm here to train you. Do it again." He straightens me like I'm a puppet, adjusting my arms and legs to his liking. This time, however, he doesn't mess around with my concentration— clearly realizing I can hardly handle the weapon alone.

I shoot. My shot goes wide of the target, missing it by about three feet.

"Fuck!" I curse.

"Focus," he chides with a shake of his head. "Focus, or I'll tell Raven that I want to borrow that hairbrush of his, and I'll fuck you with it in front of everyone."

My throat dries out at the threat, because I know he'd love to do exactly that. Probably when I'm dry too.

Goddammit. I keep my feet planted where he put

them, raise my arms, tense my abs, and shoot. I barely nick the body in the ribs, but I'm immediately calling out, "That counts!"

"That counts," he concedes, "This time. But get the next shot into the body mass, or the same consequence applies."

My next four shots get increasingly better, until I nearly maintain control of the damn weapon during the kickback phase. It's still not as quick as Hawk wants me to be, though. He grabs a box of ammo that I hadn't noticed and helps me reload the gun. Then, for the next series of shots, he presses against my back again, trying to distract me. I manage to maintain focus now that I've got a rhythm going, and I continue to hit the target, though I can't say the shots land exactly where I aim.

Nearly every shot, Hawk corrects my grip or puts a hand on my hip to help me plant my feet better, though once I'm set up, he enjoys fucking with me. At one point, he even tweaks my nipples, causing my arms to swing and my shot to stray far left. It's pure luck that the slug sinks into one of the other bodies. I end up chuckling in relief, though after that shot, he leaves my breasts alone.

After a solid hour, my arms are aching and I'm starting to sweat, but Hawk doesn't let up. He simply points to a smaller gun on the picnic blanket and has me switch to it. I practice shooting for another hour, and this time, he makes me try to move as I shoot.

God, each shot reminds me of just how lucky I got with the Predators that night. I don't know if it was adrenaline or beginner's luck fueling me, but whatever it was is lacking today. Hawk ends up barking in my ear more than once when my shots go wide. Eventually, his threats go beyond that.

"Hit that fucker in the goddamned chest this time, or I swear, I'm going to tie you to the fourth post and shoot at you!" he snarls.

Shit.

I take a deep breath and step and shoot. But the shot veers right, hitting the body of the middle corpse in the shoulder instead of the chest.

Hawk's huge hand clamps down on me before I've even relaxed my stance, his fingers wrapping around my throat as he wrenches the gun away and tosses it into the dirt, where it lands with a thump. Then he yanks me toward the fourth pole. I writhe and twist, trying to get away as I say, "Fuck! Hey! I hit the corpse. I shot it!"

"Not in the chest," he replies calmly as he continues to pull me toward the pole, ignoring how my hands come up to scrabble at the back of his with my nails.

Oh, god. He's actually going to do this! He's going to strap me to that pole and shoot at me. I'm stricken by the realization that he wasn't bluffing, but I should have known it. He's a serial killer. Why would he joke about killing? God. Fuck. No wonder Raven and Eagle were so calm about sending me off with him this morning. Of all the Birds, I know Eagle likes me least and Raven still loathes me. So, did they ask Hawk to take care of me? To take me out?

A sob shakes my shoulders, but tears don't erupt from my eyes—somehow, my body has reached a point that's passed crying. This time with the Birds has changed me. Reshaped me. A wild keening noise rips from my throat but transforms into maddened laughter. Sharp spikes of sound slash through the air as Hawk pins me to the pole with one hand and his hips and then uses his other hand to yank at his belt.

I don't even flinch.

He's going to shoot at me?

Let him.

I simply cackle up at him as a smile crosses his face, the first true smile I think I've ever seen reach his eyes. Instead of the glacial freeze that normally encapsulates his gaze, I can see his pupils are blown with excitement right now. He moves rapidly, almost clumsily, pulling his belt off and then grabbing both my hands and shoving them behind me, around the pole. He circles it himself so that he can firmly bind my wrists together.

"Tighter," I tell him, when I can finally draw enough breath to speak. "Don't want me getting away, do you?"

"No, we can't have that," he responds, tone low and husky as he cinches the belt until it cuts roughly into my skin. Once he's decided that I'm secure, his hands come up to trace over the bare skin of my arms. His touch leaves a path of fire trailing behind it, and excitement gets caught in my ribs.

I should be terrified, furious, a plethora of other negative emotions . . . but not a single one manages to penetrate the near-hysterical bubble I've erected around myself. Another bark of dry, deranged laughter escapes me as I realize how close I am to death. The Grim Reaper has a face and a name.

Hawk.

When he circles me, our eyes lock, and it's as if the top of our skulls crack open simultaneously and rationality flees to the clouds. Our minds widen and stretch beyond the grip of sanity as we stare at each other. Each of us recognizes the humming, hovering wildness trapped inside the other's veins and longing to be free. Our inner beasts want to dance through the air and drop to the earth.

After all, isn't that all that life is?

His head dips toward mine and hovers, his lips a mere inch from mine. He steals my oxygen. My breath.

My eyelashes flutter, and he turns abruptly, breaking the moment and stomping hastily back to the picnic blanket, swiping an oversized rifle into his hands.

I hear him cock it only a split second before he fires. And I don't even have time to flinch as the bullet rushes past my ear, snipping my hair. Tiny strands float down my arm and tickle against it.

Oh!

The reality of what just happened smacks me across the cheek, but only lightly, because my head is still in some floaty, disjointed space right now.

I blink.

I almost died.

He almost killed me.

A second shot rips through the air, and the sound is the most real part about it because I see nothing, feel nothing. Not until there's a thump in the pole just above me and a tiny cloud of sawdust and splinters fills the air.

Somehow, the sawdust landing on my forehead and the scent drifting over me has a greater effect on me than the bullet itself. My heart throbs painfully, as if it just realized we should be afraid. My knees give out, and I sag against the pole, head lolling.

Hawk immediately runs toward me, gun still in his hand, his chest heaving as if this whole experience has affected him just as much as it has me. As if his life was on the line.

When he realizes that I'm about to pass out, the gun is forgotten, dropped into the weeds. He surges forward, and his hands make quick work of his belt, releasing my arms and roughly rubbing them, as though he can chafe the blood flow back into them. I sag against him, my head near his navel, because with his height and my melting legs, I can't reach any higher.

He scoops me up and murmurs, "Good girl," just as Hoplite guards emerge from the trees, their black uniforms swallowing up the bright sunlight. They stomp forward with guns raised.

"Time's up!" one of them shouts.

But I don't even move. I'm too busy staring up at Hawk, memorizing the soft look in his eyes.

21

NYX

A switch flicked on inside of me this afternoon, one I'm unsure how to turn back off. The near-death experience with Hawk was not only terrifying, the way I expected it to be. There was also a savage edge of exhilaration about it, a sensation I shouldn't have felt. One that's left me aching and desperate all day.

That might explain why, when Raven orders me to the center of the cabin that evening, and I kneel naked in front of the Birds just as I do each night once the sun goes down, I feel turned on. It's the first time I've felt this way —nipples hardening, thighs clenching—not from stress but anticipation. Today, I realized that being powerless can be a rush. A panicked but also euphoric rush.

I experience that sensation again as they all circle up and surround me, tall and strong, any one of them able to hold me down and keep me in place by force, which they've done before. But not tonight. Tonight, they simply stand there and expect me to submit to their degradation.

And fuck me, but I find myself wanting to. Why? It's Stockholm Syndrome, I know that. I'm not a complete fool. I'm stuck here, day after day, dependent on them for my survival. I know how it goes. But it doesn't stop my stomach from tightening or my mind from glowing deliciously.

I can't even fully explain away my emotions using psychology, because the urge inside is so strong. And I can't stop it . . . I don't want to. I just want to sink into this feeling, wade and float through the giddiness washing over me. Why shouldn't I?

My body buzzes with electric energy as their attention focuses on me. My skin pebbles with goose bumps, even as a fire sparks in my lower belly. Eyeing them, I appreciate the power dynamic in play. How they're all fully clothed, except for where they've lowered their pants to expose their dicks, which they grip in their hands as shadows cloak them.

And even though I'm physically powerless to escape this situation . . .

Every single one of them is rock hard.

I did that to them.

Every single one of them is turned on by *me*.

Instead of avoiding looking at them while they stare down at my body and use me as their own live pornographic material, my eyes raise from the floor tonight in morbid fascination at my own little self-discovery. I might enjoy this shit more than I ever thought.

I gaze at their cocks.

Eagle's dick is pale, and average sized, but the head on the end is bulbous. His hand grips tightly on his shaft, cinching down on it and pulling the skin taut. I find myself resisting the urge to lick my lips.

Next to him is Falcon, who's using both hands stacked so that I can barely see the pink head of his cock, but precum leaks onto his fingers as he slides his palms up and down. I know from experience that he always comes a lot, jerking crazily at the very end, as if his cock is just as unhinged as he is.

I tilt my head as I watch Hawk, who's merely using his fingertips to surround the tip of his dick, teasing himself, smiling down at me with that cold, eerie grin as he does. He likes to draw things out, see if he can finish last.

Vulture often competes with him. The torturer has a wider stance than the others, his thick shaft emerging from a nest of dark curls. One hand squeezes his balls, while the other grips the base of his dick, avoiding the head. Part of me wonders if he can't resist torturing himself at times. If it's so embedded in his personality that it invades every last part of him.

Raven's dick, to my surprise, is pierced. He's got a fucking iron cross that looks both intimidating and possibly amazing on his thick cock. I've never experienced a pierced dick, but women at my old jail had and they always sang praises of pierced members.

"Cup your tits." Raven issues the first order of the night, just like he has for the past few nights. They like to have me pose for their viewing pleasure.

Tonight, I'll be posing for my pleasure too.

A wicked little thrill rushes through me at the fact that I've got this new secret. I raise my hands to comply with his demand, letting my hands gently circle the outsides of my breasts twice before I reach beneath them and squeeze, lifting and offering up my peaked nipples.

"Fuck." Vulture's hand moves from just gripping his shaft to sliding all the way up and down. "Do that again."

I repeat the process, though this time, I pause to pinch my nipples before moving down to cup my breasts, and the sensation zips pleasurably down my spine. My eyelashes flutter, and I swallow back a shallow pant of pleasure.

"This isn't for you," Raven immediately snarls. "This is for us, since these idiots decided to keep you, and fucking you would fuck up their desperate little heads even more. So, don't fucking think you're going to get off."

His rage normally makes me quake. But he's under-mined himself because he's said two very important things. The other Birds want to keep me. And they're desperate.

For me.

That knowledge makes the heat in my lower belly pulse, and I bite my lip as I turn my eyes to the floor, not wanting Raven to realize my reaction to his words.

"On your back, little killer," Falcon coaxes gently. "Legs spread."

I quickly move to do as he asks, lying on my back in the center of the cabin, spreading my thighs. I can feel their eyes dragging over me. My breathing grows shallow as I make eye contact with Vulture, and his head tilts as he realizes that tonight is different from the other nights. Unlike Raven, he doesn't disparage me. Doesn't order me to stop. Just stares down at me in a way that has my insides clenching and desperate for him.

Eagle gives the next command. "Lift your hips."

I plant my feet on the floor and raise my ass, my arms straight down on either side of my body as I lift my pussy up closer to their eyes. They typically make me hold this pose as they finish . . . which can take anywhere from two minutes to thirty, depending on how long Hawk and Vulture want to compete.

For a minute, the steady thwack of their hands sliding up and down their dicks is the only sound in the room.

But then, Hawk decides to stir the pot. To tempt me and all of them. "Reach down and spread your lips. I want to see inside you."

Fuck.

God.

His filthy fucking mouth and the crazy afternoon we had together dogpile inside my brain and leave me in a crumpled, aching heap. I have to squeeze my eyes shut as I reach down to touch myself—because I want to come so badly, but I know if I do it in front of Raven, I'll be severely punished.

My fingers find my wet folds and slide along them, and intense thrills scream up my back, flare along my hips, burst inside my belly to put me close to the edge. As wild and unhinged as the desire is, I wish one of them would lose control and just kneel down and fuck me while the others watch.

I've never been fucked in public, but the mental image of it is as delicious as chocolate. The way the other men's eyes would light with jealousy, how their gazes would trace over my body, watching the way my breasts bounced with each thrust, the way my pussy gaped open as cum dripped out of me after. Warm, sticky cum. Fuck. Wetness pools down below, and I can feel it sliding down my folds as I gently position my hand on either side.

Can they see it? Can they see how turned on I am right now?

It's impossible to hide. I can't control my shallow panting or the way my body is begging to be filled.

I pull myself apart and feel a pulse down there. Raw and needy. Muscles clenching. Searching for a dick.

Any of their dicks. All of them.

They could fill me one by one. God. Yes.

"She wants to be our cum dumpster. Look at that. Pussy begging for us." Raven rips the words right from my brain, though his sneering tone is all wrong.

"That pussy is mine, pet. Say it," Falcon orders.

"It's yours," I breathe, just as Vulture starts to argue.

"We agreed no fucking."

My eyelids crack open, and I turn my head to see the torturer glaring at Falcon.

"But that doesn't mean her pussy isn't mine. She's my

pet. I found her." Falcon's tone is calm, unconcerned about the other man as his eyes focus on my cunt. "Slide your fingers up and down," he instructs.

"But don't fucking come," Vulture adds grumpily, before his eyes focus on my hand, on the wet sound of my skin. "Don't you dare let that pretty pussy come. You're going to tease yourself right to the edge and fucking stop, or I'll whip your ass until you won't be able to sit down."

Dammit all to hell. Even his threat sounds good right now, when my mind is a disconnected haze, and my body is full of strobe lights and fog and the impending crescendo of a naughty song.

My hand slides up and down, and my hips pump of their own accord. I thrash my head from side to side, curl my toes, stomp my feet and grit my teeth—anything to stop the orgasm that's right fucking there.

"Fuck!" Raven is the first to come, splattering his cum all over my belly.

Falcon follows shortly after, stepping forward and deliberately spraying his massive amounts of cum between my thighs, all over my hands, along the seam of me. "That's it, pet. Rub my cum into your cunt."

I pulse around nothing. I bite my tongue and turn my head away from him, trying not to let his words affect me.

"Come, and I'll shove a nail right into your ass before Vulture whips it," Raven threatens, and I know that's exactly what he'd do. I try to think of horrible things, terrible nights stuck under the bridge—but Eagle ruins my focus.

"Come here and suck me. You owe me."

His order sends me scrambling to my knees, my hand still between my legs, sneakily swiping a few passes across my clit as I crawl toward him. If they won't fuck me, I can at least get this. A semblance of sex.

But just as I part my lips, Eagle sprays them with cum. Only the first jet is strong enough to reach me; the ones after that drip onto the floor. But my mouth is coated in his taste, and my tongue darts out, lewdly lapping up the flavor as I touch myself.

Vulture steps forward and grabs my hair, wrenching my head back. "Hands off our cunt." His grip only relents when I reluctantly remove my fingers. He smiles cruelly when I glance resentfully up at him. "Pissed, Nicholette? You wanted to suck his dick, didn't you? You wanted to have a cock inside you. Bet you want us to fill all three holes at once, don't you? Eagle in your mouth, Falcon in your pussy, Hawk reaming your ass?"

A grunt sounds behind me, and warm drops splatter along my spine. I can hear Hawk panting in the aftermath.

Vulture gives the other Bird a superior look before pulling quickly on his own dick. He yanks my hair even harder a second before he spurts all over my breasts, painting them white.

When he releases me, I'm not sure if I want to cry or laugh.

Because even though they all just used me for their pleasure again, even though I didn't get to come, my body is belting out a glorious high note, every pore infused with a deranged melody.

I set out to endure the Birds' cruelty, but, ironically, I've ended up craving it.

22

HAWK

T he dream begins the same way it always does.
I'm crouching in a bush, spindly needles poking against my skin as I stare at my target. Plump, middle-aged, with brown curly hair that cascades down to the middle of her back, she stands in front of the open window, utterly oblivious to my presence as she tosses her shirt over her head and throws it onto the bed. Her cotton bra comes off next, and I watch in rapt fascination as her tits spring free, her nipples beaded.

It's almost as if she senses my presence, as if she's putting on a show. That's a game I like to indulge myself in every once in a while, but not today. Not now.

When her hands move to the waistband of her jeans and slowly slides them down her shapely thighs, my cock hardens in my pants. Her panty-clad ass faces me as she bends forward.

The routine is always the same.

I'll wait until she falls asleep before sneaking through

the window, a silent shadow in the form of a beast. And
then . . .

And then the fun will begin.

Her room goes dark as she switches off the light,
though I don't move from my spot crouched in the bushes.
Instead, I do what any predator does when faced with
prey.

Wait. Watch. Listen.

Needles, loose dirt, and rough patches of grass dig into
my knees, but I don't relax my taut position. The muscles
in my neck strain from keeping my head up for so long. All
around me, a night as dark as pitch stretches like a tent
over the peaceful, serene neighborhood, the inhabitants
completely unaware of the monster lurking within their
depths. Crickets chirp in every direction, and somewhere
in the distance, a dog barks.

When I'm certain an ample amount of time has
passed, I jump to my feet and race from the bush to her
window. A child's playset rests ominously to my left,
shrouded in darkness, and I swear I can hear the phantom
giggles and whispers of children.

The window opens on silent hinges—the result of my
constant greasing over the past few months—and I easily
pull myself inside the sparsely furnished bedroom.

One I have visited many times before.

My target is fast asleep on the bed, the blankets
wrapped around her waist, baring her tits to my hungry
gaze. She murmurs something in her sleep—a name—
and a surge of smug male satisfaction rumbles
through me.

"Edward . . ." She coos the fake name I've given her aloud, writhing at whatever sex dream plagues her sleep.

I drop to my knees beside her and slowly bring my mouth to one of her breasts, my beard grazing the sensitive nub. My hand moves to caress and squeeze her other tit as moans escape her.

"Oh . . . oh . . ." With a gasp, she jerks upright, almost dislodging my lips from her nipple. She reaches for her bedside lamp, and immediately, the room is engulfed in golden light. Her fearful expression turns into one of lust and heat when she sees who's sucking on her tit. "Edward! How the fuck did you get in here?" She giggles, attempting to be coy, as her hand tangles in my short black hair, attempting to hold me to her.

I release her with a dramatic pop and smile disarmingly. In my perfected French accent, I purr, "I've come here to see you, mon amour."

One of my hands snakes down her stomach to strum at her clit, and she instantly opens herself to me.

"Yes, Edward. Yes!" she begs.

"You've been a naughty girl, haven't you?" I graze her nipple with my teeth while keeping my eyes locked on her face. Sweat glistens on her skin as her head rolls from side to side. Pleasure is etched across her features, pleasure only I'm capable of putting there. "Naughty, naughty girl. You deserve to be punished, don't you?"

"Yes! Punish me! Yes!" she all but begs.

They always beg for their punishments like good girls.

They know they've sinned, and now, they're willing to repent.

I bite down even harder on her nipple, and her cries of pleasure quickly turn into ones of pain.

"Edward, a little too hard—"

I release her tit and roll myself so I'm hovering over her body. The stupid cunt is still staring at me with lustful eyes.

She doesn't realize that, even after three months together, I still don't know her name. But tonight's the night that this game ends. Tonight's the night she faces the truth about what she is and what I am.

"You don't think I know you hit your kids? That your daughter went to school with a black eye because of your drunken rage? That your son broke his arm when you pushed him?" I allow darkness to seep into my voice, allow her to see through my eyes the evil that has been in her home, in her bed, for the last few months. She thought she found her soulmate, her Prince Charming, but I'm no fairy-tale prince.

I'm a monster. The devil. The scary story passed down from generation to generation.

"Edward . . .?" The first hint of fear trickles into her voice, but her terror only amplifies my bloodlust. My hands move up her curvy body and close around her scrawny neck. I love the way her eyes bug from their sockets, like a startled little frog.

And then I begin to squeeze.

And squeeze.

And squeeze.

And squeeze.

She writhes at first, limbs flailing wildly, thumping

against the mattress. But her children won't notice. Since I entered her life and played my part, they're used to mattress thumping noises.

Excitement fills me up as life bleeds from her vibrant green eyes and her face turns blue. Terror splays itself across her abusive, piece-of-shit face before it gets frozen there forever.

Victim number fifty-seven.

My view shifts—the image flickering from the bedroom to a courtroom with wood-paneled walls—and I stare up at a judge who toggles between a courtroom robe and a bright-green golf shirt every time I blink. I see the glare of the bright lights on his glasses as he reads from a sheet of paper. But I don't hear what he says, other than the word, "guilty."

Fifty-seven was my final victim, and the one who unwittingly led to my downfall. Who would've thought that a neighbor happened to be peeking out his window the exact same fucking time I snuck inside? The picture of the neighbor's snub-nosed face as he testified, shaking and quaking, appears, surprising me. I just see his head, not his body, and it's floating in midair and describing what he saw as I grind my teeth to nubs in frustrated anger.

I had an iron-clad alibi lined up, for fuck's sake, and while investigators scratched their heads, trying to figure out who killed fifty-seven, I'd planned to move to the next town and start charming my next victim. I wish I could pop his head like a fucking balloon. He has no idea about the work I do.

Rapists. Abusers. Pieces of shits.

They all deserve the death I so graciously provide them.

The neighbor fades away, and I'm back in that bedroom again, hands around fifty-seven's throat.

The girl beneath my body changes.

One second, she's plump and middle-aged, and the next, she's lithe and petite, but for her breasts. Her dark hair cascades around her face like a halo crafted of sin as her eyes peer up at me, unblinking.

Nyx.

My hands loosen around her delicate throat. My own heartbeat doubles as I wait to hear that little thump, wait to feel the press of life flowing under my fingertips.

Something inside my chest collapses like a house of cards, and I'm not sure I'm breathing, either, as I wait.

I question my reaction. Why don't I want to kill her?

The idea of seeing the life drain from her eyes . . .

Maybe Falcon knew what he was talking about when he decided not to kill her.

Maybe I want to keep her.

I WAKE up with my hands around a pale neck.

Squeezing. Squeezing. Squeezing.

Shit!

I immediately loosen my grip a fraction but don't let go.

Did I sleepwalk again? Fuck. I haven't done that for months. I stare down at Nyx, wondering what she's thinking, wondering why my body was drawn to her, even in sleep, wondering if murder is so ingrained in my bones that I can't stop.

Maybe it is. After our shooting session a week ago, I'd nearly come just from shooting at her. And she'd let me.

She let me nearly kill her. For no reason at all.

I note the way my thick, dark fingers look against her soft skin, the way my hands can collar her lithe neck.

So beautiful.

She doesn't claw at me, doesn't cry out, doesn't try to scream for help from the others in the cabin.

Nyx simply stares back at me with half-mast eyes, lust emanating from those smoky depths.

What the . . .?

Her hips jerk upward, almost of their own accord, and she rubs against my rock-hard cock straining against my sleep pants. She's not naked any longer. She's wearing one of Falcon's white T-shirts, but I can see those nipples pebbling underneath the shirt, and I'm reminded of the shower she took earlier tonight. It was my night to watch her, and the intense pangs of lust I'd felt as her panties had become transparent rush back to me.

Nyx must be running out of air, but there's not a hint of fear on her gorgeous face. Only grim acceptance and something akin to lust as we stare at each other in the shadows.

Almost experimentally, I gyrate my hips, allowing my cock to press against her heat, and her eyes roll back into her head. She wants it.

Fuck.

I pause to make sure, but as soon as I cease my motion, her hips pick it back up and she rubs herself against me.

I have no idea why she's doing this. Is it the choking and the fact that she seems into it? Or am I grinding on her because my own lust needs an outlet after that dream? The entire night as she scrubbed our cabin with that luscious ass on display, crawling under each bed, the sexual tension and the dirty comments from the other Birds building and building . . .

Is that why she crept into my dream? Is that why my body dragged itself over to her corner on the floor of the cabin?

Is she horny because of all the naughty things we whispered at her tonight as she cleaned the floor and we jerked off over her? Part of me doesn't want *their* whispers to have affected her at all. I want it to be my touch. Me. I want it to be me.

Harder and harder, I squeeze her throat, and harder and harder, I jerk against her, a hot frisson of pleasure threading down my spine. Her eyes blaze and her hands claw at the floorboards on either side of her. She doesn't even try to stop me from choking her.

The fact that she likes it, the fact that I can feel how wet she's getting even through the boxers I'm wearing, makes me wild. I dry hump her with abandon, not caring that we're slowly sliding backward across her freshly scrubbed floorboards.

My balls tighten, my cock straining, and before I realize what I'm doing, I blow my fucking load right into my pants like a pre-teen boy seeing a girl's tits for the first time.

Nyx's entire body convulses as she orgasms, though her face still takes on an unnaturally blue tint. And I think to myself . . .

I can end her right here and now.

Squeeze until the life drains from her gorgeous eyes. Snap her neck. Rip her head clean off her shoulders with my bare hands.

But just like in my dream, I find that I don't want to.

Just like the time I shot at her, I don't want to end her.

I just want to ride that edge with her, hover in that delicious, delirious space between life and death.

My pulse thrashes inside my veins as my hungry gaze rakes over her body. Her shirt has slipped up during our little session, and I can see her wet slit and one dusky nipple, along with a smooth, soft expanse of belly. Fuck, she's like every wet dream I ever had combined, every dirty fantasy I know I shouldn't have bundled up into one perfect woman.

And apparently, she's batshit crazy enough to get turned on by me. By this perversion of mine.

Slowly, gradually, I release her throat, one finger at a time. My hands don't leave her skin, though, but instead, travel down to her plump breasts. I reach the exposed one, tracing the edge of it lightly.

She gasps as soon as I let go of her, desperately inhaling the air I denied her. Me.

I just controlled whether or not she breathed,

whether or not she died, and whether or not she came . . . and that power is heady.

Intoxicating.

Just like the woman beneath me.

I wasn't supposed to let her come. But I can't find it in me to give a shit about that. I like the fact that she came as I nearly took her life. Love it.

But will there be consequences?

For the first time, I look at my surroundings, at the space I wandered to in my sleep—the corner of the cabin where we make Nyx lie. No blankets. No pillows.

Just wood.

The rest of the cabin is sound asleep—though, if they are awake, they know better than to interfere when I sleepwalk.

The only bunk empty is Vulture's, which is nearly always empty from the bastard's insomnia, and I imagine he's taking a midnight stroll through the jungle. It's technically not allowed—he'll be shot on sight if he gets caught by the guards patrolling—but that doesn't stop him.

"Hi." I grin down at the tiny female, who simply stares up at me. I can't quite read the expression in her gorgeous, huge brown eyes. Anger? Lust? Confusion?

"Bad dream?" She cocks a brown brow as my hands caress her curvy body, fascinated by those big, soft breasts. Better than any body I ever had the pleasure of touching, caressing, fucking.

She's not corrupted like the others.

Raven has talked all about her crimes, and they're

so . . . petty. So small. Nothing like the women I've been with.

I'm not touching her as a means to an end. Not because she's a target. I'm just . . . enjoying it. I don't think I've ever done that before.

I want to fuck her so bad, it's like there's a tether inside of me connecting my cock to her pussy. Even though I just came, I can still feel the stirrings of lust in my lower belly, telling me that once my cock revives, he wants another chance to touch that slit. The invisible string between us drags me to drop my hips back down on top of hers, loving the way her rounded hips fit between mine.

"You don't need to concern yourself with that, sweetheart," I tell her, adopting a Southern accent, my personal favorite.

"I do when you decide to sleepwalk to my corner of the cabin and choke me," she retorts, and the sass in her voice has my cock at full mast once more. That fire . . .

Damn, I want to keep her.

Make her my girl.

A wave of unbridled possessiveness cascades through me in an icy wave. It's unlike anything I've ever experienced before. It distorts my vision, narrowing my focus until all I can see is her, and darkens the room in a red sheen.

I don't want Falcon or Vulture or Eagle or Raven to have her.

I want her to be mine.

"What if I make it up to you with a nice and comfy

bed?" I suggest in a Russian lilt reminiscent of Eagle's. The accent belongs to a new character I came up with after I met the dumb brute—Alexi. Alexi is Russian, of course. Orphan, because why not? Desperate to avenge his dead wife and children.

"A bed." Nyx's eyes narrow suspiciously as she parrots those two words, and I can't exactly blame her for her distrust. I wouldn't trust myself either.

"A bed for the pretty lady." Back to Southern. Dallas Steele. Cowboy, obviously. Never been in love. Never met a woman who truly kept his interest before now. Hmm . . . he might not be the right character for tonight.

"Are you going to choke me again?" She tries to sound angry, but there's a breathy quality to her voice that hints at her fear. Damn.

Why does that turn me on so much?

"You gonna come like a freight train again?" Boston. Marcus Peters. Lawyer. Picket-fence life. A wife and two kids. Secretly fucks women on the side, because he's not a good guy, despite his claims to be otherwise.

"Fuck you." Her tone is sassy and shoots a ray of sunshine into the dark spaces inside my chest because that sass means she's still unbroken.

I smile brightly, jumping to my feet and all but pulling her onto hers. Without giving her a chance to argue or object, I move us both to my bunk and lie down, tugging her until she's sprawled out on top of me like a luscious little blanket. She holds herself stiffly, tension lining her body, but I simply smile and hold her tighter against me.

God, she feels good. Those big, soft breasts. That long hair sweeping down my side. The curves of her legs, even her little feet, which end in the middle of my calves.

"Goodnight, love." British. Tom Brothal. Ex-intelligence agent. Lone wolf.

So many characters. So many masks.

But all of them . . .

All of them are intrigued by her.

No one is more surprised than me when, a few days later, Jayce arrives in the cafeteria at breakfast and demands to speak with me alone.

The sight of him is like a punch to the gut, but his demand is a blow right to the skull. Is he insane, calling me out like this in public? And on a day when all the Birds are here at once, no less?

Raven arches a skeptical, suspicious brow at me while Falcon pouts like a toddler. Eagle simply glares at the blond guard, and Vulture taps his fingers against the tabletop, the only outward hint of his distress. Only Hawk seems unperturbed by today's turn of events as he flashes a beatific smile at Jayce.

"Howdy, sir. How are you doing this fine morning?" he asks in an over-the-type Southern drawl. He's been twice as persistent with the accents lately, ever since that night we had.

A night we never speak about.

It's almost as if we believe that, if we don't acknowledge it, then it never happened. But it most definitely *did* happen. My body still tingles just thinking about it, something I abhor and love in equal measure.

Jayce ignores the serial killer—and I can't decide if the move is the ballsiest or the stupidest thing I've ever seen—before resting his piercing gaze on me.

"Nyx." He folds his arms over his chest, his biceps rippling and flexing in a way that captures my attention. "Now, please."

I pretend to moan and lament to the Birds, but inside, something fizzles to life. Something new and exhilarating and terrifying, in equal measure—a soda can that has spent a lifetime rolling around in the back of a semitruck before being popped open, the liquid exploding in every direction.

I've found that I enjoy my time with the arresting guard. Probably more than I should. A part of me wonders if it's because he's one of the very few people on this island who doesn't stare at me as if I'm an object to covet, trade, and then discard when he tires of me. He sees me as a person, and that, in itself, is a feat.

I slowly untangle myself from Falcon's lap, where he's practically draped around me. Just before I can leave his lap completely, though, he grabs my wrist and pulls me toward him and then nips at my ear hard enough to elicit a squeal from me. I spin toward him in alarm, but he merely offers me a self-satisfied smirk that's more beast than human. Those dark eyes of his twinkle with something distinctly wicked.

"Don't forget about me, pet," he practically purrs.

I rein in the urge to roll my eyes. "Kind of hard to do when you stalk me all the time."

Falcon tilts his head to the side contemplatively, though that mischievous twinkle never leaves his striking eyes. "Stalking . . . following you around . . . sniffing your underwear . . . Is there really a difference?"

"Wait . . . you sniff my underwear?!"

He waves a hand in the air dismissively. "Semantics."

"Stalkers sniff underwear," Vulture points out, frowning.

Falcon places his arms on the table and leans forward to give the torturer a salacious eyebrow waggle. "Yes, but do stalkers also hide in bushes and watch their pets?"

"Yes," Vulture and Raven both say at once, Vulture sounding pissed and Raven appearing irritated.

"Huh." A thoughtful look paves its way across Falcon's face. "Maybe I *am* a stalker."

"Nyx." Jayce's no-nonsense voice breaks through the chatter like the crack of a whip, the barb digging into my skin and peeling away flesh. "Now, please."

I finally remove my wrist from Falcon's grip and immediately follow Jayce out of the cafeteria, ignoring the lewd stares from the other prisoners. A part of me wants to look back at the Birds, but it's a small, stupid part that craves to belong somewhere in this fucked-up, dissonant world. I tell that piece of me to take a running

nose-dive right off the nearest cliff and become intimately
familiar with the rocks at the bottom.

Questions settle on the tip of my tongue, but I hold
off on unleashing them while we're still near the other
prisoners and guards.

I know today isn't another orientation class, so why
did Jayce call on me?

The traitorous flutter in my chest—the one that feels
an awful lot like butterfly wings—begins to flap inces-
santly. I mentally stomp on that damn sensation until the
feelings are dead, buried, and forgotten.

Finally, we reach the edge of the forest, where some
of the guards' buildings reside. Trees rise from the ground
like giant wooden swords, intent on protecting the
wilderness contained beneath its boughs. There are pines
here, though other parts of the island are full of tropical
plants. Staring at the mismatched tree types, I once again
wonder where we are in the world.

"Where are we going?" I can't help the way my voice
trembles ever so slightly, but come the fuck on. Everyone
knows that the prisoners who enter the guards' sacred
buildings don't leave them alive.

Terror grows inside of me like a poisonous cloud
eroding my bones.

"Relax." Jayce's lips twitch in the beginnings of a
smile, but I don't know what the fuck he finds amusing
about this. It's my life on the line, after all. Not his.

I wonder if he's taking me to the records room to steal
that damn pen. Is that what this is about? Is he risking my
life for a stupid deal?

My anger sits on a powder keg with a long fuse, just waiting for it to finally explode. I ball both of my hands into fists as that forbidding anger swirls inside of me, a tornado waiting to be unleashed.

But Jayce surprises me when we bypass the building I know houses the records room and we approach a small, decrepit one beside it. This building is still five times bigger than the cabin I share with the Birds, but there's a large crack running through the front wall and the windows are covered in a thick film of dirt.

I cock an eyebrow, and he smirks.

"Scared, little phoenix?" he asks in a teasing voice, and my stomach does a low, hard flip at the nickname.

I scoff and jut my chin out imperiously. "No, of course not."

Liar.

Jayce simply smiles, like he can see the deceit in my eyes, before pulling open the door and gesturing for me to enter ahead of him.

The first thing I feel is cold air blowing my brown tresses away from my face.

Air conditioning.

Actual, honest-to-God air conditioning.

Is it wrong that I come a little in my pants?

I squeeze my eyelids shut and tilt my head up, reveling in the way the frigid air caresses my skin. Goose bumps pebble on my arms and my nipples harden, but I'm unsure if it's because of the cold or the orgasm I'm surely about to have.

A low, husky chuckle breaks me out of my reverie. I

turn to see Jayce staring down at me, his eyes twinkling with unencumbered amusement. "Enjoying yourself?"

"Do you know how long it's been since I felt air conditioning?" I don't wait for him to respond before plowing ahead like a verbal freight train intent on self-destruction and complete annihilation. "Way too long. This is better than sex." The last words leave my lips entirely unbidden. I swear, if I was in the correct state of mind, I wouldn't have said them, especially to Jayce, the hot-but-utterly-unavailable guard.

But alas, I seem to have air conditioning, near-orgasm-addled, brain.

He chokes on his own spit and throws me an incredu-lous stare. That same glimmer from before materializes in his eyes and softens the harsh angles of his face. It's a star-tling contrast to the almost devious tilt of his pink lips.

"Maybe you just haven't had good sex before," he rumbles, and a flood of heat shoots through me.

Oh. My. God.

Is Jayce . . . flirting?

No.

He can't be. He wouldn't flirt with a prisoner. I've been here for weeks. Alone with him in that orientation room for days. If he wanted me, he'd have just grabbed me.

Right?

Except, there's an expression on his face right now that I've never seen before, one that's raw and masculine, with hooded eyes.

I'm probably gaping at him like an imbecile, but

words evade me. The pleasure-infused lightning cascading through my veins is the only thing keeping me upright when my knees threaten to wobble.

"Um . . ."

Jayce blinks, and whatever heat I swore I saw in his eyes dissipates as if it was never there to begin with. He gently nudges me with a hand on the small of my back and rasps out, "Come on, inmate. She's waiting for you."

She?

I must've said that word out loud because Jayce glances at me out of the corner of his eye, his expression unreadable.

"All female inmates are required to meet with her once a month to ensure nothing . . . uncouth is occurring," he explains, his features pinching ever so slightly. "For some reason, a session wasn't scheduled for you last month, but she was able to put you on the rotation starting today."

I cringe, not only because I honestly don't think Hoplite gives a single shit about my well-being, but because I'm going to have to have an awkward conversation about my body like I'm a schoolgirl learning about bad touch. If she has a goddamned doll, I'm walking out of there.

"And who is this mysterious 'she'?" I ask as Jayce leads me to a room at the end of a long hall.

He doesn't answer as he slows to a stop, mumbles an apology, and then procures handcuffs connected to his belt.

Wait, what? I'm with him for hours every single day. He knows I'm not a threat!

When I give him a look of disbelief, he simply says, "Protocol." As if to soften the blow, his hand trails over my lower arm, his fingers wrapping gently around my wrist and pulling it forward until it rests near my belly. My breath catches when he does it a second time, pulling my hand up. His thumb swipes over my thudding pulse once, and I hear him suck in a breath. He steps closer, and all the air in the room evaporates. I grow dizzy for a second as I inhale the spicy scent of his cologne. Our eyes collide.

But then he remembers himself and steps back. As if to punish himself and me for that little moment, Jayce proceeds to lock me up tighter than a nun's asshole. I huff in indignation but allow him to chain me up, secretly wishing we were doing this in another, more intimate setting.

Down, hormones.

Now isn't the time.

Once he's satisfied that I'm secure, he pushes me into a room and gently closes the door behind me while he remains outside.

I take a moment to survey the small office—a large mahogany desk, a leather couch in the center of the room, a bookshelf pressed against one wall, and a Pride flag on the windowsill.

And then my eyes land on the woman staring back at me with an amused and not-at-all-surprised expression.

A rather *familiar* woman.

"Mari?" I ask in disbelief as I blink at her. Am I hallu-cinating? Do I have something in my eyes that is causing me to see shit that isn't actually there? Did the Birds drug me?

But no matter how many times I blink or gape like an idiot, the woman before me doesn't change or fade away like a mirage in the desert.

"Nicholette." She folds her arms over her chest and cocks a manicured eyebrow. "What in God's name are you doing in this hellhole?"

Mari.

Mariana Lopez.

My next-door neighbor when I was a child and one of my closest friends . . . until she moved across the country when I was ten years old.

I didn't talk to her for years until she friended me on Facebook my junior year of high school. Even then, we never messaged or talked, except for the occasional comment on a post or a like on a picture. The last time I scrolled through my feed—which was forever ago, now that I think about it—she was living in New York with her girlfriend, Beatrice.

What the hell is she doing here?

I want to say that she looks exactly as I remember her, but that would be a lie. Mari has transitioned from a lanky, too-thin girl into a striking young woman. Her dark brown hair, almost black in certain lights, cascades down her shoulders in loose, natural waves that used to make me ridiculously jealous. It frames a face with high cheek-bones, a small nose, and piercing green eyes.

Piercing green eyes that are currently locked on me with a strange emotion I can't quite decipher emanating from them.

"You can imagine my surprise when I was scrolling through my case files and discovered that my old friend Nyx is now an inmate in one of the worst prisons in the world." She *tsks* her tongue and shakes her head. I notice, somewhat belatedly, that she doesn't look scared of me, merely confused and even a little amused. "What the hell did you do, *chica*? Murder someone?"

I snort before I can stop myself. "Nothing that fancy." I absently pick at one of my fingernails as I give a loose shrug and flop down on the couch. "I simply . . . stole something."

"Stole?" Both of her brows rise, touching her hairline. "What the fuck did you steal? Nuclear codes?"

A bark of harsh laughter escapes me. "Try a diamond."

She blinks. Frowns. Blinks again. Frowns. Blinks a third time.

"A . . . diamond," she parrots dumbly.

"A diamond." I give a decisive head bob.

"And did that diamond belong to the president?"

"Unless the president was hiding it in the jewelry store I was in, then no." I give another shrug, suddenly uncomfortable with this conversation. Her line of questioning just serves to remind me that I don't fit in here. I don't belong with the insane prisoners roaming this island.

Mari seems to be on the same wavelength as me. "How the hell did you end up here, then?"

She doesn't question my story or call me a liar. I can see in her verdant green eyes—brimming with empathy and pain—that she actually believes me.

Warmth blossoms inside of my chest as I regard my old friend. "I don't know," I answer honestly. "I wonder that myself every day."

A few things that come to mind . . .

They messed up my paperwork with someone else's —a vicious murderer, perhaps, or a terrorist.

They misspelled my name, and some chick named Nicole Butterfield is supposed to be here.

I have an evil twin sister who somehow evaded capture.

Mari steeples her fingers together and regards me with a curious gaze. Before she can ask one of the dozens of questions I can see tumbling around in her brain, I blurt out, "How the hell are *you* here?"

Those green eyes regard me with an emotion I can't read before she leans back in her chair with a sigh. "You know you're not supposed to ask guards about our lives outside of the island, *chica*. You could get us both in a lot of trouble."

Actually, I didn't know that. It must be a part of the manual I haven't gotten to yet. Or maybe I glazed over it, since copying crap down is the most inane part of my day, and I spend way more of my time secretly sneaking looks at Jayce.

I open my mouth to apologize for asking about her

life when Mari smirks wickedly and waves a hand in the air. "But you know I'm always down for breaking the rules." She shrugs a delicate shoulder. "You know how I was working in that counseling office in New York?" When I nod, she continues. "Well, about a year ago, some men in suits approached me about a job, and let me tell you, girl, the pay they offered me was fucking amazing. Nearly three times what I was making."

"And you counsel . . . the women here?" I ask, trying to wrap my head around all of this.

If Mari still lives in New York, then does that mean the island is located off the coast? Are we near the United States?

I don't know how to ask her that without drawing attention to myself and my all-consuming curiosity.

But if we are nearby and I could steal a boat, I could escape. I swallow hard at the hopeful lump that's suddenly blocking my airways. I fight to keep a neutral expression on my face.

Meanwhile, a dark thundercloud rolls over Mari's. "I don't agree with Hoplite's decision to bring women here to begin with. I'm the biggest feminist you'll ever meet, but fuck! Twenty men to one woman aren't good odds, you know? My job here is to make sure that every woman who falls on the island has someone to talk to if things get . . . bad. And their definition of bad isn't the same as mine." Her lips compress into a tight line. "There were more female suicides than male suicides before I arrived here, despite the fact that there are fewer of you."

A chill skates down my back at her ominous words.

It could always be worse.

Haven't the Birds always said that?

Now, Mari's reinforcing it.

I suppose I have to be grateful to the Birds. If they hadn't taken me in . . . I shudder at the possibilities. So far, aside from the time Vulture teased me, the time Raven touched my pussy, and the night I dry-humped Hawk, none of the guys have done anything except look at me. And jerk off on me. Dress me. Feed me. Make me crawl. Watch me shower. Yes, it's degrading and humiliating, but I'd rather be ogled at than raped. I know I'm a sex object to them, but they don't actually treat me the way I expected they would. The way they could.

My god . . . is this going to be my life now?

Being grateful that the prisoners who took me in are only looking instead of touching?

What does it mean that I've started to like their looks? Heated shame colors my cheeks because, today, I sat myself right down on Falcon's lap. Happy to sit there. Craving his attention.

But then I get defensive. I peer down at my hands and knot my fingers because I'm not just some victim to them. I'm not just a victim in my own head, dammit.

Vulture has started including me in his pranks against Eagle. Last night, I giggled with him as we strung up fishing line he'd procured from god-knows-where. We'd tied it to all the trees at ankle height and then I pretended to run away, through the forest, while Vulture screamed for all the Birds to help. Eagle fell on his face, getting a mouthful of mud. And Vulture scooped me up in his arms, spinning me around as we laughed and laughed.

I know they use me.

I know what they started was against my will.

But I chose to stay.

I could have ended it, but I chose to stay.

I don't regret it.

I don't mind being used for pleasure. In return, I use them for protection. Tit for tat, right? I might be rationalizing. But I don't care. This is my life now. I'm a Bird.

I know what Mari is going to ask even before she opens her mouth.

"I haven't . . . They haven't . . ." I swallow and take a deep breath. "They haven't raped me, if that's what you're worried about. They've just touched and looked." Shame floods my body at my confession. Saying it aloud affects me far more than I thought it would. All this rationalizing and arguing I just did inside my head suddenly loses its weight, and I can't meet Mari's eyes. Yes, I'm a Bird now. But am I proud to be one? No.

Here I am, sitting in front of this woman, who was a girl I befriended and respected when we were both kids. Now, she's a psychologist at a prison, and I'm the damn prisoner she needs to check in on.

I never expected my life to turn out like this.

Instead of being ashamed of being a Bird, or of what's happened to me, I feel ashamed to just be me.

I haven't felt that way for a long time.

Instead of meeting her probing gaze, I continue my perusal of her small office. It lacks any memorabilia or

pictures, but I know that's on purpose. I doubt Mari
wants any of these prisoners to know the faces of her
friends or family.

I wouldn't.

"Nyx . . ." Mari's voice is sympathetic, and it slices at
something raw and bleeding inside of me. I fucking *hate*
pity.

"I know it's your job and all, but I don't want to talk
about it."

"But Nyx—"

"Please, Mari," I interrupt, a tiny tremor working its
way through my body as I hold her emerald stare.
"Just . . . drop it. Lie in your files or whatever and say that
I talked until I lost my voice, but please."

She considers me in that warm, assessing way she
always did, even back when we were kids—like she
recognizes a part of me that I'm too terrified to look at
closely.

Finally, she nods and stands abruptly. She moves
across the desk until she's able to reach for the cuffs
securing my wrists together. Without preamble, she
reaches into her pocket, grabs a key, and places it into the
lock. The metal manacles fall to the ground as I gape
at her.

"Um . . ."

"Come on." She tosses her dark hair over her
shoulder and opens the door to the office. When I just
continue to stare at her like she fell on her head one too
many times, she arches a perfectly manicured brow and
jerks her head to the side. "Come."

I follow, trepidation warring with excitement in my chest. "Where are we going?"

"You'll see."

As we step out of her office and move down the hall, I notice with a pang of disappointment that Jayce no longer seems to be in the building. But my initial disappointment is eclipsed by wonder when Mari steps out of the building without a care in the world and waves toward one of the guards on duty. He gives me a dubious look but allows us to pass without comment.

"Mari . . ." I scurry to catch up.

"Oh, come on, inmate." Her tone is almost teasing as she turns to stare at me over her shoulder. "Live a little."

I huff but obediently follow along behind her, shocked as shit when she enters the building Jayce indicated holds the records room.

"Where are we . . .?"

"Shush."

Mari holds open the door for me to step inside, and once again, the chill from the air conditioning has every hair on my body standing at attention. I shiver and resist the urge to rub at my arms.

"Mariana?" a cold voice demands from behind a desk in the center of the room. A beautiful woman glares back at us with an almost incandescent fury, haughty disdain written clearly across her face. "What are you doing here with an inmate?"

"Hello, Sarah," Mari says with false cheerfulness. "How are you today?" When Sarah doesn't answer, possibly too angry to speak, Mari continues, "You know

I'm allowed to bring my patients wherever I feel is necessary for their healing."

Why do I have a feeling that's total bullshit?

Sarah seems to think so too, for her right eye begins to twitch.

"Inmates aren't allowed here," she hisses, dipping her gaze to my freed hands. "Especially without handcuffs."

Mari rolls her eyes and continues on her way without even a backward glance at the blonde, muttering under her breath in rapid-fire Spanish. When I remain rooted to the spot, my joints frozen over, Mari gives me a look. "You coming?"

Face whatever it is Mari has planned for me . . . or an angry, blonde bimbo?

The answer's simple.

I take off after Mari at a sprint.

We don't walk for long before Mari pushes open a door leading into a large room with a table, over a dozen seats, a fridge and microwave, a plush couch, and a flatscreen TV rooted to the far wall.

"The . . . breakroom?" I ask in disbelief as Mari kicks off her high heels and moves toward the fridge.

"Don't worry so much, *chica*." She bends over to rummage through the fridge. "No guards will be in here for at least another hour. Hoplite likes to pretend they're unpredictable, but we all know that's the biggest load of horseshit I've ever—ha! Here it is!" She straightens a second later with a half-eaten chocolate cake in her hands. "It was Lucas's birthday yesterday, and we have some of this delicious goodness left over."

My mouth begins to water as I stare at the huge cake lathered in frosting.

When have I last eaten chocolate?

Cake?

Mari grabs two paper plates from the counter, some silverware, and then proceeds to cut two slices of cake. As I stare at her in disbelief, she nods toward the remote on the table in front of the couch.

"Why don't you put something on?" she asks as she settles on the couch and passes me a plate. "I haven't watched TV in forever. What are the kids watching nowadays?"

I can't think, can't breathe, can't do anything but gape at her.

Is she being serious?

Is this a test?

I've never known Mari to be deceitful, but then again, I don't know this grown-up version of her. It's been years since I last laid eyes on her in person. A lot can change.

I know that more than most.

"Well?" She waves her fork in the air impatiently. "What are you waiting for? We only have an hour before we need to vacate the premises, so put something on before I do it for you. And I can promise you that you won't be a fan of my Spanish soap opera. Spoiler alert— Dante's the baby's father, but Savannah is secretly in love with Mario. But Mario loves Savannah's identical twin sister, though he is having an affair with the babysitter."

Still at a loss for words, my mind reeling and tripping

over itself, I take the seat beside Mari and turn on the television.

———

FIFTY MINUTES—AND two episodes of *The Office*— later, Mari leads me out of the break room, chatting excit- edly about Pam and Jim. That girl is truly a believer in love at first sight and soulmates.

Gag.

Sarah remains behind the counter and glowers at me, her eyes spewing poisonous vitriol. Her hand tightens around the object she's holding, and it takes me only a second to realize what it is.

A pen.

The pen.

A lump forms in my throat.

"You're going to get in trouble, Mariana," Sarah hisses, flicking her gaze to me.

"Am I, now?" Mari sounds utterly unconcerned with Sarah's passive aggressive threat. If anything, amusement bursts to life in her green eyes, and I swear, if I were into girls, I would fall head over heels in love with Mariana Lopez right then and there.

I have to bite down on my lip to hide my growing smile.

Sarah drops the pen onto the desk, and I watch out of the corner of my eye as it rolls a few inches to the left.

"You think you can get away with so much just because—"

"Enough." Mari's voice is as sharp as I've ever heard it. Her eyes blaze hotly as she snarls at the other girl, "What I do with my patients is none of your concern."

Sarah huffs irritably and folds her arms over her chest. Her lip pushes out in an honest-to-God pout that makes her look like a constipated kitten. If I still had a phone and social media, she'd live to regret that face.

Behind her, a second television blares, "Touchdown!"

And I see my opportunity.

Pretending to be engrossed in the game, I take a step closer and peer over Sarah's shoulder.

"Football." I allow a bit of my wistfulness to seep into my voice. "I haven't seen a game in so long. Who's playing?"

"You actually watch that crap?" Mari asks with a sniff.

I snort and turn toward her. "Not anymore, obviously."

A tentative, fleeting smile—one painted in sadness—appears on Mari's face before fading. She sighs heavily and moves to take my arm. "Maybe next session, we can watch a football game. It's a sacrifice I'll willingly make for you."

I pretend to think about her offer before saying, "Nah. I'm too invested in Pam and Jim's relationship. I need to know what happens next."

"A woman after my own heart."

Sarah mutters something I can't quite hear before slumping down in her chair with an irritated huff. Mari ignores the other girl's temper tantrum and gives her a tiny wave over her shoulder.

"Bye, Samantha," she coos.

"It's Sarah."

"That's what I said."

Mari opens the door for me yet again, and we step outside.

But this time, the Hoplite pen I just stole is firmly tucked away in the waistband of my pants.

I wake to the sound of Raven screaming.

Jolting upright from the floor, I smash my shoulder into Falcon's bed frame.

Fuck!

I grab my sore limb and moan as pain radiates down my arm and makes it feel almost numb. Clenching and unclenching my fingers in an attempt to shake off the pain, I glance around the cabin, my eyes searching for a threat, only to see Raven standing on top of his mattress, swearing and pointing at Eagle.

"Get that motherfucking thing away from me! Goddammit!" His voice has an edge to it that's far more panicked than his normal paranoia, though when I glance around the rest of the cabin, the other Birds don't seem to share his fear.

Only Eagle looks mildly concerned, his eyes directed down at his own leg. Hawk's sitting up in bed. His back is to Raven, and I can see the huge man rolling his eyes before lying back down and pulling the covers over his face. Falcon is still asleep. He hasn't even twitched. Apparently, the sound of screams isn't enough to rouse him. And Vulture? He's not in the cabin, though he rarely is at dawn. He seems to sleep the least of all the men, wandering outside at all hours.

My gaze focuses back on Raven, whose brilliant black hair is disheveled from sleep. His gorgeous face is contorted in disgust and his fists are clenched.

"Now, I'm going to have to trade for fucking bug spray. Maybe shots. What if you get goddamned Lyme disease?" His fingers unclench and come up to fork through the strands of his hair as he shakes his head, running through a list of possibilities aloud.

Meanwhile, I rub the sleep from my eyes and sit up straighter, leaning forward so I can peer at Eagle's leg. I see a tiny black dot on his calf.

"A tick?" I murmur. All this over a tick? I want to roll my eyes like Hawk, but I know better.

"Phoenix!" Raven's spotted that I'm up. "Get over—"

Before he can even finish his command, I'm on my feet, because I know what's expected of me. If there's a menial task to be done, Raven will make me do it. If there isn't, Raven will invent one and make me do it. Honestly, he's lucky he's so damn smart that we apparently need him for these upcoming games, otherwise I would have attempted murder out of sheer annoyance. Out of all the Birds, he's the one who's still constantly hostile.

Eagle looks down at me, his jaw clenched and his expression stoic—as always.

Instead of looking back at Raven, whose glare is currently burning the side of my face, I stare up at Eagle. "Do we have tweezers?"

He shakes his head.

Great. Gross.

Eagle reaches into his pocket and retrieves a packet of matches, holding them out to me. I stand, stretching briefly before I pad over to him. Falcon's shirt—a.k.a. my nightshirt—glides over my thighs as I walk.

I've stopped asking where the Birds get things. They always seem to have access to secret treasures, the sorts of things it was impossible to get in the women's prison. I learned long ago that there's no point asking for information. The Birds will tell me exactly what I need to know —no more, no less. It's irritating as hell, but honestly? The predictability of it almost makes it . . . comfortable.

Taking the matchbook, I glance back up at the Russian. "What do I do with this?"

"Light the match. Blow it out. Place it—"

"That's old-school and doesn't work. Can I just use the nails under your bed and treat them like tweezers?"

"What?"

"Look. I lived rough for a while. I know how to deal with ticks," I tell him. I don't go into the details about living in the brush down by the river after a group of homeless guys took over the bridge I was sheltering underneath. The ticks were easier to deal with than those bloodsuckers.

"You." Raven's tone turns even more accusatory, if that were even possible. "You and your long hair. You probably brought them in here." He turns and glares down at me with all the authoritative cruelty he can muster while standing on his bed like a child. He can never resist a chance to put me down, to grind me under his heel. To blame me for anything and everything.

At first, he nearly broke me, the constant barrage of insults and degradations slicing through my skin like serrated knives. But, at this point, his wild accusations have become almost mundane, having the opposite effect of what he hopes. He's hardened me. Given me a shell. A coat of armor.

Sometimes, I wonder if his callous words are his foreplay. I imagine he'd blow a nut if I ever suggested that to him. The thought almost makes me smile.

Almost.

I open my mouth to retort, but Eagle gives the most minuscule shake of his head, as if he's warning me not to. The Russian rarely intervenes—on my behalf or anyone else's—so he must have a reason. Closing my lips, I turn back to the former arms dealer and repeat my request to get the nails Vulture pranked him with. He nods.

I head over to his bed and dig underneath it, extracting a box full of nails. The possibilities for what I could do with this tiny treasure trove of weapons are endless, but I don't dwell on them now. Not when every Bird but Vulture is in the cabin and staring right at my ass, where it peeks out from the side of the bed.

I slither back out and make my way over to Eagle, clicking the tips of the nails together like chopsticks.

Is it horrible that a part of me hopes they're rusted with age? That they'll lead to an infection?

But then I figure that Raven will cut off my head if he believes I murdered his favorite Russian. Alas, I rather like my head firmly in place, thank you very much.

Still, a twisted bit of satisfaction reverberates through me at the macabre thought.

What are these Birds doing to me? It won't be long now before I'm huddled in a bunker with my feral cats, sewing together the skins of my enemies and cackling like a hyena over the men who jaded me.

Eagle doesn't smile, only stares steadily as I sink to my knees in front of him. It's a position I've become all too familiar with. Only last night, he had me kneeling just like this in front of all the others before their jerk-off session. He's been holding that blow job over my head—literally—nearly every day. He'll make me crawl to him and take up position, unzipping his pants and taking his dick out. But then he'll always find some reason not to let me start. He hears something outside that could be the Predators. My hands are too cold. The reasons are endless.

Last night, Vulture groaned and said, "Fuck, man. I'll take the blow job if you won't." And both Raven and Eagle laid into him, snarling with an almost rabid fury.

This morning, though, as sunlight streams softly through the windows and Hawk walks over and opens the front door in order to let even more light cascade into the space, I'm not kneeling at Eagle's feet and staring up at him, waiting for a new rejection. I'm studying his calf and the smattering of hair on it, along with the tiny swollen bug stuck to the inside of his leg.

"It's not that big. It can't have been there for long," I say.

"It shouldn't be there at all," Raven rants from behind and above me, still perched on his bed, as if that's going to save him from the "infestation" he thinks is going on. I wonder if he believes this is a bioterrorist attack against him and his people? Knowing Raven, it wouldn't surprise me. Everything is a conspiracy with him, and the entire world is out to end his life.

I do roll my eyes now that I know he can't see me. "Maybe the guards conned you with sugar water instead of bug spray," I toss out, knowing exactly the effect that little statement will have. If there's one thing I've learned about Raven, it's that he doesn't trust anyone.

"Those fucksticks!" A thump on the floor tells me he's jumped down from his bed, and quick footsteps sound behind me as he walks toward the front door. He's no doubt headed for the secret location where he keeps the stash of all the special items he trades with the guards for—everything from underwear for me to the styling gel for his hair. Now that I've planted the seed of possibility in his brain, he's got to go check to see if it's true.

As soon as he leaves the cabin, it feels like everyone lets out a collective breath. Raven's never easy to get along with, but when he works himself up, he's down-right unbearable. I'm pretty sure that not even the others can stand him when he's in a mood. Eagle's his closest

friend of all the Birds—if psychopaths can have friends—
and even he looks relieved that Raven's no longer around.

I take a deep breath myself and lean forward over
Eagle's leg, angling my head so that I can better see the
little tick and figure out where its head dug in.

"There," I murmur, positioning the nails carefully. I
breathe in one more time to center myself and then to
exhale as I squeeze—

"AHHHHH!" A horrified yell sets every hair on the
back of my neck alight. My hands jerk automatically, and
I watch in horror as I accidentally stab the nails right into
Eagle's leg.

"FUCK!" The Russian jerks away from me before I
can yank the nails back, and the tiny, pointed shards of
metal follow him for a second before tumbling to the floor
with innocent little clinks.

A trail of blood starts to follow them.

Vulture stands in the doorway, where he just
screamed like a maniac but is now clutching at his
stomach as he erupts into laughter. "Got you, fucker!" He
points across the room at Eagle, who narrows his eyes and
clenches his jaw.

"Did you?" Eagle's expression turns flinty, his eyes
hardening before a tiny, mean smile tilts his lips. "Ever
wonder how I got the tick? Why I in brush all alone to get
bitten?"

Vulture's relaxed posture stiffens, and he straightens
in the doorway. "You didn't."

My eyes dart between the two of them. Eagle wears a
smug little grin as Vulture whirls around in the doorway

and stomps out, footsteps quick, as if he's hurrying off to check on something.

With a raised brow, I glance up at Eagle from my spot on the floor. "What did you do?" I ask, the desire to know so strong that I can't conceal it.

"Does not involve you," Eagle returns, moving back to stand near me. "Now, get this bug. Then clean leg."

This time, I carefully yank the little bug out, though who can tell if its mangled little mandible is still buried under the skin? Then I go to the sink and use a corner of my sleep shirt as a rag. I'm cleaning off the stab wounds I gave Eagle when Hawk and Falcon both wander out of the cabin to take their morning pees out in the bushes—because even though we have a toilet in here, these men still like to mark their territory like animals.

Once they're gone, Eagle's hand comes to my chin, and he lifts it. "Now." He says one word, just the one. But I know what he wants, because he's been dancing around it forever.

I sigh, annoyed as I reach for his pants and tug them down, his underwear along with them. I find his length already hard as I lean closer. I don't want to admire his cock, but I can admit he's big. Much bigger than Douchebag or any of the other guys I've been with in the past. Not only is he long, but he's thick, the hard muscle underneath contrasted by the velvety soft skin. I'm not even sure I'll be able to wrap my hand around his entire length.

How the fuck am I supposed to swallow that monstrosity?

And is it wrong that a twisted, demented part of me is up for the challenge?

"You sure. Now? Without an audience?" He normally makes the other Birds watch me crawl to him, enjoying their jealousy. "Do you even like blow jobs?" I ask, because he's seriously turned me down so many times that I'm starting to question whether this is just a game or if some woman bit and permanently scarred him.

If so, she deserves a medal.

Except, if she did scar him, I'm not paying the price for that mental hang-up he's got.

"Look, we had a bet, but you can't just keep—" I begin.

Eagle shoves his dick right down my throat without warning, and I gag, my eyes watering as he fills my mouth. He pulls back slightly, so that he's not in my throat, though he's still so thick that my jaw is open as wide as it can go.

"What was that?" He shoves back inside before I can answer, pressing deep, putting a hand on my head. "That's it, *kotenok*. Swallow that dick like a good girl."

I gulp around his cock, not prepared at all for this complete one-eighty. He's never taken things this far before, and I'm still stuck in shock, unable to switch gears and become an active participant.

But suddenly, Eagle pulls out, shaking his head. "Nah. I decided not today."

Frustrated and reeling, I barely resist punching him in the dick. "You can't hold this over my head forever."

"I can. And I will," he assures me, not a single ounce

of humor on his face when I glare up at him. "I burned hammock Vulture use when he no sleep. And I'll do worse to you if you stop me from getting what I'm...." He pauses, as if he's mentally translating his next word to English. "Owed." In contrast to his words, his fingertips trace gently over my chin, over my swollen lips. Heat flares to life in his eyes, a banked fire. They seem at odds with his previously frosty words. "Pretty."

Then, suddenly, he turns on his heel and stalks out of the cabin, stuffing himself back into his jeans and zipping up as he goes.

I'm left stunned, silent, and utterly confused. Was that a promise or a threat?

"Nicholette, come here." Vulture's voice slices through the brush as I stride away from my evening shower, Eagle having supervised me today.

The Russian walks languidly down the dirt path behind me as I stroll closer to Vulture, who's standing in front of our cabin, shirtless, his shirt bunched in his hand. His demeanor is serious, his lips pressed into a solemn line as he stands with his feet shoulder width apart in an almost militaristic fashion.

He looks angry but also commanding in the dim light of evening. The sun has already set, and the shadows trace every muscle in his body, as if he's been sculpted out of darkness. Perhaps he has.

I try to ignore the tingle that darts up my spine as I draw closer, but I can't hide the way my nipples pebble. It's become an automatic reaction to this new routine Vulture's created. For the past week, I've had to come to him every night just after my shower. I've had to watch the fireflies flit among the trees while he uses the lame excuse that I need to be checked for ticks in order to examine every inch of my body because Raven's gone off on three paranoid rants about Lyme disease ever since Eagle's tick.

Lyme Disease, my ass.

I've never loved and hated a bug so much as that singular tick.

These little examinations have become the most delicious torture I could have ever imagined.

I lick my lips as I draw closer, staring up at him, his gaze warming me even more than the humid night air around us.

Almost there.

My shirt already feels too heavy on my shoulders, and I can't wait to shed it.

Vulture first insisted that I walk naked from the shower all the way to him before I grumbled like a dumbass the second evening, telling him that I was more likely to pick up ticks walking through the underbrush naked because I didn't like branches snapping against my bare thighs. He hadn't cared until I'd sarcastically tossed out, "Well, I guess I'll just let Old Twinkle have a free show, then."

His eyes burned like embers then, and he stepped forward, hand snapping out to grab my chin roughly and yank it up. "What?"

"That man likes to perv on my showers," I lied

because jealousy looks good on him—brightening his eyes with a violence that makes my stomach flutter.

I'M NOT sure Old Twinkle is interested in any person like that—men or women. He seems content to play with his dolls. I don't even want to think about what he uses them for.

Now, I get an escort who bangs around the woods with a machete the entire time I wash off, looking for an old man who isn't there. It gives me a moment's reprieve from the Birds, so I get to enjoy the water in peace and, after, I walk down the path with my clothes on as I anticipate the way Vulture's hands are going to feel as he caresses every inch of my body. Actually, it's been a win, win, win situation.

Tonight, he looks particularly good. I'm surprised that Falcon isn't leaning against the cabin behind him to supervise. Sometimes, he likes to watch. And I would never say it aloud, but I like him watching, his gaze sweeping over all the parts of my body he won't touch himself.

"Hurry!" Vulture's barked command sets my feet to jogging, and when my hands come up to support and cover my bouncing breasts—because Falcon still won't let me wear a bra—he snaps, "Hands down!"

I watch his eyes dip to my chest for the remainder of my run to him, and though I ache afterward, there's also a hint of sexual tension in the ache, since Vulture likes to make me hurt, just a little. Not nearly as much as Hawk.

No. Vulture's torture is far more psychological. He doesn't want to push me to the brink of death—he wants my mental breaking point.

That's why he always uses that goddamned name.

The name my father gave me.

When I reach Vulture, I'm breathing hard, as I'm sure the bastard intended. He doesn't even bother to look at my eyes, just reaches forward and tweaks one of my nipples as my chest heaves. A spark travels down my spine, but I swallow any sound of pleasure, knowing that will make him more likely to stop than to encourage him. No, the trick I've learned with Vulture is that I have to pretend he's not affecting me at all.

"Get it over with already." I roll my eyes and fight a grin when he tugs my nipple harder, sending a thrill down to my lower belly. It's actually become quite a heady game, pretending to be unaffected by him. One that we play each night as he continues to do this useless check for bugs that we both know is only pretense.

He starts the game now, releasing my nipple to yank my shirt off over my head. He instantly proceeds to cup my breast in his hand, hefting it. Squeezing. I try to adopt a snobby expression, the kind I saw often enough in my youth. Meanwhile, tiny, buzzing tingles are darting around inside of me like errant kites caught up in a chaotic wind.

Vulture has learned just how to touch me, how much pressure to put, how much twisting my nipples can take. His years of subtle observation as he no doubt tortured hundreds of victims are put to good use when he plays with my body. And right now, I can't bring myself to regret all those hours he spent, because it means I get to experience him like this.

Cruel.

Commanding.

Captivating.

When I clench my jaw, his eyes fill with a dark sort of satisfaction. He brushes a finger across my nipple as he squeezes harder, the tiny tickle offsetting the pain.

Dammit. I gave myself away, but it was either clench my jaw or moan in pleasure, and the latter would have made him pause until my body cooled down.

As it is, his hand releases my breast, letting it fall before he traces the underside using only his index finger. He repeats the process with my other breast, pinching, hefting, squeezing and stroking, tracing. By the time he's finished, I'm wet—and not because of the shower I just took.

I breathe very slowly and carefully. Not shallowly, the way my body is urging me to.

Eagle stands behind me, watching as Vulture circles me. Though he's typically quiet—unless he's ordering me to crawl to him and unzip his pants in front of the others, always stopping just short of ordering me to give him a blow job, just enjoying holding the fucking promise over my head—his eyes study me a lot. I find it hard to read his expressions. I have no idea what he sees when he looks at me.

But tonight, once Vulture is standing beside him and they are both behind me, it feels as if both their eyes burn lines onto my back. I stare at our cabin door, and my nerve endings are scorched by their attention, torrid anticipation making my thighs clench. Vulture drags a single finger up from the base of my spine all the way to my neck, using his other hand to swipe my hair to the side. Then his finger travels back down, dips beneath the waistband of my prison-issue pants. He presses against the very top of my crack for a second, letting me know he's going to be touching me there, before sliding it around my waist.

I suck in a breath because his touch caresses my tickle spot, just as he knew it would. He's been tracing the same path for days.

"Was that . . . a bug?" His fingers backtrack, and he glides again and again over the same spot until I'm writhing, silently fighting a laugh. Fighting the urge to playfully hit him as if he's flirting and not deliberately tormenting me.

When a tiny screech finally rips from my lips, and he knows he's victorious, Vulture leans forward and nips at my ear, whispering, "That's a good girl. Just a little more to examine."

Fuck.

Immediately, my tingling nerve endings switch from humor back to naughty expectation, because I know what's coming next.

He quickly circles to the front of my body and removes my pants, kneeling to pull them off, then tossing them over his arm next to his shirt and my shirt. I've never bothered to ask why he thinks he needs to do this examination shirtless. I'm too busy enjoying the delicious display of pecs and his tattoos. The sight of him on his knees in front of me is almost too much for my poor brain to handle.

He glances up from underneath his lashes, knowing exactly how much I love the next part of his public examination.

"Put your foot on my shoulder," the torturer orders.

I eagerly lift my right leg and set it on the wide expanse of muscle on his shoulder. Staring down at his dark hair, which is shorn on either side but holds a thick dark strip down the middle, I'm tempted to pull on it. But I did that once, three days ago. And then he halted his examination to spank me and handed off my favorite part of all to Raven, who'd snapped on plastic gloves and touched me with all the medical precision of a male gynecologist.

Nope.

Not giving up Vulture's touch tonight.

I lick my lips and try to keep my back stiff and straight. I suck in my belly as Eagle steps up behind me.

"Hold her shoulders," Vulture orders. "Keep her still."

The Russian's hands clamp down on me harder than necessary, and I clench my teeth against the pressure he uses to press down on me. Unable to completely fend him off, my knees sink a bit, bending slightly, making me lean closer to Vulture, my panties edging nearer to his face.

Today's panties are a purple lace set of bikini briefs. Vulture glides his hands over my calves, circles his fingertips along the sensitive backsides of my knees, and then drags his palms over my thighs as I stand there, trying not to tremble, soaking in every single touch.

He glances up at me, waiting until my eyes meet his, letting the silence build up the moment until it reaches full potency before he says, "I'm just going to need to check along the edges here, okay?"

"Okay," I respond, the words a breathy gasp. But he forces me to say them every time. He won't continue his exam without them. And Raven won't let me into the fucking cabin without an exam. I have no choice, though, even if I did, I'm not sure I'd want one.

Vulture slides his hand slowly up over my right knee, his touch cruising leisurely over my skin. My eyes are glued to his fingertips, hungry, ravenous as I watch them approach my panty line.

And there! Yes!

Those fingers skim the edge of the lace, gently tracing along my inner thigh.

Fuck.

Heat pulses inside of me, and I feel a sudden desire to reach up and clamp on to Eagle's hands on my shoulders, digging my nails into his skin until it bleeds. I'm not allowed to touch Vulture, but is the other Bird off the hook?

I've never tried that before. I don't know. I don't want to risk it, though.

I fight the urge to buck when Vulture's fingers move to the other leg, gliding over my panties until I'm panting. I can't hide it, don't bother to try.

I've lost the game of pretend at this point, and I don't even care.

Vulture has been doing the exact same thing to me every single night, so I know what's coming. I want it—desperately—even though I simultaneously loathe it. I want him to torture me. Want him to drag this out. Want to experience this madness every evening for the rest of my existence . . . but I want the ending to be different.

I want him to let me come.

He's always stopped when I'm just on the edge, leaving me drunk, teetering, willing to crawl on my knees through broken glass if he'd just finish me off.

He always stands up, a knowing smirk on his face as my expression begs him, my lips plead with him.

But each night, he lets me get a little bit closer.

He gives me just a little more, as if he's having trouble resisting the sight of me screaming out his name.

Will tonight be the night?

Will he finally let me tip over the edge?

Maybe. Maybe if I'm good. I bite my lower lip so hard, I'm certain I'm going to draw blood.

Vulture's next line is one I've already got memorized. One I replay on a loop whenever I'm bored. "I need to look a little closer, baby."

Fuck.

Fuck.

Those words send a pulse through my entire erogenous zone.

"That okay?" he asks, tone gruff with sexual tension.

"Yes," I pant. Inside, I'm full of neon lights, strobes,

fireworks—but not the big, bright, colorful bursts far over-head. I'm full of Black Cats—loud, ear-piercing snaps of sound that are as fast as a snare rush. My nerves hiss and pop and pulse brilliantly.

He reaches up. He grabs my panties and pulls them slowly away from my body, making me appreciate just how wet I've become. The panties pull tight against my ass and make me doubly aware of every square inch of my body, though none so much as the few inches hovering so close to Vulture's face.

"Let me just see . . ." He leans forward deliberately, as if there's anything he can see in this dim light. His breath ghosts over my sensitive area, and I let out a small whimper that leaves him grinning.

"Eagle, I need a little more give in these." Vulture pulls at my panties until the threads are stretched to the extreme, the edges along my ass digging into my skin almost painfully. He's ruined quite a few pairs of panties this past week, though I don't think he regrets it one bit.

I know I don't.

One of the Russian's big hands evacuates my shoulder and drifts down to my ass. I suck in a sharp breath when his huge hand slides over the curve back there and Vulture simultaneously reaches out to trace a finger near my slit.

Both of them are touching me at once. I'm pinned between two dangerous men who are toying with me . . . and I adore it.

Eagle's fingers pinch my ass, and I yip, barely managing to avoid smashing my lady bits into Vulture's face, a foul that I know will end this little game of ours. A game I want to go on forever.

Fuck.

The pinch on my ass changes solely to a pinch of my panties as Eagle drags the hem from one side into the crack of my ass, piling the fabric there. He repeats the entire process, including the pinch, on the opposite side. When he's done, Vulture yanks the gusset of my panties forward another inch, shoving his face closer to my opening, so close that his warm breath steams my skin.

Heaven.

Did I think this island was hell?

I was wrong.

Right now, I've got wings. I'm glowing. I'm fucking incandescent.

Vulture's finger traces right next to my seam.

And heat engulfs me. Pleasure blasts through me, whipping in any and all directions as a brilliant orgasm bubbles up and spills over, splashing through my system. My hand does reach up then, grabbing the hand of Eagle's that's still on my shoulder and digging in, clawing viciously at him as sensation ripples through me. My other hand darts out and around Vulture's head, smashing his face right into my writhing body. I grind against him, and pleasure spreads for a moment before I feel his teeth viciously clamp down on the sensitive skin near my pussy.

"Fuck!" I screech, the sound piercing the night.

But even the pain doesn't erase the pleasure. It only enhances it, so I don't release my hand against Vulture's face. I keep him there, continuing to buck against his bites until my knees give out and my hands go limp as I fall backward into Eagle's arms.

That was amazing.

To my surprise, the Russian doesn't drop me on my ass but gently holds me, wrapping his arms around my waist. He stares down at me and then looks over at Vulture.

"Did you . . .?" His tone is almost accusing.

"No! I didn't touch her clit. Fucking Christ."

"Then how . . .?" Eagle glances back at me, questions still lingering in his eyes.

"Spontaneous orgasm," I tell him with a shrug.

"Spontaneous fucking orgasm," Vulture spits in disgust, brow lowered, as if my fun has suddenly ruined his. Maybe it has. "Is that even a thing?"

Eagle looks at him with a shrug.

Honestly, I don't care what they think. That orgasm is going right into my top ten. I don't think I've ever had a spontaneous orgasm before, though I heard about them while I was in the women's prison. Most women had them only in their sleep, but Vulture's been edging me for days on end.

"Well, you can only tease a girl so many times before she comes on your pretty little face," I quip merrily.

When I'm tossed over his shoulder and then dropped and shoved against the side of the cabin to get spanked for my sass, I don't even care. I brace myself and wear a wide, smirking, post-orgasm grin the entire time. I also find the bravery to threaten Vulture a little, since I'm so happy. I give an exaggerated moan and say breathily, "Careful. I'm close. You wouldn't want to make me come again for you, would you?"

When the swats stop and he swears in frustration, I have to swallow a joyful, brimming laugh.

This spontaneous orgasm thing is going to be an ace up my sleeve.

He knows it.

So do I.

When a reluctant Raven and a solemn Eagle drop me off at orientation the next morning, I'm surprised to see that Jayce isn't the only person there.

Instead, all the desks are filled with snarling, rabid-looking inmates. Some have bandages on their foreheads; others have casts on their arms, legs, and ankles. And one even appears to be missing his right hand.

What the fuck?

I remember, belatedly, Jayce telling me that the other new inmates have been in the hospital after that fateful night when we were all pushed out of the airplane. Are these the ones who survived?

I'd wondered why Jayce told me not to show up to class the last few weeks. I thought, perhaps, he was giving me special treatment. My bleeding heart wanted him to think of me differently than the other rough men and women on this island. But now, everything makes sense. He wasn't giving me extra time for combat preparation.

He didn't want me to show up, because he was giving these new inmates time to catch up.

My heart bangs like a snare drum as half a dozen sets of eyes turn to glare at me, lewd expressions painted on their faces. Some look as if they want to bend me over the nearest desk and fuck me senseless. Others simply stare at me the way Raven does—like I'm a gnat they wish to squash beneath their boot.

A cold, sinister grin tugs up the corners of Raven's luscious mouth.

"Ahh. The sheep have arrived, I see," he murmurs in a voice almost too low for me to hear.

Nice to know he's enjoying this. I should be. I should be glad that I get a moment's reprieve from the Birds. But this is nothing like my counselor. This is being stuck in a tiny, stuffy classroom filled with the scent of sweat and several other fucked-up monsters.

Eagle chuckles wanly and reaches up to ruffle my brown hair. I try to duck away from his outstretched hand, but he simply tugs at a stray lock and pulls roughly, forcing my head back. I stare into his dark, apathetic eyes and try to ignore the way my stomach knots itself. I can see Jayce watching us from the front of the room, but his eyes are unreadable, his lips compressed in a straight line.

"Try not to fuck the other prisoners, okay?" Eagle whispers, his accented voice like silk that caresses my skin. Goose bumps explode on my arms, the only indication that his sultry tone affected me. "Birds don't like to share their toys." His eyes drop to my lips for a split-second, and I wonder if he's including himself with those other Birds. If he thinks of me as his toy too. If he wants me. If I'm unopposed to the idea of him wanting me.

Raven snorts derisively. "Perhaps she should fuck these other men. Maybe then Falcon, Vulture, and Hawk will realize she's just another useless slut who will sleep with anyone to survive."

A wave of shame sweeps over me before I can stop it. I want to refute Raven's offhand remark, but there's no denying the truth of that statement.

Isn't that what I'm doing with the Birds?

Selling my body and soul in exchange for my life?

Is it even worth living, if I don't have autonomy over such crucial pieces of myself?

I push the thought to the deepest recesses of my mind and focus instead on Jayce.

Jayce, who has been nothing but kind to me since I first dropped onto this island.

Jayce, who may be my only ally in this cesspool of violent criminals and psychopaths.

Jayce, who makes my heart thunder with just one eloquent look—a look that makes words almost unnecessary.

I ignore Raven and Eagle as I yank my hair from the Russian's grip, disregarding the strands left behind in his fingers, and take a step forward, heading toward the desk near the front that has remained empty. Before I can move more than a few feet, though, Eagle grabs my arms and yanks me back to him.

"Aren't you forgetting something, *kotenok*?" he practically purrs.

I'm working to formulate a witty response when he grabs two handfuls of my ass and gives it a squeeze. He then leans down until he's able to nuzzle my cheek, his bristled face gliding against my skin like sandpaper.

Oh my god.

Is he . . . marking me?

There's something distinctly possessive about the way he holds and rubs against me. It reminds me of a cat attempting to scent its territory.

Hoots and jeers ring out in the classroom, and Jayce barks out for everyone to settle down, or he'll use his Taser. I notice that he doesn't call out the Birds for touching me, though—perhaps even my one ally among the guards is afraid of what they'll do to him.

He doesn't move, though his jaw ticks tightly shut, and his eyes narrow with displeasure at the scene we're making. I can't tell if his ire is motivated by irritation or jealousy, though a tiny sliver of me wants it to be the latter.

"Be a good girl and go to Raven," Eagle murmurs in my ear, leaning forward so he can nibble on the lobe. I hate the sparks that shoot through my bloodstream like fireworks at his touch. And I hate it even more when a tremble works its way through me, divulging my lust.

And then Eagle's words register.

Go to . . . Raven?

The Raven?

The one who's currently looking at me as if he wants

to wrap his perfect hands around my neck and strangle it?

But Eagle doesn't seem perturbed by my wide-eyed stare as he gives my ass one more squeeze and then releases me, shoving me in the other man's direction.

Raven remains ramrod straight, his chest heaving, his eyes dark and impassive, his hands balled into fists. That pouty pink lip of his pulls away from his teeth in a snarl.

My heart's nothing but a bloody lump of meat that has been carved up by a butcher. Fear pumps directly into my bloodstream as I take another step closer, dragging my feet, unsure of what to do, what to say. I'm keenly aware of both Eagle and Jayce watching me. I imagine the former looks amused, but the latter? I desperately wish I could see his expression.

"Give him a hug, *kotenok*," Eagle says, glee ringing in his voice. "What's the saying? Don't hit the bush? *Ya?*"

"Don't beat around the bush," I murmur under my breath, though the words are half-hearted, at best.

Intense anger eats into my flesh like acid.

Is the damn Russian trying to get me killed?

But when Raven doesn't protest or argue—simply staring at me with dark eyes framed by ebony lashes—I pull up my big girl panties and breach the short distance separating us. My hands lift cautiously, and I lean forward. Just before my arms can wrap around his waist, however, Raven reaches out and snags them, shoving them together so he can grip both of my wrists in a vise-like hold and hisses in my ear, "Keep your whore hands away from me." He shoves me away like unwanted trash, and embarrassment burns in my bloodstream like a wild-fire. That feeling is only amplified when the guys begin to laugh and hoot, and even Eagle releases a dark chuckle.

Fuck him.

Fuck Raven.

Fuck everyone here.

Raven's mouth is a savage slash across his face as he glares down at me.

"Aren't you such a good whore, always looking for attention and validation?" he mocks. "Is it because you didn't get enough as a child? Or is it because you got *too much*?"

Tears burn the backs of my eyes like they've been branded there with hot pokers. Still, I don't allow a single one to fall. I refuse.

What's that saying?

Give them an inch and they'll take a mile? I suppose that sums up this situation perfectly. If I allow the Birds to see even a sliver of my true emotions, they'll use them against me, wielding my own feelings into the perfect weapon, intent on destroying and eliminating.

Anger erodes all coherent thoughts. Survival instinct has been replaced by vengeance.

"You really like the word *whore*. Is it because it takes one to know one, Raven?" I say lightly, keeping my voice just loud enough for the others to hear. I know I'm playing a very dangerous game, but Raven has pushed me too far this morning. His insult stings with the keenness of a wasp—painful but survivable. He didn't break me; he made me stronger. "Do you like getting down on your knees for the guards?" I continue. "You like being their little bitch?"

Stunned silence falls over the room, though I don't pull my attention away from Raven's face to see anyone's reaction. The vitriol he aims at me with his eyes simultaneously cuts through and burns my skin like poisoned daggers, but still, I don't look away. It's like that game you play as a child—the first one to blink loses.

And I won't lose to Raven.

Not now.

Not ever.

At first glance, I may think that Raven is completely unaffected by my words. Other than the anger emitting from his eyes, his features remain carefully placid. But there's something in the twitch of his lips, the tightening of his jaw . . .

With an almost blistering speed, Raven reaches up and grabs a handful of my hair and yanks it. Hard. Much harder than Eagle did only a few minutes earlier.

Of all the guys, Raven's the shortest, so I only have to stare up slightly to be face-to-face with him. Those swirling dark orbs seem to be composed of darkness itself —twin abysses you could get lost in, falling head over feet, swirling in an endless tornado, ricocheting from side to side.

His hot breath brushes against my ear, eliciting a violent round of shivers.

"If you continue to be a bratty girl, I'll have no choice but to put you over my knees and spank you until you're red," he hisses into my ear. This time, his words are low

enough for the others not to hear. I'm not even sure if
Eagle heard, despite standing right next to him. "And I
won't be gentle like Vulture is. I will make it hurt, my
little bird, and you won't be able to walk for at least a
day."

Heat blazes across my skin before slipping beneath to
singe and bubble my blood.

I shouldn't feel such an instinctive reaction to Raven,
of all people, but I can't help but visualize his
threat . . . and like it.

The cold, eruptive wrath boiling inside me only
moments before has receded, replaced by something far
more insidious—lust. And I fucking hate it.

I shouldn't be lusting after Raven. I shouldn't.

But I am.

His scowl full of malice, Raven pushes me away and
absently rubs his hand down his pants, almost as if he's
trying to rid them of cooties.

"Your bitch needs to know her place!" someone calls
from behind me, chuckling.

Abruptly, Raven stalks away from me, grabs the
newbie by the back of the neck, and slams his face into
the desk. Blood gushes from the prisoner's nose, and a
pained cry escapes him.

"Don't you dare act like you know a thing about my
whore," Raven seethes, his voice brimming with possession. The hairs along my arms turn to spikes at his words.
Raven, still gripping the prisoner by the back of the neck,
turns his glacial gaze toward Jayce. "Are you going to
control your inmates?"

Jayce's face could've been carved from granite. His jaw clenches tightly, and a slash of sunlight only helps emphasize the hard set of his chin before gleaming on the embroidered Hoplite symbol on his chest.

I want to ask why he's allowing Raven and Eagle to walk all over him—he's the guard and they're the prisoners—but I have a feeling this is just another dynamic of the island I'm missing. Jayce may be the one with the gun, but he's under no illusions he's in control. I don't think anyone is here.

This is a new, dangerous world, one characterized by lawlessness and power.

A prickle itches over the back of my neck as Jayce and Raven engage in a silent stand-off. Blood continues to drip from the back talking prisoner's nose, but he doesn't speak, simply staring straight ahead in wide-eyed terror.

The other prisoners' gazes volley between the two men, and the silence is deafening. Roaring. It's the loudest silence I've ever heard. Sweat begins to trickle down the back of my neck, and it's not from the oppressive heat but from the tension.

Eagle stands beside me with his arms crossed over his chest. It's a clear intimidation tactic—he may not be in the midst of the fight, but he won't hesitate to step in if he needs to.

"Yes," Jayce finally grits out, his jaw clenched so tightly I'm surprised he doesn't chip a tooth. "I'll make sure they all behave."

That seems to appease Raven, because he releases the

prisoner and steps back, once again wiping his hands down the front of his shirt.

"Good. Come." He gestures to Eagle, who barely spares me a glance as they leave.

All the other prisoners in the room swivel their gazes to the two Birds, like dogs acknowledging the alpha of the pack.

But Raven *does* look back, and the gritty taste of sand in my mouth intensifies. Why is it so impossible to read the expression on his face? Why do I even want to?

"Behave yourself, Nicholette," he warns in a silky, dangerous voice. I can hear the unspoken words at the end of that sentence.

Behave yourself . . . or I'll make good on my threat.

I swallow and nod once.

And with that, Eagle and Raven step out of the classroom, leaving me alone with five angry prisoners and a furious, red-faced guard.

Fuck.

JAYCE

It takes every ounce of self-control I possess to remain where I'm standing and not rip those damn inmates apart with my bare hands.

Righteous indignation on Nyx's behalf and an almost elemental fury cascade through my bloodstream. My hands ball into fists of their own accord by my sides.

I've never considered myself a bloodthirsty person before, but just now, I have a vivid daydream of punching both Silas Wilson, a.k.a. Raven, and Ivan Petrov, a.k.a. Eagle, in the face repeatedly until their bones shatter and I'm painted in their blood. I don't think anything would be more appealing than feeling their blood rush across my busted knuckles.

And more potent than the anger coursing through me is . . . jealousy. That crippling, insidious emotion sneaks up on me entirely unbidden. It causes a green sheen to tint my vision and steal the breath from my lungs. The sight of them touching Nyx like that . . .

I study the beautiful woman, searching for any sign that she's upset or hurt by what just transpired, but her eyes are pure steel, and her chin juts up in a way that has my cock hardening.

Wait, what?

I curse myself internally. It's been too long since I left this damn island. I just need to find a nice girl to lose myself in for one night, and then I'll be able to forget all about the broken phoenix with the haunted eyes and sinful lips.

As Nyx moves toward her vacant desk, her hips swaying in a way I can't help but think is intentional, I scan the new inmates. More than one stares at her with lust emanating from his eyes, and I decide quickly that they're going to be the first to die on this island. Most of the men and women here know that, if someone is claimed by a team, everyone else needs to back the fuck off.

And that's even more true with the Birds of Prey. They rarely take on new recruits, but when they do . . .

I think of the guard who once propositioned that shit face "Raven." Within a day, the guard's body was found ripped apart in the woods. And though there were no witnesses to state what happened, we all knew the Birds were involved. It became abundantly clear to not only me but the rest of the residents here that the Birds are off-limits. You can't touch them, can't breathe on them, can't even talk to them without facing punishment. Over the years, they even pushed the Dragons off their throne of power, though I'm not sure how long that'll last. The

Dragons recruited two of these inmates to their team during the last hunt—burly men with teardrop tattoos and scarred skin.

A fly buzzes noisily into the room as I clear my throat to garner the inmates' attention, trying to ignore the way my heart hammers in my chest. This . . . this is the one part of the job I hate more than anything else. I never considered myself an overly fearful person, but there's something about being in a room with half a dozen prisoners that always has my pulse skittering in trepidation. Any of them could lunge for me, and inmates have on more than one occasion. I hate using the gun currently tucked into my holster, but I will.

God help me, I will.

Instinctively, I rest my hand on the gun, taking comfort in the familiarity of its presence. I have a Taser and stun baton as well, though I know from experience that those weapons don't always stop an inmate when they're on the hunt. More than one guard here has perished because they were hesitant to take a life.

But I won't be another body bag leaving this island. I refuse.

I came to this island for a reason, and I'll be damned if I leave it before I've completed my mission.

Six faces turn to stare at me with varying degrees of annoyance, anger, and blind hatred. Only Nyx keeps her eyes downcast, already prepared for what she has to do.

I allowed her to take the last couple of weeks off in order for the other inmates to catch up, and a part of me didn't want to even invite her back. I don't want her in this room full of vile, conniving, murderous assholes who all see her as nothing more than property. A toy. I have no doubt that, if any of them were to catch her alone, they wouldn't hesitate to do unspeakable things to her. I've read their files extensively, and their charges make bile scorch my throat. Sexual assault. Rape. Murder.

Only the worst of the worst is invited to Wicked Island, after all.

The worst of the worst . . . and Nyx, a simple thief.

For the hundredth time since I met her, I wonder why she was sent here. I'm suddenly desperate to get to her file. What secrets are Hoplite hiding? This may just be the smoking gun needed to destroy Hoplite once and for all.

"You guys know the drill," I announce airily, feigning nonchalance as I cross my arms over my chest. But it's all an act. I can't afford to let my guard down for even a second.

One of the inmates—a recruit for the Dragons, with bulging muscles, a bald head, a red goatee, and four missing front teeth—slams his fist down on the table.

"Are you fucking joking?" he asks in his deep, accented voice. Fury paints lines across his scarred face and creases his brows. In a punk move by his recruiters, he's apparently named Toothless, after some dumb kids' movie. "This isn't goddamn school."

I once again reach for the gun at my hip, tension radiating through me and freezing my joints.

"Are we going to have a problem, inmate?" I ask tightly. Directly underneath my desk is a panic button, though I've never needed to use it before. I can't help but admit that the idea is appealing right now. If he were to attack, Nyx would be caught in the crossfire. Maybe I could—

I curse myself for thinking of Nyx yet again. She's a damn sliver embedded directly underneath my nail that I can't remove, no matter how hard I try.

The man's eyes emit almost palpable fury, but he doesn't respond. Toothless simply tightens his grip on the pencil before forcing his gaze back to the manual open in front of him.

This inmate . . . he might be a problem. The Dragons are ruthless already. I can't imagine how much worse it'll be with him in their ranks. His rap sheet makes most of the men here look like Girl Scouts.

"Does anyone else have any concerns?" I bark harshly, trailing my gaze over all the inmates—except for Nyx. I don't want to stare at her. The second I start, I won't be able to stop. My eyes will become drawn to the smooth column of her neck, the generous swell of her breasts, the gentle curl of her hair . . .

Fuck.

Fuck!

Apparently, I'm a sucker for pain.

Before I can stop myself or think better of it, my gaze travels to her and sticks there.

Like the others, she's bent over her book, meticulously copying lines from the manual.

But she's not holding a pencil.

A wicked smirk dances across her plush lips, as if she

feels the heat of my stare on her, but she doesn't look up. She just continues to do her work with an almost impassive calm.

All I can focus on is the Hoplite pen in her tiny hand —the pen I had her steal for me.

My own smile is quick and grim.

Nyx . . .

Phoenix . . .

She may just be the exact thing I was looking for— someone capable of finding that smoking gun and stealing it for me.

WHEN ORIENTATION IS OVER, the rest of the inmates leave without a second glance, but Nyx remains behind, scuffing her shoe against the dirty cabin floor. Her eyes fasten on the gun at my hip before slowly lifting to meet my own. She bites down on her plush lower lip as she ventures a tentative step up the aisle between the desks.

I flick my gaze over her shoulder, ensuring that none of the assholes from the Birds are here yet to pick her up, and then meet her near her desk. I can't help but gawk at the pen in her hand.

"How did you . . .?" I shake my head in disbelief when she only flashes me a smug smirk.

Never mind. I don't even want to know.

Her smile is so fucking contagious that I find my lips twitching up instinctively as I grab the pen from her hand, my fingers grazing against the soft skin of her palm. I swear her body shivers at the connection, and goose bumps pebble on her bare arms. "You know you could get into a lot of trouble if you're caught stealing on the island," I murmur conversationally.

One of her brown brows arches. "Oh, yeah?" She takes another step closer until she's forced to tilt her head back to maintain eye contact. This new position show-cases her pebbled nipples and hints that she's not wearing a bra.

Lust percolates in my stomach, and my cock twitches in a way that's almost painful.

Everything about Nicholette is designed to lure me in. She's every dirty fantasy I've ever had, every wet dream that has plagued my nights when I'm stuck alone in my cabin, with only my fist for company. She was carved by Lucifer himself, designed to drag men's souls straight to hell. That's the only explanation for the sinful twist of her lips and the supple curves that commandeer my attention.

"Are you going to turn me in?" she practically purrs, her eyebrow lifting even higher.

Dangerous game, Jayce.

Dangerous game.

Back away.

Back away.

"I should." My voice is softer than I mean it to be. Almost . . . husky.

Another one of those wicked smirks curls up the corners of her mouth. Maybe I was wrong before. Maybe she truly *does* belong on this island. She's just as deadly as the rest of them.

"I've been learning a lot since I've been in this hell-hole," she begins, cocking her hip to the side. She flutters her long lashes at me, this enticing combination of sass and sexuality. "I think you're underestimating me, Jayce." Her voice practically caresses my name. "Everyone here does."

"And they're wrong to do that?" My fingers twitch by my sides, desperate to touch her, to push up her shirt to rub at her hips and toned stomach, to trail down her smooth neck.

Something hard enters her eyes. All she says is a simple, "Yes."

That's it. Nothing else. No explanation.

From what I can see, Nyx appears demure and docile around the Birds and other inmates. She sits on their laps, comes when they call, and acts like the pretty puppet the rest of the inmates covet and desire. But there's a fire in her eyes that refuses to diminish, no matter what they put her through. There'll be a time when she snaps, and I can't help but think the world will burn when that happens.

Fuck, will it be beautiful.

I find myself unable to look away from her penetrating stare. I wonder if this is what it feels like to be sucked into a black hole—to lose yourself in the fathomless abyss of darkness, swirling around and around with no hope of escape, no hope of freedom. Something about her ensnares me as effectively as a hunter's trap lying in the woods, catching unsuspecting prey.

She's beautiful, yes, but it's not just that. There's a sort of vulnerability that lures me in, making it impossible to look away. At first, I thought it was merely the fact that she was a defenseless girl on an island full of criminals, but now, I know it's more than that. There's just something about Nicholette that grips me by the balls and refuses to let go.

I want to worship her body.

I want to drop to my knees and bury my face between her tan thighs, feeling her hands in my hair as she tugs—

I clear my throat awkwardly and take a step away, praying she doesn't see the way my cock presses against my cargo pants.

Fuck.

"I may have another . . . job for you," I begin, moving so I can sit behind the desk. This new position hides my boner from view, thank fuck.

Her brows furrow, and she glances around in dismay, checking the corners, as if she expects cameras to be hidden there. "A job?"

I wave my hand at her. "There are no cameras in here, if that's what you're worried about." I don't understand how she can act so nonchalant about stealing the pen and then blatantly flirt with me, but the second I mention a job, she clamps up tighter than a nun's asshole. I'll never understand women. "Well, there are cameras, but they're never on." I don't know why I'm telling her that. It's a well-kept secret among the guards. Although there are hundreds of cameras on this island, only a few are kept on throughout the day. This makes it easier for us to watch and easier to hide things we don't want watched.

The training grounds, the cafeteria, the boathouses . . . those are always on, but the rest? Nope. They'll only begin recording if someone presses one of the various hidden panic buttons.

"In the coming weeks, there's going to be a file I'll need you to . . . procure for me." I choose my words very carefully, not wanting to give away that the file I'm searching for is her own. Yes, eventually, I'll need to find the information I require concerning my family, but I have no idea where to even begin looking for that.

Some of that familiar sass from before makes a reappearance on her heart-shaped face. "And what do I get for my trouble?"

I hesitate before saying, "I can . . . make your life . . . better." Fuck, I hope she understands my meaning. "There are certain . . . things . . . I can help you with."

She blinks at me. "Why can't you just speak normally?" She throws her hands up with an exasperated huff. "I thought you said there were no cameras here."

I give her a look. "Fuck off. I was trying to be mysterious."

"You were being annoying."

A smile tugs up my lips before it flattens. I lean forward and brace my arms on the table. "Look, I know about your . . . situation with the Birds." I don't wait for her to respond, even as she winces almost imperceptibly. "You'll need an ally, if you want to deal with them."

"And you'll be that ally?" She eyes me dubiously, and goddammit, that feels like a kick to the balls. It's almost as if she doesn't trust my ability to protect her.

Not that I blame her. I haven't given her any reason to.

Yet.

I hold her stare, infusing sincerity into my next words. "You may be the thief here, but there's one thing you can't steal—loyalty. You help me, and I'll help you. No matter the consequences." My heart ricochets against my rib cage as I extend a hand for her to shake. "Do we have a deal?"

She hesitates, a furrow manifesting between her brows, and I wonder if she has grown fond of the assholes who claimed and tormented her. Stockholm Syndrome, perhaps? I make a note to talk to Mari about this.

But then her face hardens, and the fire I noted earlier enters her eyes, two banked flames.

Keeping her gaze trained on me, she reaches forward and takes my hand in hers.

Just like that, a deal has been made.

S urrounded by women in a way I haven't been
since high school, I shift uncomfortably in my
folding chair and wish for the stupidest thing
imaginable—to be back in my cabin with the Birds.

Yes, life with those men is just a step above terrifying.
I'm trapped somewhere between sex slave and torture
victim most days, but that still somehow seems preferable
to enduring the judgmental stares of these four women.
Even though most of these ladies are tattooed and clearly
badass instead of girly, they still somehow give off a vibe
just as uncomfortable as the one given off by a room full
of perfumed debutantes as we all awaited our "debuts"
into society. And they seem to hate me for some reason.

I scuff the toe of my shoe along the ground as I
pretend I'm listening to Mari's group therapy spiel.

"We face common challenges in male-dominated
environments, this one in particular. I want you to see
one another as allies—"

"We do. Except her," the head of the Dollies states matter-of-factly. I glance over at Chucky, the woman sitting on my left, taking in the eyeliner smudged around her eyes, giving her a raccoonish appearance. Her bright red hair is frizzy in the humidity—possibly like mine would be if Raven didn't have expensive product and Falcon didn't steal it regularly when he brushes my hair.

Today, he braided it, and I find my fingers reaching self-consciously up to touch the woven strands, well aware of the difference between my appearance and that of the other women on this island. They're much more raw, some might say unkempt, but there's a ferocity in their eyes that I wish wasn't currently aimed at me. It's the sort of ferocious gleam I've always tried to emulate, though I'm unsure if I've ever been able to truly capture it the way Chucky has.

Another Dolly, an overly tan brunette with braids, who appears to be in her forties and introduced herself only as Annabelle, cocks her head to the right at a creepy angle as she glares at me across the "conversation circle" we've made with our chairs in this empty counseling room.

The scent of burned bread fills the air, and I know we'll get to look forward to blackened toast at our next meal, courtesy of those with kitchen duty. I don't know how the guards decide which inmates do what jobs—and which ones are allowed to work with knives and meat cleavers—but I do know the Birds have never been selected, whether that was their choice or due to the fear of them, I'm not sure.

Next to Annabelle, a woman flosses her teeth with a black string that looks like it was pulled right from the hem of her ragged shirt. I can't look directly at the third woman, because her eyes face in two different directions.

I wonder if it's any better when I'm not here or if Mari always gets the same toxic and hostile vibes that I am.

Glancing over at my former classmate, I clear my throat. "If you want, I can leave. I don't think I'm helping—"

"No. No. Stay, princess. We want to hear all about how you're getting along with those Birds." Chucky slings her arm over the back of my chair and yanks sideways to pull it closer to hers, the wide grin on her face predatory, and it's not made any less vicious by the fact that two of her bottom front teeth are missing.

I swallow hard, because when she stuck that arm out above me, I could see fresh track marks. She's a user, and she's clearly able to get a supply out here on the island. I'm unsure if she's as powerful as Raven—the Birds keep me rather insulated—but she is powerful, that much is clear.

I turn from Mari and toward the leader of the Dollies, meeting her stare. If I've learned anything during my time in prison, it's that you get respect when you lack fear. And, sometimes, when you tell the truth.

Do I want to put all my eggs in the Birds' basket? No fucking way.

And if I ever want a chance to stab Raven in the eye socket the way he deserves, it may not hurt to make another friend or two. Jayce says he can help me, but I saw the way he backed down when it came to the head of the Birds. I believe he can help me navigate some of the guard issues here, the expectations, maybe even get me put on a work rotation that isn't godawful. But to get revenge the way I want? I need someone a little wilder. Fiercer. So, that's why I say, "It's going about as well as you'd expect. I'm the bitch—bottom-of-the-totem-pole in a cabin full of men prone to violent outbursts."

Mari sucks in a breath behind me, but I don't turn to look at her.

Though she's leading this session on the surface, everyone else in this circle knows who's really in charge of this room.

"Violent outbursts? That's it?" Chucky asks.

"You know it's not." I answer without answering—a skill that served me well on the streets and once I was in jail. My level, give-no-fucks stare tells the head of the Baby Dolls everything she wants to know.

"Is there anything you want to talk about, Nyx?" Mari's tone takes on a shade of true concern.

"I'm fine, thanks." I turn and give her a genuine smile that falls off the second I turn back to Chucky. None of these women need to know about my connection to the counselor, our past. That could open another can of worms. Mari gave me a precious moment of peace, it's true. But her ability to help me survive day-to-day life here is absolutely zero.

Besides, the last thing I want to do is make her a

target. I have no doubt that both the Dollies and the Birds would use her as leverage if they thought it would hurt me.

"Why don't you leave them?" Chucky tilts her head to the side. Her expression is more calculating than curious, as if she's attempting to decipher a difficult math equation without a calculator.

"When has an inmate successfully left one team for another?" I ask. It's been a question on my mind since the moment the Birds chose to spare me and spurred on many of my questions about the other prisoners and which group they belong to during mealtimes. So far as I've been able to discern, no one ever changes teams and lives.

Chucky quirks a brow in acknowledgement of my point. Then she gives a smile, and as the skin of her lips stretches, I notice something about her I hadn't before. Dotting the entire length of her mouth, both under and above her lips, there are small circular scars—as if she once had her mouth sewn shut.

My fingers automatically come up to touch my own lips, and I see Chucky's expression immediately cool, as if I just asked about those scars rather than had an involuntary reaction to them. I can see all the progress I just made with her vanish in a puff of smoke as she tilts her body away from me and turns back to Mari.

Fuck me.

A tiny surge of panic bolts up my throat, because if I were ever to have a chance with another group, or the ability to make an ally, this group is it. As far as I can tell, I'm just meat to the rest of the men on this island.

Goddammit, Nyx! I curse myself.

Mari opens her mouth and starts to ask us all a question about our childhoods, no doubt to prod into the psychology of what made us who we are today. But the tail end of her question is interrupted when the door behind her slams open, all the way into the wall, and a dark silhouette fills the doorway.

Old Twinkle stands there, clearly having come from swim practice, wearing only his tight underwear. Water sluices down his matted chest hair, and his teeth are grinding in frustration.

Mari turns in her chair, grabbing the back and looking up at him calmly, unlike the rest of the women in the circle, who are openly gaping at the various Barbie-style dolls he's attached to his person. He has tied some of the dolls' hands to his chest, using that thick chest hair. Others, he's tucked into his underwear. Doll body parts are braided into the old man's hair this morning, and a detached leg sticks up from the left side of his head like a plastic feather. Even for him, this is a bit extreme. I wonder what the dismembered doll did to offend the lunatic.

Mari breaks the silence. "Fred, our session is later."

"Can't wait," he responds tersely.

"Well, I can't help you right now." Mari gestures at our little group, as if it's important or progress is actually being made here. "This is the women's session."

"I got a women's issue."

"You do?"

"Yeah. Darla wants to report a sexual assault." Old Twinkle—Fred—turns around and shoves down his underwear, mooning us. But lodged firmly up his ass, feet first, head protruding, plastic hands on his hairy cheeks, painted eyes staring right at us, is a doll.

VULTURE

"Hide-and-seek with guns. What an unoriginal fucking choice," Raven declares, his nostrils flaring as we follow him out of the gate.

The guard, Micah, is one I've traded with for basics on occasion. He's got a paunch and a disinterested disposition, but right now, with Raven staring at him and the way the guard's eyes are avoiding us, I'm guessing he's not quite as disinterested as usual. I smother a grin because Raven's talent for digging up skeletons is legendary around here, and no one wants to be his target. This asshole clearly has something to hide. Good to know.

We tromp through the forest, not following any path, just following our fearless and slightly unhinged leader. The green light filtering through the trees appears cool and calm but does nothing to hide the sticky, ball-sack level of humidity in the air. I swear my dick is as damp as if it's been freshly sucked. But this weather gives me zero pleasure. It's so muggy that just breathing is a chore, not to mention ignoring the swarms of mosquitos looking for a snack.

I don't want to be out here, but Raven has arranged for a special practice for us today, so we can get ready for the upcoming island-wide game. A stupid ass deadly game created to showcase our skills to the rich fucks who might pay Hoplite to send us to the far corners of the globe to die painfully for their causes.

From what I overheard, I think Raven had to hack into some North Korean missile launch codes and hand them over to the warden in order to obtain this little session of hide-and-seek. That means he's going to expect us to make the most of it.

"It's unoriginal but fucking effective," I mutter. Guns usually are. If I could choose the games, they'd be so much more creative. I'd love a good game of real-life Operation . . . I can just imagine carving into the Mountain or one of the Baby Dolls, extracting a still-beating heart.

Next to me, Falcon gives a lighthearted little head bobble. "I'm kind of disappointed, actually." I glance over at him, and he widens his eyes as his lips push forward into a pout. "Seekers can't shoot to kill."

The rules are simple enough. One player from each team is the designated "seeker" and must find inmates from opposing teams, using weapons gifted to them by the guards. At the end of an hour, the team with the most members still hiding will be declared the winner. Usually, winning teams receive a plethora of special privileges, at least for a few days. Raven is determined to never, ever lose an island game.

"Ummm, isn't that worse?" Nicolette's sweet voice pops up, far too innocent to be involved in this discussion with us. Yet, here she is. Our little bird. Our tiny Phoenix, so full of fire and life-force. All eyes swivel down to stare at her tiny figure, which is still in Falcon's arms. He insisted on carrying her out here because the fucker thinks her legs don't work or some shit. Doesn't he notice the muscle tone she's gained since arriving?

My eyes drift to the way her legs are wrapped around his waist right now, his hands under her thighs, not her ass. Never her ass, because Falcon only ever touches her innocently. Delicately.

She taps his shoulder, and he lets her slide down his front in a way that doesn't look so innocent from where I'm standing.

Is it her or him doing that? Making it provocative? I study them closely, tilting my head as a strange sort of tightness invades my throat.

She glances up at him, and though I'm at an angle behind his shoulder, I can see a soft look in her eyes as she gazes up at him. The kind of look she's never given to me. With me, there's always sass and defiance, never that gentle submission. Part of me loves that fierce side of her, the one that dares to stand up to me, that remains unbroken, no matter how we try to crack her open and wear her down.

But suddenly, I feel as though there's another side of her.

One I don't have access to.

One she doesn't share with me.

My fingers curl against my pants, tightly pinching the seam as my eyes drift over to the other Bird. Falcon's lucky we aren't practicing with guns today.

Those tantalizingly beautiful doe eyes of Nicholette's look my way.

I give her a wink just to mess with her, but she doesn't respond, her eyes looking at me but not really taking me in as her gaze sweeps across each of the guys in turn. We've ended up in a huddled circle, with her in the center.

It's always her in the center now.

Nicholette swallows as she realizes we're all still staring down at her after her comment, and, for a moment, I wonder what she's feeling.

Does the intensity of our combined concentration make her knees go weak? Or is she used to it at this point? Does she realize how much she's changed the dynamic of our little group? How our goals have shifted because she's here?

We used to think only about winning at all costs. Winning and avoiding getting assigned to a mission until Raven declares it the right one. One we could survive. But now . . . each and every one of us fantasizes about ways to break her. Break her until she's sobbing so beautifully in our arms.

Only, now I'm wondering if Falcon and his gentle little touches, all that innocent worshiping bullshit, is actually buoying her up.

Is he the reason she can take our shit?

Bend repeatedly without breaking?

A vision of her dripping with cum and tears, sunk to her knees in front of me and begging me for mercy, appears in my head—just like it has every night since she arrived on this little island, falling from the sky like an angel cast to hell. I get a halfie thinking about it. But then, it's suddenly shoved aside by a different image. One where her eyes are shy but also dancing. One in which she reaches up, and that tiny hand of hers glides along my jaw before she lifts onto her toes and offers me a kiss.

Fuck.

Fuck.

Fuck.

No.

I don't do that shit.

Emotions are for the weak. I don't want her soft and simpering. I want her under my control.

That's all I want. It's all I've ever wanted.

It's why I fumed when she had that spontaneous orgasm and stole that control away from me.

But now, I can see clearly. The root of the problem isn't her.

It's him.

Falcon's the one dulling the knife, so it doesn't slice through cleanly. Protecting her fragile ego. That delicate heart that I want to bite into until I taste the blood gushing down across my chin.

Nostrils flaring, I suck in far too large a breath for this

goddamned weather and nearly drown myself with the air itself. Bullshit tropical island.

Raven gathers us all in. "You each have thirty minutes. I want five viable hiding spots from each of you." He tosses the duffel bag from his shoulder onto the ground and unzips it. He pulls out rolls of colored string from inside. He tosses one to each of us, though he holds on to the ends himself. "All right. Make like Theseus." He performs a shooing motion with his free hand.

We all stare blankly at him. "Oh, for fuck's sake. Let me dumb it down. Hansel and Gretel. These strings are your breadcrumbs. Make a trail out. Cut it when you find a good hiding spot. Follow it back. Is that basic enough for you bitches?"

Eagle flips him off but is the first to comply and start unwinding a roll of yellow twine as he walks off in one direction.

Hawk leaves next, a trail of red following the serial killer. I don't even know why he bothers to find a hiding space. He's always the seeker for our team whenever hide-and-seek is the chosen game of the quarter.

I watch Falcon walk off, whistling, white string left in his wake.

Nicholette has hot-pink string, and she chews her lip for a moment before heading out with soft steps in the direction of the distant beach. My eyes trail after her as I roughly unspool a roll of black thread.

"Vulture." I turn to look over at Raven, who's glaring at Nicholette's ass. His body is stiff as a board before he inhales, forcefully exhales, and drags his eyes up to mine. "Follow her."

I give a sharp nod, though the ruthless predator inside of me is howling with delight at this little turn of events.

Falcon's the real villain here for making our girl immune to our demonic charms and lifting her up when the rest of us are trying to drag her down. But I don't mind working out my angry aggression on Nicholette's delightful curves while I wait for the perfect opportunity to smash his skull in, bit by bit. Maybe I'll use a hammer and chisel on him.

She trots off ahead of me, her eyes scanning side-to-side, dutifully looking for a hiding spot. Have we really trained her that well? I highly doubt it. Where's that defiant little spark right now?

Is she truly scared about the upcoming game? She shouldn't be. The Birds survive each set of games because we all will do anything it takes to win. Anything.

My intuition prickles, and I wonder if our pretty little phoenix will try to escape.

Fuck. I hope so.

I imagine dragging her by her hair back through the undergrowth, letting the branches nick and slice her skin while she screams. Think of all the things that Raven would green-light me doing to her then. My pants grow uncomfortably tight as I stalk her through the trees, staying back just enough so I can watch her, but she can't hear me.

Waiting.

Hoping.

Planning.

Gliding like a snake, I follow her into a low valley, across a little outcrop of black rocks, in the direction of the beach. The sound of the surf grows louder as she investigates the rocks. But she doesn't pick one up for a weapon. She doesn't drop the spool and then sprint off toward the ocean, like I hope she will. Disappointingly, she puts the string in her hands up to her lips so that she can try to bite off the end and wander back to our starting point.

Goddammit.

Can't a guy get a little rebellion around here?

I step out from behind the tree trunk I've been lingering behind.

She jumps, and her hand flies to her chest. "Shit. You scared me, Vultch."

"Vultch." I sneer as I draw closer. First, she doesn't even give me a reason to punish and torture her, and now she's giving me a shit name, on top of it?

"Yeah, don't you like the nickname?"

She's trying to rile me in the most obvious of ways. "Of course, Nick." I give a half grin when she rolls her eyes. "Tit for tat. Speaking of tits . . ." I glance down at hers. God, we made the right choice forcing her to go without bras. I love the sight of her real shape under the fabric. How I can see every time her nipples stiffen. Just like they are now under my deliberate gaze. I wonder how those breasts would look if I took the string I've got and slowly bound them? Nice and tight. The thought of black lines striping her skin as she begs me to release her makes me hard, and I take a step closer.

"Stop." She holds up a hand, as if she honestly thinks she's capable of pushing me away. "We're supposed to be finding hiding spots. This is serious. Raven will kill you. "

"He sent me here after you."

She scoffs.

I simply stroll closer, pulling out my string and unwinding it over my palm. "He still doesn't trust you."

Her face contorts, lips pursing and twisting into a displeased little grimace. "Of course, he doesn't. He never will. Why the fuck is that? Because I have a vagina?"

There's that spitfire spirit. I try to egg her on, needling her further. "You have one? I hadn't noticed."

She sticks her tongue out at me before clamping her teeth down on the string and biting at it. As she bites, she says through clenched teeth, "Yeah. Hadn't noticed. Sure." The string snaps, and she holds the loose end as she gives me a deadpan expression. "So, it was my asshole you were looking at when you all had your group jerk off last night, huh? Is that what you stared at when you told me to lie back on the floor and spread my legs wider?"

God, her little verbal foreplay is hot. But now, I want my type of playtime. "Take off your shirt."

Her eyes widen and dart back in the direction we came from. "Vulture, he really will kill me." There's a note of anxiety in her voice.

"I know."

"Please—"

"Shirt. Now."

With a muttered curse, Nicholette bares her breasts, tossing her black T-shirt aside into the dirt. Those dusky nipples just beg for my touch. The glittering bit of diamond draws my eyes as it sparkles in the sunlight.

She's perfect. Rare. Gorgeous. Hard to scratch. Just like a diamond. "My little diamond," I murmur, low enough that she can't hear.

I slowly walk closer and drag the end of my thin line of black string up and down her chest like it's a feather, teasing her senses. She tries to hold still, but I'm patient and, gradually, I tease her well enough that I'm rewarded with a sharp inhale.

Now that she likes it, time to make her hate it. I place my hand on the center of her chest, palm flat, string pinned beneath it. Holding the spool in my free hand, I wind it around her body before tying a knot in the loop now circling her breasts. I make sure to tie it right over that glimmering bit of skin, the fragments of jewel above her heart. Once it's secure, I create another loop and another. Nice and tight rings of black string, tight enough that her flesh spills out above and below the tiny threads, tight enough that she gasps. Enough that, when I finally loop her nipples, a plea pops out of her lips.

"Please. It's too much."

I lean down and lick the tip of one of her nipples, which is currently bisected by the string. "It's never enough." God, I could do this for hours. Touching her. Torturing her. Teasing both of us.

"Raven is going to kill us if we don't find hiding

places." She returns to her old argument, as if my answer will have changed this time around.

"He told me to follow you."

"Yeah, but this? Did he really want this? He'll probably be pissed if everyone else comes up with all their hiding spots for the game, and I only have one. And what about you? You'll have none!" The words spill out of her faster and faster as the loops grow more plentiful, and her breasts are banded in tight black lines offset by tiny mounds of flesh.

"He won't do anything to me."

"Are you sure?" Her voice wavers with uncertainty. "Because if anything happened to you—"

"What?" I cut her off, my hands paused in midair, another loop in the making hovering above her shoulders. She glances down at her feet, but I reach out and grab her chin roughly, jerking her face up. "What was that?"

"Nothing," she mumbles.

"Are you trying to manipulate me?" I sneer, anger hooking my belly and making my palms blister with warmth—with the need to hurt. "It won't work."

"Oh my god. Always with the fucking manipulation. Yes. Yes, I'm trying to manipulate you the same way I'm trying to bring Raven down from the inside here. I'm just a goddamned mastermind, standing around, waiting for you fuckers to notice my evil plan." Her vitriol is pure, raw, and seems honest.

Does that mean . . . she was telling the truth?

Curiosity piqued, I undo a loop. It's always good in an interrogation to give the other person a sign of good faith if you want them to keep talking. I lick my lips, suddenly less interested in the delicious red marks on Nicholette's skin and far more interested in what she has to say. "Tell me why you don't want anything to happen to me, and I'll undo another loop," I state.

Her eyes shoot to mine, shocked at first, before relaxing into a harder, cleverer stare. "Five loops," she bargains.

I deftly undo five, letting her think she has the advantage. "Why?"

She chews her lower lip for a second before grudgingly admitting, "Because you're my favorite."

I'm only able to keep my face neutral because I've had so many years of practice, but inside, I'm reeling, as though she just punched my temple. "That wasn't even a good lie," I growl before quickly starting to wrap her up again.

"It's not a lie!"

In the middle of creating a loop around her neck, I pause. This string is too thin to do any real damage, but I let the loop fall down over her, deliberately tightening it around her throat as I lean in close. "It's not the truth."

"It's not the whole truth," she admits, staring steadily at me. "You die, I lose the only semi-sane, semi-fun person here. Or so I thought. Your sanity is now in question."

"I'm sane. I'm just also sadistic." I give her a smile, which she doesn't return. Instead, her hands come up to her neck to scrabble at the string, which I realize I've inadvertently tightened too much. I release the string, and she gasps, fingers immediately scrambling to loosen it and toss the loop over her head, ridding herself of it.

I watch her pant, watch her anger, studying it as a strange, sudden thud knocks against my ribs—my heart punching me because it wants to believe her.

Why do you think I'm fun? I find myself wanting to ask the absolutely ridiculous question. A meaningless question. Why do I care what she thinks?

I feel sick to my stomach.

Bile rises in the back of my throat, and it grows painful and hot, as if it's been charred.

I can't puke, not in front of her. But I want to. I want to puke because, for the first time since I've set foot on this godforsaken island, I'm scared of something. Someone.

I turn, barely able to paste on a sneer for the three seconds it takes for me to spin away from her and march off toward the trees.

"Where are you going?"

"Find five more hiding spots!" I yell. "And for fuck's sake, put your shirt back on!"

Her volley of curses falls short of my ears, like arrows that don't make it all the way to their mark. But she doesn't need those curse words. She doesn't need arrows.

She's hit me with something worse.

I wind through the trees, trying to shake loose this terrible fucking emotion that's somehow climbed up my leg and dug its claws into my gut and is trying to cling to me like a . . . a koala. Fuzzy fucking feelings that don't

belong in a place like Wicked Island. That don't belong
in a head like mine.

Remember Rachel, I scold myself. *Remember that
bitch who sold you out, sent you to prison.* But the
reminder, which used to make my chest burn like a
bonfire, merely causes the smallest sizzle. It's nothing
compared to the foreign invasion that's going on
right now.

An invasion of tenderness.

I want to stomp it out and kill it. Banish it from my
body. Purge it from my bloodstream.

Abruptly, rage takes the place of whatever soft,
mushy, disgusting feeling I thought I felt. It's an emotion
familiar to me—almost like muscle memory. My hands
curl into fists of their own accord, and I feel my jaw
tighten to a level that's almost painful.

Fuck the phoenix who makes me feel things I have no
right feeling, especially here.

Fuck her for making me rethink everything I've been
taught, everything I've learned.

Rachel taught me the dangers of feeling too much,
too deeply, too quickly. I can't afford to make the same
mistakes again. They may just ruin me this time around.

I find myself pivoting on my heel before I can think
better of it, moving toward where I left Nicholette
behind. Raw, unfettered fury cascades through me, this
pathway of fire that heats my veins and causes flames to
burst to life behind my eyes.

I storm out of the tree line just in time to see my little

diamond straighten her shirt, my string a pile of black web at her feet. Her eyes widen when she catches sight of me, and she takes an automatic step backward, her lower lip wobbling. That fierce glimmer in her eyes from before seems to have diminished, replaced by something akin to fear. I wonder what she sees on my face to elicit such a reaction.

But it doesn't matter.

I need to expel her from my body, cut her from my heart, drain her from my motherfucking soul. She's a poison flowing through my veins, and I'm fucking positive she's going to be my eventual damnation if I let her.

I watch as she attempts to gain control of her fear. She juts out her chin and folds her arms over her chest with a haughty sneer.

"What?" she drawls with a sardonic eye roll that only exacerbates my rage. "Did you want to talk some more? Maybe braid each other's hair and gossip? Paint each other's fingernails?"

"Shut up," I growl, finally reaching her and capturing her throat in my hand. She's so fucking tiny, so delicate, and that fact becomes abundantly clear when I see my long fingers wrapped around her porcelain skin, digging in just enough to leave tiny indents.

I love seeing my marks on her flesh.

"I think you'd look good with pink nail polish," she continues, her voice slightly raspy from the sudden pressure on her vocal cords. Her eyes spark with fear, but she doesn't let up. She doesn't back down. I don't know if I want to feed the fire inside of her or squash it. Either way,

I'm basking in those flames, relishing the way my entire body is heating up like an inferno.

I back her up until she hits a huge boulder directly behind her. It comes up to the center of her back, and I use the forward momentum of my body to bend her backward over it in a way that's probably uncomfortable. Her ass and the backs of her thighs are plush against the outcrop, though she attempts to hold herself up with her elbows.

"Vulture . . ." A sliver of fear seeps into her voice, and my cock hardens at the sound of it.

"I've hurt hundreds of people over the years," I rasp into her ear, my fingers flexing around her small, delicate throat. "Maybe even thousands." She gasps sharply, but I ignore her. "And you know what? I enjoyed every second of it. I like listening to them scream in terror, watching their eyes dilate in fear, feeling their blood splash across my face as I cut into them." I lean in even closer, until my face is a mere inch from hers, until her breathtaking features encompass the entirety of my vision. "And you want to know what I did to the ones with the smart mouths?" I grin malevolently, relishing every sharp intake of breath she makes and every shiver of fear that rattles her small body. "I cut out their tongues."

My hand leaves her throat but only to move to her brown ponytail. Quickly, I wrap the length of it in my fist and tug her head back until she's looking up at the sky, currently dominated by hefty storm clouds promising rain.

Something materializes in her eyes again. Something that nearly eclipses her fear.

Desire.

I tighten my grip on the silky strands and tug until a gasp automatically escapes her. That noise contorts into a low moan that has my dick twitching in my pants.

"Do you know what I want to do to you whenever you sass me or talk back?" I demand, though I don't wait for her to respond. "I want to shove my dick so far in your throat that you're gagging on it. And then I want you to choke on my cum." I peer down at her face—those half-hooded eyes, flushed cheeks, and slightly parted lips. "You like the thought, don't you?" I can't quite hide the wonderment in my tone. "You want to be filled with my cum?" She doesn't answer right away; defiance paints angry lines across her face. "Answer me."

"Yes," she snaps, anger flashing in her eyes at being called out.

"Say it." I tighten my grip. "Say you want to be filled with my cum."

Yet again, she doesn't respond but simply stares at me with hard, angry eyes. My rebellious little phoenix. My shiny little diamond. The need to punish her, reprimand her, remind her who's the boss, has my hand twitching by my side, desperate to connect with the bare skin of her ass.

I release her ponytail from my grip and step away from her, but for only a moment. Before she can even take a full breath, I grip her by the waist and spin her around until her stomach is roughly shoved against the rock. I grip the waistband of her oversized pants and shove them to her feet, bending low as I do. She's without panties today—I'm pretty sure Falcon stole her last pair and is now keeping them in his pocket like a damn pervert—and I allow my eyes to feast on her bare flesh.

That round ass and its puckered hole are tempting, but my gaze travels even farther. To the source of all my desire and fury.

Her pussy is glistening with the evidence of her arousal, and I lean forward and lazily brush my finger back and forth through her slit.

"What about this hole?" I murmur, keeping my attention fixated on her pink flesh. "Do you want my cum here?"

The only answer I receive is a low, ragged moan, one that nearly makes my chest cave in because my bones grow soft. No. Fucking. No. Tenderness.

"Are you incapable of speech?" I demand, desperate for her familiar fire to return.

And I get a damn inferno.

"Fuck off!" she snaps, slightly breathless as her legs shift back and forth in a desperate, primal bid to move. Despite her body's compliance, her mouth still spews insults. "You sound like Raven."

I smirk before I can stop myself, continuing to brush my finger through her slick folds. Inhaling the scent of her arousal. "Nah. If I were Raven, I would be using a microscope to look into your vagina, searching for any bugs or trackers."

Nicholette snorts before she can stop herself, but that

gasp of amusement quickly transitions into another prolonged moan as she clutches at the rock. Wanting to get a better look at her face, I move back up her body and lean over her back, pressing against her spine, listening to her tiny puffs of breath as I bring her close to the brink.

"You still never answered my question, Nick." I use the nickname only to piss her off, to keep what we have going confrontational, keep my mind occupied so that my stupid chest can't take control.

I stick a finger inside of her channel experimentally, loving the way her pussy clamps down around the digit, squeezing. I wonder what she'd feel like around my cock . . .

My entire body tenses and pulses at the thought. I've never teased myself or a woman this long before. Raven's declaration has made us all hold off. The realization hits me with the force of a falling piano, smashing right through my skull.

That's why I'm feeling fucked up. I've waited too long and built this up too much. I need to get it out of my system.

That's where these idiotic feelings are coming from. Nothing else.

"Don't want babies," she rasps, responding to my question about being full of my cum. "Don't want diseases."

"I'm clean." I lean forward to nip at her ear, probably harder than she expected. Another gasp escapes her. "The damn doc makes us all get tested regularly."

I ignore her other request. Something about filling

Nicholette with my cum has every primal instinct inside of me rearing its head. I want to capture every last drop of my cum and shove it so deep inside of her pussy that she'll never be free of me.

That thought alone has my balls tightening and pressing painfully against the crotch of my pants. The need to take her, to own her, to make her mine batters at my skull, and only sheer willpower holds it back.

"Do you want my cum inside of you?" I ask again, my finger continuing to piston in and out of her pussy. "Answer me."

She doesn't answer, and I just know she's trying to think of a retort. But then I circle her clit before gently pinching it, and all she manages to gasp out is a loud, "Yessss."

"Yes what?"

"Yes, I want your cum in me." Her voice is practically a sob, desire and need making her incoherent.

Because of me.

Because she wants me so fucking badly, she's losing her damn mind. Good. That fucking makes two of us.

Maybe this is the type of torture Nicholette will take to—winding her up until she's brainless with lust, her lips spilling every sinful secret she ever had. I don't need to harm her; I just need to touch her.

Daily.

Hourly.

Right fucking now.

"Good girl," I growl in her ear, tugging my pants down just enough to free my cock, which has never been harder. I give it a few quick tugs with my free hand, the slit already weeping precum—because I need this woman more than air—before lining it up with her entrance.

She's so wet for me.

So ready.

I never wanted any woman the way I currently want Nicholette.

I slam into her with a groan of my own, loving the way she squeezes around my cock like a vise.

Fuuuuck.

Yes. She's so perfect. Hot and soaked and the shape of her . . . her body was made for me. Fuck Raven and his stupid rules, thinking sex would only complicate things. The lack of sex has complicated shit.
This . . . this right here is what I should have been doing all along.

"You're so damn tight, Nyx," I rasp as I tug her hair back, forcing her upper body off the rock. Then I reach around her and grab a handful of her plump breast. I wish she'd left the T-shirt off, but I suppose I should reward her for listening to me before when I told her to put it back on.

I pinch her puckered nipple through the shirt as I begin to slam into her from behind. She arches her back beautifully and cries my name as her ass bounces against my hips.

I want to break her.

Destroy her.

Own her.

Worship her. That thought slips in unbidden, but I

don't even bother to banish it, because I'm riding a high that's more intense than heroin.

My hips increase in tempo, and the grip I have on her tit is probably going to leave behind finger-shaped bruises. The thought sends a kind of primitive satisfaction zipping through me.

Mark her.

Make her mine.

I can feel my balls tightening as I pound into her with ruthless abandon, not caring that she's probably getting scraped up by the rock beneath her.

A deranged, twisted part of me—the part that fits in on this island of killers and monsters—wants to hold her orgasm hostage. It's what she deserves, after all. For all the shit she's put me and my team through, I don't want her to come. For all the jumbled shit she's made me feel.

But I'm a man first and foremost, and I want nothing more than to feel her pulsate around my cock.

I drop her hair and bring that hand down to her ass, smacking it once before reaching beneath her to pinch at her clit.

If she does orgasm, it's going to be on my terms and only because I allow her to. I own this damn girl. She's mine to do with as I please—torture, use, fuck.

Mine.

All mine.

"Come for me, Nicholette," I growl in her ear. "I want to feel you clamp down on my cock. I want to fill you with my cum."

"Oh fuck . . ." Her pussy flutters as she orgasms, and

she screams. I rut into her savagely, wanting to prolong this moment but knowing I can't hold back my own release, not when she tightens around my cock so deliciously.

I explode inside of her with a roar, every muscle in my body locking tight.

Nyx releases a soft breath—the noise between a moan and a pant—and for some reason, I stiffen behind her.

Because when she makes that sound . . .

I want to wrap her in my arms.

Cuddle her.

Kiss her.

I want to *goddamn kiss* her.

Something dark and insidious takes hold of my heart and squeezes. I shouldn't be having these thoughts about Nicholette. No. Not her.

I pull out of her quickly, not even able to appreciate the way my cum looks as it drips down her bare thighs.

No.

Fuck no.

"Vulture?" Confusion creases Nyx's brows as she turns toward me, but my mask is already in place. Impenetrable. Impassive.

I allow a cruel smirk to tug up my lips even as her own turns down. "I suppose Raven was right," I taunt, feeling as if someone has reached into my chest and rearranged all my internal organs. "You really are nothing but a desperate whore."

Hurt flickers across her face, flaying me open, before it's quickly overshadowed by something bitter and ugly.

Anger.

"And I suppose the Baby Dolls were right." She reaches for her pants around her ankles and tugs them up, not seeming to care that she's still covered in both of our cum. The sight makes my damn dick hard all over again. "You're a shit lay."

I grit my teeth but refuse to retort.

Instead, I rearrange my own pants and stomp away from her without a backward glance.

For my own sanity, I need Nicholette to burn. I need her to become consumed by the flames. Maybe then, and only then, my life will get back to fucking normal.

Restless anticipation crawls directly beneath my skin like a bursting nest of spiders as I toss and turn on the floor. Nude beneath the tiny excuse of a blanket, warmth evades me.

When the sun comes up . . . it's time.

The night before a job, I never used to sleep. But this island-wide game of shoot-and-seek is so much more than a burglary, it's like comparing children's blocks to the stones that built the pyramids. I chew my lip and stare at the scratched metal leg of Falcon's bed, contemplating my mortality until I hear a thud.

Turning my head, I see Hawk standing up in the darkened cabin. With practiced ease and none of the stiffness that always invades my limbs after I sleep on the hard ground, he stalks across the room toward me, wearing only pajama pants. The thick bands of muscle on his arms are visible, even in the dimness.

Without a word, without even a sound, he crouches down and scoops me up—blanket and all. The fact that I'm naked and still covered in droplets of dried cum from the Birds' evening jerk-off session makes me cringe, but he doesn't seem to notice or care as he carries me bridal style back to his bed and sits down on the mattress with me in his arms.

What is he doing? What does he want? Is he worried like me? They all talk with bravado and confidence, but in the dead of night, does the idea of facing the Reaper cut into the skin of Hawk's chest too? Fill his throat with dread?

I stare at him in the darkness, trying to study his facial expression in the shadows, but the moment I open my lips, he presses a finger to them to silence me. His deep brown eyes drift over my face for a second, and I think he's about to say something. But he just swallows and then lies back on the mattress, pulling me down on top of his chest, his arms wrapping around me and cinching me close.

My cheek pillowed against his pecs, his heartbeat gently and rhythmically tapping near my ear, I close my eyes and inhale his orange blossom scent. When his huge hand comes up and cups the back of my neck posses-sively, fingers squeezing once against my pulse before relenting and simply holding me against him, I find my muscles unclenching, my body melting.

His dominance—even his violence—is reassuring in this moment. Whatever we face tomorrow, we're facing together.

I yawn against his chest as our skin presses together and we trade warmth. No promises or empty words about winning. But we share heartbeats.

My eyes watch the shadows in the room shift as I listen to Raven's snores and the steady breathing of the other Birds. A roomful of misfit men who will hurt me, torture me, but also fiercely protect me from outsiders. In a sick and twisted way, I find a kind of grim satisfaction in knowing that. Happily ever afters aren't real things—I've known that since the first time my father snuck into my room after dark. But loyalty . . . that's something I still believe in. And maybe, just maybe, I've found it. That revelation brings me a sense of peace, allowing my jittering mind to settle gently, like the snow inside a snow globe.

After a while, I fall asleep cradled in the arms of a serial killer.

"Get up!" The door smashes open and light streaks in, slapping at my eyes and forcing me to squint at the silhouette in the doorway.

Who the hell—

"Get the fuck out!" Falcon yells at the intruder.

Meanwhile, Hawk's huge hands are mauling the bed as I blink to clear my vision. I finally realize what he's up to when he snatches up my blanket, which must have fallen off me while I slept on him. Quickly and roughly, he wraps that worn bit of gray cloth over my ass, pulling it tight, yanking my body into his. Our hips grind together, and my eyes pop up to look at him.

What the hell is his problem?

But he's only got a glare for whoever is standing in the doorway. I turn to see a figure with his hands on his hips, staring impassively back. That man takes a step inside, and my eyes bounce from the Hoplite logo on his shirt up to his face. Jayce.

My shock is only topped by the wave of furious jealousy that seems to heat the very air. As I glance around the room, the hostility drips from every Bird's expression, from Vulture's to even Raven's.

"Game time," Jayce announces in a cool, smooth tone, as if he's utterly unaffected by the rage poisoning the gazes of everyone around me. In fact, when his blue eyes reach mine, his expression holds a tiny little smirk before his eyes drop and deliberately skate over the length of my figure.

If we were back in Shakespeare's day, Jayce's actions would have just declared a duel. As it is, with these fuckers, he's probably signing his own death warrant.

I'm torn between amusement and horror that he's got the balls to do this and that he's willing to risk said balls.

Falcon stands and, with his eyes locked on the guard, walks over to Hawk and deliberately places himself in front of me. In a swift move, he reaches behind himself as he grabs his black T-shirt and yanks it over his head. He tosses it backward so that it lands on top of my head, and I have to peel it off.

"Put that on, pet. He doesn't deserve to see you," the psychopath hisses through his teeth.

Oh god. My cheeks heat, even though I have to keep an eye roll in check because, with the amount of testosterone currently pumping through their veins, I'm pretty certain I've got a group of wild primates instead of men on my hands right now.

They're already trigger-happy motherfuckers, prone to violence at the drop of a pin, and I don't need them killing off the one guard I've managed to win over and make an under-the-table deal with . . . though said guard has yet to deliver.

Vulture clears his throat and narrows his eyes at me when I don't move fast enough for him. I wrestle my head through the shirt and move to sit up, pressing on Hawk's chest so that I can lean up before wrangling my arms through the armholes.

My movement jostles Hawk, and the blanket slides down the top of my ass.

Eagle's sharp voice immediately cuts through the room. "Wait outside."

"I have to collect you—" Jayce begins to protest.

"Outside!" all the Birds yell at once, tones feral.

"Two minutes," Jayce commands before slamming the door shut behind him.

The second he's gone, Falcon is turning and gathering me up from Hawk's lap, ignoring the fact that I've only gotten one arm through his shirt. He carries me over to the bathroom area and states, "No time to take care of you today, pet. Today, I need you to be a little killer again. Okay?" He reaches forward and cups my cheek for a millisecond, those brown eyes of his digging like spades right into my chest.

Then he turns and, for the first time in weeks, leaves me to get ready by myself.

Rattled, I complete my caretaking needs as quickly as I can, but not quickly enough for Jayce, who smashes the door right back open on the one-hundred-twenty-second mark, just as I'm shoving a toothbrush between my lips.

The fact that even Raven lets the guard be so brazen, when normally our asshole leader is the one pulling all the strings, makes my heart pound against my rib cage, the repetitive metronome doing nothing to quell the shake reverberating through me. The tension from the guys radiates throughout the room, and the severity of today's game crashes down on me all over again.

I'm panicked and teetering on hysterical as my eyes ping-pong around the room. When I realize that none of the Birds even take a second look at Jayce, I finish brushing at warp speed, recognizing just how tightly the guys are strung, and not only about possessing me. They're tense.

Of course, they are. It's game day.

Knowing it's coming and the fact that it's finally here are two utterly different experiences.

Our practice session in the woods three days ago and the Birds frantic midnight meetings in the cabin to decide which other prisoners to seek and shoot—because the game is political as well as brutal—has all been theoretical up to this point. It's all been tomorrow's problem.

Now, tomorrow has come and brought death with it.

My mind can hardly fathom this reality. Dazed

sparkles are continually leaping into my field of vision, as if I just hit my head. I pinch myself, but it's all too real.

The Birds finish getting ready quickly and efficiently as I scramble into my pants, socks, and shoes with shaking fingers. When I glance up after tying my laces, Vulture's eyes are black pits zeroed in on me, and his expression— to anyone else—would appear murderous.

But somehow, I sense sorrow layered underneath that furious veneer.

Part of me wants to take a step toward him, to touch him. Reassure him.

I don't move. Neither does he. We simply inhale and exhale at the same time, our breathing nearly synchronized, before we turn to face our fate.

We march in, single file, behind Jayce, over to the far side of the prison, Raven leading the way. Of course, I'm at the back. As we walk, we're joined on the main road by other groups, all also following a guard like giant black ducklings.

If lightning were caused by tension instead of electricity, the entire prison would be a crackling ball of white energy.

All the tattooed, angry ducklings converge into one mass of black uniforms near a wooden pavilion set in the grass. It's a long platform set atop four steps that looks like it would work equally well for announcements and hangings. While the platform itself is nothing to look at, it's filled with an impressive number of Hoplite guards this morning, who are all wearing long-sleeve collared shirts, undermining the fact that they are carrying machine guns strapped to their shoulders.

I don't have time for further observations or any questions, though, because we're herded along. The prisoners fan out along the front of the pavilion steps, like spokes around a wagon wheel, and the guards move to the back of each line.

That places Jayce directly behind me.

The Birds tense, and Falcon glances back once, nostrils flaring But a Hoplite employee steps onto the stage and pulls his attention back to the front, to the middle-aged, silver-haired man with the buzz cut that I vaguely recognize as the warden of our little paradise. I've never seen him in person before, but I see his name each time I flip open the orientation manual. Warden Mogwai. His narrow eyes grow even thinner as he glares out at the crowd.

A speaker crackles as Mogwai lifts a cordless microphone to his lips, and feedback erupts, making all of us cringe in place.

Hushed murmurs and curses travel across the space as several people scurry to fix the sound system, all attention on that—all attention, except for Jayce's.

Cool fingers gloss over my wrist, and a hard body presses lightly against my spine. Stiffening when I feel Jayce's breath on my ear, I try to pull away subtly, so as not to draw attention and the Birds' wrath.

But his words make me freeze in place. "Stick to the north. There are fewer traps there."

Traps.

Traps?

What kind of fucking traps? None of the Birds have mentioned anything about traps!

I want to ask him what he means. I want to spin around and stare up into those bright blue eyes and see if he's telling the truth. I want to beg him to get me out of this.

But wants and wishes are both useless right now.

Begging will only make me look like an easy target.

I clamp my lips together, and he steps back as the warden says, "Good morning! Welcome to our newest game! I'm sure some of you are already familiar with the rules, since this particular game tends to be a popular choice—"

"Yeah, because you're a twisted fuck," Eagle grunts under his breath in front of me, but I clearly hear every word.

"—but there are some new faces here, so let me remind everyone of the rules."

Silence reigns for a few moments as the asshole takes his time scanning the crowd. He acts like he's the fucking ringmaster at a circus, building up the excitement. "The rules are . . . One seeker per team. No hiding in groups. You must hide alone. Seekers will have their guns programmed to function only with their own fingerprints. So, don't bother trying to steal a gun, hiders. You can't use it, and any attempt to do so will end in a very painful, very public death. On the opposite end of the spectrum, seekers, you cannot shoot to kill. Everyone will wear this beautiful bit of jewelry." He pulls a collar from his pocket, and my eyes widen at this twist, though there are no exclamations of surprise from any of the other prisoners. This must be par for the course.

Dog collars? How on the nose.

I find myself pressing my lips together in disgust, because it seems like the sort of bullshit thing my parents' friends would have considered funny—to enslave and degrade others.

"Remember, you'll have to make it back here on time. A gong will sound, and you'll have five minutes to return, or this baby will give you the shock of your life. The final shock. That same thing will happen if you kill any of the other inmates. Do you understand?"

Does he mean . . .?

Glancing around and seeing only grim expressions, I can tell I'm right. The warden means exactly what I think he does.

He continues, "And, as a little twist, today's game will come with some fun surprises for all. The prize for the winning team is a brand-new mattress." His hand gestures to his side like a game show announcer, and when I stand on tiptoe, I can just make out the top edge of what looks like a queen-size mattress.

Whispers go up among the prisoners, but I don't join them. Even if the Birds win, I know I won't get to sleep on that plush motherfucker.

"Goddammit," Eagle curses in front of me, leaning to one side to exchange a dark look with Raven, who has turned back to stare at the Birds. "Surprises?"

I peer over to see Raven's mouth twist into a grimace.

Immediately, it feels like ice-cold water has been poured down my spine. The Birds definitely don't interpret surprises to mean the mattress. Could it be the traps Jayce mentioned? Did the guard just hand me valuable information that I can give to the Birds?

Hope perches on a rib inside my chest and gives a tentative little chirp.

"You have five hours." The warden gives us a grand smile. "Choose your seeker!"

The teams turn and form tight little knots to decide who gets the gun. Each team chooses one member to be a seeker. That person is then escorted by the guards over to the ammunition station set up just past the warden, and that grand-prize mattress, and must remain in place for five hundred seconds.

Everyone else gets to grab a mask and then disperse to hide throughout the island. After the countdown ends, the seekers will be set loose to find members of the other teams. To prove that they've been found? A gunshot wound. Anywhere on the body—aside from the head and chest, to limit the number of fatalities. Limit. Not eliminate.

A worried anthem plays between my ears because, between the remaining two Predators and the Baby Dolls, it's very likely that I could have an unforeseen "accident" and get shot in the gut . . . left to bleed out.

Our team chose Hawk to be our seeker days ago. According to Raven, Falcon's our best hider—no surprise —and Hawk is incapable of being stealthy but *is* able to track like no other. The few times they played this game before, the psychopathic serial killer "found" twenty-two inmates.

The idea of being found makes my stomach churn, and I'm glad we didn't have time for breakfast.

Eagle claps Hawk on the arm and says, "Break a leg."

Vulture chimes in, "Or two."

Hawk doesn't plaster on his normal fake grin. He doesn't use a posh British accent to dust off his shoulder and make some snarky James Bond comment. He simply turns and stares at me with all the intensity and heat from last night in his dark brown eyes.

My throat threatens to collapse under such intensity.

Then he turns on his heel and marches off through the crowd, a random guard emerging from the throng and plastering himself to the serial killer's side. My last sight of Hawk is his wide shoulders pushing others aside, and a dark, venomous part of my mind wonders if that's the last sight of him I'll ever have.

Dragged along with the surging crowd toward the station for hiders, and leaving Jayce behind, I stand shoulder to shoulder with Falcon and Vulture as I bounce on the balls of my feet. Nervous energy keeps me moving. Eagle stands directly behind me, and Raven takes the lead. His shoulders are rigid beneath the fabric of his black shirt.

"We can't lose this game," Raven murmurs curtly, though he doesn't bother to turn back around to address us directly. "The Dragons have been too close to winning games lately. We need to fix that."

Vulture leans sideways toward me, his mouth tickling my earlobe, his beard grazing my hair. "When a team wins an island game, they receive a prize and special privileges," he explains as a delicious shiver works its way down my spine. All I can think about when he talks to me is his hot mouth on my skin and his cock—

Focus, Nyx!!!

Even my internal chiding can't stop the tremors of pleasure racing through my body. Probably a reaction to all the nerves. I've always had a thing for adrenaline-fueled situations; they've always gotten me closer to orgasm than any former lovers . . . the men before the ones on this island, of course. The Birds have opened my eyes to cravings I never knew I had.

Because even now, though I'm terrified and quivering, a hedonistic jolt accompanies each flicker of fear.

"The last game we won, we got ice cream," Falcon purrs from my other side. He, too, leans forward, pressing against me as he licks the side of my face from chin to eye. "I love ice cream, pet. Almost as much as I love your taste in my mouth."

My heart begins to do aerobics in my chest at his seemingly innocent words—though I know, with him, they're anything but. With him, they aren't necessarily even dirty, because Falcon is so twisted that he might like the taste of my blood more than the taste of my cum. My nipples shouldn't stiffen over that, but they do. His smile says he's noticed my reaction as I'm pressed by him on one side, Vulture on the other.

The torturer grabs my hands and interlocks our

fingers, but instead of holding gently, he squeezes tight, tighter, painfully hard, until my eyes glide over to him.

"And we also got to choose what mission we were assigned to that year," Raven barks, unaware of the Phoenix sandwich the guys have created behind him. "That's the only reason we all came back in one piece."

"Two pieces," Eagle corrects in his thick accent. He leans forward to whack Falcon, who's pawing at my hair like a damn gorilla searching for bugs, upside the head. "Do you remember, buddy?"

"I was able to sew it back on," Falcon dismisses, still intensely focused on my hair. "You don't even see the scar anymore. Besides, it's just a toe. Toes aren't that important."

"You lost a toe?" I ask in disbelief, and his fingers pause where they're knitted in my hair as I turn back to him.

"Are you worried about me, pet?" Hope ignites in his eyes, and he leans in even farther. "Because I can promise you, I'm okay. Do you want me to take off my shoes and wiggle all my toes for your perusal?"

I don't have the heart to tell him that an itty-bitty piece of me kind of hopes he's still missing a toe. You know—cosmic justice. As much as I might be starting to crave the Birds' attention, a tiny sliver of me still knows it's sick and disgusting. A tiny sliver of me still loathes it.

"You're just looking for an excuse to get your shoes off," Vulture points out with an eye roll. To me, he says, "I swear, Falcon thinks going shoeless is the same as being naked. It's almost sexual to him."

"Feeling sand between your toes is a very sensual sensation," Falcon protests seriously. "But if you're trying to convince me to take off all my clothes . . ."

"Can we focus?" Raven barks, having reached the table with our masks. He scoops up the lot and turns, immediately glaring at Falcon and Vulture, who release me. Our angry leader hands out our wooden masks and then swivels his head pointedly in both directions. All the other teams are lined up at the edge of the forest, waiting for the signal from the guards to enter. For the count-down to begin.

I spot the familiar cherubic masks of the Baby Dolls and the distinct coyote mask of one of the Predators— Wolf must be their seeker, if Coyote is set to run and hide. To the far right of us is a cluster of Dragons—red, azure, orange, yellow, green, blue, and black. Next to them is Everest, who's too fucking big to hide anywhere. Beyond him, Old Twinkle is donning a sparkling mask that resembles something one would wear to Mardi Gras. It has sequins and purple feathers.

The Birds are the only ones not yet wearing their masks. But the collars . . . those we strap on one by one, Falcon affixing mine to my neck. The weight is heavy, and I can feel the metal wires encircling my throat, ready to crackle with electricity at a moment's notice.

I try not to focus on that.

Somewhere behind us, Hawk is with the other seek-ers, grabbing their weapons under the watchful eye of a fleet of guards. A part of me wants to scan the crowd for Jayce's golden hair, but I don't want to draw attention to my...*kinship* with the handsome guard. I don't even want to think about what the Birds would do to him if they discovered our secret flirtations. Our little arrangement.

I force myself to shove away all thoughts of Jayce and instead revisit an earlier topic of conversation as the Birds carefully start to slide the masks onto the top of their heads, though they don't pull them down over their faces just yet.

"You mentioned your missions," I say to no one in particular. "Have you guys been on a lot?"

Surprisingly, it's Eagle who answers, his booming voice sounding from directly behind me. "Some. But more in future. We don't die."

"What my eloquent friend means to say," Raven begins, finally shooting me a dark look over his shoulder. His eyes are unreadable. "We've been hired out to various organizations and governments over the years, but I've been able to use my connections on the island to ensure the jobs are survivable." A muscle in his jaw jumps. "Most teams leave this island and never come back."

"Suicide squad, remember?" Vulture murmurs with a derisive sneer.

"Most of the teams on the island have been around for years—they just go through members at a fast pace," Raven continues, his face utterly deadpan as he stares at me. "Because, my annoying pest, people die on this island. People die off this island. Once you've stepped foot on our little slice of paradise, you're basically sentenced to death."

The cold smile on his face shoots bullets through my

chest. I have to stop myself from physically stumbling back a step.

"And will I be going on these . . . missions?" I hate that my voice trembles.

Vulture's face is carved from granite when he responds. "If you survive today?" He quirks one brow and radiates a sort of smugness that turns my kneecaps to ice. He's got the same air of superiority that my parents' friends used to have, as if the world tilts to their will. "Once you pass orientation, then yes."

"And I'll be with you guys?" Once again, my damn voice betrays my fear, wobbling near the end. I hate that. I hate that I'm back to being pathetic. Every time I think I've gotten past it on this fucking island, something else grabs my throat and spits in my mouth so that I can never get rid of the acrid taste of fear.

That only causes Raven's grin to broaden. "What's wrong, Nicholette? Afraid?"

"Of you? Abso-fucking-lutely."

There's no denying it. If I have to put my trust in Raven, then I'm so, so screwed. He's never made his hatred for me a secret. He's not the type of man to stab me in the back—he'll stand directly in front of me, type something into his stupid computer, and then a damn drone strike will smite me where I stand. The last thing I'd see would be that infuriating smirk of his.

Vulture releases a surprised chuckle at my candor, and Falcon huffs out a laugh against my neck. When did he even start nuzzling the skin there? Have I gotten so used to Falcon's incessant touch that it doesn't register anymore?

"Don't worry, pet. Soon, you'll be one of us. And we protect our own."

"Yes . . ." Raven muses with a calculating expression. "One of us."

This is it. My chance to mention the traps. To gain favor. Prove I'm one of them. "We need to stick to the north side. I think all the surprises are in the south," I tell the leader of the Birds, hoping that tiny sliver of information is enough to garner a bit of goodwill from Raven.

His eyes immediately harden suspiciously, and he stares at me with an intensity unmatched by any man I've ever met. My eyes glide down to my own mask, a newly carved bird face painted with swirls of yellow and orange. Swirls of fire.

"Is that so?" Raven's words are sharp, and I feel as though I've been tossed into a blaze myself as I pull the mask up on top of my head.

"Yes." I give him the truth. It's up to him if he wants to believe it.

"We'll find out, won't we?" Raven replies sharply as he reaches up to grasp the side of his mask.

As if on cue, all the other guys reach for the wooden masks resting on the top of their heads, and all four of them slide the masks into place simultaneously.

A raven.

An eagle.

A vulture.

A falcon.

And . . . me.

A phoenix without wings.

I can't see Raven's face, but his smile is clear in his tone when he says, "Let the games begin."

I'm not sure if he's referring to Hoplite's games or his own.

JAYCE

I can't focus on anything but the gritty taste of sand in my mouth.

That's been the one constant for me since I left Nyx behind to begin today's game.

No . . . that's a lie.

I've been feeling like that since I walked into the Birds' cabin this morning and spotted Nyx draped over Hawk's chest like a damn blanket.

The psychopaths glared at me with unabashed jealousy, but it was *me* who felt as if my heart had been cut up by the butcher. It was me who felt like I was breathing vinegar instead of air. It was me who felt jealousy so intense that it took everything within me not to storm across the room, grab Nyx, and carry her out of that cabin of horrors.

But I resisted.

God, it took every ounce of meager self-control I

possessed, but I didn't go all "caveman" on her glorious, naked ass the way I so desperately wanted.

Now, I regret my decision.

I should've run with her when I had the chance.

I should've found a way to take her off this damn island and away from these malicious games.

I should've—

"Jayce!" Stevie, one of my co-workers, waves his arms in the air to garner my attention. Halfway between the cafeteria and the guard quarters, where those of us with overnight shifts spend the night, I stop walking. It's one of the only areas on the island that's restricted from the inmates. And for that reason alone, it's currently teeming with employees.

No guards are allowed to patrol the island grounds during a game.

Because if an inmate finds a guard . . .

The guard won't just be shot. The inmates don't give a damn about the consequences of their actions. They'll torture, maim, and kill, if it means exacting vengeance.

It's as if the second the warden yells, "GO!" all the men and women on this damn island revert into primordial beasts out for the kill. They lose their sense of self. More than that, their will to live. In a kill-or-be-killed world, I don't think any of the inmates care which direction the pendulum swings for them. Either they kill everyone in sight, or they accept death with contented smiles on their faces. They have two choices —become the Grim Reaper or embrace him with open arms.

It's actually kind of scary how the games can change a semi-sane person.

And Nyx . . .

The thought of her in the midst of all this has vomit scorching my throat like lava in a volcano.

I shouldn't want her the way I do, but that doesn't change the way I feel. I'm ice, and she's fire. We're destined to collide, until one of us is inevitably destroyed. Why am I nearly one-hundred-percent certain that person will be me? That her fire will consume me, and I'll happily jump headfirst into her flames?

If something were to happen to her . . .

Anger and desperation grip me by the throat, but I push both emotions away to focus on Stevie. His curly hair looks like a sodden mop out here in the heat, and his expression is far too pleasant for the day's events.

"Hey, man," I say offhandedly, already hurrying past him. Though I don't use the dorm assigned to me on the island often, I'm determined to sleep in it tonight. I need to know that Nyx is okay. I need to see with my own two eyes that she survived all the horrors the island chose to throw at her. I can't return home until I'm positive she's all right. Somehow, the little thief I hardly know has stolen a disproportionately large portion of my thoughts. I don't even want to think about the proportion of my heart that's currently beating just for her.

I thought my dismissal was abundantly clear, but Stevie doesn't seem to take the hint. He quickens his pace to stay beside me, a wide smile on his scarred face.

"Boss man wants to see you," Stevie continues,

nodding his chin toward the far shore of the island—the area guarded more intensely than any of the others. Inside a large warehouse on the slender slip of sand is the only transportation both on and off the island. Boats, helicopters, and even a few jet skis, in the case of an emergency. Over twenty guards protect this shoreline at all times. They have strict orders not to just capture—but to kill—any rogue inmates in the vicinity.

It's there that the warden resides, in a large home more befitting downtown Charleston—a multistory clapboard mansion with three levels' worth of covered porches—than an island full of dangerous criminals.

I've only ever seen him once or twice in all my years working here.

Fear uncoils in my chest like a venomous snake. I can't help but think of the reasons why he would want to see me.

Does he know about my budding relationship with Nyx?

Does he suspect the reason I'm truly here?

Is it something else?

Stevie must see the unspoken questions on my face, because he shrugs. "No idea what for, man. But I suspect he wants some added security. Roger's sick with the flu, and Patricia has this week off."

Security?

My shoulders loosen a fraction, and I realize how they'd coiled tight.

I suppose it makes sense that he'd want more security. After all, the games bring out the worst in all the inmates, which is kind of the point. We want them vicious and desperate never to return before we send them on dangerous missions. It wouldn't surprise me if more than one of them decides that escape is a viable option today and beelines for this area.

I heave out a breath and run my fingers through my hair. Exhaustion hangs over my eyes like a mask, and my eyelids feel like cement. All I want to do is collapse on the uncomfortable bed in the dorm room and wait until word emerges about the end of the game.

About Nyx's fate.

But I suppose it wouldn't hurt to be in the middle of the action. I don't know what I'll be able to do to ensure Nyx survives this unscathed, but I'll do . . . something if the need arises.

I nod in Stevie's direction, murmur a quick, "Thanks, man," and then take off in the direction of the warden's home and office.

I swear the security here is tighter than Fort Knox. I have to show my ID a total of five times, have my eyes and fingerprints scanned, and go through more than one metal detector. By the time I'm finally at the shoreline, I'm sweating profusely from the sweltering summer heat and cursing every person in existence.

What the fuck? Is the warden holding the crown jewels in his backyard or something? Why is this such an issue?

This particular section of the island consists of a long beach, interspersed periodically with large, jagged boulders and overgrown weeds. Dark blue water laps at the sand, turning the golden grains a dark brown. To one side rests a building labeled the administration block—which is weird because we already have an administration block near the center of the island—while the other holds the warden's home and office. Both buildings are constructed out of red and brown bricks. The former's entrance, however, is fronted by two huge columns that hold a white-painted roof, giving it a more industrial look than the other building.

I make an immediate beeline toward the warden's office but stop when a hand lands on my shoulder.

I turn, marginally surprised to see Sergio, the head guard, glaring down at me. A familiar pang of trepidation reverberates through me, but it softens somewhat when I remember that he's always scowling. I swear the man has resting I-want-to-kill-you-all face.

"Albrecht, you're with me." Sergio's grip on his machine gun tightens as he moves toward the helicopter pad between the two buildings.

My brows furrow.

"Are we expecting new inmates, sir?" I ask, hurrying to keep pace.

Unlike Sergio, I don't have a machine gun with me, but I do have my trusty handgun. I unholster it and hold it tight, my finger hovering over the safety.

"No," Sergio answers evasively. That's it. No other explanation.

Over a dozen guards are already standing at attention, watching the helicopter pad intently. I move to join the ranks as confusion rattles me. My brain feels like a damn pinball machine with no hole for the ball to drop out of; it just keeps pinging around and around.

What the fuck is going on?

A deafening roaring sound has every muscle in my body tensing. I squint against the blinding sun to see an object moving closer.

A helicopter.

None of the other guards look confused, so I hold my ground, my body as taut as a bowstring, my mouth desperate to ask a thousand questions but my brain warning me against it. Heat blazes against my skin before slipping beneath to singe and bubble my blood. I swear the higher-ups like to torture us by forcing all of the employees to wear long sleeves and pants in the humid, one-hundred-degree weather.

It takes fifteen minutes for the helicopter to land. During that time, none of us dare to even move. Sweat drips freely down my face, but I don't lift a hand to push it away.

Sergio and the warden both rush over to open the helicopter door.

Who in the world . . .?

I don't know who I expect to see exiting the aircraft, but it's definitely not a five-foot tall woman with gray hair cinched tightly in a bun. Deep lines bracket both of her eyes and the corners of her mouth—currently set in a scowl that only makes the wrinkles on her skin more pronounced. She wears a maroon pantsuit that has to be stifling in the summer heat, though she doesn't appear to be even breaking a sweat.

"Miss," Sergio murmurs as he helps her out of the helicopter, his voice laced with a reverence I've never heard from him before.

The woman barely spares him a second glance as she turns her ice-cold glare toward the warden. Her voice is clipped and precise when she says, "Is everything set up?"

"The viewing room is ready to go," he declares with a respectful head bob.

The woman nods sharply and begins to move across the helicopter pad, her two-inch-high heels clicking against the stone.

A man exits the helicopter a second later.

He's significantly larger than the woman in both weight and height. Dark black hair, peppered liberally with gray, cascades around his chin in thick strands. He wears a light-blue dress shirt and khakis that appear at odds with the macabre environment of this death island. It's a look more befitting of a tropical paradise than a prison for deranged inmates.

He ignores Sergio's outstretched hand and moves to follow the woman, a wide smile on his face. When he reaches the warden and the unknown lady, he elbows the former in the stomach with a mischievous grin.

"I heard there's a new player this time."

The warden nods stiffly. "Several new inmates."

"Aww, you old bastard. That's not what I mean. I heard there's a girl." He chuckles. "Mind telling an old friend how many have bets on her?"

Bet?

New player?

Is he discussing the games?

I don't get to hear the warden's response, as they move just out of hearing range.

Something unsettling unfurls in my gut, and I find myself leaning over to whisper to the guard beside me. Richard, I believe his name is. "Who are they?"

Richard doesn't seem upset by my question. He simply heaves out a breath, as if he's bored with this entire day and says, "That woman is Melissa Castoff." He gives me a pointed stare, as if he expects me to know who that is. When I simply quirk an eyebrow, he elaborates, "The owner of Hoplite Defense Services."

"The owner . . .?" I gape. I'm not necessarily surprised that the owner is a woman—that would be sexist—but I suppose I can't picture this five-foot-nothing waif of a woman running an operation such as this. Who the hell is she to have created such an empire? My shock quickly morphs into fury because I've finally discovered the puppet master in this warped little corner of the world. The woman who indirectly gave me the life I have and decimated the one I had long ago . . .

But this is not the time.

"And the guy?" I nod my head toward the grinning man who has now disappeared inside the administrative building with Melissa, the warden, and Sergio.

"Some hot-shot tech billionaire." Richard waves a hand dismissively. "Don't remember his name. They're all the same to me."

"What the fuck is a tech billionaire doing here?" I

ask, confused. This seems like the exact place someone like him would steer clear of.

"I think he's a donor or something." Richard shrugs negligently. "Don't know for sure, but he's the fifteenth rich fuck to arrive today."

"Huh?"

The hair along my arms turns to spikes, and a chill races up my back.

I feel as if I'm missing something, something important, something crucial to complete this unfinished puzzle . . .

But every thought I begin to formulate drifts away like ash in the breeze.

I suppose it's not unusual for Hoplite's most esteemed donors to visit the island and check out their investment. But why today, of all days? And what did that man mean when he spoke of games and bets and—?

Something cold settles in my gut.

It couldn't be . . . could it?

No.

My gaze slides to the so-called "administrative building" as I try to control my rampant heartbeat.

I always thought I'd find my answers in the records room—and maybe I still will—but now, I wonder if the location I truly need to seek has been right under my nose this entire time.

Just what are they hiding?

And why do I have the distinct feeling that what I'll uncover will change everything?

Though it's midmorning and the birds are singing up a frenzied storm as I step beneath the branches of the forest, it might as well be a dark and stormy night.

The hair on the back of my neck stands at attention, my armpits are already soaked in nervous sweat, and my throat is parched. It's hard to force my limbs to move, because they suddenly feel heavier than lead, but the Birds set a quick and steady pace, veering left as soon as they can.

"Don't worry, pet. Stick to the plan," Falcon reassures me as he tromps off in front of me, ignoring the under-growth slapping at his thighs as he makes his way toward the area where we practiced finding hiding spots several days ago. He casually brushes back his brown hair above his mask, as if this isn't the most terrifying day of his life.

Nodding mutely, I'm unable to make my vocal cords produce any sort of sound, not even a whimper. I don't feel the rocks underneath the crappy soles of my cheap, prison-issue shoes. I don't feel the fronds caressing my arms or the branches that scratch at my hair. I *do* feel a spiderweb when I walk through one, but I swipe it away dazedly, instead of frantically searching for its weaver.

I exist in a tiny, panicked pocket inside my own mind. I'm being hunted like a duck or a deer, and I'm well aware of the fact that nature has unfairly gifted the other bastards on this island with ruthless cruelty.

I can't focus on what's going to happen or things I can't control right now, or I'll end up spiraling, so I try to turn my mind back to the plan. Something I can do.

The plan is that I'll stick near one of the guys. Not close enough that Hoplite will accuse us of hiding together, but close enough that they can help me if anything unexpected occurs.

My eyelids crash down, and I have to give myself a moment because I know "unexpected" is just a euphemism for if I get shot. Of course, my mind spirals back to the last time I was shot. Betrayed and shot, left for dead . . .

It won't be like that. This won't be like Cartier.

The sweat sliding down my spine tells me that my body doesn't believe me. Why would it? I'm surrounded by killers.

"I've got first round of babysitting," Falcon reminds me as we come closer to a cluster of imported trees, a wild collection ranging from blue spruce Christmas monstrosities to oaks.

I don't even have the willpower to be offended by his

comment as he shucks off his shoes, tying the laces together so that they dangle from his hand. Then he pulls off and balls up his socks and shoves them into each shoe. He puts the knotted laces into his mouth, a shoe dangling down on either side of his face as he turns to gaze at me, his eyes blinking through the almond-shaped slits in his mask, his ridiculous beak dipping down a little before he turns and starts to climb an oak tree the size of my waist, walking his hands and feet up it like a sloth would.

"Let's stick to the north," I remind him, glancing around nervously as other prisoners crash through the underbrush, hurrying to get as far as possible from the prison gate. In comparison to them, the Birds seem almost leisurely. I want to scream at them, tell them to hurry, but I don't say anything, because Raven's giving me a look of contempt, one I can't see through his mask but I can feel on my shoulders as surely as a sunburn.

"Let's stick to my plan, unless you care to reveal your source of information," Raven quips.

I suck in a breath because I know lying to him will just exacerbate his mistrust for me, and earning his impossible trust is the key to long-term survival with the Birds—whatever long-term might mean in this godfor-saken place.

"You'd kill them," I say.

It's the truth. He knows it. So do I.

"They could tell us something else again. So, why would I want to out someone stupid enough to feed us information?" I hedge.

Raven makes a scoffing noise, but it's Vulture's reaction that startles me. He grabs my neck, under my mask, and squeezes. "Did you fuck someone?" His thick fingers dig in deep, and I'm suddenly no longer worried about guns or seekers . . . because he's going to kill me where I stand.

"N-no!" I manage to sputter.

He releases his hold but shoves me back, as if he thinks I might be lying.

"I wouldn't!" I gasp, my fingers reaching up to cradle my throbbing throat. "You think I want to be fileted alive? For a fucking ten-second orgasm?" My anger in the air should rightfully make the trees shrivel, but they're somehow immune to my fury.

A gunshot sounds, and my head whips in the direction of the noise.

"Do . . . do they have a starter pistol?" I ask breathily.

"No," Falcon calls out cheerily above me. "Someone just got shot."

Fuck.

Fuckity fuck.

"Split up now," Raven orders. And then he adds, begrudgingly, "And see if staying north is helpful at all."

We fan out, and I glance up to track Falcon before heading in the same direction he is. That insane man moves through the trees like a wraith, soundless and quick. Compared to him, I'm a bull in a china shop, running and stumbling through the undergrowth, cringing at every sound I make.

"Smile for the camera!" Falcon calls out softly after a few minutes of high-stress sprinting on my part.

I glance up, batting a sweaty strand of hair that's gotten stuck to my mask to glare up at a tiny black box affixed to the tree that Falcon's in. He's standing balanced on a wide branch, not even holding on to anything—the crazy bastard. And his hand is pointing definitively at a camera about a foot above the branch. As I catch my breath, he drops his pants and squats, giving the device a full-frontal shot.

Shaking my head at his ridiculousness, I pivot away from him because I have no idea if his shenanigans will upset the guards, but I don't want to be associated with him if they do. *Idiot.*

My annoyance at him causes my fear to fade, but only briefly. Another gunshot sends birds flying from the trees, and potent reality smashes right back into me.

I need to hurry. Need to hide. Animal instinct starts to consume the edges of my rational mind, like a flame licking at the edge of a sheet of paper.

Veering left, giving myself about thirty or forty feet of distance from Falcon, I move over a rise toward one of the pre-planned hiding spaces the Birds found the other day. Though it's one of our weaker spots, a hollowed-out tree trunk that would provide no protection from bullets and leave one a sitting duck if discovered, it's still twice the security of stumbling around down here in the open, waiting for a bullet to bite me.

A break. I just need a break from running and clenching my shoulder blades, certain that something's coming up—

"Shit!" A woman's voice cuts through my thoughts,

and I duck down, crouching, eyes scanning. I spot an open bear trap half hidden by an overgrown plant, points gleaming cruelly. Those assholes. Guns aren't enough?

There's a series of rustling noises off to my left, and that has to be her. A Dolly has come out here, all this way.

A gunshot cracks through the air. By the sound of things, she's in trouble.

God.

Fucking.

Dammit.

My heart pounding viciously, veins throbbing with anxiety, I force myself to move slowly, to slide one foot to my right and get behind a thick bush that provides good cover. I lick my lips underneath the mask. A part of me wants to rip it off for better visibility, but I also don't want to make any big moves right now. A seeker would have no motivation to make noise. Noise will just cause any of us hiding to draw farther away. No, noise right now is a result of desperation—it's the involuntary reaction that occurs when death draws near and smiles at you.

My eyes scan the ground for weapons, and I see none. I search the trees . . . and spot a bit of deadfall, a thick forked branch hanging upside down, caught on a branch below it.

I glance around once, searching the treetops for Falcon, but he's nowhere to be found.

What the fuck! What happened to the plan?

Inside my chest, panic dumps over a gallon of gasoline and lights a match, letting it hover over the puddle.

My pulse pounds so hard that I feel like I might literally die of fright, and I have to fight against every instinct to even squeeze out a single thought.

Swallowing hard, I contemplate whether I should run, hide, or fight . . . because it looks like those are my only options right now.

I leap, swiping at the branch, my fingertips grazing the bark. It sways but doesn't come free.

Swallowing a curse, I try again, my ears on high alert as the rustling underbrush grows into distinct footsteps. Jumping a second time sends my mask askew, and my limited vision is suddenly cut in half. But my fingers brush against something, and I blindly grasp at it, sweaty, nerve-riddled fingers struggling to clutch it.

There!

I pull it down and attempt to ignore the fact that my arms feel made of Jell-O. Shallow breaths saw in and out of my lungs, each exhale serrated and sharp as my eyes scan the green landscape, looking for any shadows, any patches of black prison clothing. I take a step back and hear leaves rustle behind me.

Whirling, I finally spot the Baby Doll sprinting through the forest, heading right for me. Her mask is thumping against her chest, still strapped around her neck but no longer covering her stricken face.

Chucky.

Her waist-length red hair is flying out behind her, and underneath her standard raccoon-style eyeliner, her eyes are blank with panic, an expression of fear that reminds me horribly of the time I fell off a bridge when I was eighteen. Drunk, shoved by another homeless man when I wouldn't put out, I remember the way my mind was utterly wiped clean as I fell—knowing it was probably the end, that I could do nothing to stop it, that I was just waiting for impact. That night, I'd gotten lucky. I'd hit an embankment only a few feet down and ended up rolling several feet. I sprained the shit out of my ankle and broke several toes. I don't think Chucky is going to get that lucky . . . not when I spot Wolf only five paces behind her, gun raised, a malicious cackle erupting from behind his mask. He could shoot to kill from where he is, but he's enjoying the hunt. Devouring her fear.

I know the second the crazy bastard sees me, he'll aim all that ire my way, but I can't seem to stop myself. In this moment, I don't see her. I see my younger self . . . and I desperately want to help. I know Chucky wouldn't do the same for me, but maybe that's what sets me apart from the other inmates on this island—empathy.

Damn my conscience.

"Duck!" I scream when she's nearly on top of me.

I step out from behind the tree, swinging the branch before I even stop to register that she's heard me. The branch is massive, and I swing around with it—the weight carrying me forward, making me off balance as I lean out. Her eyebrows shoot up, arching into startled red rainbows before she drops to the ground and rolls to the side. My abdominals tighten and brace themselves . . .

The impact is delayed due to the length of the branch. I see it smash into Wolf's neck before I register feeling it. I see his mask splinter along the nose line before I register hearing it. I scent the coppery aroma of blood before I register seeing it. His head snaps to one side, and a drop of blood drips down the side of his face to dangle from his earlobe. But my eyes quickly move from his head down to his hands.

They're empty.

Where's the gun?

He must have dropped it.

I spot a tiny sliver of black underneath a large fern, but then I see Wolf bending, reaching for it. Panic wells up inside of me, and I lift the branch again. But it's too heavy—I'm not swinging downward, like I was before. Gravity is my enemy this time, and I can immediately tell I won't be able to smash him as hard again. So, I change tactics, treating the branch like a broom and slamming it into the side of his kneecap, sweeping him off his feet, sending him sprawling—away from the weapon.

It's the best I can do. It's all I can do, because if I kill him, I'll be zapped where I'm standing.

My hands tingling from the impact, I drop the branch.

I turn to Chucky and mutter a single word, "Run."

33

NYX

Wavering in indecision, I stare down at the Predator I just felled and wonder what to do next.

Chucky took off without a backward glance or a thank you, not that I expected one. I've become far too familiar with this place and its cruel nature, a stripped-down and raw version of the real world, all the social fakery shredded and tossed aside.

There are no pleases or thank yous here. The animalistic kill-or-be-killed mantra is the only one that applies in the steamy, sultry jungle.

I swat at a fat, black bug that swoops down right in front of my nose as I scan the trees for Falcon. But he's nowhere to be found, and Eagle, who was supposed to take me next, according to their plan, isn't lurking nearby, either. Of course not. The unreadable Russian only likes to be around when he's torturing me about owing him a blow job.

Why would my protection be his priority when he's running for his own life?

The stark reality of Raven's claims—that I'm a liability and not worth the hassle—weighs me down, though one glance over at Wolf tells me I'm not nearly as pathetic as I was when I landed here. No, day after day of combat practice, and night after night of degradation, has hardened me.

I'm still not quite as impenetrable as the diamond flecks in my chest, however, because the idea that Eagle might be annoyed about watching me, or might even be avoiding me, presses on a very raw nerve inside. One that's tender for reasons I don't want to examine.

A scream in the distance sends my leg muscles jolting forward.

I wade through the scratchy underbrush as quickly as I can, trying to put distance between myself and Wolf, though the part of me corrupted by this island wants to turn back around and kick him in the ribs repeatedly . . . until I know he won't rise. So long as he and Coyote are alive, I'll be hunted for killing their teammates. I'll be a target.

A thud sounds off in the distance to my left, and I jerk hard, pulling a sharp right. My muscles push hard, and soon I'm sprinting along the path, panic guiding me far more than any sense of direction because I simply have to get away from that sound.

Any noise not made by me is a threat, a danger, and could mean a bullet's headed in my direction.

I spot a noose dangling from a tree as I hurry. Then

another. And another. What the fuck is that? Is it supposed to tempt people . . . but I find my answer when I see a man limp right up to one of the dangling cords and tighten it around his neck.

Faster.

I force myself to move faster before I have to see what happens next.

A metallic snap, and my head jerks left as a cage flies up into the air with a prisoner in it. He's barely had time to yelp in surprise before—BAM—the front of his forehead splatters into the bars.

Fuck. There's a hunter here.

Quicker. Go!

Sweat beads on my brow, and my breath starts to come in shallow pants that fill my ears. The sounds of nature even set me off, causing my body to startle at the slightest noise. The trill of a cicada. The call of a bird. Both stiffen my spine and make my fists clench.

Keep moving. Keep moving.

Where am I?

The terrain starts to look unfamiliar, with more scrubby bushes and thicker trees with giant canopies but trunks spaced out farther . . . providing more coverage above from the sunlight but far less coverage below, far fewer places to hide from the seekers.

Shit.

I don't like this.

I don't like it one bit.

Nervousness grows like a creeping vine, treating my

spine as its trellis, winding up each bone until it unfurls its broad leaves inside my skull.

Fuck.

A new sound—one I haven't ever heard in real life before—sends that nervousness bursting into a fragrant bloom of bright red terror.

The growl of a cat.

Not a tabby cat, nothing domesticated. But the wild, feral sound of a hunting cat.

My bladder threatens to expel its contents, and only the knowledge that, if I piss myself, I'll basically give the fucking animal the scented equivalent of a spotlight pointed in my direction, keeps me furiously Kegeling while I run. Where the hell did a wild cat come from? No guard or prisoner has ever mentioned that fucking shit to me. Ever. I've been here for months. Someone would have let it drop.

Surprises. Was this what the warden meant by surprises?

That fucking bastard.

Traps and goddamned motherfucking wild animals!

Bile rises inside my throat and singes it, and I hurry on with a sour stomach, my eyes scanning this way and that. A security camera set high in a tree pans with an electronic buzz, lens following me as I scurry past. The guards are watching us. Probably laughing, those bastards. Is Jayce among them? Is he laughing right now?

The sour taste inside my mouth turns metallic as I bite down hard on the inside of my cheek at the thought of Jayce mocking me. But I swipe the thought away, or at least attempt to. Panic is bringing up old insecurities, the kind that used to plague my teenage years as I walked the halls at school and was convinced all my friends could see right through me.

No.

That's not real, idiot, I critique myself. *What's real is there's a fucking puma or some shit out there about to eat you. Focus.*

I worry that I've somehow made my way down to the south part of the island . . . the part that Jayce warned me against. But I'm so disoriented now, so far from the prison and the other parts of the forest that I've been to before, I have no idea how to wind my way back. Maybe I need to find the ocean and walk back up near the shore.

Having decided on a strategy, I listen.

But a gurgled scream overpowers any sound of distant waves. The sound of tearing flesh fills my ears, and I stumble, my hand smacking against the rough bark of a tree trunk. I press against it as I try to avoid sinking to the ground, since the muscles in my legs are threatening to give out.

A mindless panic that's beyond rational thought drives my body to lurch through the trees, and while I see my surroundings, it's through a haze. My brain isn't functioning beyond a basic level. Apparently, the thought of an actual beast hunting me is a trigger far worse than anything I've been subjected to thus far in my short and brutal life. Humans—even terrible, horrible humans with morals blacker than a moonless night—are capable of reason. Can be persuaded not to kill.

A wild cat?

There's no reasoning with one of those.

I stumble and glance down at my stupid feet, only to slowly blink at the ground and realize a branch tripped me. No. Not a branch. A severed black arm. The hand is jagged, fingers missing, a chunk torn from the palm . . . chewed.

Fuck.

Fuck.

"Fuck!" Just ahead, I hear a familiar voice cursing, and I rush blindly toward it—any sort of familiarity is a comfort in a moment like this.

Bursting through a feathery frond, I spot Raven's angry face. His mask has fallen down and is hanging against his chest. There's a streak of drying blood across his forehead, and I'm unsure if it's his blood or not. His eyes appear pitch black, and his mouth is curled into his typical sneer, but there's an anger vibrating from him that's more intense than his normal disdain. A fury that creates its own hideous aura. In his hands, he's holding a wooden shield. Even though that shit doesn't look like it would do a bit of good against a bullet, I still feel bitter jealousy rise inside of me, festering in my chest.

What the fuck is that? He gets protection? And we have to hide?

That goddamned bastar—

My curse is cut off when Raven's eyes meet mine for a split second. His lips thin before he turns and stomps off to the left, not even beckoning me to follow, just assuming I will like a pathetic dog. Angrily, I begin to trail after him when, suddenly—he drops. One second, he's walking. The next, he's fallen . . . into a pit.

A pit!

Carefully, my eyes glancing side to side for that fucking wild cat, I edge closer to him, only to see a four-foot-wide square hole that seems to be about twelve feet deep, double his height as he stands. Leaves are still fluttering down into the hole from whatever covering was used to disguise it.

Jayce's whisper echoes in my ears. Traps. Traps.

It looks like our fearless leader just stumbled right into one.

I could walk away. I could leave Raven here . . . let the timer run out . . . let that collar on his neck fry his big, paranoid brain like hamburger meat at a cookout. The other Birds actually seem to like me. Well, except for possibly Eagle. Jury's out on him. But Raven's the only one who's been absolutely vicious in his hatred of me. The only one who's never let up on the contempt. He's the only one who's brought up my father and used my trauma as a weapon against me.

I could walk away, and he'd deserve it.

But the other Birds wouldn't.

He might hate me, but he protects them. His knowledge gives them access and privileges they couldn't get on their own. He keeps them safe, which, ultimately, keeps me safe.

And so, as much as a huge, throbbing, vindictive part of my heart would love to laugh in his face before abandoning him . . . I can't.

Fuck me. I guess I'm not quite as hardened as I thought.

No. No. We're going to go with strategic. I'm being strategic right now. Not soft, I tell myself as I glance around and ensure no beasts are lurking just out of sight before lowering myself onto my hands and knees and crawling toward him.

"Those goddamned motherfuckers. When I get out . . ." Raven's muttering under his breath as he uses his wooden shield to chop away at the packed dirt surrounding his makeshift prison.

"Raven," I interrupt him as I lean down on my belly and stretch my hand out to him.

His head jerks up, and his expression morphs from startled to instantly suspicious, calculating—almost like he thinks I had something to do with digging this damn hole. "What the—"

"Shut up and grab my hand. There are wild animals out here."

"I saw a tiger rip off a Dragon's face. I'm aware," he snipes as he ignores my hand and continues to dig at the side of the pit with his shield.

"Do you want my hand or not?"

His lips twitch before he says, "You really think your spaghetti arms are going to pull me out of here?" He doesn't even bother to look up as he hacks at the sidewall and chips out a small foothold for himself, the kind that rock climbers use, before moving up a bit and starting a new one.

I grab a pebble and chuck it at his head. "Fine. I'll just leave."

There's a crash nearby and a yell goes up, a man's voice that transitions to falsetto as he screams, "Help. Fuck. Ahhhh! Help!" The low growl of some type of animal sweeps away all the solidness of my bones. They simply turn to dust upon hearing a human being devoured alive.

"Goddammit. Give me your hand." Raven shoves his foot into the first foothold he's carved out, and his hands fly up the side of the pit, reaching for me.

I swing my hand back down toward him, digging my toes into the dirt, bracing myself and trying desperately to ignore the prickling on the back of my neck, the mental images playing through my brain that conjure a fucking bear coming up right up behind me and using his long claws to scoop a chunk right out of my lower back. My fingers close on Raven's forearm, and his fingers get a death grip on mine, squeezing painfully. Panting, I pull, trying to wriggle backward over the dirt. But Raven's pulling too, trying to climb me or something, pulling so hard that he ends up yanking me forward.

I pitch face-first over the edge and plummet into the pit.

The landing smacks the air out of me, and I have to spend a second splayed out, face in the dirt, not even moving to swipe away the mud that's gotten into my mouth. My hands and ribs ache, and my left foot got twisted somehow, a low throb pulsing inside it. Once I can finally breathe, finally move, I have to do so gingerly, carefully unfurling my body like a roll of ancient parchment. I use the inside of my shirt to swipe at my mouth as I roll over onto my ass and earn a curse and a small kick in the shins from Raven.

"Watch out."

I don't even have the energy to argue with him right now. I just blink up at his infuriatingly beautiful deep brown eyes fringed with the luxurious lashes that no one deserves to naturally have.

He stares at me and shakes his head before saying, "Back onto your hands and knees. You're going to boost me."

"What?"

He rolls his eyes. "Your pathetic spaghetti arms couldn't get me out, just as I predicted. So, I'm going to climb on your back."

"God, if you only knew how much I want to smack you right now."

"Same."

We stare at each other for a moment, but he's fucking right, and he knows it. I have to boost him, and then he'll have to pull me because the other way around clearly didn't work out. We might hate one another, but in this moment, need is stronger than hate—and we definitely need each other.

I purse my lips as I roll onto my ginger hands and lift up into a table position from my knees.

"You'd better—" I'm cut off the instant he steps onto my back near my ass and then literally uses me as a springboard to jump out of the pit. I glance up, panting, to see him wriggling his calves over the edge, back on solid ground.

Pushing up to my feet proves a challenge, and I end up bracing myself against the dirt wall for support. But once I'm standing, and I don't feel like the tweak he just put into my back is going to kill me, I call up, "Okay. I'm ready." And I lift my hand.

His hand doesn't appear over the edge. But his shadow does . . . and it's not alone. Backlit by the sun, Raven and the rest of the Birds stand at the edge of the pit, their expressions grim. When the fuck did they arrive? And why didn't they help? The ache in my back turns into a low shiver as they stare down, ignoring gunfire in the distance as they loom over me.

Hawk, for once, isn't smiling. His eyes are black as pitch. Falcon simply frowns and folds his arms over his chest. Vulture's features are entirely devoid of any emotion—he could've been hewn from stone. Eagle looks annoyed with this entire ordeal, and Raven . . . Raven is smiling.

He pulls his bird mask back up into place over his face and peers down at me through it, eyes glittering and sharp. "Goodbye, Nicholette."

White hot despair spills through me, as if I've swallowed an entire waterfall. I gulp as I drown.

In utterly silent disbelief, I watch as the Birds—the group I've come to stupidly trust and believe in—turn on their heels and walk away.

34

NYX

They . . . left me.

They actually left me to die.

I can't help but think that this is all some nasty joke. Maybe some sort of hazing they put new team members through. Any second now, they'll return, pull me out, and help me finish this damn game.

But they never do.

Panic beats in my chest like a snare drum. It creates a cacophony of noise between my ears—this repetitive sluicing of blood accompanied by the pounding of my own pulse.

They left me.

They actually left me.

For the hundredth time in the last . . . hour? Two? For the hundredth time, I attempt to climb up the hole, using the footholds Raven created with his shield. I only get about halfway up the pit, my fingers still feet away from the opening, before I fall back down.

This time, I don't get back up.

I collapse onto my back and stare up at the sliver I can see of the muted blue sky, riven with clouds.

How much longer until the game is called to an end? An hour? Two?

The inevitability of my death crashes over me like a tsunami, sweeping me away in the fathomless, endless embrace of the icy abyss.

How long have they planned to betray me?

I think of all Vulture's tender touches, Falcon's soft kisses against my neck, the way Hawk held me this morning . . .

That was his version of a goodbye.

I hate that I've come to this conclusion way too late.

I don't know what pushed them over the edge, but if I had to hazard a guess, it has something to do with a snake that begins with an R and ends with -aven. Somehow, he convinced the Birds I'm a threat, a liability, a piece of trash that deserves to be discarded.

And that's how I'm going to die—like trash tossed into a landfill.

What will kill me first? The beasts lurking outside this hole, baying and growling and roaring? Or the collar coiled around my neck?

I instinctively brush my fingers across the cool metal, half expecting an electric shock to reverberate through me. A part of me wants it to. Maybe then, I can die on my own terms. I won't have to remain here, waiting, knowing, *accepting*.

I don't want to accept my fate.

But I don't seem to have a choice.

Tears prick my eyes, burning the backs of them like iron brands, and I bring my fist up to my mouth to muffle the sob that escapes. I hate that I'm crying over these bastards, but their betrayal cuts at my skin and burrows itself under my ribs. Any second now, it's going to pierce my heart, and then what will happen to me? Can a person survive with a punctured organ?

I suppose this entire situation is my fault. I stupidly trusted the Birds and believed their lies—these pretty, poisonous promises disguised as acerbic pieces of candy. How could I have been so stupid? They're criminals, murderers, the worst of the worst. To believe that they cared about me was my own fault.

Self-loathing cascades through my veins, almost more potent than the searing hatred I feel for the Birds. It's a strange sensation to hate myself almost as much as I hate the monsters who trapped me here.

I'm going to die down here, the way I should've died when Taylor shot me. My entire life has been character-ized by betrayal—my parents, my partner, and now the Birds. Soon, I'll fade away, my skin crumbling off my bones, my teeth falling out, my body decaying. But the diamond in my chest will remain, a constant reminder of one of the many betrayals that have plagued my life.

Anger surges through me at the reminder, momen-tarily pressing pause on my pity party.

How dare the Birds betray me? How dare Raven betray me, especially after I risked my ass to save him?

They're going to continue on without a care in the

world. It won't be long until they completely forget about the girl they left behind.

The girl they betrayed. The toy they played with and tired of.

But I refuse to be forgotten. I refuse to slip peacefully into the abyss that is death, not when I still have vengeance searing my blood.

Slowly, I push myself into a sitting position and stare up at the jagged bit of sky I can see, where the clouds are gathering and graying, signaling an impending storm.

I can't allow the Birds to get away with this.

I refuse.

I'll find a way out of this pit before time runs out, and I'll get my revenge. The Birds will regret ever crossing me. I don't know what I can do against a group like them —this isn't high school, where I can just tell the principal about the mean girls and get them sent to detention—but I'll be damned if I don't do everything in my power to knock them down a peg. They're not infallible, despite what they may believe. They have flaws. Weaknesses.

I just need to find them.

I *will* get out of this pit.

I *will* destroy the Birds.

I *will* make them regret this day—the day they left me to rot—for the rest of their lives.

I may be a broken phoenix, but I am rising from the ashes.

And the world will burn.

ACKNOWLEDGMENTS

Special thanks to all of the people who helped me get this dark little book together.

To family and friends.

To Autumn Reed Editing for cleaning up all the awkward.

A huge round of applause goes to alpha and beta readers for their feedback to make this depraved little gemstone sparkle. Thank you LeAnne, Lysanne, and Ivy.

And thank you Ruxandra Tudorica from Methyss Arts for the covers.

ABOUT THE AUTHOR

Well, as a secret penname, there isn't too much to say here without giving it all away. Ashlyn Hades is the brainchild of two top 100 Amazon authors who decided they wanted to dip their toes, thighs, and all their bits into a world that was a little darker than the previous ones they'd written. Turns out, they like slinking through the shadows.

Can you guess who I am?

Email your guesses and/or your thoughts about this book to ashlynhades@gmail.com or find my in my Facebook reader group: Ashlyn Hades's Wicked Books or on TikTok at @authorashlynhades.

 facebook.com/ashlynhades

Printed in Great Britain
by Amazon